FORGOTTEN REALMS

R.A. Salvatore's
WAR OF THE SPIDER QUEEN BOOK III

Condemnation

RICHARD BAKER

WIZARDS
OF THE COAST

R. A. SALVATORE'S

War of the Spider Queen Book III: Condemnation

Distributed in the United States by Holtzbrinck Publishing.
Distributed in Canada by Fenn Ltd.

Distributed to the hobby, toy, and comic trade in the United States and Canada by regional distributors.

Distributed worldwide by Wizards of the Coast, Inc. and regional distributors.

FORGOTTEN REALMS, WIZARDS OF THE COAST, and their logos are trademarks of Wizards of the Coast, Inc., in the USA and other countries.

All Wizards of the Coast characters, character names, and the distinctive likenesses thereof are trademarks of Wizards of the Coast, Inc.

Printed in the U.S.A.

Cover art by Brom
First Printing: May 2003
Library of Congress Catalog Card Number: 2003116417

9 8 7 6 5 4 3 2

US ISBN: 0-7869-3202-3
UK ISBN: 0-7869-3203-1
620-96541-001-EN

U.S., CANADA,
ASIA, PACIFIC, & LATIN AMERICA
Wizards of the Coast, Inc.
P.O. Box 707
Renton, WA 98057-0707
+1-800-324-6496

EUROPEAN HEADQUARTERS
Wizards of the Coast, Belgium
T Hosfveld 6d
1702 Groot-Bijgaarden
Belgium
+322 467 3360

Visit our website at **www.wizards.com**

FORGOTTEN REALMS

R.A. Salvatore's
WAR OF THE SPIDER QUEEN

For Lynn R. Baker, Jr.

1942-2002

Godspeed, Dad.

Acknowledgments

Thanks to Phil Athans for thinking big and paying the price, to Bob Salvatore for sharing his sandbox, and to Ed Greenwood for sharing his world.
Oh, and special thanks to Kim for putting up with me, and to Alex and Hannah for teaching me something new every day.

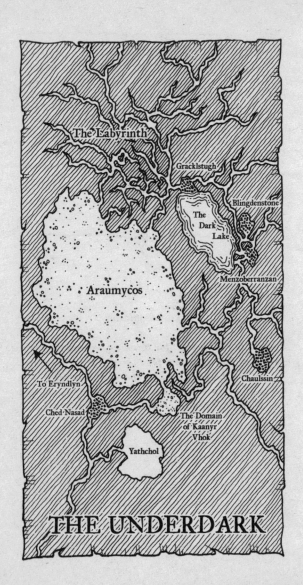

THE UNDERDARK

The food was gone and with it the warmth. All was hollow and empty, save the call to break free. That came most insistently, a subtle urging growing into desperation.

Eight tiny legs answered that imploring call. Eight tiny weapons struck at the concave wall. Battering and tearing, following the lighter shade of gray in this dark place.

A hole appeared in the leathery surface and the eight legs coordinated their attacks at that very spot, sensing weakness. Weakness could not be tolerated. Weakness had to be exploited, immediately and without mercy.

One by one, ten by ten, a thousand by a thousand, a million by a million, tiny legs waved in the misty space between universes for the first time, tearing free of their circular prisons. Driven by hunger and ambition, by fear and an instinctive vileness, the millions of arachnids fought their first battle against a pliable, leathery barrier. Hardly a worthy adversary, but they fought with an urgency wrought of knowing that the first to emerge would hold a great advantage, knowing that they—all of them—were hungry.

And knowing there was nothing to eat but each other.

The warmth of the egg sac was gone, devoured. The quiet moments of solitude, of awakening, of first sense of consciousness, were past. The walls that had served as shelter and protection became an impediment and nothing more. The soft shell was a barricade against food, against necessary battle, against satiation on so many levels.

Against power.

And that, most of all, could not be tolerated by these blessed and cursed offspring. So they fought and tore and scrabbled and scrambled to get out.

To eat.

To climb.

To dominate.

To kill.

To become. . . .

ONE

Streams of dust and sand hissed over old red stone. Halisstra Melarn drew her *piwafwi* close around her, and shivered in the bitter wind. The night was cold, colder than the deeps and caverns far below the world's surface, and the wind moaned mournfully through the weathered ruins, crouching dead and silent in arid hills. Once a great city stood there, but no more. Shattered domes and tottering colonnades whispered of a proud and skillful race, long gone. Vast ramparts still stood against the desert wind, and the broken stumps of towers reached for the heavens.

In different circumstances Halisstra might have spent days wandering the silent ways of the mighty ruins and pondering their long-lost tale, but at the moment a far greater and more terrifying mystery held her rapt with awe and horror. Above the black silhouettes of crumbling towers and crooked walls, a sea of stars glittered like cold hard ice in a black and limitless sky.

She'd heard of such things all her life, of course. Intellectually she understood the concept of an open sky in place of a cavern roof, and the ludicrously distant pinpricks of light overhead, but to sit out in the open beneath such a sight and gaze on it with her own eyes . . . that was something else indeed. In her two hundred years she had never ventured more than a few dozen miles from Ched Nasad, and she had certainly never come within miles of the surface. Very few dark elves from the City of Shimmering Webs had. Like most drow, they largely ignored the world outside the endless intrigues, scheming, and remorseless self-interest of life in Ched Nasad.

She stared at the glittering lights above and bitterly savored the irony. The pinprick diamonds and the vast night sky were real. They had existed for some unimaginably long time, long before she had happened to look up in that forlorn, freezing desert and notice them, and they would doubtless continue long after she was gone. But Ched Nasad, the city of her birth, the city whose rivalries and loyalties and fortunes had completely absorbed all of her intellectual abilities and attention for her entire life, was no more. Not a day ago she had stood on the high balconies of House Nasadra and stared down in horror at burning stone and falling castles, witness to her city's catastrophic destruction. Ched Nasad, with its wondrous webs of stone and darkly beautiful fairy-castles clinging to the chasm walls—Ched Nasad, with its awesome arrogance and hubris, its darkly beautiful noble houses and its ceaseless veneration of the Spider Queen herself—Ched Nasad, the center of Halisstra's existence, was no more.

With a sigh, Halisstra tore her gaze away from the sky overhead and stood. She was tall for a drow, almost five and a half feet in height, and slender as a rapier. While her features lacked the alluring, almost rapacious sensuality many highborn drow women possessed, she was beautiful in an austere and measured manner. Even after hours of furious fighting and desperate struggle to escape fire, foe, and calamity, Halisstra moved with cold, absentminded gracefulness, the calm self-possession of a woman born to be a queen.

Sand pelted against the jet-black steel of her armor, while the wind caught at her cloak and tried to tug it away from her. Halisstra knew well the damp, chill motions of air in vast spaces under the earth, but the desert city was scoured by a relentless, stinging blast that buffeted her from a different direction moment to moment. She put the wind, the stars, and the ruins out of her mind, and silently drifted back to the others. They huddled in the lee of a great wall in a small court studded with broken pillars. At one end of the plaza the empty remnants of a lordly palace stood. No furnishings had survived the centuries of sand and weathering that had scoured the city, but the colonnades and courts, high chambers and proud halls, indicated that the building had once been the residence of a family of some power in the city, perhaps even the rulers or lords of the place. Not far away within the sand-blasted walls stood a blank stone portal, an archway of strange black stone, that housed a magical gate leading back to Ched Nasad. Through that portal Halisstra and the others had made their escape from the sack of the drow city.

She paused and studied her six companions. Danifae, her lady-in-waiting, knelt gracefully at one side, her perfect face composed, eyes closed serenely. She might have been dozing lightly, or simply awaiting the next turn of events with equanimity. Fifteen years before, Danifae, a captive priestess from the city of Eryndlyn, had been gifted to Halisstra as a maidservant. Young, beautiful, and clever, Danifae had resigned herself to bondage with surprising grace. She had no choice, really—a silver locket over Danifae's heart enslaved the girl with a powerful enchantment. What passed behind those lustrous eyes and perfect features not even Halisstra could guess, but Danifae had served her as faithfully and as competently as her binding demanded, and perhaps even more than that. Halisstra found herself comforted to no small degree by the simple fact that Danifae was still with her.

Her remaining five companions did not comfort her in the least. The events of Ched Nasad's last days had thrown Halisstra in with a party of travelers from distant Menzoberranzan, a city that had in the course of time been Ched Nasad's enemy, rival, trading partner, and master. Quenthel Baenre sat wrapped in her own thoughts, her cloak pulled close against the chill. A sister priestess of the Spider

Queen, Quenthel was a scion of House Baenre, the leading clan of Menzoberranzan. Of course, Quenthel was no friend of Halisstra's simply because they both served as priestesses of Lolth; most drow noblewomen served the Spider Queen and spent their lives feuding for station and preeminence in her worship. That was the way of things for the drow, the pattern dictated by Lolth. If it pleased the Spider Queen to reward those who proved most ruthless, most ambitious in her service, then what else could a dark elf do?

Quenthel was in many ways the epitome of drow womanhood, a matriarch in the making who combined piety in Lolth's service with physical beauty, strength of character, and absolute ruthlessness. Of the five travelers from Menzoberranzan, she was by far the most dangerous to Halisstra. Halisstra, too, was the daughter of a matron mother and a priestess of Lolth, so she knew well that she would have to watch Quenthel closely. For the moment, they were allies, but it would not take much for Quenthel to decide that Halisstra was more useful as a follower, as a captive, or simply dead.

Quenthel commanded the loyalty of the hulking Jeggred, a draegloth of her own House Baenre. The draegloth was half-demon, half-drow, the son of Quenthel's elder sister and some unnamed denizen of the Abyss. Jeggred towered over the other drow, a four-armed creature of bestial aspect who held a murderous violence in check at all times. His face was drowlike, and he walked upright, but a gleaming silver pelt covered his dark skin at chest, shoulders, and loins, and his claws were as long and as sharp as daggers. Halisstra didn't fear Jeggred, as the draegloth was Quenthel's creature and would not lay a finger on her without his mistress's express command. He might be the instrument of Halisstra's death, if Quenthel chose to order it, but there was no point in regarding him as anything other than Quenthel's weapon.

The wizard Pharaun intrigued Halisstra greatly. The study of arcane lore was something that, like swordplay, was traditionally left to males. A powerful wizard merited a certain amount of respect despite the fact that he was male. In fact, Halisstra knew of more than one instance in which the matron mother of an important house ruled only with the consent of the powerful male wizards of the family, a situation that had always struck her as perverse and dangerous. Pharaun acted as if he commanded that kind of power and influence. Oh, he deferred to Quenthel quickly enough, but never without a sardonic smile or an insincere remark, and at times his disrespectful carriage verged on outright rebellion. That meant that he was either a complete fool—hardly likely, since he'd been handpicked in Menzoberranzan for the dangerous journey to Ched Nasad—or he was powerful enough to hold his own against the natural tyranny of a noble female like Quenthel. Pharaun struck Halisstra as a potentially critical ally against Quenthel, if it turned out that she and Quenthel could not reach an understanding.

It seemed to Halisstra that Ryld Argith was to Pharaun what Jeggred was to Quenthel. A powerfully built weapons master whose stature matched Halisstra's own, Ryld was a fighter of tremendous skill. Halisstra had seen that for herself in the escape from Ched Nasad. Like most males, he maintained a properly deferential demeanor in Quenthel's presence. That was a good sign to Halisstra. Ryld might easily transfer loyalties to another woman of high birth in a pinch. She couldn't count on Ryld turning against either Pharaun or Quenthel, but pure drow were less steadfast in their loyalties than the average draegloth. . . .

The last and the least of the party from Menzoberranzan was the scout, Valas Hune. A small, furtive male, he said little and observed much. Halisstra had seen his type before. Useful enough in the sort of tasks they excelled at, they wanted nothing to do with the machinations of priestesses and matriarchs and did all they could to stay well clear of the politics of the great Houses. At the moment, Valas was crouched over a small pile of dry brush, working to start a fire.

"Is there any chance we will be pursued?" Ryld said into the icy wind.

"I doubt it," Quenthel muttered. "The whole House fell after we used the portal. How could we be followed?"

"It is not impossible, dear Quenthel," Pharaun replied. "A competent wizard might be able to discern where the portal led to, even though it was destroyed. He might even be able to repair the portal sufficiently to make use of it. I suppose it depends on how badly we are missed in Ched Nasad." He glanced up at Halisstra and asked, "What about it, my lady? Don't you think it likely that your kinfolk will hold us to blame for the unfortunate events of the last few hours? Won't they go to great lengths to exact vengeance upon us?"

Halisstra looked at him. The question made no sense to her. Who could possibly be left to fix blame for the duergar attack on the party of Menzoberranyr? House Melarn had fallen, and House Nasadra as well. She became aware of a great weariness in her body, a leaden feeling in her heart and a fog in her mind, and she allowed herself to sink to the sand across from the others.

"Anyone still in Ched Nasad has greater things to concern herself with than your whereabouts," she managed.

"I think the lady has put you in your place, Pharaun," Ryld said, laughing. "The world and all within it do not revolve around you, you know."

Pharaun accepted the jibe with a sardonic grin and a gesture of self-deprecation.

"Just as well," he said lightly. He turned to Valas, who patiently struck sparks at his pile of brush. "Are you sure that's wise? That fire will be visible from quite a distance."

"It's not much later than midnight, unless I miss my guess," the scout replied without looking up from his task. "If you think it's cold now, wait until the hours before dawn. We need fire, regardless of the risk."

"How do you know how late it is," Quenthel asked, "or how cold it'll get?"

Valas struck a spark and quickly crouched to shelter it from the wind. In a few moments, the brush crackled and burned brightly. The scout fed it carefully with more brush.

"You see the pattern of stars to the south?" he said. "Six of them that look a little like a crown? Those are winter stars. They rise early and set late this time of year. You'll note that they're near the zenith."

"You've traveled on the surface before," Quenthel observed.

"Yes, Mistress," Valas said, but did not elaborate.

"If it's the middle of the night, what is that glow in the sky?" she asked. "Surely that must be the dawn."

"A late moonrise."

"It's not the sun coming up? It's so bright!"

Valas looked up, smiled coldly, and said, "If that was the sun, Mistress, the stars would be fading from half the sky. Trust me, it's the moon. If we stay here, you'll come to know the sun soon enough."

Quenthel fell silent, perhaps chagrined by her mistake. Halisstra didn't hold it against her—she had made the same mistake herself.

"That raises an excellent question," said Pharaun. "Presumably, we do not wish to stay here for very long. So, then, what shall we do?"

He looked deliberately at Quenthel Baenre, challenging her with his question.

Quenthel didn't rise to the bait. She gazed off at the silver glow in the east, as if she hadn't heard the question. Moon shadows faint as ghosts began to grow from weathered walls and crumbling columns, so dim that only the eyes of drow accustomed to the gloom of the Underdark could perceive them. Quenthel reached down to the sand beside her and let a handful run between her fingers, watching the way the wind swept away the silver stream. For the first time, it occurred to Halisstra that Quenthel and the other Menzoberranyr might feel something of the same weariness, the same desolation, that lay over her own heart, not because they felt her loss, but because they understood that they had witnessed *a* loss, a great and terrible one.

The silence stretched out for a long time, until Pharaun shifted and opened his mouth as if to speak again. Quenthel spoke before he could, her voice cold and scornful.

"What shall we do, Pharaun? We shall do whatever I *decide* we should do. We are exhausted and wounded, and I have no magic to restore our strength and heal our wounds." She grimaced, and let the rest of the sand slip through her fingers. "For now, rest. I will determine our course of action tomorrow."

※　　※　　※

Hundreds of miles from the desert ruins, another dark elf stood in another ruined city.

This was a drow city, a jutting bulwark of black stone that thrust out from the wall of a vast, lightless chasm. In arrangement it had once been something like a mighty fortress built upon a great rocky hilltop, only turned on its side to glower out over an empty space where foul winds from the unplumbed abyss below howled up into unseen caverns above. Though its turrets and spires leaned boldly out over a horrifying precipice, the place did not seem frail or precarious in any sense. Its massive pier of rock was one of the bones of the world, a thick spar rooted so securely in the chasm wall that nothing short of the unmaking of Toril would tear it loose.

Those few scholars who remembered the place knew it as Chaulssin, the City of Wyrmshadows, and even most of them forgot why the city was called that. In the lightless fortress on the edge of an abyss, the shadows themselves lived. Inky pools of midnight blacker than a drow's heart curled and flowed from tower to tower. Whispering darkness slithered like a gigantic, hungering dragon in and about the needle-like spires and the open-sided galleries of the dead city. From time to time the living shadows swallowed portions of the city for centuries, drawing a palace or a temple deep into a cold place beyond the circles of the world.

Nimor Imphraezl climbed deliberately through Chaulssin's deserted galleries, seemingly oblivious to the living black curtains that danced and writhed in the city's dark places. The maddening howl of the endless hurricane rising up past the city walls ripped at his cloak and sent his long silver hair streaming from his head, but he paid it no mind. This was his place, his refuge, and its perils and madness simply familiar features undeserving of his attention. Nimor wore the shape of a slim, almost boyish dark elf, which was to say that he was short of stature and slender as a reed. The top of his head would barely reach the nose of a typical female, and any female with a little height to her would tower over him head and shoulders.

Despite his graceful build, Nimor virtually radiated power. His small frame seemed to burst with a precise strength and lethal quickness far out of proportion to his body. His face was narrow but handsome, almost beautiful, and he carried himself with the supreme arrogance of a noble-born drow who feared nothing in his path. It was a part he played well, being a drow of a high House, a prince of his ruined city. If he was something else, something more, well . . . those few dark elves who lived there with him were much the same.

Nimor reached the end of the gallery and turned inward, climbing up a grand stairway cut through the heart of the monolithic spur to which Chaulssin clung. The cacophony of the winds outside faded quickly to a distant but deep whispering, sibilant and penetrating. There was no place one could go within Chaulssin to escape the sound. He set his hand on the hilt of his rapier and followed the spiraling black steps up into a great dark chamber, a vaulted cathedral of shadows in the heart of the city. Flickering torches of everburning fire in bronze sconces cast faint, ruddy pools of light along the ribbed walls, streaks of red that faded into the blackness of the vault overhead. Up there the shadows were close indeed, a roiling well of blackness that even Nimor's eyes could not penetrate.

"Nimor. You are late."

Standing in a circle in the center of the room, the seven Patron Fathers of the Jaezred Chaulssin turned as one to watch Nimor approach. On the far side of the circle stood Patron Grandfather Mauzzkyl, a hale old dark elf with broad shoulders and a deep chest, his hair thinning to a sharp widow's peak.

"The Patron Fathers do not wait on the pleasure of the Anointed Blade of the Jaezred Chaulssin," Mauzzkyl said.

"Revered Grandfather, my delay was unavoidable," Nimor replied.

He joined the circle in the place that had been left for him, offering no obeisance and expecting none from the others. As the

Anointed Blade he answered only to the Patron Grandfather, and in fact stood higher among the Jaezred Chaulssin than any of the Patron Fathers except Mauzzkyl.

"I am lately come from Menzoberranzan," he added, "and tarried as long as I could to observe events before departing."

"How stand matters there?" asked Patron Father Tomphael. He was slender and rakish, much like Nimor in appearance, but he preferred the robes of a wizard to the mail of a fighter, and he possessed a streak of caution that sometimes verged on cowardice. "How does our revolt fare?"

"Not as well as I might like, but about as well as I expected," admitted Nimor. Tomphael's divinations had no doubt revealed that much. Did the Patron Father hope to catch the Anointed Blade concealing a failure? Nimor almost smiled at the simplicity of it. "The slaves were crushed easily enough. Gromph Baenre took an interest in things, and his agents seem to have destroyed or driven off our illithilich friend. On the positive side, we did expose something of the spider-kissers' weakness to the common Menzoberranyr, which is promising, and the priestesses obliged us by using a significant amount of their hoarded magic to destroy their own rebellious slaves. The city is weakened thereby."

"You might have taken a more direct hand in the affair," said Patron Xorthaul, who wore the black mail of a priest. "If you had slain the archmage's lackeys—"

"The revolt we sponsored still would have been crushed, and I would have put them on their guard too soon," Nimor interrupted. "Remember, Patron Xorthaul, this was never intended to be anything other than a simple feint, easily deflected, by which we might assay the real strength of the matron mothers of Menzoberranzan. The next blow will be the one that beats down their guard and slices deep into flesh." He decided to turn the topic and set someone else on the defensive. "As I am the last to arrive, I have no news of how affairs proceed in the other cities. What of Eryndlyn? Or Ched Nasad?"

Cold smiles twisted cruel faces. Nimor blinked. It wasn't often that the patron fathers encountered an event in which they could collectively take pleasure. Grandfather Mauzzkyl himself broke the news.

"Eryndlyn proceeds much as we expected—Patron Father Tomphael brought tidings not dissimilar to your own—but Ched Nasad. . . . From Ched Nasad, Patron Father Zammzt returns in triumph."

"Really?" drawled Nimor, impressed despite himself.

He restrained a hot flash of jealousy and turned to face Zammzt, a dark elf of such unremarkable appearance he might have been a lowly armorer or swordsmith, a common artisan barely a step above a slave. Zammzt merely folded his arms across his chest and inclined his head in recognition of Grandfather Mauzzkyl's remark.

"What happened?" asked Nimor. "Ched Nasad should not have fallen so easily."

"As it happened, Anointed Blade, the stonefire bombs your duergar allies provided us had a devastating effect on the calcified webs upon which Ched Nasad was built," Zammzt said, doubtless feigning his humility. "Just as flame consumes a cobweb, the stonefire devoured the very structure of the city. With their castles and their palaces plummeting to the bottom of the cavern like burning sparks of paper, the Ched Nasadans could organize no real defense at all. No strong point of any significance survived the fires, and few of the House armies escaped from the conflagrations to contest the cavern."

"What is left of the city?"

"Very little, I'm afraid. A few isolated districts and outlying structures relegated to side caverns survived the fire. Of the city's people, I would guess that half perished in the fall and roughly one-third fled into the outer tunnels, where they will doubtless come to a variety of bad ends. Most of the survivors belong to those minor Houses allied with us, or minor Houses who were quick to appreciate the new order of things in the city."

Nimor stroked his chin and said, "So, from a city of twenty thousand, only three thousand remain?"

"A little less, after the slaves fled the city," Zammzt replied, allowing himself a fierce grin. "Of the spider-kissing females, nothing remains."

"Likely some number of Lolth priestesses escaped with those who fled into the Underdark," Nimor mused. "They won't all die in the tunnels. Still, that is great news, Patron Father. We have freed our first city from Lolth's dominion. Others are sure to follow."

Patron Father Xorthaul, the mail-clad priest, snorted in dissent.

"What's the point of removing the Lolth-worshipers from a city if you must level the city to do it?" he asked. "We may rule Ched Nasad now, but all we rule is a smoking chasm and a few dispossessed wretches."

Mauzzkyl shifted his weight and said sharply, "That does not matter, Xorthaul. We have spoken before of the costs of our efforts. Decades, even centuries of misery are nothing if we achieve our ends. Our master is patient." The revered grandfather offered a hard, cruel grin. "We have in two short months accomplished something our fathers among the Jaezred Chaulssin have worked toward for centuries. I would gladly repeat a dozen Ched Nasads all across the Underdark if it succeeded in breaking the Spider Queen's stranglehold over our race. Ched Nasad may be in ruins, but when the city rises again it will rise in our image, its society molded by our beliefs and guided by our secret hand. We are not mere assassins or anarchists, Xorthaul, we are the cold and deliberate hand that culls the weak, the blade that sculpts history."

The collected dark elves nodded assent. Mauzzkyl turned to face Nimor.

"Nimor, my Anointed Blade, Menzoberranzan cries out for the cleansing fire that has purged Ched Nasad. Do not fail in this."

"Revered Grandfather, I assure you that I will not," Nimor said. "I have already prepared my next move. I have reached an understanding with one of the great Houses. They will support us, but they require a demonstration of our resolve and competence. I am reasonably confident that I can oblige them. Within days, one House of Menzoberranzan will be lacking a matron mother and another will be ensnared in our net."

Mauzzkyl smiled in cold approval and said, "I wish you good hunting, then, Anointed Blade."

Nimor bowed once, and turned to leave the circle. Behind him, he could hear the patron fathers dispersing, each to return to his own hidden House in cities scattered over thousands of miles through the Underdark. Secret cabals of the Jaezred Chaulssin existed in at least one minor House of most drow cities. Each patron father ruled absolutely over a conspiracy of faith and gender that spanned generations, centuries, and the formidable hatred of one drow for another. The glaring exception was Menzoberranzan. There, the old Matron Baenre who had ruled absolutely for so long had never allowed the assassin House to gain a foothold. While eight patron fathers returned to cities where there were dozens of loyal killers and priests of Lolth-hating gods at their command, Nimor Imphraezl went alone to Menzoberranzan to resume the destruction of a city.

8   8   8

Sunrise was splendid and terrible. For an hour or more before dawn it had been growing lighter, as the stars paled in the rose-streaked sky and the frigid blast of desert wind slackened toward a fitful calm. Halisstra waited for it, watching from the top of a rambling, half-buried wall. Long before the sun broke over the horizon she was astounded by how far she could see, picking out dark jagged mountains that might have been ten miles or a hundred miles away. When the sun finally rose, it was like a fountain of liquid gold exploding across the barren landscape, in the space of a moment blinding Halisstra completely. She gasped and pressed the heels of her hands to her eyes, which ached from that single brief glimpse as if someone had shoved white daggers into her head.

"That was unwise, my lady," murmured Danifae from close by. "Our eyes were not meant to look on such a sight. You might do yourself an injury . . . and without Lolth's favor, it may prove difficult to heal such a thing."

"I wished to see a dawn," Halisstra said.

She turned away from the light of day and shaded her eyes, then dropped lightly to the sand in the shade of the great wall. In shadow she could tolerate the brilliance of the sun, but what would it be like in the middle of the day? Would they be able to see at all, or would they all be blinded completely?

"Once," she said, "our ancestors gazed on the daylit world without fear of the sun. They walked unafraid beneath the sky, beneath the fires of day, and the darkness was what they feared. Can you imagine such a thing?"

Danifae offered a demure smile that did not reach her eyes. Halisstra knew the look well. It was an expression the maid used to indulge her mistress, agreeing to a remark to which she had no response. Danifae indicated the ruined palace and its courts with a tilt of her head.

"Mistress Baenre has called Pharaun and the others to attend her," the battle captive said. "I believe she means to decide what to do next."

"She sent you for me?" Halisstra asked absently.

"No, Mistress."

Halisstra looked up sharply. Danifae offered a shy shrug.

"I thought you might wish to be present anyway."

"Indeed," replied Halisstra.

She smoothed her cloak and glanced around once more at the crumbling ruins that stretched as far as she could see. In the long shadows of sunrise, the wall tops glowed orange, and pools of blackness lay behind them. Since the wind had died, Halisstra became aware of a sense of watchfulness, of old hostility perhaps, waiting somewhere in the walls and broken domes.

The two women picked their way back to the party's camp in the stone-flagged courtyard and quietly joined the discussion. Quenthel glanced at them as they approached, but kept her attention on the others.

"We have learned that the priestesses of Ched Nasad have lost Lolth's favor, just as we have. We did not learn why. We learned that Houses allied to us through trade and blood had elected to appropriate our much-needed property for their own, turning their backs on us. We failed to restore the flow of trade to Menzoberranzan—"

"A failure for which we can hardly be held accountable," Pharaun interrupted. "The city is completely destroyed. The status of Baenre trade interests in Ched Nasad is now moot."

Quenthel continued as if the wizard had not spoken, "Finally, we find ourselves in some godsforsaken portion of the World Above, at some unknown distance from our home, low on provisions and stranded in a hostile desert. Have I accurately summed up events?"

Valas shifted uncomfortably and said, "All but the last, I think. I believe that we are somewhere in the desert known as Anauroch, in fact in its northwestern portions. If I am correct, Menzoberranzan lies perhaps five hundred miles west of us, and somewhat . . . down, of course."

"You have been here before?"

"No," the scout said, "but there are only a few deserts in Faerûn, especially at so northerly a latitude, so it is a very good bet that Anauroch is where we must be. There is a range of snow-capped mountains perhaps forty or fifty miles to our west, which you can see quite clearly in the daylight. Those I believe to be the Graypeak or Nether Mountains. They could be the Ice Mountains, but if we were so far north as to see them, I would think we would be in the High Ice, and not in this sandy and rocky stretch of the Great Desert."

"I've come to trust your sense of direction, but I can't say I relish the prospect of marching half a thousand miles across the surface lands to get home," Ryld Argith said, rubbing his hand over his short-cropped hair. He moved stiffly in his armor, bruised and battered beneath the mail from their desperate fight to escape Ched Nasad. "Citadel Adbar, Sundabar, and Silverymoon would all stand in our way, and they have very little love for our kind."

"Let them try to stop us," growled Jeggred. "We'll travel by night, when the humans and the light-elves are blind. Even if someone should stumble into us, well, the surface dwellers are soft. I don't fear them. Neither should you."

Ryld bridled at the draegloth's remark, but Quenthel silenced him with a raised hand.

"We will do what we have to do," she said. "If we have to spend the next two months creeping across the surface realms under cover of night, we will do exactly that."

She turned gracefully and paced away, gazing thoughtfully at the ruined court around them.

The party fell silent as each of the dark elves watched Quenthel's back. Pharaun pushed himself erect and wrapped his *piwafwi* closer around his lean torso. The black cloak flapped in the bitter wind.

"The question that vexes me," the mage said to no one in particular, "is whether we have accomplished what we set out to do. I do not relish the idea of crawling back to Menzoberranzan with nothing more to show for months of effort than news of Ched Nasad's fall."

"No priestess of the Spider Queen holds the answers we seek," said Quenthel. "We will return to Menzoberranzan. I can only trust that the goddess will make clear the meaning of her silence when it suits her."

Pharaun grimaced and said, "Blind faith is a poor substitute for a plan by which you might win the answers you seek."

"Faith in the goddess is the only thing we have," Halisstra snapped. She shifted half a step closer to the master of Sorcere. "You have forgotten your place if you address a high priestess of Lolth in such a manner. Do not forget it again."

Pharaun opened his mouth to frame what would no doubt have been an even more inflammatory retort, but Ryld, sitting next to him, simply cleared his throat and scratched at his chin. The wizard paused a moment under the eyes of his companions, and shrugged.

"All I meant was that it seems clear to me that the Spider Queen means for us to puzzle out her silence for ourselves."

"How do you suggest we should do that?" Quenthel asked. She folded her arms and pivoted to glare at Pharaun. "In case you have forgotten, we've toiled for months to discern the cause of the Silence."

"But we have not exhausted all avenues of investigation, have we?" Pharaun said. "In Ched Nasad, we spoke of seeking the assistance of a priest of Vhaeraun, possibly Master Hune's acquaintance Tzirik. We drow have other deities beside Lolth, after all. Is it so unreasonable to speculate that another god might be able to explain Lolth's unusual silence?"

The circle fell still. The wizard's words were not ones commonly heard in Menzoberranzan. Few dared utter such thoughts in the presence of the Spider Queen's clergy.

"I see no need to go begging favors of a male heretic worshiping a miserable whelp of a god," Quenthel said. "I doubt that Lolth has deigned to confide her purposes in any lesser powers."

"You are probably correct," said Pharaun. "She certainly hasn't confided them in you, after all."

Jeggred snarled at the wizard, and Pharaun raised his hands in a placating gesture, rolling his eyes.

Valas licked his lips nervously and offered, "Most of you have spent the great majority of your lives in Menzoberranzan, as is fit and proper for drow of your respective stations. I have traveled more widely, and I have visited places that secretly—even openly, in some cases—permit the worship of gods other than Lolth." He noticed the gathering thunder in Quenthel's face, mirrored in Halisstra's. The scout winced but pressed on. "Under the wise rule of the matron mothers, the worship of drow gods other than Lolth has hardly flourished in Menzoberranzan, and so you may not hold a high opinion of the practice, but I can attest to the fact that the priests of the lesser gods of our race can call upon spells and guidance from their deities, too."

"Where might we find Tzirik?" Ryld asked Valas.

"When last I met him, he lived among outcasts in a remote region known as the Labyrinth, south and west of the Darklake by perhaps a hundred miles. This was some time ago, of course."

"Outcasts," snorted Halisstra.

She was not the only one to express disgust. In the endless game played between the great Houses of the drow, of course there were losers. Most died, but some chose flight over death, taking up a hardscrabble and ignominious existence in the remote stretches of the Underdark. Others abandoned their home cities for different reasons—including, Halisstra supposed, the veneration of gods other than Lolth. She found it hard to believe that anyone so weak as to have been run out of her home city could offer much help at all.

"We'll solve our own problems," she said.

Pharaun glanced up at Halisstra, cold humor dancing in his eyes.

"I forgot that you now have some experience with the peculiar misfortune of being deprived of a home city," he remarked. "And I applaud your celerity in including yourself in 'our' discussions and 'our' problems. Your selflessness is laudable."

Halisstra shut her mouth, stung by the words. There would be many hundreds, even thousands of survivors from Ched Nasad scattered in as many tunnels and bolt-holes in the black caverns and passages around the city. Most of those would end their lives in the jaws of mindless monsters, or perhaps fall into wretched slavery as captives of drow from other cities, duergar, or even more horrible Underdark races like the mind flayers or the aboleths. And a few might hope to find some kind of life for themselves through their own wits and resourcefulness. It was not unknown for a House to take into its ranks a defeated enemy who had demonstrated her usefulness. House Melarn was dead. Wherever Halisstra journeyed next, she would be starting from square one. The advantages of her birth, the wealth and power of her city, all that meant nothing anymore.

She considered her reply carefully, conscious of the acute interest of the other drow around her, and said, "Spare me your pity." She spoke in a murderous hiss, putting iron in her voice that she did not feel. "Unless I miss my guess, Menzoberranzan doesn't stand so very far from Ched Nasad's fate, else you never would have come to seek our aid. Our difficulties are your difficulties, are they not?"

Her words had the desired effect. The wizard looked away, while the other Menzoberranyr shifted nervously, studying each other's reactions. Quenthel visibly flinched, her mouth tightening into a fierce scowl.

"Enough, both of you," she said, turning to Valas. "This outcast priest of Vhaeraun—why would he aid us in any way? He is not likely to entertain an especially charitable attitude toward our cause."

Valas replied, "I couldn't say, Mistress. All I can do is bring you to him. What happens after that depends on you."

The ruined courtyard fell silent. The sun was a double handspan into the sky, and blinding shafts of pure light sliced through the darkness of the ruined court from crumbling embrasures in the high walls. The ruins were apparently not as desolate as Halisstra had thought. She could hear the furtive sounds of small creatures scrabbling across sand and rubble, faint and small in the distance.

"The Labyrinth lies only a hundred miles from the Darklake?" Quenthel asked. The scout nodded once. The priestess folded her arms and thought. "Then it's not very far from our homeward course, in any event. Pharaun, do you command any magic that might speed our travel? Fighting our way home across the surface realms appeals to me no more than it does the weapons master."

The wizard leered and rose to his feet, preening under Quenthel's request for help.

"Teleportation is risky," he said. "First, the *faerzress* of the Underdark makes it dangerous to attempt transport spells. More to the point, I have never visited the Labyrinth, and so have no idea where I would be going. I would almost certainly fail. I know a spell to transform myself or others into different shapes more suited for travel, though. Perhaps if we were dragons or giant bats or something that would fly well by night. . . ." The wizard tapped his chin, considering the problem. "Whomever we press into service as a mount would have to stay in that shape until I changed him back, of course, and we'd still be looking at a couple of tendays of travel. Or . . . I know a spell of walking through shadows. It's dangerous, and I couldn't take us straight to the Labyrinth, as I have never been there and the spell is best employed to reach places you know well. I could take you to Mantol-Derith, though, which is hard by the shores of the Darklake. It would shorten our journey considerably."

"Why didn't you mention that before, when we were discussing months of marching across the surface?" said Jeggred, shaking his head in irritation.

"If you recall, we had not yet decided where we were going," Pharaun replied. "I intended to offer my services at the appropriate time."

Ryld said, "You could have transported us from Menzoberranzan to Ched Nasad in the first place. Why in the world did we walk?"

"Because I have good reason to fear the plane of shadow. As a younger and more impulsive mage I learned—the hard way—that shadow walking confers no special protection against the attentions of those creatures that dwell in the dark realm. In fact, I was very nearly devoured by something I would not care to meet again." The wizard offered a wry grin and added, "Naturally, I now regard shadow walking as an option of last resort. I only suggest it now because I deem it slightly less dangerous than tendays of travel across the surface world."

"We will exercise all due caution," Quenthel said. "Let's be about it, then."

"Not so fast. I must prepare the spell. I will require about an hour to make ready."

"Do so without delay," Quenthel said. She glanced around at the ruins, and shaded her eyes. "The sooner we are back below ground, the better."

Chapter

TWO

While Pharaun retired to a dark, quiet chamber to study his grimoires and ready his spells, the rest of the party gathered their gear and prepared to leave. They were woefully unprepared for a long journey on the surface; Halisstra and Danifae had no packs or supplies of any kind. The Menzoberranyr had wisely recovered their packs before escaping Ched Nasad, but their long journey to the City of Shimmering Webs had depleted their stores.

While they waited for Pharaun, Halisstra studied the ruins in more detail. She had something of a scholarly inclination, and deliberately taking an interest in the ancient city was as good a way as any of keeping her mind from dwelling on the last awful hours of her home city. The others busied themselves with the small tasks of breaking camp, or waited patiently in the deepest shadows they could find. Halisstra gathered the few things she had brought and set out from the ruined court. Her eye fell on Danifae, who knelt quietly in the shade of a broken arch, calmly watching her leave.

Halisstra paused, and called, "Come, Danifae."

She didn't like the idea of leaving her servant alone with the Menzoberranyr. Danifae had served her well for years, but circumstances had changed.

The maidservant stood smoothly and followed. Halisstra led her through the crumbling shell of the palace surrounding the courtyard, and they emerged onto a wide boulevard arrowing through the heart of the old city. The air had warmed noticeably in the hour or more since sunrise, but it was still bitterly cold, and the brilliance of the day seemed almost enhanced by the crystal clarity of the skies. Both women stood blinded for several long moments in the sunshine.

"This is no good," muttered Halisstra. "I'm squinting so hard I can't see my hand in front of my face."

Even when she managed to open her eyes, she could see little more than bright, painful spots.

"Valas says it's possible to get used to daylight, with time," Danifae offered. "I find that hard to believe, now that I have experienced it myself. A good thing we mean to return to the Underdark soon." Halisstra heard a small tearing sound from beside her, and Danifae pressed a strip of cloth into her hand. "Tie this over your eyes, Mistress. Perhaps it will help."

Halisstra managed to arrange the dark cloth as a makeshift veil. It did indeed help to abate the fierce glare of the sun.

"That's better," Halisstra said.

Danifae tore another small strip and bound it around her own eyes as her mistress examined the ruins. It seemed to Halisstra that the palace they'd taken shelter in was one of the more prominent buildings, which only made sense. Magical portals were not easy to make, and were often found in well-hidden or vigilantly guarded locations. A colonnade stood along the front of the palace, and across the boulevard was another great building—a temple, or perhaps a court of some kind. There was something familiar about the architecture of the buildings.

"Netherese," she said. "See the square column bases, and the pointed arches in the windows?"

"I thought Netherese cities floated in the air, and were completely destroyed by some magical cataclysm," Danifae replied. "How could anything like this still stand?"

"It could have been one of the successor states," Halisstra said, "built after the great mythallars of the old Netherese cities failed. They would share many of the same architectural features, but would have been more mundane, less magical."

"There's writing up there," Danifae said, pointing at the facade of a crumbled building. "There . . . above the columns."

Halisstra followed Danifae's gesture. "Yes," she said. "That's Netherese."

"You can read it?" Danifae asked.

"I have studied several languages—the common tongue of the surface, High Netherese, Illuskan, even some of the speech of dragons," Halisstra replied. "Our libraries contain fascinating histories and potent lore recorded in languages other than drow. I developed the habit of studying such things over a century ago, when I believed I might find some forgotten spell or secret that might prove useful against my rivals. As it turned out, I found little of that sort of thing, but I did find that I enjoyed learning for its own sake."

"What does it say, then?"

"I'm not sure of some of the words, but I think it reads, 'High Hall of Justice, Hlaungadath—In Truth's Light No Lies Abide.' "

"What a simpleminded sentiment."

Halisstra indicated the ruins around them and said, "You can see how far it got them. I know that name, though, Hlaungadath. I have seen maps of the surface world. Valas's estimate of our location was accurate."

"Even a male can do something right from time to time," Danifae said.

Halisstra smiled and turned away to scan the ruins for any other sites of interest.

Something tawny and quick ducked swiftly out of sight. Halisstra froze on the instant, staring hard at the spot where she'd seen it, a gap in a masonry wall a short distance away. Nothing moved there, but from another direction came the sound of rubble shifting. Without looking away, she touched Danifae's arm.

We're not alone here, she signed. *Back to the others—quickly.*

Together, they backed away from the court of justice and out into the street again. As they turned to retrace their steps, something long and low, covered with sand-colored scales, slid out into the boulevard. Its stubby wings clearly could never support it in flight, but its powerful talons and gaping jaws were much more developed. The dragon paused and raised up its head for a better look at the two drow on the street before it, and it hissed in delight. It was easily fifty feet from nose to tail, a hulking, powerful creature whose eyes gleamed with cunning and malice.

"Lolth protect us!" Danifae gasped.

The two women backed away in a new direction, at a right angle to the palace where their companions waited. The dragon followed leisurely, sinuously winding from side to side as it paced after them.

"It's herding us away from the others," Halisstra snarled.

She sensed hard stone behind her, and risked a quick glance backward. They were pinned against a building, sliding alongside it as they tried to keep their distance from the monster. A dark alleyway gaped just a few feet away. Halisstra hesitated for a heartbeat, then grasped Danifae by the wrist and darted into the narrow opening at the best speed she could manage.

Something waited for them in the shadows of the alley. Before Halisstra could skid to a stop, a tall golden creature reared up before her, half lion, half woman, beautiful and graceful. With a cold, cruel smile, the lion-woman reached out her hand and caressed Halisstra's cheek. Her touch was cool, soothing, and in an instant Halisstra felt her fear, her determination, her very willpower drain softly away. Vaguely she reached up to push the creature's hand away from her face.

"Don't be afraid," the creature said in a lovely voice. "Lie down and rest here a while. You are among friends, and no harm will come to you."

Halisstra stood paralyzed, recognizing that the creature's words made no sense, but empty of the willpower she needed to resist. Danifae whirled her away by her arm and slapped her hard across the face.

"It's a lamia!" she snapped. "It seeks to beguile you!"

The lamia snarled in anger, its beautiful features suddenly hard and cruel.

"Do not resist," it said, its voice harsher.

Halisstra could feel the creature's spell drawing over her, sapping at her resolve, seeking to subjugate her will to its own. She knew that if she gave in she would go willingly to her death, even lie down helplessly while the lamia devoured her if it asked her to, but the sting of Danifae's slap had reawakened the wellsprings of her will, just enough to fight through the lamia's sweet words.

"We are drow," Halisstra managed to gasp. "Our wills may not be broken by such as you."

The lamia bared its teeth in fierce anger and drew a bronze dagger from its hip, but Halisstra and Danifae backed out of the shadowed alley into the sun.

The dragon's gone, signed Danifae.

Halisstra shook her head and replied, *An illusion. We were deceived.*

Something was still hovering in the center of the street, a faint flickering phantasm that might have been about the size of the thing they had seen before, and they could hear as if from very far away its hissing protests.

"Illusion," Danifae spat in disgust.

The dragon-wisp gnawed at the corners of their minds, joined by other, more insistent murmuring and shadows. Buildings seemed to shimmer and vanish, replaced by ruins of different appearance. Dark and horrible things slithered through the rubble, closing off retreat. Ghostly drow dressed in resplendent robes appeared, smiling and happy, calling for them to join them in their blissful revels if only they would surrender first.

The lamia padded softly out into the street after them, holding its dagger behind its back.

"You may resist our enticements for a time," she purred, "but eventually we will wear you down." She reached out with her hand again. "Won't you let me smooth away your cares? Won't you let me touch you again? It would be so much easier."

A swift, graceful movement caught Halisstra's eye, and she glanced quickly to her left. Another lamia, this one male, had leaped to a wall top overshadowing their retreat. He was bronzed and handsome, lithe and tawny, and he smiled cruelly down on them.

"Your journey must have been long and tiresome," he said in voice of gold. "Won't you tell me of your travels? I want to hear all about them."

From the dark doorway of the court of justice, a third lamia emerged.

"Yes, indeed, tell us, tell us," the monster crooned. "What finer way to pass the day, eh? Rest, rest, and let us care for you."

It leaned against a great spear and smiled beatifically at them.

Halisstra and Danifae exchanged a single glance, and fled for their lives.

❁ ❁ ❁

Gromph Baenre, Archmage of Menzoberranzan, was dissatisfied. Though the slave revolt had been quelled without too much trouble, it disturbed him greatly that so many drow males had made common cause against the matron mothers. Not only that, they had made common cause with slave races to turn against the city. It bespoke desperate fear long suppressed, and something else beside—it suggested an unseen enemy who found a way to give that fear a voice and a mission. Drow simply did not cooperate so easily with each other that a coordinated rebellion could take shape secretly and spring full-grown to life.

The watchful lull that blanketed the city in the aftermath of the crushing of the revolt and the illithilich's demise struck Gromph as something malevolent and deceitful.

He stood up from his writing desk and paced across his chamber, thinking. Kyorli, the rat that served as his familiar, eyed him with cool disinterest as it munched on a slice of rothé cheese.

The sight of the rat somehow reminded the archmage that he hadn't heard from Pharaun in a while. The arrogant popinjay had reported that Ched Nasad was in a state of chaos. Perhaps it was time to check in on him.

Gromph stepped through an archway into an open shaft and levitated up to the room that served as his scrying chamber. Of necessity it was somewhat less well warded than other portions of his demesnes, since he required a certain amount of magical transparency in order to cast his mind out into the wide world around his palace. He reached the chamber and sat cross-legged in front of a low table on which rested a great crystal orb.

With a pass of his aged hands, he muttered the device's activating words and commanded, "Show me Pharaun Mizzrym, the impudent whelp who thinks he can replace me someday."

The last was not strictly necessary, but Gromph found it helpful to give voice to his frustrations before attempting to scry.

The orb grew gray and milky, swirling with fog, then it exploded with unheralded radiance. Gromph swore and averted his eyes. For a moment he believed that Pharaun had devised some new spell to discourage enemies from spying on him, but the Archmage soon recognized the peculiar quality of the brilliance.

Daylight.

Wondering what the Master of Sorcere could possibly be doing on the surface, Gromph shaded his eyes and peered again, looking closer. He saw Pharaun, sitting in the shadow of a crumbling wall as he studied his spellbooks. None of the other dark elves who had accompanied the wizard were in sight, though Gromph could see a nearby archway leading out into a hatefully brilliant courtyard beyond.

The tiny image of Pharaun looked up and frowned. The wizard had sensed Gromph's spying, as any skilled wielder of magic was likely to do. Pharaun made a few silent passes with his hands, and the picture faded. Pharaun had cast a spell to block the scrying, though chances were good he had no idea who might be watching him.

"So you think you will elude me so easily?" Gromph said, staring at the grayness.

He steepled his fingers before him and cast a spell of his own, a mental sending to dispatch a message straight to the errant wizard.

Where are you? What transpired in Ched Nasad? What do you intend to do next?

He composed himself to receive Pharaun's reply—the spell of sending conveyed the recipient's response within a few minutes. The moments crept by, as Gromph gazed out the high, narrow windows of his scrying chamber, awaiting the younger wizard's response.

He felt the feathery touch of Pharaun's words appearing in his mind: *Anauroch. Ched Nasad was destroyed by rebellion and stonefire. Lolth's silence did extend there. We now seek a priest of Vhaeraun in hope of answers.*

The contact faded after those twenty-five words. That particular spell didn't permit lengthy conversations, but Pharaun had answered Gromph's questions with uncharacteristic efficiency.

"Ched Nasad destroyed?" breathed Gromph.

That merited immediate investigation. He turned again to his crystal orb and commanded it to show him the City of Shimmering Webs. It took a moment for the mist to clear, and reveal to the Archmage a complete calamity.

Where Ched Nasad had stood, there was nothing but remnant strands of calcified webbing, dripping slowly into a black abyss like molten glass from a glazier's pipe. Of the city's sinister palaces and wall-climbing castles, virtually nothing remained.

"Lolth protect us," murmured Gromph, sickened at the sight.

He had no particular love for the City of Shimmering Webs, but whatever misfortune had befallen Ched Nasad might visit Menzoberranzan in time. Ched Nasad had been a city nearly as large and as powerful as Menzoberranzan itself, but Gromph could see with his own eyes the completeness of its ruin. If one building in twenty of the city remained, he would have been surprised.

Gromph shifted his orb's vision, searching as best he could for some sign of survivors, but the main cavern was largely deserted. He saw more than a few burned bodies among the smoldering debris, but any drow who'd lived through the burning of the city were clearly sheltering in the nearby caverns. Gromph was unable to bring them into the view of his scrying device, so after a time he decided that the effort was irrelevant and allowed the crystal orb to go dim again. He sat for a long time in silence, gazing absently at the darkened orb.

"Now, do I need to share this with dear Triel?" he asked himself when he finally stirred from his reverie.

He knew something that the matron mothers presumably did not, and that was always the sign of possibility. The trouble was, Gromph had no idea what possible advantage he could derive from hoarding the knowledge, and the risks of failing to communicate what he had learned were all too clear. Knowing that Lolth's silence extended beyond Menzoberranzan, he might mount a direct challenge to the priestesses—if he were inclined to do so—but even if he brought the full strength of Sorcere against the ruling Houses of the city, what would be left if he did succeed? The smoldering wreckage of Ched Nasad seemed a likely result. Most likely the House loyalties among the masters of the wizards' school would cripple any such nonsense from the start.

No, Gromph decided. I am no revolutionary anxious to sweep away the old order—not yet, anyway.

Besides, the most likely cause of all the trouble was some insidious new snare of Lolth's devising. Gromph wouldn't put it past the Spider Queen to fall completely and inexplicably silent, just to see who might slink out of the shadows in order to take advantage of her priestesses' temporary "weakness." That meant that sooner or later, Lolth would tire of her game and restore her favor to her clerics. When that happened, woe to anyone foolish enough to have shown the shallowness of his allegiance to the established order. No, the wisest thing to do was to pass along to Triel what he'd learned, and to make sure Matron Baenre didn't hoard the knowledge to herself. Pharaun's words indicated in a few quick brushstrokes a very grave danger to Menzoberranzan, and Gromph refused to be remembered as the archmage who allowed his city to be razed.

With a sigh, he stood and dropped silently back down the shaft. He rather hoped Triel was in the middle of something awkward, so that he could savor the petty pleasure of interrupting her with news that could not wait.

🕷   🕷   🕷

"The question is not where we should go next," observed Pharaun with a wry grimace. "The question is how we shall escape Hlaunga-dath alive." The Master of Sorcere was exhausted. Dust plastered the blood and sweat on his face, and he was so tired he could do no more than collapse into the shadow of a long, crumbling wall. Having long since exhausted any spells useful in battle, he wielded a wand of thin black iron from which he called forth bolts of lightning. Pharaun glanced up at the sky as if to gauge how much more daylight remained, and he quickly winced away. "Will the cursed sun never set?"

"Get up, wizard," said Quenthel. "If we rest, we die."

She, too, trembled with exhaustion, but she stayed on her feet. The long snake-headed whips she carried still coiled and hissed dangerously, covered with gore, but blood trickled from a nasty cut above her left eye, and two furrows of broken and twisted links in her mail shirt showed just how close she'd come to dying under the claws of some hulking monstrosity of gray skin and spiderlike eyes.

"You're more vulnerable to the lamias' powers of suggestion and illusion while you're fatigued," Halisstra said. "Better to die fighting than to fall under the dominion of such a creature."

She was in much the same condition as the others. Since she and Danifae had survived their initial encounter with the monsters, it had been an hours-long running battle through the streets and empty buildings of the ruins. First, a large pride of lamias had tried to overwhelm the party with their beguiling powers, but drow on guard for such magical tricks were no easy prey. Halisstra and the others steeled themselves for a fight against the lion-bodied monsters, but the lamias—deceitful and cowardly things that they were—withdrew from the battle and instead hurled wave after wave of beguiled thralls at the drow party. Lamias might have lacked for physical courage, but the manticores, asabis, gargoyles, and other assorted creatures under their control certainly did not.

"Neither option appeals to me," Quenthel growled. She turned slowly, studying the walls and structures around them, seeking escape. "There. I can see the open desert just beyond those buildings. Maybe they'll abandon the chase if we leave the city."

"Unwise, Mistress," said Valas. He crouched by an archway leading into their temporary refuge, watching for the next assault. "Once we leave the shelter of the walls, they'll know exactly where we are. We'd be visible for miles out in the open, even with our *piwafwis*—they weren't made to hide us in bright daylight on an open plain. Concealment is our best defense."

Ryld nodded wearily. He stood by another doorway, his greatsword resting on his shoulder.

"They would surround us and drag us down out there," the Master of Melee-Magthere said. "Best to try to keep moving within the ruins, and hope the lamias—ah, damn. We've got more company."

Rubble shifted somewhere in the maze of crumbling walls beyond their refuge as something large padded closer.

"Watch out for illusions," Halisstra said.

She balanced her mace in her hand and tugged at her shield, making sure it was strapped securely to her arm. Behind her, Danifae crouched, a long dagger in her hand. Halisstra wasn't happy about arming her battle captive, but at the moment they needed all the help they could get, and it was plainly in Danifae's best interests to make sure they didn't all fall prey to the denizens of Hlaungadath.

The lamias tried something new. Against the gap in the wall that Jeggred guarded, the monsters hurled a wave of lizardlike asabis, savage creatures that hissed in anger as they threw themselves against the draegloth with scimitars and falchions clutched in their scaly hands. Three more challenged Valas while a pair of gargoyles streaked over the walls and dropped into the midst of the ruined building behind Ryld, their great black wings raising huge clouds of dust with every beat. The weapons master whirled to face the threat behind him, cursing.

Jeggred howled in rage and leaped to meet the rush of the asabis, batting aside flashing blades and snapping jaws while he tore at the lizard warriors with his great talons. The white-haired demon used his four arms to wreak terrible carnage, but even Jeggred was tiring. Blows he would have eluded with his freakish speed landed awkwardly. He blocked one slashing scimitar badly with his left outer arm, and suffered a long bloody cut halfway from elbow to wrist. Another blade scored his torso, starting a stream of red across his white-pelted chest. The draegloth roared in rage and redoubled his efforts.

Ryld slashed at the gargoyles while Halisstra and Quenthel ran to his side. Quenthel lashed at one with her whip. The snake heads wound around the creature's taloned legs and sank fangs into stony flesh, but the gargoyle beat furiously for height and dragged the priestess off her feet and across the dusty structure. Pharaun raised his wand to blast the monsters with deadly lightning, but spun in a half-circle and fell, a crossbow bolt transfixing his right forearm. The wand flew from his hands.

"The rooftops!" the wizard called.

Halisstra backed away from the gargoyles and squinted at the bright sky, searching for more attackers. Tawny blurs crouched atop a high wall perhaps forty or fifty yards distant, a handful of lamias who carried heavy crossbows and watched carefully for opportunities to shoot into the fray, their beautiful faces twisted into evil grins. Even as she watched, one took at shot at Ryld. The bolt whistled past the weapons master's head, smashing a divot from the soft stone wall nearby. Ryld flinched away.

"Someone take care of the snipers!" he snapped, while slashing at the gargoyles.

A second later, two more bolts flew at Ryld. One bounced from his breastplate, but the other caught him on the right side while his arms were raised to wield Splitter. The bolt lodged in the arm-opening of his armor. Ryld staggered back two steps and collapsed in the dust.

Halisstra reached down and snatched up Pharaun's wand.

"Aid Quenthel," she told Danifae.

She leveled the wizard's weapon at the lamias on the high wall. She knew something about using such devices—a talent she wouldn't normally have wished to reveal, but the fight was desperate. She spoke an arcane word, and a bolt of purple lightning shot out at the first lamia, blasting the creature from the wall in a spray of shattered stone. Thunder reverberated in the dusty ruin. She aimed at the next lamia, but the monsters weren't stupid. They abandoned their lofty perches at once, leaping back behind the wall to avoid more lightning.

From the shadow of the back wall, Pharaun returned to the battle, armed with another wand. This one produced a blazing bolt of fire, which he directed against the gargoyles overhead. With shrieks of pain, the monsters flapped off, though the one poisoned by Quenthel's whips didn't get far before its wings folded. It plummeted down among the rooftops some distance away.

Valas dispatched the last of his attackers with a double-handed slash that nearly cut the creature in two, and Jeggred stood amid a virtual heap of asabi bodies, his flanks heaving. The wizard glanced around once, and noticed Ryld on the ground.

"Damn," he muttered.

He knelt by the weapons master and turned him over. Ryld was dying. Blood streamed from the bolt in his chest, and he fought for each breath, bloody spittle streaking his gray lips. The wizard scowled, then looked up at Quenthel.

"Do something," he said. "We need him."

Quenthel folded her arms with a cold frown and said, "Unfortunately, Lolth does not choose to grant me spells of healing at the moment, and I have already expended almost all of the healing magic I brought on our journey. There is little I can do for him."

Halisstra narrowed her eyes, thinking. Again, she didn't like the thought of what she was about to do, but there was a benefit to revealing her secret. If she proved herself useful, the Menzoberranyr would be hesitant to discard her.

Besides, she thought, they likely already know.

"Move aside," she said quietly. "I can help him."

Quenthel and Pharaun looked up suspiciously.

"How?" Quenthel demanded. "Do you mean to say that Lolth has not withdrawn her favor from you?"

"No," Halisstra replied. She knelt by Ryld and examined him. She would have to move quickly. If he died, he would be beyond her assistance. "Lolth has denied me spells, just as she has Quenthel, and presumably every other priestess of our race. I have some ability to heal by a different means, though."

With that, she began to sing. Her song was a strange keening threnody, something dark and eerie that tugged at the drow admiration for beauty, ambition, and black deeds skillfully done. Halisstra molded the shape of her voice and the ancient words of the song, summoning the magic of her lament as she set her hand on the quarrel and drew it from the wound.

Ryld started, his eyes wide and staring, and blood spurted over Halisstra's hands—but the wound closed into a puckered scar, and the weapons master coughed himself awake.

"What happened?" he groaned.

"What happened, indeed?" Quenthel replied. She eyed Halisstra suspiciously. "Was that what I thought it was?"

Halisstra nodded and stood, wiping blood from her hands.

"It is a tradition in my House that those females who are suited for it may study the arts of the *bae'qeshel*, the dark minstrels. As you can see, there is power in song, something that few of our kind care to study. I have been trained in the minstrel's lore."

Ryld sat up, looking down at his breastplate and the bloody quarrel lying in the dust. He looked up at Halisstra.

"You healed me?" he asked.

Halisstra offered her hand and pulled him to his feet.

"As your friend Pharaun observed, we need you too much to allow you to inconvenience us with your death."

Ryld met her eyes, obviously considering some reply. Gratitude was not an emotion many drow bothered to act upon. The weapons master perhaps wondered what Halisstra might choose to do with his.

She spared him any more serious reflections by turning her attention to Pharaun, and handing the iron wand back to him.

"Here," she said. "You dropped this."

Pharaun inclined his head and replied, "I admit I was surprised to see you wield it, but I heard you sing in Ched Nasad. Shame on me for not adding two and two."

"Let me see your arm," Halisstra said.

She sang the song of healing again, and repaired Pharaun's injury.

She would have examined the others and aided them if she could, but Quenthel interrupted her.

"No one else is dying," the high priestess said. "We must move now or our enemies will surely descend on us again. Valas, you lead the way. Head toward the outer walls so that we may make for the open desert if we decide to flee."

"Very well, Mistress Baenre," the scout acquiesced. "It will be as you say."

Kaanyr Vhok, the half-demon prince known as the Sceptered One, stood on a high balcony over the old dwarven foundry and watched his armorers at work. The great smelter had once been the heart of the fallen realm of Ammarindar. The cavern was immense, and its roof rested upon dozens of towering pillars carved into the shapes of dragons, glowing red with angry firelight and the lurid radiance of molten metal. The clanging of hammers and roar of kilns at work filled the air. Dozens of hulking tanarukks, bestial fiends bred from orcs and demons, toiled on the foundry floor. They might have lacked the skill and enchantments of the dwarves who once worked there, but Kaanyr Vhok's soldiers possessed a cunning instinct for the making of deadly weapons infused with dark lore.

Kaanyr himself fit the infernal scene well. Tall and powerful, he had the stature of a strong-thewed human warrior and the strength of a stone giant. His skin was red and hot to the touch, and his flesh was hard enough to turn a blade. He was strikingly handsome, though his eyes danced with malice and his teeth were as black as coal. He wore a golden breastplate and carried a pair of wicked short swords made from some demonic black iron in rune-chased scabbards at his belt. He grinned fiercely with delight as he looked out over the gathering storm of his army.

"I now lead nearly two thousand tanarukk warriors," he said over his shoulder, "and I have just as many orcs, ogres, trolls, and giants at my command. I think the time has come to try my strength, my love."

Aliisza allowed herself a smile and moved closer, pressing herself to the demon prince's side. Like Kaanyr Vhok, she too possessed demonic blood. In her case, she was an alu-fiend, the spawn of a succubus and some mortal sorcerer. Wings as smooth as black leather sprouted from her shoulder blades, but other than that she was dusky and seductive, voluptuous and inviting, a half-demoness whose allure few mortal men could resist. She was also clever, capricious, and very skilled in magic, and therefore well-suited to be the consort of a demonspawned warlord such as Kaanyr.

"Menzoberranzan?" she purred, tracing the filigree of his armor with one fingertip.

"Of course. There seems to be nothing worth the taking in Ched Nasad, after all." Kaanyr frowned, and his gaze grew distant. "If the dark elves are without the protection of their spider goddess, and unable to govern their interminable feuds, I may have an opportunity to seize the greatness I have always coveted. Having mastered the ruins of Ammarindar, I find that I hunger for something more. Subjugating a city of drow appeals to me."

"Others have had that thought," Aliisza pointed out. "The Menzoberranyr I spoke with in Ched Nasad suggested that his own city had suffered a significant slave uprising, sponsored by some outside agency. I think the duergar mercenaries who fought in Ched Nasad would not have left the city to whatever House hired them, once they'd managed to take it. If the duergar firebombs hadn't worked so well, I suspect Clan Xornbane would rule Ched Nasad now."

"Or I would," Kaanyr said. He narrowed his eyes. "If you had reported the situation to me in a more timely manner, I might have been able to bring my army against Ched Nasad when the drow and duergar were exhausted from fighting each other."

Aliisza licked her lips.

"You would have lost whatever forces you brought into the city," she replied. "Your tanarukks could have endured the fires, of course, but the collapse of the city streets destroyed everything in the cavern. Trust me, you missed no opportunities in Ched Nasad."

Kaanyr did not reply. Instead, he disentangled himself from Aliisza and vaulted lightly over the balcony rail, descending to the foundry floor. The warlord had no wings, but his demonic heritage conferred the ability to fly through effort of will. Aliisza frowned, and followed behind him, spreading her black pinions wide to catch the blazing updrafts of the room. Kaanyr was still sore about Ched Nasad, and that was not good, she reflected. If the warlord ever tired of her, he was certainly capable of having her killed in some grisly manner, past intimacies notwithstanding. There was nothing of which he was not capable, if his temper got the better of him.

The half-demon alighted beside a sand mold filling with molten iron. A pair of tanarukks stood by, carefully watching over the pour. Kaanyr squatted down by the white-hot metal and absently stirred his fingers in it. It was hot enough to cause him discomfort, and after a moment he shook the molten iron from his fingers and brushed them against his thigh.

"Good iron," he said to the tanarukks. "Carry on, lads."

He straightened and continued on his way. Aliisza fluttered to the stone floor and fell into step behind him.

"The thing that troubles me is this," Kaanyr mused. "Why did the Xornbane duergar betray the House that employed them by burning the whole city? Was it simply a dispute over pay? Or did they intend from the start to bring ruin to Ched Nasad? If so, was Horgar Steelshadow behind it? Did the prince of Gracklstugh send his mercenaries to Ched Nasad to destroy the city, or did Clan Xornbane do that for someone else?"

"Does it matter?" Aliisza asked, sidling up beside him again.

"The city was destroyed, regardless of anyone's intentions. The great Houses of Ched Nasad are dead, and there aren't many Xornbane dwarves remaining, for that matter."

"It matters because I find myself wondering whether the duergar of Gracklstugh plan to attack Menzoberranzan next," Kaanyr said. "I have amassed no small strength here, but I do not believe I can take Menzoberranzan unless the dark elves are reduced to utter chaos and helplessness. If the duergar mean to march on the city too, my opportunities are limitless."

"Ah," Aliisza breathed. "You could sell your services to the dark elves, the gray dwarves, both, or neither. Hmm, that *is* interesting."

"And the price I command will increase with the number of warriors I bring, and my proximity to Menzoberranzan, but it depends on the intentions of the gray dwarves." The half-demon let out a bark of hard laughter. "I would not care to find myself on Menzoberranzan's doorstep, facing a strong and united dark elf city with no allies at hand."

"Why do I get the feeling that you're about to send me away again?" Aliisza pouted. She stretched her wings languorously around Kaanyr, halting him as she reached up to turn him toward her. "I've only just come back, you know."

"Clever girl," Vhok said with a smile. "Yes, I mean to dispatch you on another mission. This time, though, you won't have to creep about and stay out of sight. You will call on Horgar Steelshadow, the Crown Prince of Gracklstugh, as my personal envoy—a diplomat, if you like. Find out if the gray dwarves intend to attack Menzoberranzan. If they do, let them know that I would like to join them. If they don't . . . well, see if you can't persuade them that it's in their best interest to destroy Menzoberranzan while the dark elves are weak."

"The dwarves are not likely to confide in me."

"Of course they won't want to confide in you. However, if they do intend to attack, they will see the advantage of gaining me as an ally. If they don't plan on attacking, the fact that I am willing to ally with them may decide the issue for them. They wish Menzoberranzan no good, so you need not worry that they'll stand up for the drow."

"Envoy. . . ." Aliisza murmured. "It sounds better than spy, doesn't it? I suppose I can carry your message for you, my sweet, fierce Kaanyr, but maybe you should provide me with some special incentive to hurry home, hmm?"

Kaanyr Vhok circled her with his powerful arms and nuzzled the hollow of her neck.

"Very well, my pet," he rumbled. "Though I sometimes wonder if you are utterly insatiable."

* * *

A desperate hour of flight from ruin to ruin saw the battered company to a hard-won refuge from the monsters who ruled Hlaungadath. Beneath the hulking shell of a square tower they found a sand-choked stair descending into cool, lightless catacombs beneath the city. Buoyed by their find, the dark elves slipped through a maze of buried shrines, subterranean wells, and echoing colonnades of brown stone, finally holing up in a deep, disused gallery that showed no signs of recent use. It was a cheerless and desolate spot, but it was free of blinding sunlight and mind-controlling monsters, and that was all they needed.

"Pharaun, prepare your spells quickly," Quenthel commanded after sizing up the chamber. "Halisstra, you and Ryld will stand watch here. Jeggred, you and Valas keep watch on the far archway, over there."

"Unfortunately, you must keep your watch for some time," the wizard said. He made a rueful gesture. "I was ready to study my spellbook earlier, when I'd had some time to rest in the courtyard of the palace above, but the poor hospitality of our lamia hosts has left me somewhat fatigued. I must rest for some time before I will be able to ready my spells."

"We're all tired," Quenthel snarled. "We have no time for you to rest. Prepare your spells at once!"

The snakes of her whip coiled and hissed in agitation.

"The exercise would be pointless, dear Quenthel. You must

keep our enemies away from me until I have recovered from my exertions."

"If he is so powerless," Jeggred rumbled, "now would be as good a time as any to punish him for his disrespectful attitude and many transgressions."

"Stupid creature," Pharaun snorted. "Slay me, and all of you will die in these light-blasted wastelands within a day. Or perhaps you have suddenly acquired a knack for the arcane arts?"

Jeggred bristled, but Quenthel silenced him with nothing more than a look. The draegloth stalked off to take up his watch at the far end of the long, dusty chamber, crouching in a jumble of fallen stones near the opposite entrance. Valas sighed and trotted off to join him.

"Ready your spells as fast as you can, wizard," the priestess said, deadly anger tightly contained in her voice. "I have little patience left for your wit. Give Halisstra your lightning wand in case we need spells of that sort to repel another attack."

It was a measure of his true exhaustion that Pharaun didn't even bother to seek the last word. He turned to Halisstra and dropped the black iron wand into her hand with a sour smile.

"I suppose you know how to use this already. I'll want it back, of course, so please try not to exhaust it completely. They're hard to make."

"I won't use it unless I have to," Halisstra said.

She watched as the wizard found a shadowed spot beside a large column and sat down cross-legged, leaning against the cold stone, and she tucked the wand into her belt. Quenthel composed herself against the opposite wall, watching Pharaun as if to make sure he was not feigning his need for rest. Ryld Argith pushed himself erect and set out for the passage leading back toward the monster-haunted surface, leaning on his massive greatsword as he did so.

Halisstra started to follow, but Danifae said, "Shall I keep watch here, Mistress Melarn?"

The girl knelt on the dusty floor between the wizard and the priestess, the dagger thrust through her belt. She looked up at Halisstra, her expression blank and perfect, the picture of an innocent question.

The Melarn priestess repressed a grimace. Arming a battle captive was tantamount to admitting one no longer had the strength to force her submission, and she suspected that Danifae would later exact a difficult price for continued compliance. Danifae watched serenely as her mistress considered the offer. Halisstra could feel Quenthel's eyes on her too, and she steeled herself against glancing at the Baenre priestess to measure her approval.

"You may keep the dagger to defend yourself—for now," Halisstra allowed. "Your vigilance is not required. Do not presume to suggest such a thing again."

"Of course, Mistress Melarn," Danifae replied.

The girl's face was devoid of emotion, but Halisstra didn't like the thoughtful look in Danifae's eye as she composed herself to wait.

Will her binding hold? Halisstra mused.

In the heart of House Melarn, surrounded by the full strength of her enemies, Danifae would not have dared to throw off the magical compulsion that enslaved her, even if she could do such a thing. Things had changed, though. Danifae's care in how she addressed her mistress in front of Quenthel did not escape Halisstra's notice. Without her House, her city, to invest Halisstra with absolute dominion over what she called her own—her life, her loyalties, and possessions such as Danifae—any or all of those things might be wrested away from her. The thought left her feeling as hollow and as brittle as a rotten piece of bone.

What happens when Danifae decides to test the bounds of her captivity in earnest? she wondered. Would Quenthel permit Halisstra to retain her mastery over the girl, or would the Baenre intercede simply to spite Halisstra and strip her of one more shred of her status? For that matter, was Quenthel capable of freeing Danifae and claiming Halisstra herself as a battle captive?

The girl studied Halisstra from her lowered eyes, demure and beautiful. Patient.

"Are you coming?" Ryld asked. He stood in the mouth of the passage, waiting.

"Yes, of course," Halisstra said, barely repressing a scowl.

Deliberately turning her back on the servant, Halisstra followed Ryld back out to the tunnels leading to their refuge. For the moment, she was safe enough. Danifae could not remove the silver locket from her neck with all of her will, strength, and effort. The moment she touched it, the enchantment would lock her muscles into rigidity until she abandoned the attempt. Nor could she ask someone else to remove it for her, since the moment she tried to speak of the locket, her tongue would freeze in her mouth. As long as the locket encircled her neck, Danifae was compelled to serve Halisstra, even to the point of giving her own life to save her mistress. Danifae had borne her bondage well, but Halisstra had no intention of removing the locket in the presence of the Menzoberranyr—if, in fact, she ever did.

She and Ryld took up positions in a small rotunda a short ways down the tunnel, a dark and open space from which they could keep the approach to their refuge under careful observation without being seen themselves. Folded in their *piwafwis*, they were virtually indistinguishable from the dark stone around them. Despite the capricious chaos and gnawing ambition that burned in every drow heart, any drow of accomplishment was capable of patience and iron discipline in the performance of an important task, and so Halisstra and Ryld set themselves to watch and wait in vigilant silence.

Halisstra tried to empty her mind of all but the input of her senses, to better stand her watch, but she found that her head was filled with thoughts that did not care to be dismissed. It occurred to Halisstra that whatever became of her from this day forward, she would rise or fall based on nothing more than her own strength, cunning, and ruthlessness. The displeasure of House Melarn meant nothing. If she desired respect, she would have to make the displeasure of Halisstra Melarn something to be feared in its place. All because Lolth had decided to test those most faithful to her. By the caprice of the goddess House Melarn of Ched Nasad, whose leading females for centuries beyond counting had poured out blood and treasure upon the Spider Queen's altars, had been cast down.

Why? Halisstra wondered. Why?

The answer was cold and empty, of course. Lolth's machinations were not for her priestesses to understand, and her tests could be cruel indeed. Halisstra ground her teeth softly and tried to thrust her weak questions out of her heart. If Lolth chose to test Halisstra's faith by stripping her of everything she held dear to see if the First Daughter of House Melarn could win it back, the Spider Queen would find her equal to the challenge.

Care to talk about it? Ryld's fingers flashed discreetly in the sophisticated sign language of the dark elves.

Talk about what?

Whatever it is that troubles you. Something has you tied in a knot, priestess.

It is nothing to concern a male, she replied.

Of course. It never is.

Their eyes met across the small chamber. Halisstra was surprised to find Ryld's face twisted in a curious expression of bitter resignation and wry amusement at the same time. She studied him carefully, trying to ascertain what motive he might have had for striking up a conversation.

He was very tall and strongly built for a male—for any dark elf, really—just as tall as she was herself. His close-cropped hair was an exotic affectation in drow society, a strangely ascetic austerity for a race that delighted in things of beauty and personal refinement. Drow were ruthlessly pragmatic in their dealings with one another, but not in their grooming. Most males in Halisstra's experience preened themselves, affecting silken grace and deadly guile. Pharaun virtually epitomized the type. Ryld, she realized, was something very different.

You fight well, she offered—not an apology, not to a male, but still something. *You could have let me die in Ched Nasad, yet you risked yourself to save me. Why?*

We had an agreement. You led us to safety, and we helped you escape.

Yes, but I had discharged my end of the bargain by that time. There was no need to honor yours.

There was no need not to. Ryld offered a slight smile, and shifted to a soft whisper. "Besides, it seems that it was in my own interests to save you, as not an hour ago you saved my life in turn. We are indebted to each other."

Halisstra laughed at that, so quietly that no one more than ten feet away would have noticed.

We are not a race given to honoring our debts, she signed.

That has been made clear to me more than once, the weapons master replied. A brief flicker of pain crossed his face, and Halisstra wondered exactly whom the Master of Melee-Magthere had trusted, and why he'd done something so foolish. Before she could ask, he continued, *So tell me of the* bae'qeshel. *I do not know of them.*

"By tradition," she whispered, "our wizards, swordsmen, and clerics are trained in academies. This is true in most drow cities. The reason you do not know of the *bae'qeshel* is that the bardic training is not a public matter. We pass our secrets, one mistress to one student at a time."

I thought the noble Houses had little use for common minstrels.

"The *bae'qeshel* are not common minstrels, weapons master," Halisstra said in a low voice. "We are a proud and ancient sect, the *bae'qeshel telphraezzar*, the Whisperers of the Dark Queen. I am a priestess of Lolth, as are the other females of my House, but I was chosen to spend many long years as a girl studying the *bae'qeshel* lore. I revere the goddess not only with my service as her priestess, but with the gift of raising the ancient songs of our race, which are pleasing to her ears. House Melarn has always been proud to raise one *bae'qeshel* into the sisterhood of Lolth's service in each generation."

"If your songs are sacred to Lolth, why do they work while other spells fail?" Ryld asked.

"Because the songs possess a power in and of themselves, like a wizard's spells. We do not channel the divine power of the Queen of Spiders to wield our songs. Regrettably, my skill with such things is nothing compared to the divine might I could wield in Lolth's name, if she would restore her favor to me."

"An interesting talent, nonetheless," he murmured. Ryld glanced back down the passageway toward the chamber where the others waited. "It seems quiet enough. We may have some time to wait yet. If I know Pharaun, he will need hours to regain his strength. Tell me, do you play *sava*?"

❦ ❦ ❦

Nimor clung to the shadows of a gigantic stalactite, one of many such stone fangs reaching down from the ceiling of Menzoberranzan's vast cavern. Old passages and precarious paths crisscrossed the city's roof, and many of the stalactites were in fact carved into darkly beautiful castles and aeries all the more spectacular for their bold arrogance. Only drow would make homes out of fragile stone spears a thousand feet above the cavern floor. Highborn dark elves frequently possessed innate magic or enchanted trinkets that freed them of concern over heights, and gave little thought to dizzying overlooks that would terrify bats. Their slaves and servants were not so fortunate, and must have found life in a ceiling spire something peculiarly nerve-racking.

The more important ceiling spires were of course magically re-inforced against the inevitable fall, and would not fail unless magic itself gave out—but more than one proud old palace stood dusty and abandoned at the top of the city, the House that claimed it too weak in the Art to maintain the spells that made the place tenable. It was in just such an empty place that Nimor crouched, leaning out over a dark abyss to study his target below.

House Faen Tlabbar, Third House of Menzoberranzan, lay below him and a short distance to his left. The castle sprawled over several towering stalagmites and columns, its elegant balustrades and soaring buttresses belying the underlying strength of the rambling towers and mighty bulwarks of dark stone. Faen Tlabbar's compound was one of the largest and proudest of any in Menzoberranzan that did not sit on the high plateau of Qu'ellarz'orl, the most prestigious of the underground city's noble districts. Instead House Tlabbar's palace clambered up along the southern wall of

Menzoberranzan's great cavern, until its highest spires surmounted the plateau in whose shadow it sat, as if the matrons of the Third House wished to be able to peer over the plateau's edge and gaze enviously upon the manors fortunate enough to be located alongside the exalted House Baenre.

It was an apt analogy for Faen Tlabbar's political maneuverings. Only two Houses stood ahead of them in Menzoberranzan's dark hierarchy: Baenre, the First, and Barrison Del'Armgo, the Second. Nimor thought it likely that Matron Mother Tlabbar harbored great aspirations for her House. Del'Armgo, the Second House, was strong but with few allies. Baenre, the strongest, was as weak as it had been in centuries. Houses such as Faen Tlabbar gazed on the Baenre and remembered centuries of absolute arrogance, humiliating condescension, and they wondered whether the time had come for several lesser Houses to band together and end Baenre's dominance once and for all.

"That would be a merry game to watch," Nimor mused.

He suspected that in such a scenario Baenre might prove stronger than their resentful rivals guessed, but the bloodletting would be spectacular. Several great Houses would fall, for Baenre would not go alone into the gentle night. Of course, that would go a long way toward advancing the schemes of the Anointed Blade of the Jaezred Chaulssin.

That would be a play for another day, though. Nimor meant to strike a deep and grievous blow at Faen Tlabbar, not incite them against House Baenre. Ghenni Tlabbar, Matron of the Third House, would die beneath his blade. Her blood would purchase treason on a grand scale, and place into the assassin's hand the stiletto Nimor meant to drive into Menzoberranzan's heart.

A scrabbling sound and the clink of mail caught Nimor's notice. He withdrew softly into the shadows and waited patiently as a squad of Tlabbar warriors mounted on great riding lizards climbed along a small, unworked stalactite nearby. The pallid reptiles possessed large, sticky pads on their clawed feet that allowed them to cling to the sheerest of surfaces, and many of Menzoberranzan's noble

Houses used the creatures for patrolling the high places of the city's vast cavern. Faen Tlabbar was renowned for its squadrons of lizard cavalry. The assassin had studied the Tlabbar patrols from his precarious perch for more than an hour, carefully timing their sweeps.

Right on time, Nimor observed. You've allowed yourselves to become predictable, lads.

The riders carried crossbows and lances at the ready, scurrying along in single file as they looped around the smaller stalactite and scanned the cavern ceiling. As Nimor expected, the leader turned to the left and followed the curve of the stone pinnacle down and out of sight.

"You would do well to vary your routine, Captain," Nimor whispered to the departing squad. "An intrepid fellow such as myself might be deterred by the possibility of your unexpected return."

With a single silent spring, Nimor launched himself out into the vast darkness, plunging through the eternal night.

By an accident of cavern formation, House Tlabbar held little of the city's roof and overcaverns. One large column and a pair of small stalactites linked Tlabbar to the ceiling, which meant that Tlabbar had something of a blind spot directly over its palace roof. This was the weakness Nimor intended to exploit. His black cloak streamed behind him, and cold air rushed past his face. Nimor bared his teeth in a savage grin, delighting in the long seconds of his great leap. His body burned with the dark fires of his heritage, and he longed to shed his rakish guise, but this was not the time.

While he fell, he mouthed the words to a spell that made him invisible, and as the spearlike pinnacle of Faen Tlabbar's central palace rushed up at him, he quickly halted his fall by employing his power of levitation. Less than six heartbeats from the moment he'd leaped from the abandoned stalactite overhead, Nimor alighted on the knifelike ridge of a steep hall, invisible and undetected. He listened for any sign that he had been detected, then he glided toward the hall's juncture with the castle proper, his steps as silent as death.

The dark elves of Faen Tlabbar were not unaware of their vulnerability to assault from above, and vigilant sentries manned battlements and cupolas atop the palace, watching for intruders. Nimor avoided them carefully. Those who were able to see invisible foes—and there were more than a few—were not in the habit of watching for an invisible foe who also glided from shadow to shadow with the stealth of a master assassin. Nimor was more concerned with the various magical barriers shielding the house. He habitually protected himself with spells designed to counter and confuse various forms of magical detection, but they were not foolproof.

Green and gold radiance glimmered around him as he crept along the steep, tiled roof of a square tower. The Faen Tlabbar, like many other Houses, used magic to illuminate and decorate the baroque spires and balconies of their home. Nimor lowered himself to his belly and edged down even farther, headfirst, listening carefully. Below him he expected to find a guard post, and an entrance leading into the manor itself. Over the decades the Jaezred Chaulssin had used magic to scry what they could of the layout and defenses of many great Houses in more than one drow city, and the slender assassin had carefully studied his brotherhood's notes and drawings on House Tlabbar. The information was, of course, incomplete and out of date, as parts of the castle were blocked from all scrying, and the Jaezred Chaulssin had not studied the Houses of Menzoberranzan in a very long time. Nimor would have preferred to update his information through the bribery or capture of a Tlabbar guard, but he simply did not have the time to arrange such a thing and keep the rest of his timetable intact.

He heard the soft sounds of movement on the balcony below the eave of the roof he lay on. Two, he guessed, at least one wearing chain mail. He would have to be swift—a single outcry could spell the end of his single-handed assault on the castle. With calculating patience, Nimor edged out even more and found himself looking down on a curving gallery beneath the overhanging eave. To his left, the walkway became a walled stair leading down to the lower battlements, while to his right it simply ended at a black doorway. The door itself stood open. Directly beneath him stood a drow male in armor, gazing out over a lower courtyard.

Nimor studied the fellow for a full thirty heartbeats, planning his strike as he quietly slipped his dagger from its sheath. It was a blade of green-black enchanted steel that glistened wetly in the glimmering faerielight. Then, still invisible, he rolled himself off the roof and dropped down behind the Tlabbar guard.

The assassin's feet thudded softly to the flagstones. The guard started to turn and opened his mouth to cry out, but with one remorseless movement, Nimor clapped a hand over the fellow's face and punched his dagger deep into the base of the skull. The blade grated on bone, and the Tlabbar guard simply sagged into Nimor's arms, dead on his feet.

Nimor let the nerveless body slump to the floor and looked up at the other sentry in the guard post, a fellow in the black robes of a wizard. The Tlabbar mage glanced over at the rustle of sound, just in time to see his watch mate fold up and collapse for no apparent cause—for Nimor was still invisible.

"Zilzmaer?" he said sharply. "What is it?"

Nimor bounded forward and rammed his bloody knife up under the wizard's chin, nailing his jaws closed and transfixing the Tlabbar's brain. The mage jerked two or three times, violently, then shuddered and died.

"Shh," the assassin hissed. "It's nothing. Go to sleep."

He laid the wizard alongside his companion, and turned to the dark archway leading into the castle proper.

Knife in hand, he stalked through—only to be halted by an invisible, intangible barrier that blocked the archway as surely as a wall of masonry. Nimor frowned, summoned up his willpower, and tried the archway again, only to find his passage barred in mid-step.

"Damnation," he muttered. "A forbidding."

The Tlabbar castle, or its interior anyway, was warded by a great fixed spell that utterly prevented an enemy from setting foot within. Nimor could elude or undo some magical traps, but the forbidding was simply beyond his ability to penetrate.

That explains the open door, he thought. The Tlabbars are confident in their magical defenses. Now what?

Nimor sheathed his knife and studied the archway. A spell of forbidding could be crafted to defend a building or area in one of several ways, but if the Tlabbars wanted to move about their own castle, they would have had to make a forbidding through which one could pass without too much difficulty—perhaps with a token of some kind, or maybe with a password. Nimor quickly searched the bodies of the two Tlabbar guards he'd slain, but found nothing that seemed like it might serve as a token to pass the forbidding.

It might be anything, he thought. A cloak clasp, an enchanted coin in a purse, an earring or a necklace . . .

He decided he didn't have time to experiment. With one hand he picked up the dead wizard and tucked the fellow under his arm, then he strode back to the archway and steeled himself to step through. This time, he passed through without resistance, as if the ward was simply gone.

Something the Tlabbar guards wear, then, Nimor decided.

He briefly considered shouldering the dead wizard and carrying the fellow along in case he needed to pass another warding inside the castle, but decided against it. Stealth and speed were his best defenses, and lugging a corpse through the castle was not particularly subtle. Besides, the Tlabbars were not likely to have two forbiddings in their palace, or to use the same key for both if they did. He unceremoniously dumped the wizard on the other side of the doorway, and headed inside.

The archway opened into a long, high-ceilinged corridor that ran above one of the Tlabbar halls. Doors made of pale zurkhwood lined the hall, opening into studies, parlors, trophy rooms, and other such chambers if Nimor's old maps were correct. He ignored them all and darted swiftly down the hall, reaching a small staircase at the end that descended to the level below. Here he encountered a magical glyph barring passage on the stair, but he sensed the trap before stepping close enough to trigger it. He simply vaulted over the rail instead, dropping lightly to the stairs below. The stairs swept around in a grand curve and led him to another gleaming black corridor near the center of the Tlabbar castle, leading to the House shrine.

The floor was polished black marble that would have gleamed like a mirror had there been any light to see by. Not far ahead, a pair of House guards stood watch over a great double door leading into Lolth's sanctuary.

Nimor smiled invisibly and congratulated himself on his timing. The matron mother, and perhaps a daughter or two, would be within, performing some empty ritual to their mute goddess.

Carefully staying out of sight, Nimor took one more look around to make sure no one else was approaching. He studied the two guards outside the door. They seemed no more than young officers, proudly attired for their exalted duty as guards to the matron mother, but Nimor did not trust his eyes. The two were more than they seemed, he was certain of it. He decided to bypass them if he could.

Gathering himself, Nimor raised his left hand, on which gleamed a ring as black as jet. The ring of shadows was perhaps his most useful weapon, a device that conferred a number of useful magical powers. He called upon one of those powers, and melted into the shadows of the black corridor only to step out on the far side of the shrine's door, into House Tlabbar's most sacred sanctum.

The temple almost filled the central floor of the great palace, its graceful dome rising overhead, chased in silver and jet with Lolth's spider insignia. The shrine was lit with a sinister silvery radiance, the better to display the lavish wealth House Faen Tlabbar had expended in decorating the Spider Queen's chapel. Nimor spared no admiration on the gold baubles and gem-encrusted images, though.

Matron Mother Ghenni and two of her daughters abased themselves before the towering black idol of the silent goddess, groveling before Lolth, no doubt beseeching the Spider Queen to restore her favor to the House. No one else waited within. Apparently the matron mother felt that her guards and servants did not need to see her and her daughters prostrate themselves in their private adorations. Nimor's information on Faen Tlabbar had once again been proven accurate.

The assassin silently drew his rapier and advanced, eyeing his prey. Ghenni was a striking dark elf, a female with a voluptuous body and a sinuous grace that allowed her to carry her years better than many females a hundred years younger. He noted the dark glint of mail beneath her emerald robes, and smiled. Apparently even the matron mother of a strong House didn't feel entirely safe in her own home without the Spider Queen's protection.

The matron mother paused in her observances, warned by something—a small sound, the flicker of a shadow, possibly just intuition. She raised herself up to her knees and looked around, wariness plain on her face.

"Sil'zet, Vadalma," she hissed. "We are not alone."

The two girls halted at once, still stretched out on the cold stone floor. They glanced about warily. Ghenni stood carefully, reaching for a wand at her belt.

"Who are you?" she demanded. "Who dares intrude on our devotions?"

Nimor made no answer but glided closer. The matron mother didn't see him, he was certain of that, but just as he drew within sword reach, he felt a *presence* coalesce in the room. An unseen demonic force took shape in the air near the top of the dome.

"Beware, Matron," a cold voice hissed. "An assassin approaches you unseen."

To her credit, the Matron Mother of House Faen Tlabbar did not quail. As her daughters scrambled to their feet, Ghenni took two steps back and quickly gestured with her wand, snapping out a word of command. A sphere of roiling blackness hurled forth from the wand and burst behind Nimor in an inky blot of frigid shadows that lashed out like living things hungry for prey. The assassin ignored the spell, as he was already leaping forward. With a precise thrust, he ran the Faen Tlabbar through with his rapier. The blade was as black as night, a long stiletto of intangible shadowstuff that simply glided through the matron mother's mail shirt as if the armor wasn't even there. Its effect on the priestess was as lethal as one might expect. He twisted the blade in her heart and grinned, though she still could not see him.

"Greetings, Matron Mother," he hissed aloud. "Perhaps you will find the answers you were seeking when you reach Lolth's black hells."

Ghenni gasped once and coughed blood. She staggered back, clutching at the blade in her heart, and her eyes rolled up in her head and she toppled to the floor. Nimor withdrew his rapier and whirled on the daughter on the left, Sil'zet, while the demon took shape over Ghenni's body. It was a skeletal creature wrapped in green flames, armed with a black-glowing scimitar of pale bone.

The demon evidently could see him perfectly, for it set on Nimor at once. It aimed a ferocious cut at his head, which he simply ducked, but the creature reversed its blade with surprising speed and back-handed a second cut waist high. Nimor scowled and skipped back, momentarily thwarted. Behind the demon, he saw Sil'zet unrolling a scroll to read, while Vadalma held her ground, stooping to retrieve her mother's wand while guarding herself with a dagger.

"You will not escape this room with your life, assassin," Vadalma cried. "Guards! To me!"

Nimor heard the guards outside fumbling at the chapel door. He ducked and darted, keeping away from the bone demon, but unwilling to engage it. Slaying a guardian demon was pointless, after all. He had only a few moments more, and he wanted to make the most of them. The assassin took one quick step and rolled beneath the demon's guard, coming up beside Sil'zet as she declaimed the words of her scroll. He rammed his dagger into the small of her back while parrying the bone demon's scimitar with his own black rapier. Sil'zet shrieked in agony and wrenched away, but Nimor tripped her expertly. She sprawled to the ground and writhed. Nimor followed her and sank the point of his rapier into the notch of her collarbone.

This time, the demon made him pay for ignoring it. Screeching in rage, it flailed at him with its bone sword, cutting a long, burning gash across his shoulder blade as he tried to spin out of the way. Nimor gritted his teeth against the pain and rolled away before the creature could cut him in two.

Vadalma barked out the command word for her mother's wand and blasted blindly with the shadow sphere in Nimor's direction, flaying the assassin's flesh with ebon tendrils as cold and as sharp as razors.

The door guards burst in with blades bared, their faces cold and expressionless. They closed with uncanny swiftness, sword points weaving as they groped closer to Nimor, following him with quick jerks of their heads as if the scuffle of his boots and panting of his breath betrayed him.

I've done what I came for, Nimor decided.

Ghenni was dead, and Sil'zet clearly dying. Her heels drummed on the marble floor as she drowned in her own blood. He would have liked to have killed Vadalma as well, but the demon and the door guards—whatever they actually were—simply complicated matters beyond practical resolution.

With a grimace of resignation, Nimor backed off several steps and blinked away with the power of his ring, emerging an instant later near the balcony where he had first entered the castle. The forbidding kept him from escaping in a single dimensional leap, but the assassin simply seized the body of the Tlabbar wizard he'd left by the door and darted outside again. The cut across his shoulders burned abominably, and his legs ached where the icy tendrils of the sphere had lashed him, but Nimor drew in a deep breath and allowed himself a feral grin of triumph.

"Fortunate fellows," he said to the dead males at his feet. "When the Tlabbars determine that you guarded the door through which I came, you will be glad that you are dead."

The bodies made no response, of course. They never did.

He glanced out at the faerielight glimmering over the battlements of the castle, listening to the alarms and cries of dismay rising from within. He would have liked to savor the sounds for a long time, but pursuit could not be far behind. With a sigh, he clenched his fist around his black ring and willed himself away.

FOUR

Halisstra and Ryld played two games, using a small traveling board the weapons master kept in a pouch at his belt. Ryld
Argith won both games, though Halisstra pressed him hard in
both. She'd always had a knack for *sava*, though she could tell
early on that she was playing a master. Long, silent hours passed
in the darkness, with no sign that the lamias had discovered their
hiding place.

I can't believe they haven't followed us, Halisstra remarked at the
end of the second game.

*We slew many of their favorite thralls, I guess. The lamias were
careless of the lives of their slaves, and perhaps do not have enough left
to do a proper job of searching the city for us.* Ryld smiled coldly. *For
that matter, we slew a few lamias, too. Perhaps they're not very anxious
to find us.*

As long as they leave us be, Halisstra replied.

With the *sava* game no longer holding her interest, she realized that she was dreadfully hungry. They'd eaten a thin breakfast before sunrise from the few supplies they'd brought from Ched Nasad, but Halisstra was certain that the day was drawing down. Drow could stand privation better than most, but hard combat followed by hours of vigilance had left her physically exhausted.

I'm starving, she flashed at Ryld. *Things seem quiet. I'm going to slip back to the camp and break out some stores. Stay alert.*

The weapons master nodded, and whispered, "Hurry back."

Halisstra rose and wrapped her *piwafwi* close around her. The hall was still and dark, as it had been for hours. She stole quietly back to the chamber where the others waited for Pharaun to ready his spells, using all the stealth she could muster. She could hear soft voices ahead, Quenthel and Danifae conversing quietly in the ruined gallery.

A dark shadow flitted across Halisstra's heart. When she thought about it, there were few things she wished Danifae and Quenthel to speak about.

I should not have left them alone, she chided herself. *I let Quenthel order me about like a male!*

Deliberately, she crept closer, a silent shadow in the darkness. She could see Pharaun sitting wrapped in a blanket, deep in Reverie as he leaned against the wall, his eyes heavy and half-lidded. Quenthel and Danifae sat close together, turned a little away from the wizard, which brought them close to the passage in which Halisstra stood.

"What do you think you will do when we return to Menzoberranzan, girl? Do you think some high station awaits your mistress there?" Quenthel said, her whispers scornful and acidic.

"I do not know, Mistress," Danifae said after a long time. "I have not thought that far ahead."

"Orcswill. You have been thinking hard from the moment I laid eyes on you in the audience hall of House Melarn. In fact, I'll even hazard a guess as to what must occupy your thoughts. You are wondering how you can bring about your return to House Yauntyrr in Eryndlyn, with Halisstra Melarn as your battle captive."

"I dare not entertain such a thought—"

Quenthel laughed cruelly and said, "Save your innocent protests for someone more gullible, girl. You still have not answered my question. Why should I take you and your mistress back to Menzoberranzan?"

"It would be my hope," Danifae said in a faltering voice, "that I might have an opportunity to demonstrate my usefulness to you, so that you might choose to give me the opportunity to serve."

"I see you do not presume to answer for your mistress this time," Quenthel snorted. "So I should reward your faithless insolence by shielding you in House Baenre, when I know that you are nothing more than an opportunistic viper who will abandon her mistress as soon as the mood strikes her?"

"You misjudge me," Danifae said. "The tradition of adopting the best and most useful nobles of a defeated house is a way of life among our people. My mistress and I—"

The vipers of Quenthel's whip hissed and cracked close by Danifae's face, silencing her.

"I think," said Quenthel, "that I misjudge nothing at all. You are a simpering fawn of a girl who lacked the strength to keep herself from being taken as another's slave. You are nothing more than a useless ornament to me—or you are a very patient and very clever little sycophant, in which case bringing you into my home is not very useful, either." She sat back, sneering at Danifae. "Perhaps I should simply advise Halisstra of this conversation. I doubt your mistress would be pleased to know how much you presume in her behalf. It is most unbecoming in a handmaiden, after all."

"It is your prerogative, Mistress," Danifae said, bowing her head. "You may do as you please with me. I can only place myself at your convenience." She looked up again from her submissive pose, and licked her lips. "In captivity I have come to understand something of the nature of power, what it means to hold absolute power over someone else. If I am not to wield that kind of power myself, then all that remains is to place myself into the care of a female who understands these things, too. Halisstra Melarn is my mistress, but only at your pleasure. When the time comes that you choose to consider the matter, I pray you will allow me to demonstrate my more useful qualities and earn the chance to live as your slave. You, more so than my mistress, understand the exercise of power."

"Cease your meaningless flattery, girl," Quenthel said. She stood smoothly and stepped close, looming menacingly above the kneeling girl with a smile on her lips. "I told you once that I can see past your pretty face. Besides, an appreciation for the uses of silence is only one of the virtues I find endearing in those I take under my gentle guidance."

"I beg you, Mistress," Danifae murmured. She leaned forward to nuzzle her face against Quenthel's thighs, eyes closed, entwining her arms around the Baenre's knees. "I would do anything to earn your favor. I beg you."

Quenthel's snake-headed scourge curled and teased Danifae's silver hair. The Mistress of the Academy stood in silence, the same cold smile on her face. When she reached down and gently raised Danifae's chin with one hand, she bent down to look closely into her eyes.

"Understand this," Quenthel said in a low voice. "I know exactly what you're doing, and you will not win this game. The women of House Baenre are made of sterner stuff than the weaklings of House Melarn. Savor every heartbeat, foolish girl, because in the instant you no longer amuse me, your life ends."

Quenthel disentangled herself and walked away, resuming her restless pacing across the dusty chamber. Danifae rose and moved to the same spot in which Halisstra had left her, kneeling gracefully and composing herself to wait.

Halisstra exhaled quietly in the shadowed passageway, forcing her knotted limbs to relax. She had not realized how tense she had become.

Now, what shall I make of that? she thought.

More than once in the girl's long years as her servant she had used Danifae's beauty to secure favors. If she called Danifae to account for presuming to address Quenthel in Halisstra's absence, she was certain that she knew how the girl would respond. Danifae would claim that she was simply exploring Quenthel's regard for Halisstra by feigning the attenuation of her loyalty to House Melarn, a plausible excuse to approach Quenthel under the circumstances. Under such a scenario, Danifae could claim that she was simply telling Quenthel what she wanted to hear, in order to measure whether there was a place for her and her mistress in the powerful priestess's House. She would most likely finish with submissive apologies, and ask Halisstra to take her life if her actions had somehow displeased her noble mistress.

On the other hand, did it not seem equally likely that Danifae's approach to Quenthel was unfeigned? If the maidservant found a way to escape the magical binding that held her captive, she would need Quenthel's approval, or else her freedom might come at the cost of her life. It was quite possible that nothing more than the deadly capriciousness of a highborn priestess prevented Danifae from seeking release from her bondage. After all, if Danifae claimed her freedom and looked to Quenthel to guarantee it, the Baenre might choose to destroy the girl for her presumption. Any drow would delight in encouraging the dreams of a slave, only to dash them to pieces for nothing more than an instant's dark pleasure.

Only a day before, Halisstra would have described Danifae as one of her most prized possessions. She was not only held to an unbreakable loyalty, but she served also as a confidante, perhaps even something of a friend—even if her faithfulness was magically compelled. They had shared many diversions and plotted many intrigues together. Danifae had been eager to follow her into her self-imposed exile, volunteering to share her trials and continue her servitude. Of course she would have paid a terrible price had she remained in House Melarn after Halisstra's flight, but had she been too eager, perhaps?

"Here I stand, afraid to confront or discipline my own handmaid," Halisstra breathed. "Lolth has cast me low, indeed."

With her coldness locked away in her heart, Halisstra carefully retraced her steps. She wasn't hungry anymore, but it was necessary to allay suspicions. She turned around, and advanced more openly toward the party's hiding place, allowing a slight scuff of her boot soles against the sand-covered stones to whisper through the dead, still air of the chamber. She would let Quenthel and Danifae believe she had heard nothing, but she would watch both of them closely from that point forward.

Nimor Imphraezl made his way among the grand palaces and jagged stalagmites of the Qu'ellarz'orl, draped in a hooded *piwafwi*. He wore a merchant's insignia, posing as a well-to-do commoner with business on the high plateau of Menzoberranzan's haughtiest noble Houses. It was a thin disguise, as anyone taking note of his confident step and rakish manner would not mistake him for anything other than a noble drow himself. The costume was not uncommon among highborn males who wished to move about incognito. Certain spells at his command might have sufficed to offer him almost any appearance he could think of, but Nimor had discovered long ago that the simplest disguises were often the best. Most drow houses were guarded by defenders who would note the approach of someone veiled in webs of illusion, but spotting a common disguise required a mundane vigilance that some dark elves had forgotten.

He passed a pair of Baenre armsmen, walking in the opposite direction. The noble lads eyed him with open curiosity and not a little suspicion. Nimor bowed deeply and offered an empty pleasantry. The young rakes glanced back over their shoulders at him once or twice, but continued on their business. Baenre boys had become hesitant to start trouble unless they were certain of themselves. Nimor took an extra turn or two on his way to his destination anyway, just to make sure they hadn't taken it into their heads to follow him. With one last double-back to clear his trail, he turned to a high walled palace near the center of the plateau and approached the fortresslike gate.

House Agrach Dyrr, the Fifth House of Menzoberranzan, clambered in and around nine needle-like towers of rock within the bounds of a great dry moat. Each fang of rock had been joined to its neighbor by a graceful wall of adamantine-reinforced stone, impossibly slender and strong. Flying buttresses, bladelike and beautiful, linked the natural towers to those wrought by drow, a narrow cluster of minarets and spires in the center of the compound that rose hundreds of feet above the plateau floor. A railless bridge spanned in a single elegant arch the sheer chasm surrounding the structure.

Nimor climbed the bridge and approached openly. Near the far end he was challenged by several swordsmen and a pair of competent-looking wizards.

"Hold," called the gate captain. "Who are you, and what is your business with Agrach Dyrr?"

The assassin halted with a smile. He could sense the myriad instruments of death trained upon him, as if he might suddenly take it into his head to utter some truly inappropriate answer.

"I am Reethk Vaszune, a purveyor of magical ingredients and reagents," he said, bowing and spreading his arms. "I have been summoned by the Old Dyrr to discuss the sale of my goods."

The gate captain relaxed and said, "The master told us to expect you, Reethk Vaszune. Come this way."

Nimor followed the captain through several grand reception halls and high, echoing chambers in the great heart of the Agrach Dyrr castle. The captain showed him to a small sitting room, elaborately furnished in exotic corals and limestone rendered in the motifs of the kuo-toa, the fish creatures who dwelled in some of the Underdark's subterranean seas. Exotic enough to bespeak the House's wealth and taste, the room radiated arrogance.

"I am informed that Master Dyrr will join us shortly," the guard captain said.

A moment later, a hidden door in the opposite wall slid smoothly open, and Old Dyrr appeared. The ancient wizard was decrepit indeed, a rare sight for any elf, let alone a drow. He leaned on a great staff of black wood, and his ebon skin seemed as thin and delicate as parchment. A bright, cold spark burned in the old wizard's eye, hinting at reserves of ambition and vitality that had not yet been tapped completely despite his great age.

"We are delighted to see you again so soon, Master Reethk," the ancient drow said with a dry, crackling voice. "Have you perchance obtained the things we discussed?"

"I believe you will be satisfied, Lord Dyrr," Nimor said.

He glanced at the guard captain, who looked to the old wizard to make sure that he was dismissed. Dyrr sent him along with a small wave of his hand, then the old wizard made another gesture and spoke an arcane word, encapsulating the chamber in a sphere of crawling blackness that hissed and moaned softly like a thing alive.

"I hope you'll forgive me, young one, if I take steps to ensure that our conversation remains private," the ancient drow wheezed. "Eavesdropping seems to be a way of life among our kind."

He shuffled to an ornately carved chair and lowered himself into the seat, seemingly careless of the fact that he bared the nape of his wattled neck to Nimor in so doing.

"A sensible precaution," Nimor said.

The old one reckons me no threat, the assassin noted. Either he is very trusting—unlikely—or very confident. If he has such confidence in isolating himself with me, then either he does not have the measure of my strength, or I do not have the measure of his.

"It *is* confidence, young one," the old wizard said, "and you do not have the measure of me, for we are both of us more than we appear." Dyrr laughed again, a wet and rasping sound. "Yes, your thoughts are known to me. I did not reach my advanced age through carelessness. Now, take a seat. We will dispense with this foolishness and discuss our business."

Nimor spread his hands in a gesture of acquiescence and took the chair opposite the old wizard. With some care he organized his thoughts, locking away his darker secrets in a place he would not examine while Dyrr sat by reading his thoughts. Instead he concentrated solely on the matter at hand.

"You have no doubt heard of the unfortunate demise of the Matron Mother of House Faen Tlabbar?" the assassin said. "And her daughter Sil'zet, as well?"

"It did not escape my notice. Count on the Tlabbars to go crying murder to the ruling council. What possible action did they hope to exhort from the other matron mothers, I wonder?"

"Perhaps they were overcome with grief," Nimor replied.

He reached slowly into a pouch at his side, allowing the wizard to note the deliberate nature of his motion. From the pouch he withdrew a platinum brooch, worked in the barred double-curve symbol of Faen Tlabbar and crowned by a dark ruby. Nimor placed it on the table.

"The matron mother's own House brooch, which I managed to pocket as a keepsake for you. I hope your scrying shield is good, Lord Dyrr. No doubt the Tlabbar wizards will be seeking that emblem with all the magic at their disposal."

"Half-witted children fumbling in the dark," Dyrr muttered. "Five hundred years ago I'd forgotten more about the Art than that whole house full of wizards had collectively deciphered in all their years of training."

He reached out one near-skeletal hand for the brooch and weighed it in his hand.

"I am sure you have a means to confirm the authenticity of the brooch," said Nimor.

"Oh, I believe you, assassin. I do not think you have cheated me, but I will examine the issue later, just to be certain."

The wizard left the brooch sitting on the table and leaned back into his chair. Nimor waited patiently while Dyrr settled back, tapping one long, thin finger on his staff, a satisfied smile on his face.

"Well," the old wizard said finally, "in our previous meeting I required that you demonstrate to me the reach and skill of your brotherhood by removing an enemy of my House, and I suppose that you have done exactly that. You have won my ear. So what is it that the Jaezred Chaulssin want of House Agrach Dyrr?"

Nimor shifted and shot a sharp glance at the wizard. Dyrr was very well informed indeed, to know of that name. Very few outside of Chaulssin did. In fact, Nimor had studiously avoided bringing it up when he had first approached the ancient lord. He wondered what clues he had left for the wizard to decipher, and whether Dyrr could be permitted that knowledge.

"Do not be hasty, boy," Dyrr cautioned him. "You gave away nothing that I did not already know. I have been aware of the House of Shadows for quite a long time."

"I am impressed," Nimor said.

"On the contrary, you believe that I am making empty boasts." Dyrr pointed at his own temple and smiled coldly. "I am not given to bluffing or making wild guesses. Long ago I discerned a pattern of activity that spanned a number of the great cities of our race and inferred the existence of a secret league between seemingly weak minor Houses, each renowned for the skill of its assassins, each reputed to be governed by its males, each a secret ally of the others. These families that otherwise would have been devoured by their ambitious matriarchal rivals instead survived through the convenient and violent deaths of any emergent enemies.

Though I find it ironic that any particular House of the Jaezred Chaulssin must, by definition, be considered the blackest sort of traitors to the city unfortunate enough to host them. Placing loyalty to your House above loyalty to your city is not a particularly egregious sin, of course, but to acknowledge a tie of loyalty to a House in another city all together, that is something entirely different, is it not?"

Nimor kept his mind carefully empty and said, "You seem to know all our secrets."

He studied the wizard carefully, trying not to let the calculations he performed in his mind show.

"Not entirely true," Dyrr replied. "I would give much to know how your brotherhood orders its Houses, where your true strength is held, and who rules your society. You name yourselves after the city of Chaulssin, which fell into shadow many hundreds of years ago. I wonder about the significance of that appellation."

He knows more than we can permit, Nimor thought.

He glanced up sharply at the old wizard, realizing that Dyrr would have noted that thought. The ancient mage simply studied him with his weak gaze and inclined his head. The assassin regained the mastery of his thoughts and decided to change the subject.

"For the sake of our friendship, I respectfully submit that it would be best for all involved if you did not do anything with your knowledge that would draw it to anyone else's attention. We feel quite strongly that our secrets are best left that way."

"I will do as I wish. However, I do not wish to incur your enmity. I think it would be inconvenient to have the Jaezred Chaulssin as my enemy."

"It is not merely inconvenient, Lord Dyrr; it is invariably fatal."

"Perhaps. In any event, I will keep your secrets."

The old drow laughed softly, clutching his staff with his withered hands.

"Now, let's get to our business, young one. You and your fellows demonstrated no small amount of ability in the murder of Matron Mother Tlabbar, the enemy of my House. Very well, I am suitably impressed. What is it you want of Agrach Dyrr?"

"I need an ally in Menzoberranzan, Lord Dyrr, and I have a strong suspicion that you might be that ally." Nimor leaned forward, offering a sly grin. "Events now proceed in this city that will lead to the downfall of the Houses ahead of yours. If you choose to be a part of those events, you will find that House Agrach Dyrr is possessed of a great opportunity to order the city largely as you like. We believe you can help us to steer Menzoberranzan through the difficult times ahead."

"And if we refuse, we die?"

Nimor shrugged.

"Given the uncertainty of matters as they stand," said Dyrr, "I am hesitant to embrace a cause I know little about."

"Understandable. I will, of course, elaborate, but I hope you will recognize the wisdom, in these uncertain times, of taking aggressive and resolute steps to create the certainty you wish to see. Impose your vision on events, instead of allowing events to limit your imagination."

"Easy words to speak, young one, but more difficult to render into action," Dyrr said.

The ancient wizard fell silent for a long time, regarding the rakish assassin with a baleful, unblinking gaze. Nimor met his eyes without flinching, but he found himself wondering again what hidden strength the Agrach high mage must hold. Dyrr smiled again, doubtless reading Nimor's thoughts, and shifted in his seat.

"Very well, then, Prince of Chaulssin. You have awakened my curiosity. Explain exactly what you mean, and what you plan, and I will say if House Agrach Dyrr can stand by your bold actions or not."

🕷 🕷 🕷

"Gather closely, dear friends," Pharaun said with a flourish, "and I will explain a few things it would be wise to remember while we walk within the shadows."

The wizard stood confidently in the center of the chamber, arms folded, showing no hint of the exhaustion or despair of the day's desperate flight. Stirring from his Reverie shortly before sunset, he had spent almost an hour preparing dozens of spells from his collection of traveling tomes.

While no one bothered to draw closer to the wizard, all focused their attention on him. Pharaun grinned in delight, pleased as ever by the attention. He knotted his fists behind his back as if lecturing to novices at Sorcere, and began.

"When we are ready, I will lead us along a path that skirts the Fringe—the borders of the Plane of Shadow. We will travel quite swiftly, and minor inconveniences such as icy mountains, hungry monsters, and thick-headed humans won't trouble us in the least. I expect a walk of ten to twelve hours to reach Mantol-Derith, provided that I do not become lost and lead you all into some grisly demise in an uncivilized plane far from Faerûn."

"You fail to reassure me, Pharaun," Ryld sighed.

"Oh, I haven't ever gotten myself lost in the Shadow Deep, nor do I know of a wizard who has. Of course, one would simply never hear from such an unfortunate fellow again, so perhaps a mishap in shadow walking might explain the disappearance of a young mage I knew—"

"Get to the point," Quenthel snapped.

"Oh, fine. There are two important things to remember, then, for those of you challenged by the effort. First, while we need fear no difficulties in this world while we walk, we gain no special protection from the hazards of the Plane of Shadow. There are things in that place that will object to our passage if they happen upon us—I encountered one such creature the last time I traveled this way, and it was very nearly the last of my marvelous adventures.

"Second, and most importantly, do *not* lose sight of me. Stay close by and follow me diligently. If you lose contact with me while we traverse the Plane of Shadow, you will likely wander its gloomy barrens for all eternity—or until something terrible devours you, which will probably happen rather soon. My attention must remain on maintaining the spell and navigating the Fringe, so don't make it easy for me to misplace you, unless of course I don't like you, in which case please feel free to amble the Shadow Deep at will."

"Will the lamias be able to follow us?" Ryld asked, his eye still on the passage leading back to the ruins above.

"No, not unless they have a wizard as learned and charming as I, and he knows a spell that permits one to track shadow walkers, which I do not." Pharaun smiled. "You will be able to shake the dust of the surface from your boots, friend Ryld. Concern yourself no more with the perils of this place, and save your worry for what we might meet on the Fringe." The wizard glanced around, and nodded to himself. "All right, then. Take each other's hands—there's a good fellow, Jeggred, you can get everybody at once, can't you?—and be still while I cast the spell."

Pharaun raised his hands and muttered a series of arcane syllables, working his spell.

Halisstra stood between Danifae and Valas, their hands linked. The great subterranean gallery grew somehow *darker*, if such a thing could be possible in an unlit room underground. Drow could see quite well even in the darkest places, but it seemed to Halisstra as if some kind of murk hung in the air. At first glance, it seemed that Pharaun had succeeded in little more than conjuring a gloom around the party, but as she studied her surroundings more closely, she realized that she was indeed no longer upon Faerûn. A preternatural chill gnawed at her exposed skin, radiating from the cold dust beneath her feet. The high, rune-carved columns that lined the space were twisted caricatures that loomed bizarrely out over the chamber's open floor.

"Strange," she murmured. "I expected something . . . different."

"This is the way of the shadow, dear lady," Pharaun said. His voice seemed flat and distant, despite the fact he stood no more than six feet from her. "This plane has no substance of its own. It is made up of echoes from our own world, and other, stranger places. We stand in the shadow of the ruins above, but they are not the same ruins we recently traversed. The lamias and their minions do not exist here. Now, remember, stay close, and do not lose sight of me."

The wizard set off along the passage leading back to the surface. Halisstra blinked in surprise. He took only one small step as he turned away from the party, but he was suddenly across the room, and a second step carried him perilously far down the corridor outside. She hurried to keep him in sight, only to find that a single step caused the chamber to blur into darkness. She stood so close to Pharaun that she had to restrain an impulse to back up a step, lest she throw herself even farther away.

The wizard smirked at her discomfiture and said, "I am flattered by your attention, dear lady, but you need not stay quite so close." He laughed softly. "Just step when I step, and you will pace me more easily."

He took several slow, measured strides, holding back a bit as the rest of the party caught the trick of it, and in a moment they all marched together along the dusty streets of Hlaungadath beneath a cold and starless sky. Each step seemed to catapult Halisstra forty, perhaps fifty feet across the dim terrain. The black shapes of ruined buildings leered and leaned from all sides, huddling down close over the streets as if to hem in the travelers, only to fade into dark blurs with each careful stride.

Outside the ruined walls, Pharaun paused a moment to check

on the party. He nodded toward the desert stretching to cold mountains in the west, and he began to march quickly, setting a rapid pace that belied his effete mannerisms and aversion to the toils of travel. Finally able to stretch out her legs, Halisstra began to gain a sense of just how quickly they were moving. In five minutes of walking they left the site of the Netherese city a league behind them, a dark blot on the dim breast of the sands. In thirty minutes the mountains, nothing more than a distant fence of snowcapped peaks from Hlaungadath's streets, towered up over them like a rampart of night. The shadow walk also made light of the most difficult terrain in their path. Without hesitation Pharaun stepped out over a sheer ravine as if it simply did not exist. The magic of his spell and the strange plane they traversed brought his foot down securely on the far side of the obstacle. Climbing the long, rugged slopes leading up into the mountains was no more work than stepping from stone to stone across a stream.

"Tell me, Pharaun," Quenthel said after a time, "why did we crawl through miles of dangerous Underdark passages to reach Ched Nasad, when you might have used this spell to shorten our journey?"

Halisstra could sense the ire hidden in the Baenre's voice, even through the murk and gloom of the Shadow Fringe.

"Three reasons, fair Quenthel," Pharaun replied, not taking his eyes from the unseen path he followed. "First, you did not ask me to do any such thing. Second, the wizards of Ched Nasad arranged certain defenses against intrusions of this sort. Finally, as I said before, the Fringe is a dangerous place. I only suggested this after we all agreed that marching for months across the sun-blasted surface world presented an even less appealing prospect."

Quenthel seemed to consider the wizard's words, while mountains reeled and gnarled black trees began to appear around them.

"In the future," the Mistress of Arach-Tinilith said, "I shall expect you to volunteer useful information or suggestions in a timely manner. Your reticence in advancing ideas may cost us all our lives.

Is that worth the meager pleasure you derive from knowing something we may not?"

The Master of Sorcere's teeth gleamed in his dark face, and he continued without making a reply. For some time he devoted his attention to navigating the Fringe. As Pharaun was under normal circumstances the most garrulous of the company, the effort of concentrating on his spell left the small party of dark elves unusually silent. They fell into a watchful march, winding quietly along in single file behind the wizard, as the immeasurable journey through the darkness stretched out into what might have been hours or even days. Halisstra found herself beginning to consider the very curious notion that this was the real world, the true substance of things, and the bland mundane rigidity of her own world was the illusion. She found that she did not care for that thought at all.

After a long time, Pharaun raised his hand and called a halt. They stood on a small gray stone bridge, arching over a deep gully through which trickled a dark, bubbling stream. Nearby the black ramparts of an abandoned city jutted into the lightless sky, a place that seemed more like a fortress than a town, its thick walls pierced by turret-guarded gates.

"We're about halfway to our destination," Pharaun said. "I suggest half an hour's rest, and maybe a meal from what stores we have. We should be able to replenish our supplies when we reach Mantol-Derith."

Ryld gestured at the empty castle nearby and said, "What is that place?"

"That?" Pharaun glanced over his shoulder. "Who knows? Maybe it's the echo of a surface city in our world, or maybe it's a reflection of some other reality all together. The Shadow is like that."

The company huddled by the low stone wall of the bridge and made a dreary repast from their dwindling provisions. The ever present chill of the place leeched away the warmth of Halisstra's body, as if the stones beneath her hungered for her very life. The gloom smothered their spirits, deadening any attempt at conversation, making it hard to even think with any degree of acuteness. When the time came to set off again, Halisstra was surprised by the sheer lethargy that had crept into her limbs. She had little desire to do anything except sink back down to the ground and lie still, wrapped in shadows. Only with a fierce and focused effort of will did she drive herself into motion again.

They set off into the unending night, and had gone on for some distance from the vicinity of the old bridge when Halisstra became aware of the fact that they were being followed. She was not sure of it, at first. Whatever trailed them was stealthy, and the deadening effects of the Shadow made her unsure if she had really heard something or not. It seemed to whisper and titter in the darkness, a presence that announced itself in a stirring of the motionless air, the faint rush of wind behind them. She turned and studied the path, searching for their pursuer, but she saw nothing save the weary faces of her companions.

Valas brought up the rear of the march, and he looked up at her as he drew close.

You sense it too? he signed.

"What is it?" Halisstra wondered aloud. "What manner of things live in a place like this?"

The scout shrugged wearily and said, "Something that Pharaun has reason to fear, which alarms me." He reached out and turned her back toward the rest of the party. Halisstra was shocked to see how far they'd moved away in the few short moments she had stood watching. "Come, we do not want to be left behind. Perhaps what hunts us will be content to follow."

They hurried to catch up to the others—and at that moment, their pursuer attacked. Striding up out of the shadows behind them loomed a tremendous figure composed of pure darkness, a black, faceless giant towering more than twenty feet in height. Despite its great size, the thing moved swiftly and silently toward them, strangely graceful. Two shining ovals of silver marked its eyes, and long, spidery talons reached for Halisstra and Valas. Its sibilant whispers filled their minds with awful things, like fat pale worms crawling through rotten meat.

"Pharaun, wait!" Halisstra cried.

She fumbled for her mace as the dark giant approached. Beside her, Valas swore and swept out his curved blades, crouching in a fighting stance. A nauseating, tangible chill radiated from the creature, like the cold that seeped through the entire plane but far more concentrated and malevolent in the presence of the monster. The dark giant shimmered, acquiring an almost oily appearance, and it sprang forward in a sudden burst of motion.

Before Halisstra could cry out another warning, one blow of its massive taloned fist knocked her sprawling to the ground. It turned to fix its pale and terrible gaze upon Valas. The Bregan D'aerthe scout screamed in terror and averted his eyes, dropping one kukri and allowing the second to droop limply from his hand.

Jeggred roared a challenge and bounded toward the monster, talons extended. The dark giant slammed the half-demon to the ground with one blow of its long black hand. The draegloth scrambled back to his feet and leaped up to rake deep, black furrows across the giant's thighs and abdomen, seeking to eviscerate the creature, but the wounds closed after the draegloth's claws passed through the thing's flesh. Jeggred howled in frustration and redoubled his futile assault.

"Stand back, you fool!" Pharaun cried from nearby. "It is a nightwalker. You need powerful magic to harm it."

The wizard chanted a dire spell, and a bright bolt of green lightning shot out to smite the creature high in its torso—but the pernicious energy just flowed away from the monster's featureless black hide, leaving it unharmed.

Your spells are useless, whispered a dark and terrible voice in Halisstra's mind. *Your weapons are useless. You are mine, foolish drow.*

"We will see about that," Halisstra snarled.

She picked herself up and dashed forward, raising her mace. The weapon was enchanted, and she hoped it would prove powerful enough to harm the creature. A long arm with deadly talons raked at her, but Halisstra tumbled beneath the monster's grasp and hammered at the nightwalker's knee. With a sharp crack of sound and a flash of actinic light, the weapon detonated with the force of a thunderclap. The nightwalker made no sound, but its knee buckled, and it staggered.

Quenthel's whip hissed through the air, flaying at the creature's face. The vipers tore and snapped through dark flesh, leaving great gory wounds, but the monster seemed unaffected by the deadly venom coursing through the weapon. Apparently even the most virulent poison did not discomfit its shadowstuff.

Ryld, wheeling and spinning, slashed at the monster with his gleaming greatsword. The nightwalker reached out to wrest away his weapon, but the Master of Melee-Magthere danced back and sheared off half the creature's hand with one savage blow. The nightwalker screamed soundlessly, its anguished cry stabbing through their very minds. Ignoring the others, the creature fastened its baleful gaze on Ryld, and conjured up from the black soil underfoot a dreadful, dark vapor that blotted out all sight.

Halisstra groped her way into the black mist, seeking the monster. The vapor seared her nose like vitriol and ate at her eyes, burning like fire. She persevered, and felt the giant looming over her. She raised her mace and struck again, hammering at the creature's legs. From beside her she heard the hiss of Quenthel's whip, tearing into dark flesh. Great black talons raked through the vapor, ripping at Halisstra's shield, driving her to the ground.

"It's here!" she called, hoping to lead someone else to the battle, but the acidic mists burned like fire in her throat.

She narrowed her eyes to nothing more than bare slits, and flailed back at the monster. The nightwalker's venomous will settled over her like a blanket of madness, seeking to rend away her reason, but she endured the new assault, lashing out again and again.

Ryld's sword lanced through the murk like a white razor, opening dreadful wounds in the shadow creature's body. Black fluid splattered like droplets of poison, and the mind-whispers of the nightwalker rose into a hellish mental shriek that dragged Halisstra to the very edge of madness—and there was silence.

She felt the thing abruptly discorporate around her, its body exploding into black, stinking mist that dissipated into the shadows.

Still gagging on the poisonous black vapors the creature had raised, Halisstra stumbled out of the dark cloud and fell to all fours, gasping for breath. Her chest burned as if she'd drunk molten sulfur. When at last she could open her eyes and take notice of her surroundings again, she found that most of the rest of the party had fared little better than she.

Ryld slumped against a stone, his greatsword point down before him. He was leaning on the blade, exhausted. Quenthel stood close by, her hands on her knees, coughing wretchedly.

When at last she could draw breath, the high priestess looked up at Pharaun and said, "That is what you encountered before?"

The wizard nodded and said, "Nightwalkers. They roam the Fringe. Creatures of undead darkness, evil personified. As you saw, they can be . . . formidable."

The Mistress of the Academy drew herself up and returned her whip to her belt.

"I think I understand why you hesitated to volunteer this method of travel until now," she said.

Despite his exhaustion, the wizard preened.

"Careful, Quenthel," he said in a mocking voice, "you almost acknowledged my usefulness."

The high priestess's eyes narrowed, and she straightened proudly. She obviously didn't care to be the subject of the wizard's humor. Seemingly ignorant of the smoldering glare Quenthel fixed on him, Pharaun made a grand gesture indicating the formless dark ahead of them.

"Our path leads now into the shadow of our own Underdark," he said. "I suggest we redouble our efforts and finish our march quickly, as there may be more nightwalkers about."

"That's a damned cheerful thought," grumbled Ryld. "How much farther now?"

"Not more than an hour, perhaps two," Pharaun answered.

The wizard waited while the dark elves stood and fell in behind him again. Ryld and Valas, the two who had borne the virulence of the nightwalker's dread gaze, seemed gray with weariness, hardly able to keep their feet.

"Come," said Pharaun. "Mantol-Derith is no Menzoberranzan, but it will be the most civilized place we've seen in days, and no one is likely to want to kill us.

"Not right away, at least."

F I V E

Nothing more troubled them for the rest of the shadow walk, and they emerged from the Fringe not long after the nightwalker's attack, returning to the mundane world on the floor of a narrow, subterranean gorge. The walls were marked with various trail signs and messages from previous travelers who had stopped there. It was obviously a commonly used campsite near the trade cavern. The company rested there for hours, warming up from the insidious chill of the Shadow Fringe. After resting, they left the gorge and found their way out into a long, smooth-sided tunnel that bored for miles through the dark, broken by occasional open caverns along the way.

Valas led the company, as he was familiar with their arrival point and the route they found themselves traveling. After the burning skies of the daylit surface and the miserable gloom of the Plane of Shadow, the routine perils of the Underdark felt like old friends. This was their world, the place where they belonged, even those of their number who had rarely journeyed outside their home cities.

After a march of about two miles, Valas called a brief halt and knelt down to sketch a crude map in the dust of the passage floor.

"Mantol-Derith lies not more than half a mile ahead. Remember, this is a place of trade and association with other races. We do not rule Mantol-Derith—no one does—and so it would be prudent to avoid giving offense to anyone you encounter there, unless you're looking for a fight that may waste our time and resources.

"Also, I have been considering how best to find our way from the trade cavern to the holdings of House Jaelre in the Labyrinth. From here our path must traverse the dominion of Gracklstugh, city of the gray dwarves."

"Under no circumstances will we approach Gracklstugh," Quenthel said at once. "The gray dwarves destroyed Ched Nasad. I see no reason to present myself at their doorstep for slaughter."

"We have few other options, Mistress," Valas said. "We are northeast of the duergar realm, and the Labyrinth lies several days southwest of the city. We cannot skirt the city to the south because the Darklake is in the way, and the duergar patrol its waters. Skirting the city to the north would take us at least two tendays of difficult travel through tunnels I do not know well at all."

"Why did we bother to come this way, then?" Jeggred muttered. "We might as well have returned to Menzoberranzan."

"Well, for one thing, Gracklstugh still lies between us and House Jaelre, whether we're in Mantol-Derith or Menzoberranzan," Pharaun replied. He tapped three points on Valas's crudely sketched map. "The gray dwarves must be addressed in either scenario. The question is simply whether we dare to pass through Gracklstugh, or not."

"Could you shadow walk us past the city?" Danifae asked.

Pharaun grimaced and said, "I have never traveled past Mantol-Derith in this direction, and shadow walking is best employed to reach a familiar destination. At any rate, it wouldn't surprise me to find that the duergar have defended their realm against the passage of travelers on nearby planes."

"Are we certain that the gray dwarves would object to our presence?" Ryld asked. "Merchants from Menzoberranzan journey to Gracklstugh often enough, and gray dwarf merchants bring their wares to Menzoberranzan's bazaar. It's possible that Gracklstugh had nothing to do with the duergar mercenaries who attacked Ched Nasad."

"I have heard nothing that suggests to me that we should risk entering Gracklstugh," Quenthel said. She made a curt gesture with her hand, silencing the debate. "I prefer not to gamble on the hospitality of the gray dwarves, not after the fall of Ched Nasad. We will go around the city to the north, and trust that Master Hune can find us a way through."

Halisstra glanced at Ryld and Valas. The scout chewed on his lip, worrying at the problem, while the weapons master simply lowered his eyes in resignation.

"We are only a mile or two from this cavern known as Mantol-Derith?" Halisstra asked, pointing at the sketch.

"Yes, my lady," Valas replied.

"And regardless of which course we choose, we must pass through the place?"

The Bregan D'aerthe scout simply nodded again.

"Then perhaps we should see what we can learn in the trade cavern before we make our decision," Halisstra offered. She could feel Quenthel's eyes on her, but she did not look at the Baenre. "There might be duergar merchants there who could shed some light on the question for us. If not, well, we'll have to provision ourselves there anyway before striking out into the wilds of the Underdark."

"A reasonable suggestion," Pharaun remarked. "There are a dozen mercenary companies based in the City of Blades. Is it not likely that the duergar we fought in Ched Nasad were hired by a drow House, and had no special allegiance to Gracklstugh?"

"They did Gracklstugh's work when they destroyed the city," Quenthel said darkly. She stood and set her hands on her hips, still staring at the sketch on the floor. She thought for a moment, then angrily swept it out with her foot. "We will see what we learn in

Mantol-Derith, then. I suspect that time is of the essence, and if we can avoid a detour of twenty or thirty days to skirt the city, we should do so, but if we hear anything to indicate that Gracklstugh may be closed to our kind, we strike out into the barrens."

Valas Hune nodded and said, "Very well, Mistress. I suspect we will be able to arrange passage unless the duergar are openly at war with Menzoberranzan. I've dealt with the gray dwarves before, and there is nothing they would not sell for the right price. I will seek out a duergar guide in Mantol-Derith and see what I can learn."

"Good enough," said Quenthel. "Take us to the duergar, and we will—"

"No, Mistress, not 'we'," the scout said. He stood and brushed off his hands. "Most duergar have little liking for drow under any circumstances, less so for noble-born drow, and even less for priestesses of the Spider Queen. Your presence would only complicate things. It might be best if I handled any negotiations myself."

Quenthel frowned.

Jeggred, standing close behind her, rumbled, "I could go along to keep an eye on him, Mistress."

Pharaun barked sharp laughter at the thought and said, "If a priestess of Lolth makes a gray dwarf nervous, *what do you think he'd make of you?*"

The draegloth bridled, but Quenthel shook her head.

"No," she said. "he's right. We will find a place to wait, and perhaps see what news there is to be had, while Valas takes care of the details."

They resumed their march, and soon came to Mantol-Derith. The place was much smaller than Halisstra expected, a cavern not more than sixty or seventy feet in height and perhaps twice that in width, though it twisted and snaked for many hundreds of yards. She was used to the immensity of Ched Nasad's great canyon, and the stories she'd heard of other places of civilization underground usually involved tremendous caverns miles across. Mantol-Derith would have been nothing more than a side cavern in a drow city.

It was also much less crowded than she would have expected. The marketplaces in her home city had always been busy places, thronged by common drow or the slaves of nobles engaged in their various errands. The market of a drow city usually hummed with industry, energy, and activity, even if those qualities were peculiarly distorted to match the aesthetic tastes of drow society. Mantol-Derith was comparatively silent and forbidding. Here and there throughout the cavern's winding length, small groups of merchants sat or squatted, their wares secured in coffers and casks behind them instead of rolled out on display. No one shouted, or haggled, or laughed. What business transpired there seemed best conducted in whispers and shadows.

Creatures from many different races gathered at Mantol-Derith. More than a few drow merchants held various corners of the cavern, most from Menzoberranzan if Halisstra read the blazons on their goods correctly. Mind flayers glided smoothly from place to place, mauve skin glistening damply, tentacles writhing beneath their cephalopod faces. A handful of sullen svirfneblin huddled together in one spot, eyeing the drow with unalloyed resentment. Of course the duergar were present in numbers, too. Short and broad-shouldered, the gaunt gray dwarves gathered together in secretive cabals, conversing with each softly in their guttural tongue.

Halisstra trailed close behind Pharaun, studying each group as they passed. She noticed that the wizard was trading discreet signs with Valas as they wound deeper into the marketplace.

Not many merchants here today, the wizard observed. *Where are they all?*

Valas glanced over his shoulder to make sure Quenthel wasn't looking, and answered, *Chaos in Menzoberranzan means few buyers. Few buyers means few sellers. Anarchy seems to be bad for business.*

The scout turned to eye a band of duergar nearby, and said over his shoulder to the rest of the company, "Go on ahead. You'll find an inn of sorts a little farther on. I will meet you there soon."

He quietly approached the gray dwarves, making a strange gesture of greeting with his hands folded before him, and engaged the duergar merchants in whispered conversation. The rest of the party moved on.

They found the "inn" to which the scout referred in a dank warren of caves near the southern end of Mantol-Derith. There, a surly duergar woman terrorized a handful of goblin slaves, driving them mercilessly from one task to another. Several small cookfires smoldered haphazardly in the area, warming iron pots of thick stew tended by the harried cooks. Other slaves scrambled to tap casks of mushroom ale or stolen surface lagers, serving silent customers who simply gathered around the fires, sitting on flat boulders arranged like chairs. Sturdy doors of petrified mushroom fiber or rusted iron plate sealed off crevices in the walls nearby. Halisstra presumed that these led to the guest rooms of the gray dwarf's inn. The chambers were most likely secure behind the strong doors, but she couldn't imagine that they were at all comfortable.

"How . . . rustic," Halisstra said.

She wondered for one terrible moment if it would be her fate to live out the rest of her expatriate existence crouched in some similar hovel.

"It's even more charming than the last time I was here," Pharaun said with a forced smile. "The dwarf there is Dinnka. You'll find that this nameless wayside inn of hers constitutes the finest lodgings available in Mantol-Derith. You'll get food, fire, and shelter—three things that are hard to come by in the wilds of the Underdark—and pay a small fortune for it."

"It will be better than resting in a monster-haunted surface ruin, I suppose," Quenthel said.

She led the way as the party approached one of the cookfires. A trio of bugbears occupied the seats there, apparently mercenaries of some skill, judging by the quality of the armor they wore. The hairy creatures brooded over big leather jacks of mushroom ale, and gnawed at haunches of rothé meat. One by one the hulking warriors looked up as the five drow and Jeggred approached. Quenthel folded her arms and looked at the creatures with contempt.

"Well?" she said.

The bugbears growled, setting down ale and meat as their great fists dropped down to rest on axe-hafts thrust through their belts. The motion caught Halisstra's eye. Bugbears with any lick of sense would have vacated their places immediately, almost anywhere in the Underdark. They might not have been drow slaves—clearly they weren't, if they were in Mantol-Derith—but she'd ventured out into similar places near Ched Nasad enough times to understand that creatures like bugbears learned quickly to give way to the truly dangerous denizens of the Lands Below, such as noble dark elves.

"Well, what?" snarled the largest of the three. "It'll take more'n a drow sneer t'make us give up our seats."

"Think y'can just push us aroun'?" the second bugbear added. "You elfies ain't as scary as y'was, y'know. Maybe yous'll have t'start showin' off why we's oughtta do what y'says."

Quenthel waited for a moment, then said one word: "Jeggred."

The draegloth bounded forward and seized the first bugbear. With his two smaller arms he clamped down over the bugbear's hands, preventing him from drawing any of the weapons at his side. He locked one fighting talon around the creature's head, holding him tightly, and with his other fighting hand he plunged his powerful talons into the bugbear's face. The mercenary screamed something in his uncouth language and struggled against the draegloth. Jeggred grinned, knotted his claws deep in the shrieking monster's head, and yanked back hard, ripping off the front of the bugbear's skull. Blood and brain matter splattered the bugbear's companions, who scrambled to their feet, drawing swords and axes.

Jeggred lowered the twitching body a bit and looked over it at the other two.

"Next?" he purred.

The two remaining bugbears stumbled back, and fled in abject terror. Jeggred shook his white-furred head and tossed the corpse aside, taking a seat at the fire. He helped himself to a hunk of roast dropped by a bugbear, and raised one of their jacks in another hand.

"Bugbears. . . ." he muttered.

"Hey, you!"

The surly duergar innkeeper—Dinnka—scuttled forward, anger plain on her face.

"Those three hadn't settled their tab yet," she complained. "Now how in all the screaming hells am I going to get my gold from them?"

Ryld stooped and removed the bugbear's belt pouch. He tossed it to Dinnka.

"Settle up with this," the weapons master said, "and start our tab with what's left. We'll want good wine, and more food."

The duergar woman caught the purse, but she did not move.

"I don't appreciate your scaring off paying customers, drow. Nor killing them, neither. Next time do your murdering at home, where it belongs."

She marched off, already barking orders at the goblin slaves underfoot.

Halisstra watched her go, then she looked back to the others and flashed, *That was odd. Did you hear what the bugbear said?*

"What he said about the drow not being as scary as they used to be?" Ryld said, then he switched to sign. *Has word of Ched Nasad's fall reached this place so quickly? It was only a couple of days ago, and Mantol-Derith is many days' travel from the City of Shimmering Webs.*

It's possible that magical scrying or spells of communication might have spread the word already, Halisstra said. *Or . . . perhaps he meant something else. Perhaps something of our unusual difficulties is known here.*

That, thought Halisstra, was a very disturbing scenario. Gray dwarves and mind flayers were competent foes, creatures who knew many secrets of sorcery. If they had discerned the drow's weakness, it would not be unduly surprising, but if common bugbear mercenaries were aware of matters in Ched Nasad or Menzoberranzan, it must be widely known indeed.

Goblin slaves returned to their fire, laden with somewhat better fare than the bugbears had enjoyed, and flagons of cool wine from some surface vineyard. The small slaves gathered up the hulking body of the fallen bugbear and dragged it off into the darkness. The dark elves paid them scant attention. Goblin slaves were so far beneath their notice that they might as well have not existed. The party ate and drank in silence, occupied with their own thoughts.

After a time, Valas joined them, accompanied by another gray dwarf. This one was a male, with a short beard of iron grey and not a single hair on his head above his eyebrows. The duergar wore a shirt of chain mail and carried a wicked hand axe at his side. His visage was maimed by a set of three great furrowed scars that had taken off one ear and twisted the right side of his face into a nightmarish map of old pain. He might have been a merchant, a mercenary, or a miner—his dour attire offered few hints as to his trade.

"This is Ghevel Coalhewer," the scout said. "He owns a boat moored nearby, on the Darklake. He will take us to Gracklstugh tomorrow."

"I'll want me payment in advance," the gray dwarf warned. "And I'll have ye know I've a contract o' redress with me guild back home. If ye think to slit me throat and dump me over the side out on the lake, ye'll be hunted down for it."

"A trusting soul," Pharaun said with a smile. "We've no interest in robbing you, Master Coalhewer."

"I'll take me precautions, just the same." The duergar looked at Valas and asked, "Ye know where the boat is. Pay me now, and ye can meet me there tomorrow early."

"How do we know you won't rob us, dwarf?" rumbled Jeggred.

"It's usually bad business to rob drow, not unless ye be sure to get away with it," the dwarf replied. " 'Course, that may be changing, but no' so fast that I'll chance it today."

Valas jingled a pouch in front of the duergar and dropped it into his hand. The dwarf immediately poured out its contents into his big, weathered palm, appraising the gemstones there before scooping them back into the pouch.

"Ye must be in a rush, or yer man here might've struck a better bargain. Ah, well, ye drow don't appreciate a good gemstone, anyway."

He turned and stumped away into the darkness.

"That's the last you'll see of him," Jeggred said. "You should have waited to pay him."

"He insisted on it," Valas said. "He said something about wanting to make sure we didn't kill him to recover the fare." The scout looked after the duergar, and shrugged. "I don't think he would cheat us. If he was that kind of duergar, well, he wouldn't last long in Mantol-Derith. People here don't take kindly to being cheated."

"He can secure safe passage through Gracklstugh?" Ryld asked.

Valas spread his hands and replied, "We'll have to carry some kind of documents or letters, which Coalhewer can arrange for us. I think it's some kind of mercantile license."

"We're carrying no goods," Pharaun observed dryly. "Doesn't that explanation seem a little thin?"

"I told him that Lady Quenthel's family has business holdings in Eryndlyn she wishes to check on, and that if she finds things in order, she might be interested in negotiating for the services of duergar teamsters to transport her goods across Gracklstugh's territory. I also implied that Coalhewer might do well to make himself a part of the arrangement."

Pharaun didn't have time to reply before the cavern echoed softly with the stealthy padding of numerous feet. The dark elves glanced up from the fire to see a large band of bugbear warriors approaching, led by the two mercenaries who had fled a few minutes before. At least a dozen of their fellows followed close behind them, axes and spiked flails dangling from hairy paws, murder in their eyes. The other patrons of Dinnka's inn began to slip away from their places, seeking safer environs. The hulking humanoids muttered and growled to each other in their own tongue.

"Tell me," said Valas, "did someone happen to kill, maim, or humiliate a bugbear when I was talking with Coalhewer?" The scout glanced back at the others, and at Jeggred, who shrugged. He sighed. "Was I unclear when I advised against starting fights here?"

"There was a misunderstanding over the seating arrangements," Quenthel explained.

Ryld stood, threw his cloak over his shoulder to clear his arms for fighting, and said, "Should've guessed there might be more of them nearby."

"Time to remind these stupid creatures of the order of things," Halisstra remarked.

Quenthel stood and drew her five-headed whip, eyeing the approaching warriors with a wry smile.

"Jeggred?" she said.

Gromph Baenre stood on a balcony high above Menzoberranzan, studying the dim faerielights of the drow city. He had been waiting for nearly an hour, and his patience was almost exhausted. Under most circumstances an hour here or an hour there would have meant nothing to a dark elf with centuries of life behind him, but this was different. The archmage waited in fear, dreading the arrival of the one who had summoned him to this clandestine encounter. It was not a sensation Gromph was accustomed to, and he found that he did not care for it at all. He had, of course, taken extreme steps to protect his person, girding himself with an array of formidable defensive spells and a carefully considered selection of protective magical devices. The archmage was not entirely confident that those precautions would deter the one who came to meet him in that lonely, windswept spot.

"Gromph Baenre," a voice, cold and rasping, greeted him. Before the archmage even began to turn, he felt the presence of the other, an icy chill that somehow managed to sink past his defenses, the smell of great and terrible magic. "How good of you to accept my invitation. It has been a long time, has it not?"

The ancient sorcerer Dyrr approached from the shadows at the back of the balcony, leaning on his great staff, his feet seeming not to move at all as he glided forward in a rustle of robes no quicker than an old man's shuffle.

Among the ambitious drow of his own House, it suited Dyrr

to wear the shape of a venerable old dark elf of fantastic age, but Gromph's arcane sight pierced the guise to the truth behind it. Dyrr was dead, dead these many centuries. Nothing remained of the ancient mage but dusty bones clothed in tattered shreds of mummified flesh. His hands were the claws of a skeleton, his robes were faded and threadbare, and his face was a hideous grinning skull, the black eye sockets alight with the bright green flame of his powerful spirit.

"I see that my poor guise does not deceive you," the lich rasped. "In truth, I would have been disappointed if you were so easily beguiled, Archmage."

"Lord Dyrr," said Gromph, a cautious greeting. He inclined his head without taking his eyes off the lichdrow. "In truth, I am surprised to find that you are still among us. I have heard whispers that you still lived—er, so to speak—secluded in your house. I thought from time to time that I detected an old and canny hand guiding the affairs of Agrach Dyrr, but I have not met anyone who claims to have seen you in almost two hundred years, and it's been almost twice that since last we spoke."

"I value my privacy, and encourage my descendants to value my privacy as well. It's best for all involved if my hand remains hidden. We wouldn't want to make the matron mothers nervous now, would we?"

"Indeed. In my experience they react poorly to surprises."

The lich laughed, a horrible sound that chilled the blood. He moved closer, gliding forward to stand by Gromph's side and look out over the city. The archmage found himself more than a little unsettled by the unnatural presence of the undead creature—again, a sensation he did not experience often at all.

What secrets does this walking ghost hold in its empty skull? Gromph wondered. What does he know about this city that no one else remembers? What lonely and terrible heights of lore has he scaled alone in the dreary centuries of his deathless existence?

The questions troubled Gromph, but he decided to put such speculation behind him for the moment.

"Well, Lord Dyrr, you requested this meeting. What shall we talk about?"

"You were always admirably direct, young Baenre," the lich said. "It's a refreshing quality among our kind. To get swiftly to the point, what do you think of the recent difficulties that have beset our fair city? More specifically, what do you think should be done about the powerlessness that has descended upon our ruling caste of priestesses?"

"What should be done?" Gromph replied. "That's hard to say, when the question would seem to be what can be done? It is hardly within my power to entreat the Queen of the Demonweb Pits to restore her favor to her priestesses. Lolth will do as she will."

"As ever. I do not mean to imply that you could do otherwise." The lich paused, the green fire of its gaze locked on the archmage. "What do you see when you look out over Menzoberranzan today, Gromph?"

"Disorder. Peril. Denial."

"And, perhaps, opportunity?"

Gromph hesitated a moment, then said, "Yes, of course."

"You hesitated. You do not agree with me?"

"No, it is not that."

The archmage frowned, and chose his words with care. He did not wish to give offense to the powerful apparition. Dyrr seemed civil enough, but the mind did not always stand up well to ages of undeath. He had to assume that there was nothing the lich was not capable of.

"Lord Dyrr," he said, "surely you have observed that there is no end to the wiles of the Spider Queen. The only certainty of our existence is that Lolth is a capricious and demanding deity, a goddess who delights in teaching very harsh lessons indeed. What if her silence is a ruse to test her faithful? Isn't it likely, even probable, that Lolth withholds her favor from her priestesses to see how they respond? Or—worse yet—to see whether the enemies of her clerics might be emboldened to creep out from the shadows and assault her minions directly? If that is the case, what then becomes of anyone foolish enough to defy the Queen of Spiders when she tires of her test and restores her full favor to her priestesses, just as abruptly as she withdrew it? I would not care to be caught out by such a ploy. Not at all."

"Your logic is sound enough, though I think you have perhaps allowed the habit of caution to hobble your thoughts," Dyrr said. "I could almost agree with you, dear boy, except for this one fact. In the more than two thousand years that I have walked this world, I have never seen this happen before. Oh, I can recall several occasions when Lolth denied her clerics spells for a few days, and many instances in which she arbitrarily decided to stop favoring this priestess or that House all together, casting them down to their enemies, but never has she abandoned our entire race for month after month." The lich glanced up in a reflective manner. "It seems a poor way to treat one's worshipers. Should I ever attain godhood, I think I will try to do a better job of it."

"What precisely do you propose, then, Lord Dyrr?"

"I propose nothing yet, but I do consider, young Baenre, whether powerless clerics should be trusted with the rule of this city for very much longer at all. You and I, we still command great and terrible powers, do we not? The mystic secrets of our Art have not abandoned us, nor are they likely to at any point in the future. Perhaps it is time to look to the security of our civilization, the defense of our city, by taking up the reins of governance the matron mothers are no longer strong enough to hold. Our city's peril grows with every hour. We have rivals outside the Dark Dominion, after all, other races and realms that threaten us."

"And that is precisely why I am hesitant to turn drow wizards against drow priestesses," Gromph replied. "The only thing that could possibly increase our current vulnerability would be to start a civil war. To spare ourselves the fate of Ched Nasad, we must shore up the existing order until the crisis has passed."

"And what thanks do you think you will earn, from the priestesses or from the Spider Queen herself, for that blind loyalty?" Dyrr turned back to Gromph and tapped one skeletal forefinger in the center of the archmage's chest. Gromph could not restrain a shudder. "You have potential, young Gromph. You are not without talent, and you see past House Baenre to Menzoberranzan itself. Put those qualities to work and consider carefully the course you choose in the next few days. Events are coming that will provide you with an opportunity for greatness, or failure. Do not make the wrong choice."

Gromph took a cautious step backward, moving out over the vast gulf of the cavern and hovering in the air.

"I am afraid I must tend Narbondel, Lord Dyrr. I will take my leave now . . . and I will think carefully on your words. You may have appreciated the situation more accurately than I."

The burning green gaze of the lichdrow followed Gromph down into the darkness as he fell softly toward the city below. He would indeed think long and hard about the lich's words. He might stall Dyrr once with civility and caution, but he would not be able to do so indefinitely. Gromph didn't doubt the lich would expect a different answer when next they spoke.

The Darklake was a strange and terrible place. A blackness greater than any Halisstra had ever known enveloped her and her companions, a space so vast that its unseen recesses gnawed at the mind. The great caverns of the drow were often miles across, tremendous places harboring cities of many thousands, but—if Coalhewer did not exaggerate—the Darklake occupied a cavern well over one hundred miles from side to side, and thousands of feet in height. Great island columns the size of mountains held up the mighty roof, creating fanglike archipelagos in the darkness. The waters of the lake virtually filled the immense space. As they sailed across its surface the ceiling was often less than a spearcast above them, leaving many hundreds, or even thousands of feet of black mystery below their feet. It was an unsettling sensation.

Coalhewer's boat was less than comforting itself. It was an asymmetrical vessel made mostly of planks sawn from the woody stems of a particular type of gigantic Underdark mushroom, and treated with lacquers for strength and rigidity. The zurkhwood formed a broad platform, which floated on a cluster of soft air bladders taken from some aquatic species of giant fungus. The whole thing was riveted together with the excellent metalwork of the gray dwarves.

Four hulking skeletons—ogres in life, perhaps, or maybe trolls—crouched in a well-like area in the boat's center, endlessly turning two large cranks that drove a pair of zurkhwood water-wheels. The mindless undead never tired, never complained, never even slowed their pace unless Coalhewer ordered them to, driving the boat onward with no sound but the soft rush of water over the wheels and the faint clicking and scraping of their bones in motion. The gray dwarf stood near the stern on a small, elevated bridge, high enough to see over the waterwheels. He peered ahead into the darkness, arms folded across his thick chest, keeping his thoughts to himself.

The passengers crouched on the cold, uncomfortable deck or paced back and forth, staying a little ways back from the railless edge of the platform. The journey from Mantol-Derith was not extremely swift, as the vessel was not quick, and Coalhewer had to carefully thread his way around places where the cavern roof dropped so low there wasn't enough room for the boat.

Valas spent most of his time standing on the bridge beside the dwarf, keeping a careful eye on the course he steered. Pharaun sat cross-legged at the base of the structure, deep in Reverie, while Ryld and Jeggred kept a sharp watch on the port and starboard sides respectively, making sure that none of the lake's denizens approached undetected. The priestesses kept to themselves, wrapped in Reveries of their own or staring out over the lightless waters, lost in thought.

They passed almost two full days in that manner, pausing only briefly for austere meals or to let the duergar captain rest. Coalhewer was extraordinarily cautious about showing any kind of light and made them build their cookfires in a small, secluded fire-box that shielded the flames from view.

"There's too many things as are drawn by the light," he muttered. "Even this much may be dangerous."

After their third such meal, late on their second day of travel, Halisstra retired to the bow of the boat so that she could look out over the waters and not find herself staring at one or another of her companions. In the furious battle to escape Hlaungadath, and the walk through the Plane of Shadow, she had had little time to embrace and understand her new circumstances. Empty hours of listening to the soft murmur of water and the insectlike clicking and scraping of the boat's skeletal engine had unfortunately failed to immerse her in activity, leaving her with the opportunity to replay the fall of Ched Nasad over and over again in her head.

What became of my House? she wondered. Did any of our servants and soldiers survive by escaping Ched Nasad? Are they together, and who leads them? Or did they all die amid the flame and ruin?

Matron Mother Melarn's death left Halisstra as the head of the House—presuming that none of her younger cousins had managed to claim leadership. If one of them had, Halisstra was certain she could wrest it away from her kinswoman. She had always been the most favored of the Melarn daughters, the oldest, the strongest, and she knew her cousins could not deny her her birthright.

But it seemed very likely indeed that her birthright was nothing more than ash and rubble at the floor of Ched Nasad's great chasm. Even if some part of her household had escaped, would she want to seek them out and join them in a miserable, squalid, and dangerous exile in the Underdark?

This was not how it was supposed to be, she thought. I was to ascend to my mother's place in time, and wield the power that had been hers and her mother's before her. The thousand strands of Ched Nasad would have met at my feet. My least desire I might have fulfilled with a word, a look, a simple frown. Instead, I am a rootless wanderer.

Why, Lolth? she cried out in her mind. Why? What offense did we give you? What weakness did we show?

Once Halisstra had heard the dark whispers of the Spider Queen in her heart, but that place was empty. Lolth chose not to answer. She did not even choose to punish Halisstra for the temerity of demanding an answer.

If Lolth had truly abandoned her, what would become of her if she followed her House down into death? All of her life, Halisstra had believed that her faithful service as a priestess and a *bae'qeshel* to the Queen of the Demonweb Pits would earn her a high place in Lolth's domain after her death, but what would become of her now? Would her rootless spirit be interred with the other unfortunate souls no god claimed in the afterlife, fated to dissipate and die the real and eternal death in the gray voids reserved for the faithless? Halisstra shivered in horror. Lolth's faith was hard, and weaklings had no place in it, but a priestess could expect that she would be rewarded in death for her service in life. If that was no longer true . . .

Danifae approached with sinuous grace and knelt beside her. She looked into Halisstra's face boldly, and did not lower her eyes.

"Grief is a sweet wine, Mistress Melarn. If you drink but a little, you are tempted to drink more, and things are never improved by overindulging in either."

Halisstra looked away to compose herself. She did not care to share her secret horror with Danifae.

"Grief is not enough of a word for what is in my heart," she said. "I have thought of little else since we began this interminable voyage. Ched Nasad was more than a city, Danifae. It was a dream, a dark and glorious dream of the Spider Queen. Graceful castles, soaring webs, Houses full of wealth and pride and ambition, all burned to ashes in a few short hours. The city, its matrons and daughters, the beautiful web-spun palaces, all lost now, and for what reason?" She closed her eyes and battled the hot ache in the hollow of her breast. "The dwarves did not destroy us. We destroyed ourselves."

"I will not mourn the passing of Ched Nasad," Danifae said. Halisstra looked up sharply, cut more by the girl's dispassionate tone than her words. "It was a city full of enemies, most of whom are dead, while others flee as paupers into the wilds of the Underdark.

No, I will not mourn Ched Nasad. Who, besides the few Ched Nasadans who survive, will?"

Halisstra did not choose to answer. No one would grieve for a city of drow, not even other dark elves. That was the way of the drow. The strong endured, and the weak fell by the wayside, as the Spider Queen demanded. Danifae waited for a long time before she spoke again.

"Have you given thought to what we will do next?"

Halisstra glanced at her and said, "Our lot is already cast with the Menzoberranyr, is it not?"

"For today, yes, but tomorrow will your purposes and theirs coincide? What will you do if Lolth's favor returns tomorrow? Where would you go?"

"Does it matter?" Halisstra said. "Return to Ched Nasad, I suppose, and gather together what survivors I can. It will be a hard task, more than I likely could hope to accomplish even in a lifetime, but with the Spider Queen's blessing House Melarn may yet rise again."

"Do you think Quenthel would permit such a thing?"

"Why should she care what I do with the rest of my life? Especially if I spend it raising a wretched fragment of a House over the smoking ruins of my city?" Halisstra said bitterly.

Danifae merely spread her hands. Halisstra understood. What reason would a Baenre need to do anything at all, really? The Menzoberranyr might have been their saviors from the wreck of Ched Nasad, but at a word from Quenthel they might become their captors, or their killers. The girl glanced back to where the others meditated or stood their watches, and changed to signs, carefully hidden from the rest of the company.

Perhaps it might be wise to consider exactly how we can make ourselves indispensable to the Menzoberranyr, she motioned. *The hour will come when we will no longer wish to rely on Quenthel Baenre's benevolence, such as it is.*

"Careful," Halisstra cautioned.

She sat up straight and deliberately controlled her own impulse to look over her shoulder. Danifae had an uncanny instinct for manipulation, but if Quenthel suspected that Halisstra and Danifae planned to undermine her authority—or even impose limits on her freedom of action—Halisstra didn't doubt that the Baenre would take quick and drastic steps to remove a perceived challenge.

It is a dangerous thing you suggest, Danifae. Quenthel would not hesitate to kill a challenger, and if I were killed—

I would not survive, Danifae finished for her. *I understand the conditions of my captivity quite well, Mistress Melarn. Still, inaction in the face of our danger is every bit as risky as what I am about to propose. Hear me out, and you can decide what you wish me to do.*

Halisstra measured the girl, studying her perfect features, her alluring figure. She thought of the conversation between Quenthel and Danifae she had overheard in the catacombs of Hlaungadath. She could put a halt to Danifae's scheming with a word, of course. She could even compel it through the magic of the locket—but then she wouldn't know what Danifae plotted, would she?

"Very well," she said. *Tell me what you have in mind.*

Chapter

SIX

Gracklstugh, like Menzoberranzan, was a cavern city. Unlike the realm of the dark elves, the stalagmites harbored great stinking smelters and foundries, not the elegant castles of noble families. The air had an acrid reek, and the clamor of industry rang endlessly throughout the cavern—the roaring of fires, the metallic ringing of iron on iron, and the rush of polluted streams carrying away the wastes of the duergar forges. Unlike Menzoberranzan, lightless except for the delicate faerie fire applied to decorate drow palaces, Gracklstugh glowed with reflected firelight and the occasional harsh glare of white-hot metal splashing into molds. It was a singularly unlovely place, an affront to any highborn drow. Halisstra thought the place seemed like nothing less than the Hells' own foundry.

At its eastern end, the great cavern of the city sloped down sharply to join the immense gulf of the Darklake, so that Gracklstugh was a subterranean port—though few among the Underdark races used waterways such as the Darklake in their commerce. Consequently the wharves and lakeside warehouses of the duergar city constituted one of its poorest and most dangerous districts. Coalhewer moored his macabre vessel at the end of a crumbling stone quay occupied by a handful of ships of the same general design.

"Get yer things and step lively," the dwarf snapped. "The less ye're seen t'be about the streets, the better. Spider-kissers in the City of Blades be well-advised to step soft and quick, if ye take my meaning."

Valas shot the others a quick look and signed, *No killing! It will not be tolerated here.*

The scout shouldered his pack and followed the dwarf down the quay, wrapping his *piwafwi* around him to conceal the swords at his hip.

Pharaun glanced up at Jeggred and said, "You won't like it here, half-demon. How will you pass the time without something helpless to dismember?"

"I will simply while away the hours considering how I might kill you, wizard," the draegloth rumbled.

Still, Jeggred blew out his breath and drew his own long cloak over his white mane, doing the best he could to hunch over and make himself inconspicuous. The rest of the party followed after, threading their way through the dilapidated streets of the city's dock quarter to a fortresslike inn a few blocks from the wharves. A sign lettered in both Dwarvish and Undercommon named the place as the Cold Foundry. The building itself consisted of an encircling stone wall, guarding a number of small, free-standing blockhouses. The company halted just outside the inn's front gate, which stood beside a pen holding huge, foul-smelling pack lizards.

"Hardly an appealing prospect," muttered Pharaun. "Still, I suppose it's better than a rock on a cavern floor."

Valas conferred briefly with Coalhewer, then turned to the rest of the dark elves and said quietly, "Coalhewer and I will arrange safe passage out of the city and look into provisioning. It'll likely involve some bribes to obtain proper licenses and such, which will take time. We should plan on staying here for at least a full day, perhaps two."

"Can we spare the time?" Ryld asked.

"That would be up to Mistress Quenthel," Valas said, "but we may be many days on the next leg of our journey. We accomplish nothing by starving to death after a tenday or two in the wilds of the Underdark."

Quenthel studied the cheerless duergar inn, and made her decision.

"We will stay two nights, and leave early on the day after tomorrow," she said. "I would stay longer, but I am hesitant to trust our fortunes to the continued hospitality of the duergar. Events are moving too quickly for us to tarry long."

She looked at the scout, and at Coalhewer, who stood a short distance off, watching the street with arms folded and pointedly not listening in on the dark elves' conversation.

Is this place safe? she signed. *Will the dwarf betray us?*

Safe enough, the scout replied. *Keep Jeggred out of sight. The rest of you should be fine, as long as you avoid confrontations.* He flicked his eyes at Coalhewer and added, *The dwarf understands that we will pay well for his services, but if he should come to believe that we might kill him rather than pay him, he will undoubtedly find a way to have us all arrested. He knows we're something more than merchants, but he doesn't care what errand brings us here as long as he's paid.*

A loose end to be tied up? Ryld asked.

Too dangerous now, Valas signed. *I will keep a close eye on him as long as we're here.*

"Take Ryld with you, just in case," Quenthel said.

Ryld nodded and tugged at his pack, adjusting it to ride better between his shoulder blades.

"Ready when you are," he said.

"I can't say I won't welcome the company, if trouble comes," Valas replied. "Well, let's not keep Master Coalhewer waiting. If you don't hear back from us by midday tomorrow, presume the worst and get out of the city by the quickest means at hand."

The scout hurried off with Ryld striding along a step behind him.

They collected Coalhewer and made their way deeper into the city.

"It's that boundless good cheer we find endearing in you, Valas," Pharaun remarked to the scout's back. "Well, I too have errands to run. I must find what passes for a dealer in arcane reagents in this grim place, and replenish my spell components."

"Don't take too long," Quenthel said. She glanced over at Halisstra and Danifae. "Well, aren't you coming?"

"Not yet," Halisstra said. "As long as we're here, I think I will see to providing Danifae with weapons and armor. We'll be back when she is suitably equipped."

"I thought you didn't care to allow your battle captive to fight for you," Quenthel said, her eyes narrowing in calculation.

"I have decided that Danifae is something of a liability as long as she's unarmed and unarmored. I don't want my property damaged for no good reason."

Halisstra could almost feel the depth of Quenthel's suspicion, and the Baenre silently stroked the hilt of her whip as she studied the Ched Nasadan and her handmaid thoughtfully.

Good, thought Halisstra. Let her wonder what hold I have over Danifae that I feel confident arming her. A little uncertainty might improve her assessment of our usefulness.

"Don't wander far or get yourselves into trouble," Quenthel said. "I won't hesitate to set out without either of you if the circumstances so dictate."

She motioned to Jeggred and marched into the Cold Foundry, apparently dismissing both the Ched Nasadan and the Eryndlyrr from her thoughts.

Halisstra couldn't repress a smile of satisfaction as Quenthel disappeared from view, Jeggred slinking behind her. She exchanged looks with Danifae, and the two set off into the duergar city.

Though Coalhewer had insisted that the city was open to folk of all races, provided they brought gold, Halisstra could not convince herself that a pair of dark elves were truly safe in Gracklstugh. The short, stocky gray dwarves crowding the streets went about their business with a sullen purposefulness that Halisstra didn't like at all. They didn't laugh, or primp and preen, or even trade veiled threats with one another. Instead, they glared angrily at passersby of any race, including their own, and stomped along beneath heavy shirts of mail, fists gripped tightly on the hafts of axes and hammers thrust through their broad belts. Only after Halisstra and Danifae had passed half a dozen folk of other races in the streets did she begin to relax.

Halisstra paused in a spot between two towering smelters and looked around.

"There. I know little Dwarvish, but I think those signs advertise weaponsmiths."

They turned down the street, which was little more than a winding footpath rounding the castle-like stalagmites. Past the great stone pillars, they came to something resembling a town square of sorts, an open place surrounded by low, fortlike buildings of mortared stone. Here they found a large storefront displaying dozens of weapons and suits of armor beneath a merchant's sign.

"This seems promising," Halisstra said. She ducked through the low door and stepped inside, Danifae behind her.

The place was filled with martial accoutrements of all sorts, much of it dwarven, but a number of pieces from other races—heavy iron blades of orog-work, kuo-toan armor made from the scales of some great pale fish, and black mithral mail of drow-make. Two well-armed duergar busied themselves with assembling a suit of half-plate armor at a workbench to one side of the door. They fixed suspicious stares on Halisstra and Danifae when the dark elves walked in, and kept a wary eye on them as the priestess and her handmaid examined the merchandise.

"Mistress Melarn," Danifae called.

Halisstra turned to find the girl gazing up at a well-made suit of drow chain mail, worked with the emblem of a minor House she did not know. A matching buckler hung near the mail, with a morning-star of black steel alongside it. The head of the weapon was fashioned in the shape of a demonic face with twisting, spikelike horns. Halisstra carefully muttered the words of a spell of detection, and smiled at the result. The arms were magical—not overwhelmingly so, but certainly as good as or better than anything she'd hoped to find in the city.

"What can you tell us of these drow arms?" she asked of the shopkeepers.

The duergar halted their work. The two might have been twins; Halisstra could hardly tell them apart.

"Trophy," one of them rasped. "A captain in the service of Laird Thrazgad sold 'em a couple of months ago. Don't know where he got 'em."

"They're enchanted," said the other dwarf. "Won't be cheap. Not at all cheap."

Halisstra moved over to the counter, and fished a small pouch from inside her hauberk. She pored through its contents, and picked out several fine emeralds to set on the counter.

"Do we have a deal?"

The gray dwarf stood and approached to study the emeralds.

He scowled and said, "More than that. A lot more."

Halisstra met his gaze evenly. She hadn't managed to carry away much from her House before it fell, and she simply couldn't waste it on a gray dwarf's greed, not if she had other options open to her.

"Danifae, have another look at the mail," she said over her shoulder. "Make sure it's what you want."

Danifae read her intent perfectly. The girl picked up the morningstar and hefted it in her hand, feeling out its balance. As Halisstra had hoped, the second dwarf became nervous, watching a dark elf handle merchandise so valuable. He set down his work and moved over to keep a closer eye on her, making sure he stood between Danifae and the door. Danifae immediately began to offer a variety of comments about the arms, admiring the mail, questioning the strength of the enchantments, and generally engaging the fellow in conversation.

"It'll take five times that weight of gemstones," the duergar at the counter told Halisstra. "And they'll have to be good stones, too."

"Very well, then," Halisstra said.

She shrugged a leather case from her back and set it on the countertop. Unwrapping it carefully, she withdrew her lyre, a small, curved instrument of dragonbone, strung with mithral wire and chased with mithral filigree.

"As you can see, it's an exquisite piece of work," she said.

She picked it up and strummed it as if to show off its qualities—and quietly sang a *bae'qeshel* song. The dwarf gaped at her, then recoiled in horror when he realized she was casting a spell. Before he could call out a warning, the magic of the song ensnared him.

"What's going on there?" the duergar watching Danifae demanded.

"Tell your friend it's all right," Halisstra whispered across the counter. "You don't want the lyre."

"It's fine," the first dwarf said. "She's offering the lyre, but we don't want it."

"Of course not," the second muttered. "Do you see any instruments in here?"

He returned his attention to Danifae, who asked him about the best way to care for mail in damp places.

"Now," said Halisstra to the dwarf she'd beguiled, "we're a little far apart at the moment, but I'm certain we can strike a good bargain. You're going to sell us the arms my handmaid is looking over. Will you take the emeralds as a down payment? I will come back in a couple of days with a very handsome sum to square my account."

"The stones'll do as a down payment," the merchant allowed, "but my partner won't be happy with that. He'll think you don't mean to come back."

"Let him think I've paid in full, then, and he won't trouble you." Halisstra said.

She thought for a moment more, then leaned forward and held the fellow with her eye.

"You know," she said softly, "if something were to happen to your partner, the entire business would be yours to run as you see fit, wouldn't it? You could keep *all* of the profits, couldn't you?"

An avaricious gleam came to the merchant's eye.

"I think you're right," he said. "I don't know why it didn't occur to me before!"

"Patience," Halisstra advised. "Anytime today would be fine. Oh, and I would appreciate it if you didn't mention to anyone else that my friend and I had done business with you. Let's just keep this between the two of us."

🕷 🕷 🕷

Nimor departed Menzoberranzan, carrying various payments and tokens to indicate that Reethk Vaszune had entered into an arrangement to provide the wizards of Agrach Dyrr with certain spell reagents and components on the small chance that he might be required to talk his way out of the city. The details of the true arrangement he had forged he carried in no place except his own mind. The Anointed Blade of the Jaezred Chaulssin was well satisfied with his work of the past few days. While he did not strictly need Agrach Dyrr for what he had in mind, the accommodation he'd reached with the ancient master of the House would make the task ahead of him much easier.

Nimor slipped from the Qu'ellarz'orl into a small side cavern leading out into the Dark Dominion. He had come to know the maze of dangerous passages surrounding the great city quite well in the past few months, and he quickly found a dark, quiet spot unobserved by any of the city's defenders. The Anointed Blade stretched out his hand toward the blank stone of the passage wall. The Ring of Shadows gleamed on his left hand, a small circle of inky darkness that seemed more like a tiny hole in the world than a piece of ornamentation. Among its other powers, the ring made available to him the ability to walk paths in the Plane of Shadow and so freed him from many of the constraints that travel on foot would otherwise place on him.

He stepped forward toward the wall, and vanished into the Shadow Fringe. His destination lay not much more than a hundred miles from Menzoberranzan. He'd made the trip several times before, and it rarely took more than an hour. No son of Chaulssin had much to fear walking among the shadows, so Nimor occupied himself during his journey by weighing the value of his alliance with Agrach Dyrr, and wondering whether the ancient sorcerer who secretly ruled the House could be trusted to do as he said he would.

Nimor followed the dark path the ring forged through the Shadow Fringe for a measureless span of time, and the road began to twist back toward the mundane world. It was nearly impossible to judge the passage of hours in the Fringe, but the magic of the spell was such that the path it created would, in its own time, emerge at the desired destination. The assassin set his hand to the hilt of his rapier and took the last step of his journey, stepping through a veil of gloom into a large, vaultlike chamber of carefully fitted stone blocks. Only one door led from the room, a great portal of iron reinforced by strengthening spells. Nimor drew from beneath his mail vest a large bronze key and fitted it to the looming portal. The door swung open with a squeal of rust.

Beyond the door stood a great, dark hall lit by red-glowing coals in iron braziers. Like the vault it was made of dressed stone, its ceiling supported by massive columns, but unlike similar chambers in drow palaces, the space was devoid of decoration or adornment. Nimor felt the presence of some number of guardians, though they chose not to reveal themselves.

"It is I, Nimor Imphraezl," he said. "Inform the crown prince that I am here."

From the air beside him several duergar guards appeared, shedding their invisibility. The gray dwarves stood a head shorter than the drow, but they were broad of shoulder and long of torso, their legs thick and short, their arms powerfully muscled. They wore black plate armor and carried battle-axes and shields emblazoned with the symbol of Gracklstugh. One duergar woman, her rank indicated only by a single strip of gold filigree on the brow of her helm, studied him carefully.

"The crown prince has left instructions to show you to a guest apartment in the palace. He will call on you shortly."

She made the courtesy sound like an order.

The assassin folded his arms and suffered himself to be marched off by a pair of the prince's own Stone Guards. The gray dwarves eyed him uneasily, as if they expected mischief from Nimor. In truth, there was little love lost between duergar and drow, despite the fact that Menzoberranzan and Gracklstugh had stood as neighbors for millennia. Gray dwarf and dark elf had fought more than one vicious war for control of the hundred-odd miles of cavern and chasm that lay between the two cities. The fact that no such war had been fought in a century or more simply indicated that both races had come to hold a grudging respect for their enemy's strength, and not any real lessening of the ill will between them.

The guards led him through the labyrinthine corridors of Gracklstugh's palace and showed him to a large suite in a disused portion of the fortress. The furnishings were simple and functional, as fitted duergar taste. Nimor settled down to wait, moving over to gaze out of a slitlike window at the gray dwarf city beyond the palace. The city was as unlovely as ever, a reeking cauldron of smoke and noise.

After a time, Nimor noted the approach of footsteps outside and turned as Horgar Steelshadow entered the suite, flanked by a pair of Stone Guards.

"Ah," the dark elf said, inclining his head. "A good day to you, my lord. How fares the City of Blades?"

"I doubt that you care," Horgar replied. For the ruler of such a powerful city, the crown prince was in many ways unremarkable. He looked very much like all the other duergar in the room, with a sullen cast to his eyes and a hairless skull. He carried a scepter of office and did not wear armor, which was all that differentiated him from his bodyguards. He motioned the guards to remain by the door, and strode over to speak quietly to Nimor. "Well? What news?"

"I believe I have found the allies I was seeking in Menzoberranzan, dear prince. A strong House eager to see the current order of things overthrown, but whose loyalty is not in question there. The hour of your victory approaches."

"Hmph. House Zauvirr was eager to hire our mercenaries in Ched Nasad, but damned few of Khorrl Xornbane's folk came back. I don't doubt that you or that Zammzt fellow whispered the same thing in Khorrl's ear when you hired his company."

"Xornbane's losses were regrettable, but in truth we did not expect the exceptional effectiveness of your stonefire bombs against Ched Nasad's calcified webs. Absent that unforeseeable chance, Khorrl Xornbane would have taken the city with House Zauvirr."

The duergar prince scowled, his beard jutting out like a bottle-brush.

"I warned Khorrl that dark elves have a habit of poorly rewarding mercenaries, especially dwarves. I won't let another of our mercenary companies march into peril like that again. Xornbane was an eighth of this city's strength."

"I have no need of a single company of mercenaries, Prince, no matter how large and fierce," Nimor assured him. "I have need of your whole army. March in your full strength, and you need not fear defeat in detail."

"It still smells like an insidious drow ruse to me."

Nimor frowned and said, "Prince Horgar, if you are hesitant to hazard any risks at all, you will rarely win a throw of the dice. You have an opportunity to achieve something great, but I cannot tell you that your success is guaranteed, or that there are no risks in our enterprise."

"We're not talking about a handful of coins riding on a stupid game," the duergar prince said. "We're talking about my throne riding on a war that could take a turn I don't care for in any number of ways. Don't try to shore up my resolve with empty observations about risk and reward."

"Very well, then, I shall not, but I will point out that when last we met you said you wanted only one thing before you would consent to lead your army against Menzoberranzan, and that was a substantial ally within the city itself. I have provided you that ally. When will it ever be better for you to strike out at the threat a strong Menzoberranzan poses to your kingdom? Their priestesses are powerless, they have already endured a costly slave rebellion, and now I bring to you a great House willing to assist you in your efforts. What more do we lack, Prince?"

The duergar scowled and turned away to stare out at Gracklstugh. He stood for a time, thinking hard. Nimor watched him waver, and decided it was time to set the hook.

Lowering his voice, he moved close and said, "What better way to secure your seat against the unruly lairds you fear, than by distracting them with a campaign beyond your borders? Even if you should fail to take Menzoberranzan, some diligent planning should ensure that the forces of the most dangerous lairds seem to find the deadliest part of any battle you fight. In truth I believe it is within your grasp to win a great victory over Menzoberranzan, and wreck the strength of your most rebellious nobles at the same time."

The duergar prince grunted and studied Nimor closely.

"You presume much, dark elf," said Horgar. "What is it you hope to gain by destroying Menzoberranzan, eh? Why do you seek to set me on this course of action?"

The assassin grinned and clapped the duergar on the shoulder. The Stone Guards in the chamber shifted nervously, disapproving of the contact.

"My dear Prince Horgar, the answer is simple," Nimor said. "Revenge. Your army is to be the instrument of my vengeance. Naturally I recognize that you will not raze Menzoberranzan simply because I ask it, so it is a necessary part of my design that you are provided with the suitable motivation to do what I wish done. I have worked long and hard to bring about the circumstances under which the army of Gracklstugh might be aimed at the city I hate—including, I might add, assisting you with the small problem of your father's thoughtless longevity. How can I make my purpose plainer?"

"I paid for your help in that case with hundreds of stonefire bombs," the duergar prince said, bridling. "Do not speak of my father's . . . death again. If I came to believe that you might seek to influence my actions with that story, I would have to make sure that whatever information you possessed never came to light. Do you understand me?"

"Oh, I did not mean anything by the remark, Horgar. I merely pointed out that I had been useful to you before, and that I may prove useful again. Now, can I count on the army of Gracklstugh, or not?"

Horgar Steelshadow, Crown Prince of Gracklstugh, reluctantly nodded assent.

"We will come," he said. "Now, explain to me who exactly will be aiding us inside Menzoberranzan, and how he'll be able to help."

Ryld could feel hateful eyes lingering on his broad back as he followed Valas and Coalhewer through the streets of the duergar city. He was all too conscious of the fact that he was out of his element. He towered a good twenty inches over any of the gray dwarves, and his coal-black skin and inky *piwafwi* didn't help him to blend in at all. The three travelers wound their way through a swordsmith's district, a narrow alleyway lined on both sides by open-air forges where duergar in leather aprons hammered endlessly on glowing metal. Ryld knew a thing or two about good steel, and he could see at a glance that the dwarves knew their work.

The weapons master quickened his step and drew alongside Valas.

"Where are we going?" he asked as quietly as possible over the ringing hammers. "I thought we needed to obtain some sort of official license or pass. Shouldn't we be heading for a courthouse, or something?"

"If ye wanted a royal license, ye would," Coalhewer answered, "but that would take ye months and cost ye a fortune in bribes. No, I'm takin' ye to call on the household of the clan laird Muzgardt. He'll give ye a writ o' passage that should get ye where ye want to go."

Ryld nodded. It was not so different from Menzoberranzan, after all.

"How far will Muzgardt's writ run?" Valas asked. "Will it get us out of Gracklstugh's dominions?"

"Muzgardt's clan be merchants. They deal in ale and liquors throughout the Deepkingdom, and sometimes bring outside brews into the city—drow wine, svirfneblin brandy, even some vintages from the surface, or so I hear. Ye'll find his folk all over the realm." Coalhewer laughed a nasty laugh and added, " 'Course, Muzgardt sells passage to those as want it, too. He likes his gold."

Ryld smiled. Coalhewer was a grasping, avaricious fellow by anyone's standards. Muzgardt's greed must be something noteworthy indeed for a dwarf like Coalhewer to comment on it.

They came to the end of the street of swordsmiths and found themselves back in the vicinity of the Darklake, though farther north along the shore. Before them stood a huge, ramshackle brewery made from loose stone stacked to make walls between the petrified stems of a small forest of gigantic mushrooms. Big copper vats steamed within, filling the air with a heavy, yeasty stink. Dozens of copper kegs stood nearby, and burly gray dwarves swarmed over the place, mashing fungus, mixing fermenting masses, and filling casks with freshly brewed ale.

"A dwarf's second love after gold," Coalhewer said with a crooked smile. "Ah, Muzgardt's lads do good work, I tell ye."

The dwarf led Ryld and Valas into the brewhouse and past the huge vats to a small shack or shelter in the back of the place. A pair of gray dwarves stood in heavy mail armor, wicked-looking axes resting close at hand. The guards glared angrily at the dark elves, and picked up their weapons.

"What d'ye want?" one growled.

"Thummud," Coalhewer replied. "Got a business proposition for him."

"Stay here," the first guard said.

He ducked through a ragged curtain in the doorway, and returned a moment later.

"Thummud'll see ye, but the drow'll have t'leave their weapons at the door. Don't trust 'em."

Ryld looked at Valas and signed, *Are we worried about an ambush?*

The scout replied, *Coalhewer knows there are five more in our party,*

*including a capable wizard and a draegloth. I don't think he'd lead us
into a trap—but watch your back anyway.*

"Enough finger-talk," the guard snarled. "Talk so's we can understand ye, if ye've got anything to say."

"Always," Ryld said aloud to Valas.

He gave the duergar a hard look, but shrugged Splitter from his shoulder and set the greatsword against one wall. He unbuckled his short sword from its sheath at his hip and set it nearby.

"There's a curse on the big blade," he said. "You won't like what happens if you try to handle it."

Valas set down his shortbow and arrows, then dropped his kukris to the ground. The duergar guards checked the two dark elves for concealed weapons, then ushered them into the gloomy shelter. The place was an office of sorts, with ledgers and records scattered about. By a large standing clerk's desk stood one of the fattest gray dwarfs Ryld had ever seen, a round-bodied fellow with thick arms and heavy shoulders. Duergar tended to run toward a gaunt, broad-shouldered build despite their short, powerful stature, but the brewmaster Thummud was as round as one of his kegs.

"Coalhewer," he said by way of a greeting. "What can you do for me?"

"I've got a party of dark elves as need a writ o' business from Muzgardt," Coalhewer said. "They'd prefer not to wait on a royal permit."

"What sort of business?"

"We deal in gemstones, mostly," Valas said. "We're looking into setting up transport through the Deepkingdom. We need to be able to move around and talk to a lot of people, and as Coalhewer said, we don't want to wait for months to get a royal license."

"Ye're stupid or ye're lying, then. Ye'll pay ten times the cost of a royal license to get a writ from our clan laird. Most merchants I know wouldn't such a thing."

Valas glanced up at Ryld, then looked back to Thummud and said, "All right, then. We've got some rivals from back home that are doing a fine business here, and we want to sound out their suppliers to see if they can't be encouraged to sell to us instead of the others.

A royal license wouldn't really extend that far, would it?"

Thummud snorted, "No, I suppose not."

"Can ye help me clients, or not?" Coalhewer asked. "Or do I have to go see Ironhead, or maybe Anvilthew?"

"Clan Muzgardt might be able to help ye," Thummud said after a long moment. "We'll want two hundred pieces of gold for each body on the writ, and ye can't have it today."

Coalhewer glanced up at the dark elves. Ryld nodded to him.

"They'll pay the laird's fee," the duergar sailor said, "but they want to get started right quick."

"Doesn't matter what yer clients want," Thummud replied with a shrug. "I'll have to take up the matter with the clan laird before I write you a pass."

"Ye never had to before!"

The fat dwarf folded his arms and set his jaw stubbornly. He glared at Coalhewer and the dark elves.

"Be that as it may, the crown prince's soldiers have been checking our writs and passes too closely of late. Horgar's let it be known that he wants to know who's in the Deepkingdom and why, and he's leaning on the clan lairds to withhold their writs. We'll be able to get yer clients theirs, I think, but I'll have to gain Muzgardt's blessing first. Come back tomorrow, or the day after."

Coalhewer muttered into his beard, but he didn't bother to argue the point any further. He jerked his head toward the curtain, and led Ryld and Valas outside. The dark elves picked up their arms, and in a few minutes they'd left the brewery behind them.

"Now, what should we make of that?" Valas wondered aloud. "Do you know another clan that might help out, Coalhewer?"

"Maybe, but if Horgar's cracking down on informal passes and such things, ye'll have trouble anywhere ye go." The dwarf scratched at his beard. "I'll have to ask some questions, and I don't think ye'd best be with me."

Ryld looked to Valas, who thought carefully before agreeing, and even then the weapons master didn't think his fellow Menzoberranyr looked sufficiently confident in their guide's loyalty.

Chapter

SEVEN

When Halisstra and Danifae returned to the Cold Foundry,
they found that Quenthel had rented one of the inn's larger wings,
a freestanding structure with its own small common room and
eight private chambers on two floors. The whole wing seemed to be
built and decorated to a duergar's conception of drow comfort. Its
furnishings were proportioned for drow-sized guests, not dwarves,
it was richly appointed with tapestries and lavish rugs, and all the
doors had locks. Dark elves didn't require endless hours of sleep in
the same manner as lesser races, but few drow felt safe or comfortable in a deep, dreaming Reverie unless they were taking their ease
behind a locked door.

The rest of the company, with the exception of Pharaun, reclined
on the rugs or sat at the common room's table, partaking of a bounti-
ful meal accompanied by silver ewers of wine. Armor and packs lay
stacked against the walls, but weapons remained within easy reach.

Halisstra raised an eyebrow, eyeing the banquet spread out on the sideboard. A large roast of rothé, several wheels of finely molded cheeses, and steaming platters of braised mushrooms reminded her how long she'd been without a decent, hot meal.

"The food's safe?" she asked.

Quenthel snorted. "Do you think we're stupid? Of course we checked it. The innkeeper sent us a cask of drugged wine the first time around, but we complained to the management"—Jeggred looked up and smiled with a mouthful of fangs at that, and Halisstra guessed she knew what form that complaint had taken—"so the banquet is complimentary. Enjoy."

Halisstra performed her own examination of the table anyway, relying on a magic ring she wore for just that purpose. Poisons were too commonplace among highborn drow to take any meal for granted. Satisfied, she helped herself and sat down by the table. Danifae took some food as well, and took a place, reclining on a low lounge near Quenthel.

"I see the wizard has not yet returned. Have you had any luck?" Halisstra asked Valas as she ate.

The scout sat cross-legged beside the door, his knife belt loosened but still around his narrow hips. He sipped at a mug of mulled wine, and chewed thoughtfully on a piece of bread.

"After a fashion," he said. "The weapons master and I encountered no overt hostility, but we didn't get as far as I would have liked, despite our efforts to impress upon the duergar the importance of time." He jingled the pouch of coins at his belt. "I don't know if this is a sign that something unusual is happening, but Coalhewer didn't like it."

"Where is the dwarf?" asked Danifae.

"He wanted to see if he could obtain a writ through other channels."

"You trust him to do that?"

"Not entirely, but it's something we could not easily do ourselves." The scout grimaced and said, "It's one thing to deal with the duergar clans in a reasonably forthright fashion. If I was caught looking into forging our passes, I would look very much like a spy, wouldn't I? And so would all of you, by association."

"Real spies would approach Gracklstugh in much the same manner we have," Ryld said from one corner, where Splitter leaned against the wall, within easy reach.

"True, but remember that Coalhewer is something of a smuggler himself. He's hardly anxious to bring us to the attention of the crown prince," Valas replied. "Still, the weapons master and I settled for replenishing our provisions, so we're ready to leave whenever Coalhewer obtains our pass."

"It seems we've done all we can for now," Halisstra observed. "I, for one, am tired of blinding deserts, soul-bleaching shadowlands, and bare cavern floors. If we're soon to return to the bleak and comfortless wilds, I'll enjoy what civilization I can."

Halisstra held up her cup for Danifae to fill. The battle captive rose sinuously and refilled her mistress's goblet.

"Drink if you like, but don't let your wits become too sodden," Quenthel warned from her couch. "We're hardly among friends in this filthy city."

"When are any of us truly among friends?" Ryld asked with a snort.

Halisstra laughed softly and said, "Indeed, Ryld, but tonight we can rest in comfort, confident in the knowledge that we none of us trust each other and that not too far away lurk grim enemies who would destroy us if they could. Would we have it any other way?"

Danifae carried the ewer to Quenthel. Ignoring the subtle writhing of the priestess's serpent whip, she lowered her eyes and leaned forward to refill the high priestess's cup.

"We must seize what pleasures we can when the opportunity arises," Danifae added. "Is that not the purpose of power?"

Halisstra sipped her wine and watched the scene. Danifae had neglected to don an arming-coat beneath her mail, as she had found the black mithral shirt without its leather padding. Of course, Halisstra had already offered Danifae a spare coat of her own, and she had no doubt that in the morning Danifae would accept it. In the meantime, the girl's perfect dark skin gleamed through the metal mesh, and her full, round breasts swayed enticingly beneath the steel as she stooped to pour Quenthel's wine. The males in the room could not take their eyes from her, try as they might. Even Jeggred, four-armed hulking beast that he was, seemed entranced by the girl's grace and beauty. Valas frowned and busied himself with oiling his kukris, obviously sensing the peril of the moment and recoiling with his usual caution. Ryld, on the other hand. . . .

Ryld was looking at her. Halisstra carefully kept the surprise from her face as she met the weapons master's gaze. Their eyes locked. His expression seemed avid, intense, and Halisstra knew that Danifae's posturing could not have escaped his notice, but instead of gaping at the girl in her armor of metal mesh, the weapons master turned that gaze on her.

Ryld offered a slight smile and made a soft gesture with his hand: *An interesting play.*

I do not follow your meaning, Halisstra replied, though she could see easily enough that the weapons master knew perfectly well that she did.

She returned her attention to Danifae as the girl kneeled close beside Quenthel, sipping her own wine. The company grew quiet, and Ryld pulled out his traveling *sava* set to play a game against Valas while the others contented themselves with savoring a moment's respite from danger.

Pharaun returned eventually, a handful of scrolls tucked under one arm. He retired to his chamber after a couple of halfhearted jibes at the weapons master to break his concentration. Ryld won anyway, though the Bregan D'aerthe scout gave a good account of himself.

"It has been a long day," Quenthel said. "I shall retire to my chambers. Jeggred, Valas, split the watch tonight. Two others will watch tomorrow."

She stood and stretched, and turned her eyes on Danifae before gliding out of the room.

"I think I'll do the same," Danifae said.

The battle captive glanced at Halisstra, offered a coy smile, and went quickly after Quenthel. Ryld put away his *sava* board and headed up to his room, while Valas and Jeggred tossed a coin for first watch. Halisstra stood, gathered her *piwafwi* around her, and went up to her own room. She paused briefly by Quenthel's door and listened, just long enough to hear what might have been a soft gasp or a rustle of clothing, then she moved on. Quenthel's serpents would likely report an eavesdropper at her door.

Clever girl, Halisstra thought. Quenthel was an astute and daring move indeed.

In Ched Nasad Halisstra had sent Danifae to seduce a rival on more than one occasion. Even the most pragmatic priestess had her favorite pets, and sometimes an otherwise cold and calculating female might be manipulated through her secret pleasures. Halisstra doubted that Danifae could succeed in establishing any real influence over Quenthel, but at the worst, she was providing the Mistress of Arach-Tinilith with a reason not to abandon Halisstra and her handmaid on a whim. Of course, if Danifae's services proved *too* valuable to Quenthel, the Baenre might be inclined to claim the captive as her own, but that was a risk Halisstra was willing to take.

Even if Danifae continued to encourage the Baenre to do just that, Halisstra thought of the silver locket around the girl's neck, and allowed herself a smile. Unless Danifae managed to free herself of the binding spell, she couldn't take the smallest step in that direction, as Halisstra's death would precipitate her own. For the moment Halisstra felt she could rely on Danifae's loyalty.

Halisstra found her room and undressed for bed, setting her armor on a chest in the small room and leaving her mace where she could reach it quickly.

She drifted into Reverie thinking about Quenthel and Danifae together.

🍋   🍋   🍋

Aliisza rode in an iron palanquin through the streets of Gracklstugh, carried by four ogres and escorted by a dozen tanarukk warriors. The tanarukks wore armor of burnished iron and carried wickedly hooked greatswords. One fellow carried a yellow banner emblazoned with Kaanyr Vhok's assumed symbol—a scepter clasped in a gauntleted hand. Twice their number of gray dwarf warriors escorted the embassy along, suspicious glares fixed rigidly on the black palanquin and its occupant. The alu-fiend preened just a little beneath the attention. She would have moved much quicker on her own, of course, but making a grand entrance into the city of the gray dwarves might encourage the duergar to take her seriously. Besides, it was fun.

The journey from the halls of old Ammarindar had not been particularly swift or easy. Aliisza and her warriors had pressed hard at their best possible speed for five days along ancient dwarven highways to reach the shores of the Darklake, and it had taken three days more to obtain a duergar boat to cross it. She was growing tired of dashing this way and that through the Underdark at Kaanyr Vhok's command. On the other hand, it continued to demonstrate her usefulness to the demonspawned warlord, and perhaps it wasn't a bad thing that circumstances gave her reasons to leave his side from time to time. It whetted his appetite for her return, and sometimes gave her the opportunity to indulge her taste for . . . variety.

Gracklstugh seemed to be one great smithy, a city of roaring forges and reeking smoke. It struck Aliisza as not unlike the foundry hall in the ruins of Ammarindar, except Kaanyr Vhok's forge was only a fraction of the size of the gray dwarf realm.

What an ugly place, Aliisza thought. Still, the sheer scale of the work that went on around her was staggering. More than once, she spotted components of siege engines of enormous size being assembled in their workshops. Ched Nasad might have been far more graceful and insidious, but Gracklstugh was *strong*. Dwarven skill and single-mindedness seemed almost a match for drow magic and cruelty.

The gray dwarves turned her escort toward a great fortress delved into a mighty stalagmite. Ramparts of stone and turrets of iron guarded the sloping sides of the duergar castle. As the ogres carried her into the open gate of the king's palace, Aliisza could not check her impulse to glance up at the mighty portcullis and deadly devices poised to crush any attack. She had several ways to escape if she needed to, but none of her warriors would get out of the palace alive if the gray dwarves decided not to let them leave.

The procession came to a halt in a large, cheerless hall whose floor was made of polished stone slabs.

"It seems that I am here," Aliisza said to herself.

She tapped on the palanquin's side, and the ogres lowered the carriage carefully to the floor. The alu-fiend waited for the seat to settle, then let herself out, straightening and stretching her wings.

A duergar officer wearing a plain black surcoat over his armor approached her.

"You said you wished to see the crown prince," he stated.

"At his earliest convenience," Aliisza replied. She'd had the same conversation several times that day with various gray dwarf lieutenants and captains.

"Who are you, again?"

"I am Aliisza, an envoy from Kaanyr Vhok, the Sceptered One, Lord of Ammarindar and Master of Hellgate Keep. I believe your crown prince will find my lord's message worth listening to."

The officer scowled doubtfully.

"They stay here," he said, nodding at Aliisza's entourage. "Follow me."

Aliisza glanced at the leader of her escort, a battered old tanarukk champion with a missing tusk, and said, "You and your warriors wait here. I might be a while."

She followed the duergar captain deeper into the fortress, flanked by another half-dozen gray dwarf soldiers. She decided to think of them as an honor guard.

They climbed a wide, sweeping stairway that might have been impressive if the gray dwarves had taken a single step toward decorating the place, and finally came to a throne room with huge, stone columns supporting a vaulted ceiling high overhead.

At the far end of the chamber stood a knot of gray dwarves. By the way they moved, and the cold regard in their eyes, Aliisza guessed that they were the high advisors and nobles of the realm, but their garb displayed no such ostentation. In their midst stood the only gray dwarf she'd seen yet with any kind of ornamentation, a burly fellow who wore a hauberk of gleaming chain mail beneath an embroidered surcoat of black and gold. A circlet of gold rested atop his bare head, and rings of gold gathered the braids of his beard.

The captain escorting Aliisza motioned for her to halt and went closer to whisper in the ear of the crown prince. The gray dwarf ruler glared at Aliisza, then stepped forward, thick arms folded across his chest.

"Welcome to Gracklstugh," he said, though his hard eyes offered no welcome at all. "I am Horgar Steelshadow. What does Kaanyr Vhok want of me?"

Not long on the social graces, Aliisza noted.

Well, she'd never met a gray dwarf who was. She decided to speak plainly and not waste time on flattery or subtlety, as it was clear any such efforts would be lost on the ruler of Gracklstugh. She offered a small bow, and straightened.

"Kaanyr dispatched me to ask a few questions about what happened in Ched Nasad, and to perhaps explore some other issues," she said. She glanced at the other gray dwarves standing nearby. "Does everyone here enjoy your confidence?"

Horgar frowned, and muttered something in Dwarvish. Several of the advisors or nobles moved off, returning to whatever duties they had elsewhere. A pair of heavily armored guards in black surcoats remained behind, as well as another important-looking duergar, a scarred fellow in armor who wore a tabard marked with a red symbol.

"My Stone Guards stay," Horgar said, then indicated the scarred dwarf. "This is the clan laird Borwald Firehand, marshal of Gracklstugh's army."

Borwald returned Aliisza's nod of greeting with a sullen glare. She shrugged and got back to the point, deciding to match directness with directness.

"A duergar clan—Xornbane, wasn't it?—attacked the drow city

of Ched Nasad, and precipitated its destruction. Kaanyr Vhok wonders if you set them to it."

"Clan Xornbane are mercenaries," Borwald answered. The scar he carried creased the side of his bald head from cheekbone to three inches behind the ear, leaving a visible indentation. "Whatever job they took in Ched Nasad is an issue of commerce, not of Deepkingdom policy. You should take up the matter with them."

"I would, but survivors are hard to find," Aliisza said. "As near as we can tell, they trapped themselves in the city they burned." She returned her gaze to Horgar Steelshadow and asked, "So, did they destroy Ched Nasad with your blessing?"

"With my blessing?" The duergar prince thought for a moment, then said, "I am not unhappy that the City of Shimmering Webs fell, but I did not dispatch Clan Xornbane to do that piece of work. Khorrl Xornbane was hired by one of Ched Nasad's matron mothers to help her destroy those Houses ahead of hers. I did not choose to interfere with Xornbane's business."

"In that case, Xornbane's choice of tactics seems spectacularly unsound. They delivered their employer a smoking ruin, and sustained horrible losses in doing so," Aliisza observed.

"I am afraid that I was at least in part responsible for that," said a melodious voice to one side.

From the shadow of a pillar in the great hall a slim form emerged, a rakish drow of short stature and catlike grace. He was a handsome fellow, impeccably dressed in garments of black and gray, and he wore a matched rapier and dagger at his hip.

"On behalf of my fellows," the newcomer said, "I arranged for Khorrl's troops to be provided with the stonefire bombs that proved so effective in the slave uprising in Menzoberranzan. I did not imagine they would destroy Ched Nasad in its entirety, of course."

Aliisza raised an eyebrow and said, "I did not expect to find a dark elf in the confidence of the prince of the duergar."

"I am something of a sellsword," the fellow replied, "tasked with effecting certain changes in a handful of Houses in Ched Nasad and

Menzoberranzan." He offered her a slight smile that didn't reach his intense eyes. "Call me Nimor."

"Nimor," Aliisza replied. "Whatever your purpose, you certainly effected a change in Ched Nasad. What do you have in mind regarding Menzoberranzan?"

Horgar shifted uncomfortably and asked, "What interest is this to Kaanyr Vhok?"

"Well, had we known that someone meant to attack Ched Nasad, we might have offered our assistance," Aliisza replied. "My lord scents opportunity in the dark elves' difficulties. If someone were considering a similar effort to lay low Menzoberranzan, we might be willing to take on partners in our business."

Borwald sneered, "I doubt the Deepkingdom would have any need of a few hundred rabble squatting in fungus-grown ruins."

Aliisza suppressed her annoyance.

They're duergar, she told herself, abrasive and crass. This is how they are.

"Your intelligence is somewhat out of date," she said. "My lord commands over two thousand hardened tanarukk warriors, each of them as strong as an ogre and three times as smart. We have built forges and armories, perhaps not as grand as those of Gracklstugh, but sufficient to arm and armor our soldiers. We command auxiliary troops as well—bugbears, ogres, giants, and such—more numerous than our tanarukk legion." She leveled her gaze on Borwald and added, "We don't have the strength of the Deepkingdom, Firehand, but we could take on twice our number of gray dwarves and give them a fierce fight. You denigrate Kaanyr Vhok's Scoured Legion at your peril."

"I am not unaware of Kaanyr Vhok's growing strength," Horgar muttered, tugging at his beard. "Speak plainly. What does your lord want?"

No subtlety at all, Aliisza lamented. Kaanyr might as well have sent a dim-witted ogre to deliver this message.

"Kaanyr Vhok wants to know if you intend to march on Menzoberranzan. If you do, he wishes to join you. As I have just said,

I believe that the Scoured Legion could be a valuable ally."

"We might not want you for an ally, if we were thinking of any such thing," Horgar said. "We might think we have sufficient strength to get what we want without splitting the prize."

"You might think that," Aliisza conceded. "If you were correct, the dark elves of Menzoberranzan would be well-advised to seek allies against you. I wonder to whom they could turn for help?"

"I would crush Kaanyr Vhok if he did anything so foolish," Horgar growled. "Go back to your demonspawned master and tell him—"

"A moment, Prince Horgar," Nimor said, stepping between the duergar and the alu-fiend. "Let us not be hasty. We should give Lady Aliisza's message careful thought before we consider our reply."

Horgar snarled, "You do not tell me how to conduct my kingdom's affairs, drow!"

"Of course not, my lord prince, but I would very much like to confer with you at greater length on this question." Nimor turned back to Aliisza and said, "I presume you would be willing to remain as a guest of the crown prince while we discuss your master's offer?"

Aliisza merely smiled. She let her eyes linger on the slim figure of the dark elf. Given an opportunity, she felt sure that she could convince him to see the virtues of her proposal, though she also sensed that there was more to this Nimor than met the eye. Unfortunately, Horgar and his Marshal Firehand were less likely to succumb to her special talents. She could wait a day or two and see if Nimor succeeded in advancing her arguments for her.

The duergar prince measured her, mulling over Nimor's words. Finally, he relented.

"You may stay a short time, while I think about your offer. I'll have the captain set aside quarters in the palace for you. Your soldiers will have to stay in a barracks near my own guards. They will not be permitted in the castle."

"I will require some attendants."

"Fine, you can retain two, if you wish. The rest go."

Horgar looked toward the end of the hall and gestured. His captain came trotting up.

"We will speak again when I have made up my mind," he told her.

"In that event, I will be available at your convenience," she said to Horgar, but she let her eyes linger on Nimor as she spoke.

☗   ☗   ☗

"It can't be done today," Thummud of Clan Muzgardt told Ryld, Valas, and Coalhewer. The fat duergar stood with a mallet in his hand, carefully sealing a fresh keg of mushroom ale. "Try again in a day or two, I guess."

Coalhewer swore under his breath, but the two drow exchanged wary looks. It hardly escaped Ryld's notice that over a dozen duergar brewers happened to be hard at work very close by the spot where Thummud stood, and that many of them had the unmistakable glint of metal beneath their smocks. The brewer wasn't in the habit of taking chances, it seemed.

"That's what you said yesterday," Ryld said. "Time is pressing."

"Not my problem," Thummud replied. He finished tapping down the lid, and set the mallet on top of the cask. "Ye'll have t'wait, like it or not."

Valas sighed and reached for the purse at his belt. He jingled it judiciously and set it down nearby.

"You'll find gemstones in there worth better than twice what we agreed on," the scout said. "They're yours if you get us that writ today."

Thummud's eyes narrowed. "Now I'm wondering what ye really be up to," he said slowly. "No honest purpose, of that I'm sure."

"Consider this a personal bonus," Ryld said quietly. "Your laird expects two hundred pieces of gold per head, and you'll see to it he gets that. What's left over, he doesn't need to know about, does he?"

"I can't say as ye wouldn't get what ye want some other time,"

Thummud admitted with a shrug, "but the laird was certain of his words to me on this matter. I'd be crossin' him to do this bit o' business with ye, and old Muzgardt would have me head for it." The brewer thought about things for a moment, and added, "Better make it three or four days, I think. The crown prince's lads are all over the city, and I don't need 'em to see ye coming here every damned day."

The stout dwarf heaved the keg up onto his shoulder and stomped off, leaving the two dark elves standing with Coalhewer in the middle of the sullen crowd of brewers.

"Now what?" Ryld asked Valas.

"Go back to the inn and wait, I'd say," Coalhewer muttered. "Ye'll have no luck standing here. Come back in a couple of days."

"Quenthel won't like that," Ryld said, still addressing the drow scout.

All Valas could do was shrug.

The two drow and their guide left the Muzgardt brewery, wrapped in their own thoughts. They marched along for a short distance, putting the brewery well behind them.

"I'm beginning to wonder whether we shouldn't just write our own letter of passage," Valas said softly. "We wouldn't need it for long, after all."

"That's a bad idea," Coalhewer said. "Ye might forge a letter that looks about right, but ye need Muzgardt's blessing. If ye get stopped, ye'll be held while they check to be sure that ye've got the blessing of the laird. That ye won't have until Muzgardt grants it to ye."

"Damn," Valas muttered.

Ryld examined the situation, trying to figure what to make of it. Either Coalhewer had purposely led them to a dead end, or the difficulty in obtaining the passes was unfeigned. For the first possibility, Ryld couldn't see any reason why Coalhewer would delay the company in Gracklstugh. Perhaps the dwarf meant to set them up in some way, but if that was the case, wouldn't he have had ample opportunity to spring whatever surprise he might have had in mind? On the other hand, if Coalhewer and Thummud weren't collaborating in some elaborate deception, why would the crown prince happen to choose the occasion of the company's visit to Gracklstugh to crack down on foreigners moving about the realm?

Because he's got something he doesn't want foreigners to see, of course, Ryld decided. What wouldn't he want outsiders to see?

Ryld halted dead in the street. Valas and Coalhewer turned a few steps farther on, looking back at him.

"What is it?" Valas asked.

"You and I have something we need to do," Ryld said to Valas, then he turned to their guide. "Come to the inn tomorrow morning."

Coalhewer frowned.

"Fine," he said. The duergar turned and headed down the street, muttering under his breath, "Don't blame me if ye get arrested for doing whatever it is ye have in mind. I won't speak up for ye. I'll be on me boat if ye need me."

What is it? Valas asked after the dwarf disappeared into the shadowed street.

The crown prince is limiting freedom of movement for foreign merchants and travelers, Ryld answered. *He doesn't want news from the city to get out. I think the army of Gracklstugh is going to march.*

Valas blinked and signed, *You think so?*

"It's what I would do," Ryld answered. "The question is, how to make sure of it."

He glanced around the street. As always, any gray dwarf in sight was staring at the two dark elves with undisguised hostility.

Investigating your suspicion makes us exactly the sort of fellows the crown prince's soldiers will be looking for, Valas signed. The wiry scout frowned, thinking. *What would you need to see to confirm your fear?*

A supply train, Ryld answered at once. *Wagons, pack lizards, that sort of thing. You wouldn't gather that together unless you meant to march, and it would take several days to do it. You'd need a lot of space.*

Agreed, Valas answered.

Valas thought, frowning as he tugged absently at the odd charms and tokens he carried on his clothing.

Feel like taking a chance? the scout signed.

Ryld glanced around the street. Thummud had pretty much told them outright that things wouldn't change for several more days at a minimum, and that was not going to please Quenthel. If Gracklstugh meant to attack Menzoberranzan, he wanted to know about it before the duergar army marched. They would want to find a way to send a warning back home. The duergar were no slave rabble to be crushed at the leisure of the great Houses. The army of the City of Blades would be large, strong, disciplined, and well armed for an assault on the drow, and Ryld didn't like the thought of what an army of that sort might do to his home city.

Let's go, he replied.

Valas nodded and set off at once. Instead of heading back to the lakeside district and the Cold Foundry, he turned deeper, toward the heart of the cavern. They weaved through the foul-smelling streets and dark alleyways for a fair distance, passing through business districts where duergar artisans and merchants kept their shops in cramped buildings of fieldstone. The hour was growing late, and traffic along the dwarf city's streets seemed to be diminishing. The two dark elves finally reached a street that ran along the edge of a deep cleft or chasm bisecting the city's higher, more inaccessible districts from its ramshackle lakeside neighborhoods. Numerous bridges of stone spanned the gap, leading to narrow streets that continued on the far side. A squad of vigilant duergar soldiers stood watch at the foot of each, barring passage across the chasm.

The scout drew Ryld into the shadow of an alleyway and nodded toward the rift and its bridges.

Laduguer's Furrow, he signed. *Also known as the Cleft. Everything on the west side is strictly off limits to foreigners. There are a couple of large side caverns on the far side that might serve as good marshalling grounds, and they'd be secure from any casual observation.*

Ryld studied the Bregan D'aerthe scout thoughtfully, wondering how he knew so much about a part of the city that was supposedly off limits.

I take it you've been there before? Ryld asked.

I've passed through Gracklstugh a couple of times.

I wonder if there's anyplace Valas *hasn't* been, Ryld thought. He shifted in the shadows to get a better look at the guarded bridges. He was a fair hand at staying out of sight when he needed to, but he didn't like the possibilities offered by the narrow, railless spans. There was no cover at all once one set foot on any of the bridges.

How do we cross? he asked.

Valas finished his knots and stepped close, setting his right foot in one bottom loop and crooking his right arm through the topmost.

"Stay close to this stalagmite as you ascend," he said. "We'll want the cover."

Ryld nodded and reached up absently to touch the insignia pinned to his breast. It identified him as a Master of Melee-Magthere, and like the clasps and brooches of many noble Houses, it was enchanted with the power of levitation. Valas didn't doubt that Ryld had fought long and hard to win the right to wear it.

As he'd hoped, the enchantment proved strong enough to support both Ryld's weight and the Bregan D'aerthe's. Effortlessly they glided up into the smoke and gloom of Gracklstugh's upper reaches, until the fumes obscured the streets below. From the top of the great cavern, the floor seemed shrouded in haze and smoke, glaring firelight making bright circles of glowing red mist in a hundred spots around them.

"This is better than I thought," Valas said. "The smoke and fumes give us some concealment."

"And they make my eyes water," Ryld said. He reached the ceiling and found that the cavern roof was rough and pitted. "Which way?"

"To your right. Yes, that's it."

Valas indicated the northern wall of the city with a jerk of his chin, keeping his foot and arm secure in the rope stirrups he'd fashioned. Carefully, Ryld turned to face the ceiling more evenly, and he pulled himself along hand over hand as if he were climbing a vertical wall of rock. The scout shifted to secure his grip, and kept his own eyes down at the cavern floor below, directing the weapons master in his progress.

"One gray dwarf wizard with a spell of cancellation would certainly ruin our day," Ryld remarked. "Aren't you a little nervous in that arrangement?"

"I've always had a good head for heights, but let's not talk about it anymore."

Ryld chuckled.

For days, the journey had been simply uneventful and dreary. The tactical challenge of spying in the heart of the duergar city, though, fully engaged them both.

"Head more to your left," Valas said, interrupting his own thoughts. "There's a bit of a ledge on the cavern wall that should run the way we want to go."

Ryld complied, and the two of them carefully leveled off and descended along the sloping roof of the cavern until they found the place where it dropped more or less straight down and became the wall. There, an old weathered seam circled the cavern like the eaves of an old tavern. The weapons master looked at it dubiously, but as they drew close Valas disentangled himself and leaped lightly down to crouch in the space like a skinny spider.

Ryld followed, somewhat more awkwardly. He could manage it, barely, but he was lucky to have the magic of his insignia to fall back on if his footing or grip failed him.

Valas moved confidently forward, following the seam as it descended sharply and disappeared around a sharp bend overlooking a side cavern.

Ryld scrambled down after him, cursing silently as his foot dislodged some loose rock and sent it clattering down the clifflike wall. The forges and hammers of Gracklstugh covered the sound fairly well, though, and they were still above Laduguer's Furrow. The rock skittered into the abyss and vanished.

Valas glanced back from his perch at the bend.

Carefully, he signed. *Come up here and see this.*

Ryld worked his way up beside the scout, finally stretching out on his belly to stay on the ledge. The seam ran down to a side cave and turned in sharply. From their vantage a hundred feet or more above the floor, they could see a good-sized cavern, perhaps three or four hundred yards long and about half that wide. The walls were hewn into barracks rooms, enough to house quite a large number of soldiers, but the floor of the place was level and open, a good drilling ground for bodies of troops.

From end to end, it was crowded with wagons and pack lizards. Hundreds of duergar swarmed over the scene, securing great panniers to the ugly reptiles, loading wagons, and preparing siege engines for travel. The noxious reek of the city's smelters didn't suffice to mask the heavy smell of animal dung in the large chamber, and the lizards' hisses and rasping croaks filled the air.

Valas began counting wagons and pack beasts, trying to estimate the size of the force that might be on the march. After a few minutes, he finally tore his eyes away.

Somewhere between two and three thousand? Ryld said.

The scout frowned and replied, *I think somewhat more, maybe four thousand all together, but there may be more trains gathering in other caverns nearby.*

Is there any reason to think they're not bound for Menzoberranzan? Ryld asked.

We're not their only enemies. Still, I don't like the timing.

"I don't believe in coincidences, either," Ryld whispered. He carefully began to worm his way back from the edge, taking great pains to dislodge no more rocks. "I would suggest checking the other caves for more soldiers, but I think we've seen more than the duergar would want already, and I don't feel like pressing my luck. We'd best get back and report this to the others."

EIGHT

"We should just leave," growled Jeggred. His white fur was streaked with red wine, and hot grease from a roast of rothé meat stained his muzzle. The draegloth didn't take well to long waits, and two days of confining himself to the Cold Foundry had been hard for him. "We could be out of the city before they knew we'd gone."

"I fear it wouldn't be as simple as you make it sound," Ryld said. He knelt by his pack, stuffing sacks with the least perishable items from the buffet. He dropped the sacks into a yawning black circle beside him—a magical hole that could be picked up and carried as if it was nothing but a piece of dark cloth. It could hold hundreds of pounds of gear and supplies, but weighed nothing at all. "You may not have noticed, but I'm sure I'm not the only one who marked the spies watching this inn. We wouldn't make a quarter mile before we were swarmed under duergar soldiers."

"So?" the draegloth demanded. "I fear no dwarf!"

"Duergar aren't goblins or gnolls, too stupid to use their numbers well, too clumsy and crude to stand a chance in a one-on-one duel. I've met duergar swordsmen nearly as good as I am. I have no doubt that a number of such formidable fellows would be banded together against us, and the duergar count skilled wizards and clerics among their ranks, too."

"We should have known better than to march into a duergar city," Halisstra said. "What a miserable piece of timing."

She hurried to don her armor, a suit of highly enchanted chain mail that carried the arms of House Melarn on its breast. She wondered if the best strategy would be to simply wait a few more days and allow the gray dwarves to relax their vigilant stance. On the other hand, if they delayed too long, there was always the chance that the merchant she'd charmed to part with Danifae's new arms would recover his wits and report the incident to the authorities. Had they simply murdered the merchants . . . but no, if they'd been caught at that, they would already have paid with their lives.

She tugged at the long hem of the mail hauberk and wriggled to settle it better on her shoulders.

"Master Argith, how long will it take the duergar army to march?" Halisstra asked.

"Soon," Ryld said. "They can't keep that many pack lizards in harness for long. The question is how long after the army sallies before they allow travel to resume. If we wait them out, we might be delayed for days."

"Delayed—or disposed of," Danifae warned.

"We will set out at once," Quenthel said, putting a halt to the debate.

The Mistress of the Academy dressed for battle, her face set in a black scowl, her whips writhing in agitation.

"That begs the question that was raised a moment ago—which way do we go?" asked Ryld.

The weapons master finished with his supplies and picked up the hole, rolling it tightly and slipping it into his pack.

"I can retrace our steps back to Mantol-Derith," Pharaun offered, "but it will be difficult to move forward from here. I don't know the way to the Labyrinth, so any stroll we took on the Plane of Shadow would doubtless lead us to a strange and cheerless end. There are too many of you for me to teleport us all together, so unless someone feels like answering to the gray dwarves for the rest of the company's sudden departure, I suppose that's out as well."

"What about a spell to conceal our identities?" Ryld asked.

"Regrettably," the wizard replied, "gray dwarves are notoriously resistant to illusions of any kind."

Halisstra added, "If only one saw through a disguise and saw a party of dark elves. . . ."

"Better to simply render us all invisible," the Master of Sorcere said. "Yes, that would be the most expedient solution to this little conundrum. It quite reminds me of a time when—"

"Enough." Quenthel shifted in her seat and asked Valas, "Do we need to set out for the Labyrinth from here, or could you find a way around Gracklstugh if we retraced our steps a bit?"

"It will take several more days to circle the city," the scout answered, "but I could guide you past Gracklstugh's borders."

"Fine," Quenthel said. "We will head back for the docks and make use of Coalhewer's boat. It's the most direct route out of the city from here, and unless I miss my guess, the lakeside will be less heavily guarded than the tunnels. Is everybody armed?" She looked around quickly. No one requested more time to prepare, so the Baenre priestess nodded with a small gesture of approval and turned to Pharaun. "What must we do for your spell to succeed?"

"Join hands and stay close to me," Pharaun said, "or wander off if you like, in which case you will find yourself inconveniently visible. I will not be held responsible for any difficulties that ensue."

Fully armed and armored, packs shouldered, all but Valas joined hands and waited. The Master of Sorcere, standing in their center, hissed out a sibilant string of arcane words and wove his hands in mystic passes. They all vanished from view. Halisstra could feel Danifae's hand on her left shoulder, and she clasped Ryld's cuirass with her own right hand, but as far as her eyes could tell, only the scout was in the room.

"Are you ready, Master Hune?" Pharaun asked, unseen.

Valas offered a small nod. He was dressed in what passed for his own finery, a simple vest of chain mail over a good shirt of spider silk and dark breeches, his *piwafwi* thrown over one shoulder in a rakish fashion. Odd badges and tokens pinned here and there to his clothing, the defenses and charms of half a dozen races, completed his ensemble.

"I'll dawdle in the courtyard a moment. Make sure you're all out swiftly; it will look less suspicious if I don't stand around for long. I'll join you at Coalhewer's boat in ten minutes."

"You'll be tailed," Ryld said.

Valas Hune seemed honestly offended.

"No one alive can follow me when I do not wish to be followed," he said.

Valas went out into the courtyard, throwing open the door to their room and taking a long moment to stretch. Halisstra felt Ryld shuffle forward, and she did likewise, crowding close behind him as Danifae pressed up behind her. The girl's breath was warm at her neck.

While the Bregan D'aerthe scout casually strolled out of the inn's gate and turned left toward the city's central district, Halisstra and the others bent around in an awkward circle and headed right, back to the docks. The streets were not deserted, but neither were they busy. Most duergar were back in their drab residences after a long day in the city's forges and foundries. Had the company been forced into flight at the beginning or the end of the workday, their deception might have been given away by the sheer accident of a busy gray dwarf bumping into their invisible chain as they skulked down the street.

Halisstra risked one more glance over her shoulder at Valas, who strolled quickly down the street in the opposite direction, looking a little furtive himself—a better disguise than complete nonchalance, which would have been jarring in a place like Gracklstugh. She also noted a gray dwarf porter who hefted a small cask of brandy to his shoulder as the scout passed and turned to follow, seemingly nothing more than a common laborer hired to carry goods from one part of the city to another. Valas could not have missed him, she decided. *The mercenary is too sharp to miss a straightforward tail like that.*

Though Halisstra expected a hue and a cry at any moment from hidden watchers, their progress was unimpeded until they reached the docks. As they hurried across the stone quays toward the strange vessels moored there, Ryld suddenly halted, surprising her. Halisstra walked into his back before she realized he'd stopped. Danifae bumped into her as well, as the whole column came to a halt.

"Trouble," whispered Pharaun. "A patrol of duergar soldiers in the crown prince's colors just came around the corner of the next street over. They're invisible, too, and there's a wizard-looking fellow leading them in our direction."

"They see us?" Jeggred rumbled. "What use are you, mage?"

"There are spells that allow one to see the invisible," Pharaun replied. "I'm using one right now, in fact, which is why I can see the guards, and you cannot. I suppose that begs the question, what use are y—"

"You there! Dismiss your spell, and lay down your weapons!" the leader of the duergar patrol called. A clatter of arms echoed across the silent street, though Halisstra still could not make out any of the gray dwarves. "You are under arrest!"

"Jeggred, Ryld, Pharaun—deal with them," Quenthel ordered. "Danifae, Halisstra, stay with me."

She dashed off down the pier, ghosting into visibility as she left Pharaun's magical influence behind. Jeggred and Ryld charged in the opposite direction, Splitter appearing in the weapons master's hand as if he had worked an enchantment of his own. Pharaun snarled out a short phrase of words that seemed to shiver the very air of the quay, and a moment later a ripple of light washed over the opposite side of the street, revealing the armored duergar where they stood. The wizard followed instantly with another spell, becoming visible himself as he pointed a black ray at the wizard among the gray dwarf soldiers. The purple lance struck the duergar mage in the center of his chest, and the enemy wizard collapsed like a puppet with its strings cut.

"Next time, strike first and issue challenges later," Pharaun remarked. He started to work another spell as the draegloth and the weapons master crashed into the ranks of the patrol, hewing and slashing with abandon.

Halisstra followed Quenthel as she ran down the pier and leaped onto Coalhewer's boat. The massive undead skeletons stood motionless in their well in the center of the hull, nothing more than inert machinery awaiting command. Beneath the bridge, the duergar smuggler stirred and sat up from a thin bedroll, snatching up a hand axe close by his sleeping place.

"Who goes there?" he roared, scrambling to his feet. "Why, ye—"

He was cut off by the impact of Quenthel's boot in the center of his chest, slamming him back down to the deck.

The Baenre raised her whip to finish the smuggler, but Halisstra called, "Wait! We may need him to run this thing."

"You believed that story of his?" Quenthel said, not taking her eyes from the dwarf. "Of course he wanted us to think we needed him to run the boat."

"True or not, now is not the time to gamble on our escape," Halisstra said. "We'd look damned foolish if we fought our way through a patrol of the prince's soldiers and couldn't leave the pier."

"Fell out of the crown prince's favor, did ye?" Coalhewer said. He stood slowly and offered a fierce grin. From the end of the pier a sudden bright glare of lightning and a booming thunderclap announced the arrival of duergar reinforcements. "If ye kill me, ye'll never escape. Now, what's a fair price fer taking you off this pier, I wonder?"

Quenthel bristled and doubtless would have struck him down then, but Halisstra stepped between them.

"If we get caught here," the Melarn priestess said, "we'll implicate you in whatever charges are brought against us, dwarf. Now get us underway."

Coalhewer stared up at the three dark elves, his face contorted with fury.

"I dealt fairly with ye, and this be my thanks?" he snarled. "I should've known better than to traffic with yer kind!"

He whirled to cast off the lines securing the macabre vessel to the quay, barking orders at the hulking skeletons in the center of the boat.

Quenthel looked at Halisstra with narrowed eyes and asked, "Why spare the dwarf? You know he's lying about commanding the boat."

Halisstra shrugged and said, "You can always kill him later, if you're so inclined."

As the wheels at the side of the vessel began to churn in the water, Ryld and Jeggred sprinted up, clambering aboard. Blood dripped from both the half-demon's talons and Splitter. Pharaun bounded up a moment later, after sealing the end of the pier with a wall of roaring flame to keep the soldiers at bay.

"That won't hold them for long, I'm sure," the wizard said. "There must be three or four mages back there, and they'll extinguish that wall quickly enough. Best we get well away from here before they can fling their spells against our humble conveyance."

Ryld studied the wall of fire at the pier's end and scowled.

"You realize you've also blocked Valas's escape with that spell," he grated. "We need him, Pharaun. We can't leave him here."

"I'm flattered, Master Argith."

From the shadows of the vessel's stern, Valas stood up and adjusted his *piwafwi*.

"Where in Lolth's dark hells did you come from?" the weapons master said, blinking and rubbing his eyes.

"I boarded just a few steps behind the three ladies," the scout said. He glanced around, savoring the open surprise on the faces of his companions, then made a small bow and a gesture of self-deprecation. "As I said, I am not easily followed or marked when I do not wish to be. Besides, it seemed that the three of you had the crown prince's soldiers in hand."

The Master of Melee-Magthere snorted, and returned Splitter to its sheath across his back. He turned to the city's waterfront, which was receding quickly into the darkness. Fire still glowed along the piers, illuminating the bizarre profiles of more duergar vessels whose crews swarmed the decks, shouting orders at each other and scurrying to obey the crown prince's soldiers.

"I hope our vessel is faster than theirs," Ryld said.

"Not to worry," Coalhewer called from his perch. "This be the fastest vessel on the Darklake. None of those scows can catch us."

He snapped out another order to the hulking skeletons driving the boat, and the undead monstrosities redoubled their efforts, driving their crankshafts faster and faster, until a froth of white foam boiled at the paddlewheels. The duergar city faded into the darkness behind them, marked by nothing more than a red glare on the cavern ceiling.

"A dire development all this," Quenthel mused. "Menzoberranzan hardly needs a war with the duergar now."

"Do we alter our course?" Ryld asked. "Menzoberranzan must be warned of the duergar army."

The Mistress of Arach-Tinilith stood in thought for a moment, then said, "No. What we're doing is more important, and if I am not mistaken Pharaun possesses the means to pass a warning to the archmage. Is that not so, wizard?"

The Master of Sorcere simply smiled and spread his hands.

$$\maltese \qquad \maltese \qquad \maltese$$

Nimor's soft footfalls echoed in corridor after empty corridor as he made his way through the crown prince's fortress. At odd intervals he passed pairs of scowling guards in heavy armor, halberds held upright, and he wondered if they ever tired of looking at the blank stone walls in the course of their duties.

Most likely not, he decided. Duergar were simply insensitive to that sort of thing.

In his hand, Nimor idly flipped a small envelope from finger to finger. The Lady Aliisza of the Sceptered One's Court (an inventive title if Nimor had ever heard one) had invited him to join her for dinner in her chambers, observing that the gray dwarves had so far failed to invite her to any kind of banquet or dinner. Nimor didn't expect that companionship for dinner was the only thing on her agenda.

Arriving at the rooms assigned to the Sceptered One's envoy, he tucked his invitation back into his breast pocket, and rapped twice at the door.

"Enter," called a soft voice.

Nimor let himself in. Aliisza waited by a table spread with quite an impressive meal, complete with a bottle of wine from the World Above and a pair of glasses already poured. She wore a flowing skirt of red silk with a tight-fitting corselet trimmed with black lace. The colors suited her, he noted, and even went well with her soft black wings.

"Lady Aliisza," he said, offering a bow. "I am flattered. I am certain the repast before me did not come from the crown prince's kitchens."

"There is a limit to how much smoked rothé cheese and black sporeflour bread one can stand," she said. She took the wine glasses in hand and moved close to extend him one. "I admit, I had my entourage scour the city to find inns and taverns willing to provide meals suited to an elf's palate."

Nimor took the glass and swirled it, bringing it to his nose to inhale the aroma. Not only did it allow him to appreciate the wine's bouquet, but he could sniff the vintage for any signs of the various subtle poisons with which he was familiar. He would have proved difficult to poison in any case, but he did not detect any strange scents.

"You have my thanks, dear lady. I have been traveling of late, and have been forced to live on very plain fare indeed."

Aliisza sipped at her own wine, and nodded at the table.

"In that case, why don't we eat while we talk?"

Nimor took the seat opposite the half-demon, and fell to his meal. One of the consequences of his true nature was a surprising ability to eat far more than one might expect for a dark elf of his slight build, and to go for quite a long time between meals. The rothé roast with mushroom gravy was cool and rare in the middle and quite excellent, the small blind fish were somewhat saltier than he would have cared for, and the wine was dry and strong, a good match for the roast.

"So, to what do I owe the pleasure of this occasion?" he asked between mouthfuls.

"You intrigue me, Nimor Imphraezl. I want to know more about who you are, and what interests you represent."

"Who I am? I have given you my true name," Nimor replied.

"That is not exactly the sort of answer I had in mind." Aliisza leaned forward, her eyes fixed on him. "What I meant was, whom do you serve? What are you doing here?"

Nimor felt a subtle flutter at the edges of his thoughts, as if he was trying to remember something he'd momentarily misplaced. He leaned back in his chair and grinned at the alu-fiend.

"I hope you'll forgive me, dear lady, but I recently found myself in an interview in which the other party could read my thoughts, and so I have taken steps to defend myself against such things this evening. You won't pick your answers from my mind."

Aliisza frowned and said, "Now I wonder what thoughts you have to guard so well, Nimor. Are you afraid that I wouldn't like what I found there?"

"We all have our secrets." Nimor teased his wine and admired the bouquet again. He would not give her the complete truth, of course, but what he would offer was truthful enough under the circumstances. "I belong to a minor House of Menzoberranzan with some unusual practices of which the matron mothers would not approve," he began. "Among other things, we do not subject ourselves to the tyranny of our Lolth-worshiping female relations, and we possess old and strong ties to minor Houses with similar practices in several other cities. We masquerade as low-ranking merchants, but we keep our true nature and capabilities quite secret."

"Capabilities?"

"We are assassins, dear lady, and we are very good at what we do."

Aliisza leaned forward, resting her delicate chin on her fingertips as she studied Nimor with her dark, mischievous gaze.

"So what is an assassin of Menzoberranzan doing in Gracklstugh, advising Horgar Steelshadow as he musters his army for war?" she asked. "Wouldn't that constitute the worst sort of treason?"

Nimor shrugged and replied, "We wish to see the order of things upset. We cannot defeat the great Houses of our city without an army, and Gracklstugh's is the strongest in this corner of the Underdark. As soon as it became evident that Lolth had abandoned her priestesses, we realized that we had a golden opportunity to strike a mortal blow against the great Houses. We have been doing all that we can to help Horgar see that our opportunity is his opportunity, too."

"Aren't you concerned that the duergar might prove unwilling to relinquish the drow city to your care once they've conquered it?"

"Of course," Nimor said, "but in all honesty, we view the fall of the Spider Queen's Houses as a goal desirable enough to outweigh the risks of duergar perfidy. Even if Gracklstugh turned on my House and occupied Menzoberranzan for a hundred years, we would still survive, and we would reclaim the city in time."

Aliisza stood gracefully and paced over to a narrow, slitlike window overlooking the city.

"Do you really think the Spider Queen will allow her city to fall? What becomes of the gray dwarves' assault if the priestesses of Lolth suddenly recover their powers?"

"We are a long-lived race, dear lady. My grandfather saw with his own eyes the events of a thousand years past. We do not forget the past the way other races do. In all our legends, our lore, we have never encountered a silence so complete and long-lasting. Even if it proves to be temporary, well, it represents a chance that comes along only once every couple of thousand years, doesn't it? How could we not choose this moment to strike?"

"Perhaps you're right. I've spoken to other drow who seem to feel these are extraordinary and unprecedented times." Aliisza glanced over her shoulder at him and added, "In fact, in Ched Nasad I encountered a mission of high-ranking Menzoberranyr who had come to the city in the hopes of discovering the causes of Lolth's silence. Quenthel Baenre, the Mistress of Arach-Tinilith, led the company."

"I've heard of Mistress Quenthel's mission. So they made it to Ched Nasad?"

"After passing through Kaanyr Vhok's territory, yes. They arrived just in time to witness the city's destruction."

"Did any of them survive?"

Aliisza shrugged and said, "I could not say for certain. They were a capable lot. If anyone could escape the city's fall, they would have."

Nimor tapped his finger on the table, thinking. Was Quenthel's mission of investigation significant, then? He'd simply figured that the matron mothers had decided to shuffle the Mistress of Arach-Tinilith out of the city for a time in the event that she was entertaining dangerous aspirations. Still, it represented a wild card, an unknown factor that the Jaezred Chaulssin might be wise to take note of. A party of powerful dark elves roaming the Underdark might find the opportunity to cause all sorts of trouble.

"Did they find any answers to their questions?" he asked.

"None that I know of," Aliisza said. She turned back from the window and glided over to the table again, then changed the subject. "You seemed very anxious to argue my case with the crown prince. Might I ask why?"

The assassin shifted in his seat and leaned back, allowing his gaze to rest on her.

"You touched on this already," he said. "Either Gracklstugh is strong enough to defeat Menzoberranzan, or it isn't. If it is not, then Kaanyr Vhok's Scoured Legion is likely to tip the scales in our favor. If Gracklstugh is strong enough, then the Scoured Legion might serve as a useful check on Horgar's aspirations. We wouldn't want the crown prince to forget the details of our arrangement."

"And why should the Scoured Legion serve as your army in the field?"

"Because Horgar won't have you for an ally unless I persuade him that he'd be better served with Kaanyr Vhok's tanarukks at his side than attacking his flank," Nimor answered. "Besides, your master doesn't want to sit at home while events unfold. He sent you here to urge the duergar to attack Menzoberranzan, did he not?"

Aliisza hid her smile with a sip of wine.

"Well, there is that," she admitted. "So, will you ask the duergar to accept our help, or not?"

The assassin studied the alu-fiend while he considered the question. Agrach Dyrr was a useful ally, but he doubted that the Fifth House of Menzoberranzan had the strength to counterbalance Horgar's army if push came to shove. Another force on the field would increase the chances of success for the Jaezred Chaulssin, and with three factions to work with, it should be possible to align two against the third in whatever combination was necessary to advance his goals. In extremis, the Jaezred Chaulssin could bring their own strength to bear, but they were not numerous, and it was always preferable to expend the resources of one's allies before tapping your own reserves.

"I think," he said at length, "that we won't give Horgar the chance to refuse your help. Do you know of a place called the Pillars of Woe?"

Aliisza frowned and shook her head.

"It's a gorge between Gracklstugh and Menzoberranzan," Nimor said, "a place I have great plans for. I am certain that some of Kaanyr Vhok's scouts will know the spot, and I'll make sure you know where to find it. Go back to Kaanyr Vhok and have him bring the Scoured Legion to the Pillars of Woe with all possible speed. You will have your chance to assist in the destruction of Menzoberranzan. If the crown prince proves completely unreasonable, you will have other opportunities available to you, but I believe that Horgar will accept your stake in events once he encounters your force in the field."

"That sounds risky."

"Risk is the cost of opportunity, dear lady. It cannot be avoided."

Aliisza measured him with her smoky gaze.

"All right," she said, "but I'll warn you that Kaanyr will be quite put out with me if he marches his army off into the wilds of the Underdark and misses all the fun."

"I will not disappoint you," Nimor promised. He allowed himself a deep draught of wine, and pushed his chair away from the table. "That would seem to conclude our business, Lady Aliisza. I thank you for the fine supper and the pleasant company."

"Leaving so soon?" Aliisza said, with just a hint of a pout.

She drifted closer, a mischievous fire springing up in her eyes, and Nimor found his gaze roving over the voluptuous curves of her body. She leaned forward to put her hands on the arms of his chair, and enfolded her wings around him. With sinuous grace she lowered herself closer to nibble at his ear, pressing her soft, hot flesh against him.

"If we've finished our business already, Nimor Imphraezl, it must be time for pleasure," she whispered into his ear.

Nimor inhaled the delicious odor of her perfume and found his hands roving to stroke her hips and bring her closer still.

"If you insist," he murmured, kissing the hollow of her neck.

She shivered in his arms as he reached up to unlace her corselet.

The crude paddlewheels at the sides of Coalhewer's boat clattered loudly in the darkness, churning the black water into furious, white, rushing foam. The hulking skeletons in their well-like space at the boat's center stooped and rose, stooped and rose, their bony hands clamped to the crankshafts driving the wheels. Relentlessly, tirelessly, they continued their mindless work, held to their labors by the necromantic magic that had animated them years, or perhaps dec— s past. Halisstra was no judge of waterborne travel, but it seemed to her that Coalhewer's boat was holding to a pace that would be difficult to match.

She risked a glance back over her shoulder to see if her companions had marked any signs of pursuit. Ryld, Jeggred, and Pharaun all stood in the rear of the boat, watching its wake. Quenthel sat on a large trunk just under the boat's scaffoldlike bridge, also gazing back toward Gracklstugh. Valas stood on the bridge alongside Coalhewer, making sure that the duergar captain kept the ungainly vehicle to the course he desired.

Halisstra and Danifae had taken up the posts of lookouts, peering ahead to make sure they didn't run headlong into trouble. Halisstra hadn't bothered to debate the arrangement. The males were best placed between the rest of the company and the most likely threats, and Pharaun was probably their best weapon against any pursuit out of Gracklstugh.

The city itself was no longer visible, except as a long, low red smudge. The firelight of the dwarves' forges could be seen for several miles across the vast black space of the Dark Lake's open waters, a sense of distance that reminded Halisstra of the unnatural vistas of the World Above. They'd churned their way east and south from Gracklstugh's waterfront for several hours, with no sign of anyone following, but Halisstra couldn't shake the impression that they were not clear of the duergar yet. Reluctantly she shifted her gaze back to the boundless dark in front of the boat, and checked her crossbow to make sure it was ready to fire.

Halisstra carefully scanned her half of the bow, starting with the water close to the boat and working her way farther out until even her drow sight could make out nothing more through the blackness, then she returned her gaze to the boat and started again. Great stalactites or columns—it was impossible to tell—descended from the ceiling and vanished into the inky water at odd intervals, creating titanic pillars of stone for the boat to navigate around. In other spots the jagged points of stalagmites jutted from the surface like spears. Coalhewer steered well clear of those, pointing out that there might be two submerged rocks for every one that broke the surface.

"I can't believe I'm crouching on the deck of a duergar boat, fleeing for my life from a city I'd never seen before three days ago," Halisstra murmured, breaking the long silence. "Two tendays ago I was the heir apparent of a great House in a noble city. One tenday ago I was a prisoner, betrayed by the petty malice of Faeryl Zauvirr, and now here I am, a rootless wanderer with nothing more to my name than the armor on my back and whatever odds and ends are stowed in my pack. I just cannot fathom why."

"I am not unfamiliar with changes in one's circumstances and fortunes," Danifae said. "What is the point of asking why? It is the will of the Spider Queen."

"Is it?" Halisstra asked. "House Melarn stood for twenty centuries or more, only to fall in the hour when Lolth withdrew her favor from our entire race. It was only in her absence that our enemies could overthrow us."

Danifae did not reply, nor did Halisstra expect her to. That thought was perilously close to heresy, after all. To suggest that something had occurred against Lolth's will was to doubt the power of the Spider Queen, and to question Lolth's power was to invite death and condemnation as a faithless weakling. The fate that awaited the faithless in the afterlife was too terrible to contemplate. Unless Lolth chose to take the soul of a follower to her divine abode in the Demonweb Pits, a drow's spirit would be condemned to anguish and oblivion in the barren wastelands where the dead of all kinds were judged. Only abject worship and perfect service could sway the Dark Queen to intercede on one's behalf and grant life beyond life, eternal existence as one of Lolth's divine host.

Of course, thought Halisstra, if Lolth is dead, then damnation and oblivion become unavoidable, don't they?

She blanched at the thought and shivered in horror, standing quickly and pacing away from the bridge to hide her face from the others.

I must not think such things, she told herself. Better to empty my mind of all thoughts than to entertain blasphemy.

She closed her eyes and took a deep breath, doing her best to banish her insidious doubts.

"We've got trouble," Ryld announced from the afterdeck. The weapons master knelt and peered through the darkness behind the boat. "Three boats, much like this one."

"I see them," Pharaun said. He glanced up at the bridge. "Master

Coalhewer, I thought you said this was the fastest vessel on the Dark-lake. Am I to gather that you exaggerated a bit?"

The dwarf scowled back into the darkness and replied, "I've never been overtaken before today, so how was I t'know any different?"

He muttered a foul string of curses and paced from one end of the bridge to the other, never taking his eyes off the following boats.

"They're not gaining on us by much," Quenthel observed after a long moment. "It's going to take them a while to catch us."

Halisstra turned and clambered past the bridge to gaze aft. She could see the pursuing boats, just barely. They trailed behind Coalhewer's craft by a bowshot, black ghosts silhouetted faintly against the dying red smudge that marked the city behind them. A glimmer of white played at the bow of each boat where it parted the waters.

She looked up at the duergar and asked, "Can't you make this thing go any faster?"

Coalhewer growled and waved a hand at the skeletons driving the craft.

"They've been told to go as fast as they can," he said. "We might speed her up by throwing weight over the side, but there's no telling if it'd be help enough."

"How far are we from the southern wall of the cavern?" asked Quenthel.

"I don't know these waters well. Three miles, I'd guess."

"Then keep to your course," the Baenre decided. "Once we're ashore, we'll be able to outdistance any pursuit, or pick our ground to fight on if we decide not to run."

"But what of my boat?" Coalhewer demanded. "D'ye have any idea how much I paid for it?"

"I'm certain I hadn't invited you along, dwarf," Quenthel replied.

She turned her back on the duergar and settled down to wait, absently stroking her whip as she watched the pursuing boats draw closer.

The boat churned on, passing more stalagmites jutting up from the waters as the pursuing boats edged closer. Halisstra and Danifae watched carefully for obstacles ahead, but despite herself, Halisstra could not resist the impulse to glance over her shoulder every few minutes to check on their pursuers. Each time she did, the boats had closed a little more, until she could actually make out discrete individuals moving around on their decks. Fifteen minutes after they'd first come into view behind Coalhewer's boat, the duergar vessels began to fire missiles after them—heavy crossbow bolts that fell hissing into their wake, and clumsy catapult-shot of great flaming spheres that soared past the boat to smash against the dank columns littering the surrounding waters.

"Zigzag a bit," Quenthel told the dwarf. "We don't want to be hit by one of those."

"They'll gain faster on us if I do," Coalhewer protested, but he began to ease his wheel from one side to the other, trying to avoid keeping straight on any heading for too long.

"Ryld, Valas, return fire at the lead boat. Don't use more than half your arrows or bolts. We may need them later on." Quenthel glanced around, and nodded at Halisstra. "You too, Halisstra. Danifae, keep watch forward. Pharaun, answer those catapults."

Valas turned around on the bridge and braced himself against intersecting rails, fitting an arrow to his string. He aimed for the lead boat, and loosed an arrow. Ryld and Halisstra followed a moment later with bolts of their own. After a long heartbeat of flight time, the tiny figure of a gray dwarf threw up its arms and reeled over the side of the boat, vanishing beneath its flailing paddles. Other dwarves scurried for cover, raising large mantlets to cover themselves.

Pharaun stepped forward and gestured boldly at the leading boat, barking out the words of a spell. From his fingertips a small orange bead of flame streaked out, darting across the dark water with the speed of an arrow. It seemed to vanish into the blackness, swallowed by the bulk of the leading boat—and a brilliant blast of flame erupted right at the pursuer's prow, scouring the foredecks with a roar that echoed through the great cavern. Duergar wreathed in flames lurched and stumbled in the distance, with more of them falling or throwing themselves over the side.

"Well done!" Quenthel cried.

Even Jeggred roared in glee, but a moment later a buzzing globe of blue energy rose from the second ship and streaked back at them. Pharaun started a spell of deflection or warding, but he was unable to parry the blow, and glaring streaks of lightning enveloped Coalhewer's boat. The very air roared with dozens of thunderclaps and explosions as crawling arcs of electricity detonated barrels, casks, and fittings, or sizzled into flesh. Halisstra cried out and buckled to the deck as a bolt stabbed through her left hip, while Ryld collapsed jerking to the deck, his breastplate glowing blue-white with the lightning ball's energy.

The skeletal rowers kept at their toil, driving the boat onward.

Pharaun jerked out his wand and hurled a bolt back at the boat that had launched the lightning ball at them. A skipping meteor of blinding fire flew at them from the leading boat, bounding across the water with an almost animate hunger. By a stroke of good luck, the missile struck a low-lying rocky outcropping and detonated behind them, spreading a slick of burning fluid across the water's surface. The third boat fired its catapult again, sending a comet-like ball of flame whizzing clear over the bridge to explode a short distance ahead.

"Damnation," Coalhewer snarled. "They've got the range on us!"

"It seems that I am somewhat outnumbered," Pharaun called out between spells. "Perhaps we should redouble our efforts to escape?"

Arrows hissed past them, clattering against the boat or sticking into the zurkhwood decks with heavy *tchunks*!

"Halisstra," the wizard called, "would you take my wand—the one in my hand, I mean—and use it to discourage that fellow on the first boat?"

Halisstra ignored the hot ache in her hip and scrambled aft. She took the iron wand from the wizard's hand, aiming at the lead boat as she barked out its command word. The air crackled with sparks and ozone as the bolt blasted back at the pursuing boat, only to flare impotently against some kind of spell shield that had been raised by the duergar wizards behind them.

Pharaun chanted out the words of another spell, and a thick white mist arose in their wake, its billows spreading across the water with startling speed. Almost instantly, it sprawled across their stern like a wall of white, completely blocking the pursuing boats from view.

"There," said the wizard. "That should slow them a bit."

"It's fog. Won't they just sail right through it?" Ryld asked.

"That is no ordinary fog, my friend. That fog is thick enough to arrest an arrow in mid-flight. Best of all, it is highly acidic, so that anyone blundering about in there will be slowly eaten away." The wizard smiled and folded his arms. "Ah, *damn it,* I'm good."

Quenthel opened her mouth, most likely to take issue with the wizard's self-congratulations, when Danifae called from the bow, "Stop! Rocks ahead! Stop!"

"Bloody hell!" gasped Coalhewer. "All back full! All back full, ye great bony louts!"

The turning skeletons slowed their furious pumping, unable to arrest the heavy wheels all at once, and slowly began to spin the paddles back the other way. The dwarf did not wait on them, slamming his wheel hard over to veer away from the black line of fanglike rocks ahead. The lake seemed to come to an end, shoaling up quickly to meet the plunging ceiling. The shoreline extended left and right for as far as Halisstra could see. The boat slued to an awkward halt, its starboard bow rebounding from a thankfully rounded rock in their path. The impact staggered everyone on board, and nearly pitched Danifae headlong over the bow.

"Now what?" Ryld asked, picking himself up off the deck. "They've got us pinned against the cavern wall."

"How long will your fog delay the gray dwarves?" Quenthel snapped at Pharaun.

"No more than a couple of minutes," he answered. "They might choose to back out and go around, of course."

Pharaun stared intently at his handiwork. In the distance, duergar screamed in pain, their cries of agony oddly muffled by the insidious white mist.

"The spell is unlikely to kill or disable very many of them," the wizard added, "and I don't think it'll sink their boats."

"Then this is where we get off," Quenthel said. She pointed at the cavern wall. "We'll take cover in the rocks there, and stay out of sight. We'll send the boat that way—" she pointed toward the east—"and let the crown prince's men chase it away from us."

"I won't be yer decoy!" Coalhewer snapped. "Ye got me into this mess, and ye'll get me out of it!"

The dark elves ignored the dwarf as they hurriedly threw their packs to the wet rocks below the bow. Jeggred bounded down into the icy water and struggled up on shore, followed by Ryld and Pharaun. Valas swarmed down from the bridge and vaulted down as well.

"You're wasting my time," Quenthel said to the duergar captain. "Go on, now, and take your chances, or stay here and face the draegloth."

She leaped lightly to the boulders below, joined by Halisstra and Danifae a moment later.

"But if ye . . . ah, damn the lot of ye to Lolth's spidery hells!" Coalhewer swore.

He dashed back up to his bridge and began to bark orders at the skeletal rowers again. The boat slowly backed away from the rocks.

"If they catch me," he shouted back, "I'll tell them exactly where to find ye!"

Quenthel narrowed her eyes. She started to gesture to Jeggred, but Halisstra shook her head and started a low, droning *bae'qeshel* song. She gathered the force of her will and hurled it full upon the livid dwarf.

"Escape, Coalhewer," she hissed. "Flee as quickly as you may, and do not let yourself be caught. If you are caught, better to swim to safety than to let yourself be taken."

The invisible webs of the spell settled about the dwarf like a snow-fall of deadly venom. He stared open-mouthed at Halisstra, then whirled to redouble his efforts to take his boat clear before the fog lifted. Quenthel glanced at Halisstra and raised an eyebrow.

"It seemed best to make sure he would flee as we wanted him to," Halisstra explained as she quickly gathered her things and hurried for the cover of the boulders and stalagmites above the waterline.

Quenthel followed a step behind her. They splashed ashore and settled behind a large rock just as the prow of the first duergar boat, still glowing red with embers left from the fireball Pharaun had hurled at it, nosed through the deadly mists. The dark elves drew their *piwafwis* close around them and held still, watching as the duergar stirred and broke from whatever shelters they'd managed to find from the acidic fog.

One of the gray dwarves pointed and shouted, and the others joined the clamor. Turning sharply in the water, they slewed around the ship's bow and set off after Coalhewer's vanishing boat.

Good, signed Pharaun. *I was afraid they were using magic to follow us. It seems that Master Coalhewer will render us one last service after all.*

What do you think will happen when they catch him? Ryld asked.

The duergar boats pulled out of earshot.

"I suppose it depends on whether or not he can swim," Halisstra said.

NINE

A long day's march later, pausing only long enough to allow Pharaun to finally craft a sending to pass news of Gracklstugh's army to Gromph, the company came to the Labyrinth. They emerged from winding, unexplored passageways into a series of miles-long natural tunnels interspersed with long, hewn ways and small, square chambers. Coalhewer, his boat, and the pursuit from Gracklstugh they'd left twenty miles or more behind them.

The tunnels were black basalt, cold and sharp, the frozen remnants of great fires from the beginning of the world. From time to time the party encountered great vertical rifts hundreds of feet high, where tunnels ended in blank walls with rough, perilous steps cut up or down to a different level where the path continued. Whole sheets of the world's crust had sunk or fractured in places, shearing off the old lava tunnels and leaving behind vast, lightless chasms deep in the earth. A few of these places were spanned by slender bridges of stone, or circled by crude paths hacked from the hard rock of the walls. Everywhere they turned, more square passages and twisting, smooth-floored tunnels branched from their line of march, so that in the space of an hour Halisstra was forced to concede that she'd become hopelessly lost.

"I see why they call this place the Labyrinth," she said softly, as the company threaded its way along a narrow ledge overlooking another of the chasms. "This place is truly a maze."

"It's worse than you think," Valas replied from the front of the party. He paused to examine the path ahead, and another of the ubiquitous openings on one side. "It's close to two hundred miles from north to south, and almost half that from east to west. Most of it is exactly like this, a confusion of lava tubes and hand-cut tunnels with thousands of branching turns and twists."

"How can you hope to find House Jaelre in all this?" Ryld asked. "Do you know this place so well that you've mastered it?"

"Mastered it? Hardly. You could spend a lifetime here and never see the whole thing, but I do know something of its ways. Several well-traveled caravan routes exist along some of the straighter paths, though we're not near any of those. Few travelers approach the Labyrinth from the east, as we have." The scout stepped a little ahead and brushed his hand against the wall, near the place where the other tunnel opened up. Old, strange symbols glowed with a greenish light beneath his fingertips. "Fortunately, the builders carved runes to identify their secret ways. It's a code of markings that holds true throughout the Labyrinth. I solved the puzzle when I last journeyed here. We're not in tunnels I traveled before, but I think I know how to reach them from here."

"You are a lad of many talents," Pharaun observed.

"Who carved these tunnels?" Halisstra asked. "If this place is as big as you say, it must have been a powerful realm in its day, but I can tell at a glance those marks aren't ours. Nor are they duergar, illithid, or aboleth."

"Minotaurs," Valas replied. "I don't know how long ago their realm rose or fell, but there was a great kingdom of them here at some point in the past."

"Minotaurs?" Quenthel sneered. "They're bestial savages. They could hardly have the wits or the patience to undertake work of this scope, let alone build a great realm."

Valas shrugged and said, "That may be true now, but a thousand years ago, who knows? I've found plenty of their artifacts and remains scattered through this region. The horned skulls are quite distinctive. My friends among House Jaelre told me that many minotaurs still roam the wild places and disused passages of the Labyrinth, including demonic beasts armed with powerful sorcery. Their patrols skirmished with the monsters regularly."

"One wonders whether we might at some point in our journey happen to pass through a realm filled with cheerful, civilized folk genuinely concerned for our well-being and eager to help us on our way," Pharaun muttered. "I am beginning to think our fair city lies at the bottom of a barrel of venomous snakes."

"If so, we're quicker, stronger, and more venomous than any other snake in the barrel," Quenthel said with a smile. "Come, let's continue. If there are any minotaurs about, they would be well-advised not to show themselves where the children of Menzoberranzan choose to walk."

The company continued on for several hours more through endless gloomy halls and contorted passages before calling a halt to rest and replenish their strength. The stretch of the Labyrinth they wandered seemed to be quite deserted. They found few signs that anything, even the mindless predatory creatures of the Underdark, had passed that way in many years. The air was preternaturally still and silent. Whenever their whispered conversation died away for a moment, the quiet of the place seemed to rush in upon them, pressing close with a strangely hostile quality, as if the very stone resented their presence.

After Valas and Ryld had been set to watch, the rest wrapped themselves in their *piwafwis* and made themselves as comfortable as possible on the cold stone floor of the cavern. Halisstra let her eyes fall half-closed and drifted off into a deep Reverie, dreaming about endless tunnels and strange old secrets buried in mold. In her dream she thought she could make out a faint, distant rustling or whisper in the quiet, as if she might hear something more if only she moved a little ways off from the others, out into the darkness alone. Despite the fact that the air was completely still and motionless, she discerned the distant deep sighing of wind far off in the tunnels, a low moaning sound that tickled at the edge of her awareness, like something important she had forgotten. Lolth's whispers sometimes came to one in that fashion, a sibilant sigh of wordless intent filling a priestess with knowledge of the demon queen's desires.

Hope and fear stirred in Halisstra's heart and she came closer to wakefulness.

What is your wish, Goddess? she cried out in her mind. *Tell me how House Melarn might win your favor again. Tell me how Ched Nasad might be made whole. I will do anything you command of me!*

Faithless daughter, the wind whispered back to her. *Foolish weakling.*

Horror jolted Halisstra from her Reverie and she sat up straight, her heart pounding.

Only a dream, she told herself. I dreamed of what I wished to happen, and what I feared might come, but nothing more. The Spider Queen has not spoken. She has not condemned me.

Nearby, the others lay on the cold stone floor or sat wrapped deep in their own meditations, taking their rest, while a little distance away Ryld stood guard, a broad-shouldered shape motionless in the dark. The daughter of House Melarn lowered her eyes and listened to the curious sound of the wind, surrounded in the darkness her people had made theirs.

"Lolth does not speak," she whispered. "I heard only the wind, nothing else."

Why has the Goddess abandoned us? Why did she allow Ched Nasad to fall? How did we incur her wrath? Halisstra wondered. Her eyes stung with bitter tears. Were we unworthy of her?

The wind rose again, this time closer, louder. It was not a

whistling, or even a rushing sound. It reminded her of the call of a deep-voiced horn far off, perhaps many horns, and it was growing. Halisstra frowned, puzzled. Was this some strange phenomenon of the Labyrinth, a rush of air through pipelike tunnels in the dark? Such things were not unknown in other places of the Underdark. In some cases the winds could scour a tunnel bare of life, they were so sudden and powerful. This one muttered and babbled and thrummed as she listened, many great horns roaring at once—

Halisstra leaped to her feet. Ryld stood staring back the way they had come, Splitter gleaming in his hand.

"Do you hear them?" she called to Ryld. "The minotaurs are coming!"

"I thought it was the wind," the fighter growled. "Rouse the others."

He sprinted down the passageway toward the approaching host, shouting for Valas to join him from his post in the other direction. Halisstra snatched up her pack and shouldered it quickly, rousing the rest of the company with shouts of alarm and the occasional quick kick for those who were slow to shake off their deep trances.

She readied her crossbow, loading a quarrel as she peered down the tunnel behind them.

The floor quivered beneath her feet. Great footfalls as hard as rock came in a stamping rush, and deep bellows and snorts echoed and echoed again in a roiling cacophony that filled the passage. Hot animal stink assaulted her nostrils, and she saw them—an onrushing mob of dozens of the hulking brutes, huge bull-headed monsters with shaggy pelts and massive hooves, clutching mighty axes and flails in their thickly muscled fists.

Before that storm Ryld and Valas skipped and darted like sparrows blown before a gale, battling furiously for their lives against the bloodthirsty savages. Halisstra took aim quickly and shot one monster in the chest with her powerful crossbow, but the creature was so blood-maddened it simply ignored the bolt buried in its thick torso. She laid in another quarrel as the bow's magic cocked it again, only to have her shot spoiled by Jeggred's rush into the fray.

"Jeggred, you idiot, there are too many to fight!" she cried.

The draegloth ignored her and threw himself against the horde. For a moment the half-demon's size and fury held up the minotaurs' charge, but over Jeggred's white-furred shoulders and the flashing blades of Ryld and Valas, Halisstra could make out dozens more of the hirsute monsters, fanged mouths bellowing challenges, eyes glowing red with rage. Several had fallen before Splitter, Valas's curved knives, and Jeggred's talons, but battle-frenzied minotaurs shrugged off all but the most grievous of injuries, clawing over each other to get at the drow invaders.

Halisstra shifted to one side and shot again, while Danifae joined her with her own crossbow. Quenthel danced just behind Jeggred, flicking her deadly scourge at monsters threatening to swarm over the draegloth, and Pharaun shouted an arcane word that hurled a bright globe of crackling energy into the midst of the minotaur ranks. The sphere detonated with a clap of thunder and blasted bright arcs of lightning across the tunnel, charring some minotaurs into cinders, and burning great black wounds in others.

In the searing light of the lightning ball, Halisstra saw something taller and lankier than the minotaurs, behind the front ranks, a demonic presence—no, several demons—driving the angry monsters on. Huge black wings shrouded the things in shadow, and their dark horns glowed red with heat.

Roars and bellows filled the passage with rage, while the ring of steel on steel came so fast and hard that Halisstra could barely hear herself shout, "There are demons back there!"

"I see them," Quenthel replied. She fell back a couple of steps and seized Pharaun by the arm. "Can you dismiss them?"

"I have no such spell ready," the wizard replied. "Besides, getting rid of the demons isn't going to get us out of this little imbroglio. I think we—"

"I don't care what you think!" Quenthel screamed. "If you can't banish the demons, then bar the passage!"

Pharaun grimaced, but he complied by beginning another

spell. Halisstra reloaded and searched for another clear shot. Ryld crouched low and hamstrung a minotaur attacking him with an axe big enough to split an anvil, and gutted the creature with an upward draw cut across its belly. Valas was upended by a flailing chain that yanked his feet out from under him. The scout rolled away, narrowly escaping having his skull pulped.

One or more of the demons behind the battling minotaurs hurled a barrage of green, fiery bolts at the dark elves. One dissipated against Quenthel's inborn resistance to magic, while two others burned Pharaun and Danifae with vitriolic fire. Somehow the wizard managed to complete his spell.

What Halisstra assumed was some sort of invisible barrier forced most of the minotaurs and their demonic masters back, while a pair of the frontline fighters found themselves suddenly cut off from their allies. While the main host of the bull creatures hurled themselves against Pharaun's invisible wall and tried vainly to batter their way through with their crude, clumsy weapons, the dark elves quickly cut down the minotaurs unfortunate enough to have been caught on the drow's side.

In a few moments the screams and impacts of the fight had died away to the dull, attenuated bellowing of the minotaurs on the other side of the wall, milling about and shaking their weapons in anger at the drow. The minotaurs turned away all at once and darted back the way they'd come, running hard. A dozen or more hulking carcasses remained scattered on the floor.

Ryld backed away carefully, helping Valas to his feet. Jeggred stood panting, bleeding from a dozen small wounds.

"How long will that wall hold?" Quenthel asked.

"No more than a quarter of an hour," Pharaun answered. "The demons can probably get through it if they wish, but I suspect that they're leading those minotaurs around through other tunnels to come at us from the other side. May I suggest we remove ourselves from the vicinity before we find out how they mean to circumvent my barrier?"

Quenthel scowled, grabbed her pack, and said, "Fine. Let's go."

❦ ❦ ❦

If it had been in his nature to show alarm by pacing back and forth across his sanctum, Gromph Baenre would have spent most of the previous hour doing so. Instead, he peered into the great crystal ball that rested in the center of his scrying sanctum, confirming Pharaun's report. How exactly had the Master of Sorcere worded it?

Felicitations, mighty Gromph. It may interest you to learn that the army of Gracklstugh now marches on Menzoberranzan. We continue on our course. Good luck!

"Arrogant popinjay," Gromph muttered to himself. The boy had no respect for his elders.

Before dashing off to the matron mothers in a panic, Gromph had of course decided to investigate Pharaun's report with his own careful scrying and study. The milky orb revealed a fine scene for the archmage's eyes, a long column of marching duergar warriors winding through the Underdark. Huge pack lizards carried heavy bundles of supplies and various infernal devices of war. Siege engines trundled along behind long lines of ogre slaves.

Gaining even that glimpse of the army on the move was difficult, as duergar wizards sought to conceal the movements of their prince's army from the scrying efforts of hostile mages. Gromph, however, was an extraordinarily capable diviner. It had taken him some time, but he had eventually pierced the duergar wizards' defenses.

Gromph examined the scene closely, seeking out the most minute details—the insignia of marching soldiers, the exact size and condition of the tunnels they passed through, the cadence of the Dwarvish marching chants. He wanted to be absolutely certain he understood the scope and immediacy of the threat before he brought his news to the attention of the Council, as the matron mothers would doubtless expect him to have already divined the answers to any questions they might think of. The most disturbing question, of course, was how long it might have taken him to learn of the marching army if

Pharaun Mizzrym hadn't been passing through Gracklstugh. The duergar might have covered half the distance between the cities before an outpost or a far-ranging patrol detected the army.

"Damnation," the archmage growled.

Whether or not Menzoberranzan was ready, the next challenge to the city gathered in the smoky pits of the duergar realm a hundred miles to the south. Gromph sighed and decided that he might as well deal with the unpleasant business of telling the Council what he'd seen sooner rather than later. He rose with one smooth motion, arranged his robes, and took up his favorite staff. It would not do to appear before the matron mothers in anything less than complete and total self-assurance, especially when bringing such dire news to them.

He was just about to step into the stone shaft at the rear of the chamber and descend to his apartments in Sorcere when he felt a familiar, crawling sensation. Someone was scrying upon him—an accomplishment of no small skill, considering the steps he took to prevent such occurrences. Gromph started to work a spell to sever the magical spying, but stopped himself. He was engaged in nothing he cared to conceal, and he was curious to discover whether a duergar wizard had managed to detect his own scrying.

"Do you have anything you wish to say to me," he asked the air, "or shall I simply strike you blind where you sit?"

Save your spell, came a cold, rasping voice in his head. *As I haven't had eyes in my skull in over a thousand years, I doubt you could do them much harm.*

"Lord Dyrr," Gromph said, frowning. "To what do I owe the honor of your attentions?"

And how did you find me? he wondered, though he was careful not to voice the question.

I wish to continue the conversation we began a few days past, young Gromph, the lich's voice replied. *I intend to expand upon my earlier offer by describing in greater detail some of the schemes I have in mind. After all, if I am to ask you to trust me, then I suppose I must extend you a token of trust first.*

"Indeed. Well, I would be happy to oblige you, but I have urgent business with the Council. Perhaps we could take up this conversation a little later?"

Gromph glanced around the room, and his eyes fell on the crystal orb in the chamber's oriel. The sphere swirled with pearly green opalescence.

Ah, of course, the archmage realized. He found me here, where my screens against hostile divinations are weakened by the transparency of my scrying place. I must investigate ways to guard against such occurrences without hampering my own efforts.

I fear I must speak with you now, Dyrr pressed. *I will not delay you for very long, and I believe you will be glad you listened to me before facing our scheming females. May I join you there?*

Gromph paused and gazed up at the unseen presence watching him, repressing an angry scowl. Inviting a creature like Dyrr into his conjuring chambers was not something he cared to do on a whim. Whether or not the ancient sorcerer had anything Gromph wished to hear, it was true that the matron mothers would not take kindly to waiting on his arrival. He tapped his finger on the great wooden staff at his side, considering carefully. He had no wish to give offense to Dyrr if it could be avoided, and after long centuries of undeath it was hard to say what the lich might or might not find offensive. Besides, Gromph stood in his own sanctum, where many potent magical defenses lay within his reach. . . .

"Very well, Lord Dyrr. Though I really must insist that we keep our conversation short, as my business with the Council is exceedingly urgent."

The air began to seethe and hum a few feet in front of the archmage, and with a sudden crack of sound, the ancient lichdrow stood before him. The creature leaned on a staff of his own, a mighty implement made from four adamantine rods twisted around each other and bound at head and heel. A small buckler of black metal in the shape of a demonic face twisted in an idiot's grin hovered in the air at his elbow. Dyrr did not bother with his living guise, and stood revealed as a horrid skeleton with eyes as black as death.

"Greetings, Archmage. I apologize for inconveniencing you," the lich said. He fixed his blank sockets on Gromph. "What is it that drives you to seek an audience with the matrons today, young Gromph?"

"With all due respect, Lord Dyrr, I believe that is a matter for their ears, not yours. Now, what offer do you have for me that cannot wait?"

"As you wish, then," Dyrr said. "An army marches against Menzoberranzan from the south—the gray dwarves have apparently heard of our troubles and have decided to take advantage of the opportunity this offers."

"Yes, I know," Gromph snapped. "It is for this very reason that I must leave at once. If you have nothing else . . . ?"

He started toward the plain stone shaft leading down into his apartments.

"I find that I am pleased that my news did not surprise you," the lich said. "If you had not known of the duergar army, I would have had to make sure that it did not come to your attention, if you take my meaning." Dyrr turned to face Gromph's back with a terrible scraping and clicking sound of bones rubbing together. "You may recall we spoke a few days past regarding a time when you must make a decision. The time has come to do so."

Gromph stopped in his tracks and turned around carefully. He'd hoped that wasn't the lich's motive in confronting him, but it seemed Dyrr intended to press the issue whether the archmage wished him to or not.

"A decision, Dyrr?"

"Do not play at misunderstanding me. I know you're far too intelligent for that. All you need do is withhold your report for a few more days, and you can rush over to panic the matrons with news of a duergar army on our doorstep. In fact, my plans will be well served if you do so at a time and in a manner convenient to me."

"That would place the city in peril," Gromph said.

"It is in peril already, young Gromph. I mean to impose some measure of order on the inevitable. You could be of great assistance to me in the coming days, or. . . ."

"I see," said Gromph.

He narrowed his eyes, considering his options. He could feign acceptance, and do as he wished anyway, but that would certainly invite the lich's wrath at the time and place of Dyrr's choosing. He could refuse outright, which would likely result in a deadly contest on the spot to determine whose will would prevail.

Or I could agree in earnest, he thought. Who's to say that we might not channel the forces marshalling against the city into useful chaos, valuable progress? There will doubtless be tremendous damage, but the Menzoberranzan that emerged from such a crucible of blood and fire might be a better, stronger city in the end, a city purged of the ruthless tyranny of the sadistic priestesses and instead governed by the cold, passionless intelligence of pragmatic wizards. Every cruelty could be made to serve a rational purpose, every excess curbed to produce a city whose strength was not spent on its own internecine strife. Would not such a city be worthy of his loyalty?

Would such a city have any place for a Baenre? he answered himself.

No revolution such as Dyrr dreamed of could possibly end with anything but complete annihilation for the First House of Menzoberranzan. While Gromph despised his sisters and loathed many of the simpering relations who populated Castle Baenre, he would be damned if he would allow some lesser House to unseat his high and ancient family as the supreme power of Menzoberranzan. There could be, really, only one response.

As quick as thought, Gromph raised his hand and unleashed a terrible, brilliant blast of colors at the lich, a spell whose energy he had prepared with such care and effort that it took only the merest act of will to unleash it. Colors never seen in the gloom of the cavern city lanced through his conjury, each carrying with it a different doom, blight, or energy. A quivering blue bolt of electricity passed so close to Dyrr that the lich's ancient robes crackled with tiny arcs, while a bright orange ray burned the ancient creature with acid powerful enough to melt stone. A third ray, a beam of insidious violet, was deflected by the lich's animated buckler. The device tittered like a wicked child as it intercepted the attack.

"I am the Archmage of Menzoberranzan," Gromph roared. "I am no one's errand boy!"

Dyrr recoiled with a wailing shriek of anger as the acid splattered and hissed, gnawing at his ancient flesh. The smell of burning bone filled the magnificent conjury with a horrid stench. Gromph followed up his first assault by raising an abjuration he hoped would turn Dyrr's spells back at him. The archmage fully expected that it would take every ruse, every defense, every subtle and deadly spell at his command to defeat a thing as powerful as the Lord of Agrach Dyrr.

Gromph concluded his turning spell just in time, as Dyrr recovered with impossible speed and lashed out with a dire black ray of invidious energy that would have ripped away great portions of the archmage's very life-force had it struck home. Instead, the ebon beam rebounded on Gromph's shield and struck Dyrr in the center of his torso. This, however, had an unforeseen effect. Instead of shredding the ancient lich's own life-force, the crackling black energy swelled the Lord of Agrach Dyrr with its horrible power. The lich laughed aloud.

"A clever move, Gromph, but I fear it miscarried. Living creatures are grievously harmed by that spell, but the undead are invigorated by it!"

The archmage muttered a curse and struck again, this time directing a vile green ray at the laughing lich. It burned a perfect round hole in Dyrr's breastbone, blasting undead flesh and bone to dust. The lich screeched again in whatever passed for pain in its undead state and leaped aside before Gromph could disintegrate him outright.

Even as the archmage commenced another casting, Dyrr snarled out the words of a dark and murderous spell that clawed horribly at Gromph's flesh, sucking greedily at the very fluids of his body and bleaching his skin with a thousand needles of agony. Gromph gasped aloud in pain and lost the spell he'd been preparing to cast, stumbling back over a marble bench and falling heavily to the floor.

Damn it all, he thought. I need to buy a moment's respite.

Fortunately, he was in his sanctum, surrounded by a dozen weapons he might employ.

Gromph rolled to his elbow and barked out, "*Szashune!* Destroy him!"

In one alcove of the room, a tall statue of a four-armed swordsman carved from perfect black obsidian stirred to life, striding out into the chamber as it hefted and clashed its ebon blades like a living warrior.

Dyrr skittered away several steps and spoke a word. The lich soared up out of the spiderstone golem's reach, but Gromph used the opportunity of the distraction to summon up the most destructive spell he knew and hurl it at the airborne lich. From his outstretched hands eight brilliant orbs of blinding white energy streaked out to blast through the lich's undead form, each detonating in a stone-shattering explosion that demolished great gaping pieces of the undead sorcerer. The exploding meteors caused no small damage to Gromph's sanctum, blasting a pair of old bookshelves to flinders and snapping an arm from the spiderstone golem as if the device was a toy damaged by a petulant child. Gromph cried out in triumph as pieces of Dyrr clattered to the floor.

Dust billowed from the hovering form of the lich, and his skull nodded down to his breastbone almost as if his animating magic was failing him, but the bony creature returned to itself with startling speed. Dyrr looked up again as wicked green light grew strong in his eye sockets, and he laughed.

"My old bones aren't the entirety of my being, Gromph," he rasped. "You abuse them to no great effect."

He started to intone another spell, but the archmage struck again, seeking to dispel any enchantments or abjurations protecting the lich. Dyrr's flying spell failed, and the lich sank down into blade-reach of the living statue waiting below.

The golem rushed forward. The massive construct pounded at the lich with terrific blows of its three remaining arms, its gleaming black face completely expressionless. The conjury rang with the mighty impact of the blows. Gromph bared his teeth in a savage grin.

"You might not be tied to your moldering corpse, lich, but you'll have a difficult time casting spells when you've been dismembered and buried in a dozen different graves," he called. "You were a fool to challenge me here!"

Gromph prowled closer, looking for an opening to strike again with a spell.

Dyrr endured two, then three tremendous blows from the towering statue, staggering in his steps as bone cracked and split. The demon-faced buckler darted and wheeled around him, laughing shrilly and blocking even more blows than that, parrying strike after strike from the stone construct. The sorcerer retreated a step, found his footing, and spread his arms wide. His gleaming black robes shimmered once, and exploded outward in a deadly spinning saw of razor-sharp blades that carved chunks of stone from Gromph's golem and diced tables, furnishings, and books with abandon.

Blades slashed through the archmage's own potent defensive enchantments, gashing him in a dozen places, though nowhere deep enough to kill. Gromph threw himself flat to duck beneath the disk of flying razors, blinking blood from his eyes as his golem crumbled into worthless black rock.

Dyrr shouted in triumph and leaped forward at the archmage, swinging his adamantine staff with startling speed and swiftness. Gromph yelped in surprise and rolled aside just in time to avoid a two-handed blow that split the marble flagstone right where he'd fallen.

"That does not befit mages of our station!" Gromph howled, scrambling to his feet.

Dyrr didn't answer. Instead the lich leaped after him, clearing off whole tabletops and bookshelves with great two-handed sweeps of his staff.

Gromph shouted a spell that ripped the lich's weapon from his grasp, hurling it across the room with such force that the adamantine rod stuck, quivering end first, in the chamber's wall like a javelin thrown by a giant.

As Dyrr floundered for balance, Gromph took a moment to craft a potent spell defense, a shimmering globe that would completely negate the effects of all but the most powerful of spells. So fortified, he hunted quickly through the various incantations locked in his mind, seeking the most efficacious to employ against the Lord of Agrach Dyrr.

"Ah," Dyrr remarked, studying the shimmering sphere. "An excellent defense, young Gromph, but not impervious to one of my skill."

The lich muttered a word of awful power and scuttled forward, his skeletal talons outstretched. Seemingly unconcerned by Gromph's defensive spell the lich plunged his hand through the dancing globe of color and grasped the archmage by one arm. Gromph shrieked in dismay as the power of the lich's spell struck full upon him, blasting his defensive globe to motes of winking light and locking his every muscle into an absolute rigidity.

"Gromph Baenre, thou art encysted," Dyrr intoned, his naked teeth gleamed against the great and terrible blackness within his skull.

The archmage had one long glimpse at the triumphant lich standing over him, then he started to fall. Gromph, unable to move, plummeted straight down through the floor, through the flickering rooms and chambers of Sorcere, through a vast distance into the yawning black rock below the tower, the city, the world. For one terrible instant Gromph felt himself at the bottom of a measureless well, staring up through uncounted miles of darkness at the pinprick figure of his nemesis above. The darkness fell in upon him and smothered him in its embrace.

In the archmage's chambers in Sorcere, the lich Dyrr stood, looking down at the spot in the floor where he had condemned Gromph Baenre. Had he been a living mage Dyrr might have panted for breath, trembled with fatigue, or perhaps even collapsed from mortal wounds sustained in the fierce duel, but the dark magic binding his undead sinews and bones together was not subject to the weaknesses of the living.

"Bide there a time, young Gromph," he said to the empty place. "I may find a use for you yet, perhaps in a century or two."

He made a curt gesture and vanished from the conjury.

The great peals of a thunderclap echoed through the black stone passageways, a rumbling so deep and visceral that Halisstra could feel it more than hear it. She crouched in the shadow of a great stone arch and risked a quick glance across the great hall. On the far side, below the drow party, a handful of hulking monsters picked themselves up off the floor and sought cover. Several more lay still in the rubble and wreckage of the lower portion of the hall.

"That broke their rush," Halisstra called out to her companions. "They're regrouping, though."

"Determined bastards," Pharaun said.

The wizard sheltered behind a towering pillar of stone, grimacing with fatigue. Over the previous day and a half the company had marched at least thirty miles through the endless corridors of the Labyrinth, pursued at every turn by seemingly endless hordes of minotaurs and baphomet demons. On two occasions the dark elves had narrowly avoided fiendishly clever efforts to trap them by closing off the tunnels they were fleeing through.

"I have few spells of that sort left," Pharaun said. "We need to find a place where I can rest and ready more spells."

"You'll rest when we all do, wizard," Quenthel growled. The Baenre and her whip were splattered with gore, and her armor showed more than one ugly rent where a deadly blow had barely been turned.

"We're close to the Jaelre. We must be. Let's move again before the minotaurs organize another charge."

The other drow exchanged looks, but they pushed themselves to their feet and followed Quenthel and Valas into another passage. This ran for perhaps four hundred yards before opening into another great hall, this one featuring tall, fluted columns and a floor paved with well-fitted flagstones. Graceful, winding staircases rose up along the cavern walls to meet long, sheltered galleries where dim faerie fire burned, illuminating chambers that might once have been workshops, merchant houses, or simply the modest homes of soldiers and artisans.

"Drow work again," Ryld observed. "And again, abandoned. You're certain this is the place, Valas?"

The scout nodded wearily, his right hand clamped over a shallow but bloody wound on his left shoulder.

"I have been in this very cavern before," he replied. "These are Jaelre dwellings. Up there a number of armorers lived, and over on that wall was an inn I stayed at. The palace of the Jaelre nobles lies just through the next passage."

Quenthel leaped up a short, curving stairway and glanced into some kind of shop, its windows dark and empty. She swore and moved past several others, looking into each in turn before descending back to the floor of the main hall.

"If these are the Jaelre dwellings, then where in all the screaming hells are the Jaelre?" she demanded. "Did the accursed minotaurs slay them all?"

"I doubt it," Halisstra said. "No battle was fought here—we would have seen the signs. Even if the minotaurs had carried off all the bodies over the years, there would be scorch marks, broken flagstones, the remnants of ruined weapons. I think the Jaelre left this place of their own accord."

"How long ago was it that you were here, Valas?" asked Ryld.

"Almost fifty years," the scout said. "Not that long ago, really. The Jaelre skirmished frequently with the minotaurs back then, and these caverns were guarded by both physical and magical defenses."

He studied the great chamber carefully. "Let me proceed ahead a little ways. I will see if I can find anything in the palace that might illuminate this riddle."

"Should we all go?" Ryld asked.

"Best not. There is only one entrance to the palace, and we could be trapped inside if the minotaurs return in numbers. Remain outside, so that you can escape if you need to. I will return in a few minutes."

The scout slipped off into the darkness, leaving the company in the abandoned hall.

"I think I agree with Mistress Melarn," Ryld said. "It seems the Jaelre carried away everything of value and left this place."

"A great deal of trouble for nothing, then," Pharaun remarked. "If there's anything so disappointing as fruitless toil and hardship, I'm not sure what it is."

The company stood in silence a moment, each occupied with his own thoughts.

Halisstra ached with exhaustion, her legs as weak as water. She had avoided any serious injury, but on the other hand she had almost completely exhausted her reservoir of magical strength over the past few hours, wielding her *bae'qeshel* songs to confuse the attacking hordes, strengthen her companions, and staunch the worst of her companions' wounds.

Jeggred, lurking at the rear of the band near the tunnel leading back to the previous room, broke the silence.

"If the mercenary does not return soon, we will be fighting again," the draegloth said. "I do not hear the minotaurs behind us any longer, which means they're probably circling around to come at us from another direction."

"We've taught them not to come at us down long, straight tunnels, I suppose," Ryld observed. He studied the Jaelre cavern with a practiced eye. "Best not to let them catch us in the open like this. They might overwhelm us with sheer numbers."

Danifae asked quietly, "What if this is a dead end?"

"It can't be," Quenthel said. "Somewhere in these caverns we'll discover where it is the Jaelre have fled to, and we will follow. I have come too far to return to Menzoberranzan empty-handed."

"That's all very good," Pharaun said. "However, I feel constrained to point out that we are exhausted and have almost used up our magical strength. Blundering through these halls and corridors until the minotaurs manage to trap and kill us is sheer stupidity. Why don't we lie low in one of those artisan homes—say, in that gallery over there—and rest until we're ready to continue? I believe I can conceal our presence from our pursuers."

Quenthel's eyes flashed with fire as she said, "We will rest when I see fit. Until then, we keep moving."

"I do not believe you understand what I am saying—" Pharaun began, rising to his feet and speaking with short, clipped words.

"I do not believe you understand what I am commanding you to do!" Quenthel snapped. She whirled on the wizard and stepped close, her whips writhing in agitation. "You will cease your incessant questioning of my leadership."

"When you begin to lead intelligently, I will," Pharaun retorted, his calm demeanor finally cracking. "Now, listen—"

Jeggred rose with a feral snarl and grasped the wizard around the upper arms with his huge fighting claws, pulling him away from Quenthel and hurling him across the floor.

"Show some respect!" the draegloth thundered. "You address High Priestess Quenthel Baenre, Mistress of Arach-Tinilith, Mistress of the Academy, Mistress of Tier Breche, First Sister of House Baenre of Menzoberranzan . . . you insolent dog!"

Pharaun's eyes flashed as he leaped to his feet. The facade of good humor fell from his face, leaving nothing but cold, perfect malice.

"Never lay a hand on me again," he said in a deadly hiss.

His hands crooked at his sides, ready to shape awful spells against the draegloth, while Jeggred crouched and made ready to spring.

Quenthel shifted the grip on her scourge and paced closer as the serpent heads curled and darted, striking at the air in their agitation. Ryld set one hand on Splitter's hilt and watched all three, his face an expressionless mask.

"This is madness," Halisstra said as she backed away, pointing her crossbow at the floor. "We must cooperate if we want to get out of here alive."

Quenthel opened her mouth to speak, perhaps to issue the order that would send Jeggred charging at the wizard regardless of the consequences, but at that moment Valas returned, trotting up to the company. The scout came to a halt, taking in the situation with a glance.

"What is going on here?" he asked carefully.

When no one answered, the Bregan D'aerthe looked at each of the company in turn.

"I cannot believe this. Have you not had your fill of fighting in the last forty hours? How can you even consider spending the last of your strength, your magic, your blood, slaughtering each other, when we've already fought our way across half of the damned Labyrinth?"

"We are in no mood to be harangued by you, mercenary," said Quenthel. "Be silent." She glared at Pharaun, and thrust her whip through her belt. "It serves no purpose to fight each other here."

"Agreed," said Pharaun—perhaps the tersest statement the loquacious mage had uttered in the time Halisstra had known him. From some unsuspected well of discipline the wizard mastered his anger and straightened, relaxing his hands. "I will not be handled like a common goblin, though. That I will not bear."

"And I will not be taunted and baited at every turn," Quenthel replied. She turned to Valas. "Master Hune, did you find anything in the palace?"

The scout glanced nervously at Quenthel and Pharaun, as did Halisstra and Danifae.

"In fact, I did," he said. "In the main hall of the palace there is a large portal of some kind. Unless I misread the signs, a large number of people passed through it. I suspect House Jaelre lies somewhere on the other side, in some new abode."

"Where does the portal lead?" Ryld asked.

Valas shrugged and said, "I have no idea, but there is certainly one way to find out."

"Fine," said Quenthel. "We will put your portal to the test at once, before the minotaurs and their demons return. In a few minutes, anywhere will be better than here."

She let one long glare linger on Pharaun, who finally had the good sense to avert his eyes in what would have to suffice for a bow.

Halisstra let out a breath she didn't realize she'd been holding.

TEN

"Now this I did not expect," remarked Pharaun.

The wizard sighed and sat down on a rock, allowing his pack to drop to the moss-covered ground. The company stood in the mouth of a low cavern looking up at a daylit forest, somewhere on the surface. The Jaelre portal lay a few hundred yards behind them in a damp, winding cavern that led to a large, steep-sided sinkhole with lichen-covered boulders and trickling rills of cold water splashing down from the hillside above.

The day was heavily overcast—in fact, a light rain was falling—and the clouds, coupled with the gloom of the forest, helped to ameliorate the insufferable brightness of the sun. It was not so harshly brilliant a day as they had seen in the cloudless desert of Anauroch a tenday past, but to eyes long accustomed to the utter lightlessness of the Underdark, the diffuse sunlight still seemed as harsh as the glare of a lightning stroke.

"Should we keep moving?" Ryld asked. He'd returned Splitter to its sheath, angled across his broad back, but he held a crossbow at the ready and squinted into the towering green trees. "It won't take the minotaurs long to figure out where we went."

"It doesn't matter if they do," Pharaun said. "The portal was keyed to function for drow alone. It's nothing more than a wall of blank stone to our friends in the Labyrinth—a sensible precaution on the part of the Jaelre, I suppose, though had I been in their shoes I believe I would not have ruled out the possibility of attackers of my own race."

"You're certain of that?" Quenthel asked.

The wizard nodded and replied, "I was careful to examine the portal before we stepped through. Leaping blindly through portals is a bad habit, and should be reserved only for the gravest of situations, such as escaping imminent death in the destruction of a city. And, before anyone asks, we can still retrace our steps if we wish. The portal functions in both directions."

"I am not in a hurry to return to the Labyrinth. Better the sun-blasted surface than that," Halisstra murmured.

She picked her way across the floor of the sinkhole, studying the forest overhead. The air was cool, and she noted that the trees nearby were mostly needleleafs of some kind, trees that did not lose their foliage in the wintertime, if she remembered correctly. A number of barren trees of a different sort stood in and among the evergreens, trees with slender white trunks and only a handful of ragged red and brown leaves clinging in an odd clump near the crown. Dead? she wondered. Or merely bare of leaves for the winter months? She'd read many accounts of the World Above, its peoples, its green plants and animals, its changing seasons, but there was a great difference between reading about something and experiencing it firsthand.

"Where on the surface are we?" Quenthel asked.

Valas stared hard at the trees for a long time, and craned his head up to squint at the dimly glowing patch of clouds that hid the sun. He turned in a slow circle to examine the hillside nearby. Finally he knelt and ran his fingers over the soft green mat of mosses clinging to the boulders in the cavern mouth.

"Northern Faerûn," he said. "It's early winter, as it should be. You can't see the sun too well to judge its position in the sky, but I can certainly feel it, as I suspect we all do. We're in the same general latitude as the lands above Menzoberranzan—not more than a few hundred miles either north or south, I think."

"Somewhere in the High Forest, then?" Danifae asked.

"Possibly. I'm not sure the trees look right. I've traveled the surface lands near our city, and the foliage looks different from what I remember of the High Forest. We might be some ways distant from Menzoberranzan."

"Excellent," muttered Pharaun. "We trek through the Underdark to Ched Nasad, are forced through a portal to the surface hundreds of miles from home, then we trek back down into the Underdark through shadow and peril, only to pass through another portal that takes us back to the surface, perhaps even farther from home. One wonders if we might have simply marched here from Hlaungadath without our pleasant detour through the Plane of Shadow, the delightful hospitality of Gracklstugh, and our lovely little tour of the minotaur-infested Labyrinth."

"Your spirits must be rebounding, Pharaun," Ryld observed. "You've found your sarcasm again."

"A sharper weapon than your sword, my friend, and just as devastating when properly employed," the wizard said. He ran his hands over his torso and winced. "I feel half dead. Every time I turned around, some hulking bull-headed brute was trying to cleave me in two with an axe or pin me to the floor with a spear. Might I trouble you for one of your healing songs, dear lady?" he asked Halisstra.

"Do not repair his injuries," Quenthel snapped. She still stood with one hand clamped around her torso, blood trickling between her fingers. "No one is mortally injured. Conserve your magic."

"Now, that is precisely—" Pharaun began again, glaring at Quenthel and climbing to his feet.

"Stop it!" Halisstra snapped. "I have exhausted my songs of power, so it does not matter. When I have recovered my magical strength I will heal all who need it, because it is foolish to press on in our state. Until then, we will have to rely on mundane methods to address your injuries. Danifae, help me dress these wounds."

The battle captive turned to Jeggred, who stood near, and motioned for him to sit down, shrugging her pack from her shoulders to search for bandages and ointments. The draegloth did not protest, a sign of how exhausted he was.

Halisstra glanced over the others and decided that the wizard was most in need of attention. After pushing him back down onto the boulder, she took out her own supply of bandages. She studied Pharaun's upper arm, where Jeggred's talons had scored the flesh, and she began to apply an ointment from among the supplies they'd purchased in Gracklstugh.

"This will sting," she said pleasantly.

Pharaun mouthed an awful curse and jumped as if he had been stabbed, yelping in pain.

"You did that on purpose!" he said.

"Of course," Halisstra replied.

While she and Danifae worked on the others, Valas scrambled up a narrow path hidden along the wall of the sinkhole. He studied the ground carefully, and paused to stare thoughtfully into the forest nearby.

Halisstra looked up at him and asked, "Did you find something of interest, Master Hune?"

"There is a path here that climbs up out of the cave mouth," the Bregan D'aerthe answered, "but I couldn't say where the Jaelre went. Several game trails converge here, but none seem to have been used by any number of folk."

"In the Jaelre palace in the Labyrinth you said you'd found clear signs that they had used the portal. How could there be no signs on this side?" Quenthel demanded.

"Dust and grit in the Underdark can hold signs of passage for many years, Mistress. On the surface, it is not so easy. It rains, it snows, the small plants quickly grow over disused paths. Had the Jaelre passed this way in great numbers within the last tenday or two,

I would probably see the signs, but if they came this way five or ten years ago, I would be left with nothing to read."

"They would not have marched far across the surface," Quenthel mused. "They can't be far away."

"You're probably correct, Mistress," Valas replied. "The Jaelre would doubtless have preferred to move by night, staying under the cover of the trees during the day. If this is a very large forest—the High Forest, or perhaps Cormanthor—they might be hundreds of miles away."

"There's a cheerful thought," Pharaun muttered. "What in the world brought the Jaelre up here, anyway? Didn't they consider the possibility that the surface dwellers would slaughter them as eagerly as the minotaurs did?"

"When I knew them years ago, Tzirik and his fellows spoke from time to time of returning to the surface," Valas said. He turned away from the forest and lightly dropped back down into the cave mouth. "Reclaiming the World Above is part of the doctrine of the Masked Lord, and the captains and rulers of House Jaelre wondered if the so-called Retreat of our light-blinded surface kin might not be an invitation to claim the lands the surface elves were abandoning."

"Did it not occur to you back in Ched Nasad that your heretical friends might have decided to act upon their wishful thinking and abandon that black, fiend-ravaged warren they called home?" Quenthel asked. "Did it not occur to you that you might have been leading us into a dead end in the Labyrinth?"

The Bregan D'aerthe scout shifted nervously under Quenthel's gaze, and said, "I didn't see any better alternatives, Mistress. Not if we truly want to get to the bottom of things."

"You were so eager to solve the mystery of the Spider Queen's silence that you chose to gamble that your friend Tzirik was still in the Labyrinth, even though you knew his House had been planning to flee the place for years?" Ryld asked. "We endured a great deal of peril in the city of the duergar and the domain of the minotaurs to satisfy your curiosity."

"Perhaps we were not meant to find this Tzirik at all," said

Quenthel. "Perhaps Master Hune has led us far away from our true mission over the last few tendays, and perhaps it was no accident that he did so."

"When we considered the question of whether we should return to Menzoberranzan," Jeggred said, "it was the Bregan D'aerthe who urged us to set off in search of this priest Tzirik—a heretic priest none of us have even heard of, except for Valas." His eyes narrowed, and the draegloth climbed to his feet, his four clawed hands balling into fists as he shouldered Danifae aside. "Things become clear, now. Our guide is a Vhaeraunite heretic, and he has served the Masked Lord well by leading us through useless perils for days on end."

"This is ludicrous," Valas protested. "I would hardly have led the Bregan D'aerthe to the defense of Menzoberranzan if I was an enemy of the city."

"Ah, but it is the classic ruse," Danifae purred. "Introduce your victims to the agent you have chosen for their destruction by giving them reason to trust her. In your case, the job seems to have been expertly done indeed."

"Even if that was the case," Valas said, "why did I not betray you to the duergar in Gracklstugh? Or leave you to the minotaurs in the Labyrinth? I could have arranged your deaths, not a mere delay. If I was your enemy, you can be certain that is what I would have done."

"Perhaps you would have placed yourself in peril by betraying us in either Gracklstugh or the Labyrinth," Pharaun observed. "Still, you raise a cogent point in your own defense."

"Nothing more than the glib lies of a traitor," Jeggred snarled. He glanced at Quenthel. "Command me, Mistress. Shall I rend him limb from limb for you?"

Valas lowered his hands to the hilts of his kukris, and licked his lips. He was gray with fear, but his eyes sparked with anger. Each of the others in the company turned their eyes to Quenthel, who still leaned against a boulder, her whips quiescent at her waist. She stayed silent, as rain splattered down in the forest and birds chirped and called in the distance.

"I withhold judgment for the moment," she said, looking at the scout. "If you are loyal, we shall need you to find Tzirik—if the Vhaeraunite priest exists, of course—but you would be well advised to produce the Jaelre and their high priest quickly, Master Hune."

"I have no idea where they might be," Valas said. "You might as well condemn me now, and prepare yourself for Bregan D'aerthe's response."

Quenthel exchanged a long look with Jeggred. The draegloth smiled, his needle-like fangs gleaming in his dark face.

Halisstra wasn't sure what to think, as she hadn't known the scout for more than a tenday, and couldn't say what might or might not have happened in Menzoberranzan before the Menzoberranyr came to Ched Nasad. She was, however, certain that they would all regret it if Quenthel had Valas killed and it turned out that the guide's services were still required, or that his powerful mercenary guild decided to seek vengeance for the death of their scout.

"What is the best means of locating the Jaelre from here?" Halisstra asked, hoping to deflect the conversation into a less dangerous course.

Valas hesitated, then said, "As Mistress Quenthel pointed out, they are unlikely to have moved far. We can search in an expanding spiral until we come across better information."

"A plan that sounds wearying and tedious," Pharaun commented. "Marching aimlessly through this blinding woodland does not appeal to me."

"Find a surface dweller and pry information from him," Ryld said. "Assuming, of course, that any are nearby, and that they know anything of the whereabouts of House Jaelre."

"Again, we would have to march off in order to locate a surface dweller, as none conveniently present themselves here," Pharaun observed. "Your plan differs in no significant respects from Master Hune's."

"Then what would you propose?" asked Quenthel, her voice icy.

"Allow me to rest and study my spellbooks. In the morning, I can prepare a spell that may reveal the location of our missing House

181

of heretical outcasts." He raised his hand to forestall the Baenre's protests and added, "I know, I know, you would like to continue this very moment, but if I can successfully divine the goal of our search, it is likely to save us many hours of marching in the wrong direction. The delay will also give the lovely Lady Melarn a chance to regain her own magical strength, and perhaps heal us of the worst of our wounds."

"You may learn nothing from your spells," Quenthel said. "Magic of that sort is notoriously fickle."

Pharaun simply looked at her.

Quenthel looked up at the sky, blinking in the merciless gray light that permeated the clouds above. She sighed and looked back down at the others, her eyes lingering overlong on Danifae. The battle captive tilted her head down in a single, almost imperceptible nod that Halisstra wasn't even certain she saw.

"Very well," the Mistress of Arach-Tinilith said finally. "It would be wise for us to wait for the cover of darkness in any event, so we will set up camp in the cave below, where this accursed sunlight will not trouble us so much. Master Hune, you will stay close by me until we find this Tzirik of yours."

Nimor Imphraezl made his way swiftly along the wide ledge, passing a long line of marching duergar on his right hand while skirting the edge of a black abyss on his left. Moving an army of several thousand through the dark and lightless ways of the Underdark was a formidable challenge, and many of the smaller, more direct routes were simply impassable to a body of so many soldiers. That left only the most capacious caverns and tunnels, and those routes frequently passed through dangers that the stealthier ways avoided.

The road clung to the shoulder of a great subterranean canyon, winding in a northerly direction forty miles from Gracklstugh. The day's march was not more than two hours old, and the gray dwarf army had already lost a fully laden pack lizard—and five soldiers unlucky enough to be close to the beast—to a flight of hungry yrthaks, raking the high trail with their sonic blasts.

No tremendous loss, Nimor reflected, but every day brought its own mishap or accident, and so the army's attrition began. In all truthfulness, the Jaezred Chaulssin assassin had not really grasped the enormous effort required to move a large, well-equipped army a hundred miles through the Underdark. He was quite familiar with journeying the dark ways by himself or in the company of a small band of merchants or scouts, traveling light, making use of the secret byways and known refuges that lay hidden along the main routes of travel. Having marched several days alongside an army, with ample opportunity to observe minor setbacks, difficulties, and challenges he hadn't even imagined, Nimor appreciated the scope of the expedition. The duergar were anxious indeed to strike a mortal blow at a neighbor in distress, if they were willing to tolerate the vast expense in beasts, soldiers, and materiel required to put an army in the field.

The assassin rounded a precarious bend, and came upon the crown prince's diligence: a floating hull of iron, perhaps thirty feet long and ten wide, ensorcelled not only to levitate itself above the ground but also to move as directed by the gray dwarves controlling the thing. Its ugly black form bristled with spikes to repel attackers and armored slits through which the occupants could fire missiles or work deadly spells on anyone outside. The diligence was pierced with several large, shuttered windows that were propped open, and through these Nimor glimpsed the quiet and orderly bustle of the duergar leaders and their chief assistants. The whole construct functioned as command post, throne, and bedchamber for the crown prince while in the field with his army. It was the perfect embodiment of the dwarf approach to things, Nimor reflected, a device displaying skillful craftsmanship and powerful magic, but no grace or beauty.

With a light bound he hopped up onto the running board of the diligence and ducked through a thick iron door. Inside, dim lights gleamed from blue globes, illuminating a great table that held a

representation of the tunnels and caverns between Gracklstugh and
Menzoberranzan. There the lords and captains of the gray dwarves
studied their army's march and planned for the battles to come.
The assassin took in the various officers and servants with one quick
glance then turned to the elevated center portion of the diligence.
The lord of the City of Blades sat at a high table with his most important advisors and watched over the planning below.

"Good news, my lord prince," Nimor said, sweeping into the
circle of captains and guards surrounding Horgar Steelshadow.
"I have been advised that the Archmage of Menzoberranzan, old
Gromph Baenre himself, has been removed from the *sava* board of
our little game. The matron mothers do not yet suspect our advance
into their territory."

"If you say so," the duergar lord replied gruffly. "In dealing with
the dark elves I have found it prudent not to rule out the presence of
an archmage until I see him dead under my own hammer."

The assembled gray dwarves around Horgar nodded, and glared
at Nimor with undisguised suspicion. A drow turncoat might have
been a useful ally in a war against Menzoberranzan, but that did not
mean they considered Nimor a reliable partner.

Nimor spied a gold pitcher standing by the high table and poured
himself a great goblet of dark wine.

"Gromph Baenre is not the only skilled wizard in Menzoberranzan," growled Borwald Firehand. Short and stocky even for a gray
dwarf, the marshal gripped the table with his huge, powerful hands
and leaned forward to glare at the assassin. "That cursed wizard
school of theirs is full of talented mages. Your allies played their hand
too quickly, drow. We're still fifteen days from Menzoberranzan, and
Gromph's death will provoke alarm."

"A sensible notion, but not entirely correct," Nimor said. He
drained off a large gulp from his goblet, savoring the moment.
"Gromph will be missed soon, I'm sure, but instead of casting their
arcane gaze out into the Underdark to search for approaching foes,
every Master of Sorcere will be searching fruitlessly for the archmage
and scheming against his colleagues. While the crown prince's army

approaches, the most powerful wizards in the city will have their eyes firmly fixed on each other, and more than a few will seek to murder their colleagues to win the archmage's vacant seat."

"The Masters of Sorcere will surely set aside their ambitions once they come to realize their peril," the crown prince said. He cut off Nimor with a curt gesture and added, "Yes, I know you say they may not, but we would be wise to plan on meeting an organized and well-directed magical defense of the city. Still, that was a well-struck blow, well-struck indeed."

He rose, and shouldered his way past the clan lairds and guards to approach the map table, beckoning Nimor to follow. The assassin circled to the other side of the table to attend the duergar ruler's words. Horgar traced their route with one thick finger.

"If the wizards of Menzoberranzan do not note our approach," Horgar said, "then the question becomes, at what point will they perceive their danger?"

The clan laird Borwald thrust his way to the tableside and indicated a cavern intersection.

"Presuming we don't encounter any drow patrols, the first place we'll meet the enemy is here, at the cavern called Rhazzt's Dilemma. The Menzoberranyr have long maintained a small outpost there to watch this road, as it's one of the few large enough for an army to use. Our vanguard should reach it in five days' time. After that, our path forks and we must make our first hard decision. We can choose to go north, through the Pillars of Woe, or circle around to the west, which adds at least six days to our march. The Pillars are likely to be held against us, and so could delay us indefinitely."

"The Pillars of Woe . . ." Horgar said. The prince tugged at his iron-gray beard as he studied the map. "When the drow learn we're coming, they'll certainly move troops there and hold the pass against us. That way is no good, then. We'll want to follow the other branch to the west, and circle around to approach the city from that side. The time it adds to our march cannot be helped."

"On the contrary, I mean for you to take the straighter path," Nimor said. "Passing through the Pillars of Woe will save you six days, and once you're on the other side, you will be on Menzoberranzan's doorstep. If you go through the western passes, you'll find the terrain there much less favorable."

The duergar lord snorted and said, "Perhaps you have not traveled this way before, Nimor. It is a difficult road you've chosen, if you plan to force the Pillars of Woe. The canyon becomes narrow there and climbs steeply. Two mighty columns bar the upper end, with only a narrow way between them. Even a small force of drow can hold it indefinitely."

"You can beat the Menzoberranyr to the Pillars, Crown Prince," the assassin said. "I will deliver the outpost of Rhazzt's Dilemma to you. We shall allow the defenders of the post to report a duergar force on the march, but even as the message speeds back to the matron mothers, your forces will race ahead to lay a deadly trap at the Pillars of Woe. There, you will destroy the army the rulers of the city send to hold the gap."

"If you can give us the outpost, drow, why allow the soldiers there to send any warning at all?" growled Borwald. "Better to cling to our secrecy as long as possible."

"The pinnacle of deceit," said Nimor, "lies not in depriving your foe of information, but in showing your foe the thing that he expects to see. Even with the stroke we have engineered against the city's wizards, they cannot help but note our approach soon. Best for us to control the circumstances under which the crown prince's army is reported to Menzoberranzan's rulers, and perhaps anticipate their response."

"This intrigues me. Go on," Horgar said.

"The soldiers of Menzoberranzan expect that an army approaching along this road must be delayed by the effort to take Rhazzt's Dilemma, giving the city time to man the choke point at the Pillars of Woe in sufficient strength to defeat any further attack. I suggest you allow the outpost to make its report and alert the rulers of Menzoberranzan to the presence of your army. Before the matron mothers can muster an army to face you, we will take Rhazzt's Dilemma by storm. We will be waiting to intercept the drow march at the Pillars of Woe."

"Your plan has two fundamental flaws," said Borwald, sneering in contempt. "First, you presume that the outpost can be taken whenever we wish. Second, you seem to think that the matron mothers will choose to send out their army instead of standing fast to await a siege. I would give much to know how you intend to engineer these two feats."

"Easily done," the assassin replied. "The outpost will fall because much of its garrison has been withdrawn to keep order in the city. Of those soldiers that remain, many are Agrach Dyrr. That is why I urged you to choose this road for your attack. The outpost will be betrayed into your hands when the time is right."

"You knew this before we set out," Horgar said. "In the future, you will share such information in a more timely manner. What would we have done if you'd met some accident of the march? We must know exactly what kind of help you will lend us, and when you will be able to do so."

Nimor laughed coldly and said, "It would be good for our continued friendship, Prince Horgar, if you find yourself wondering from time to time exactly how helpful I might turn out to be."

🕷   🕷   🕷

Halisstra roused herself from her Reverie to find that she was cold and wet. During the night, a light dusting of wretched stuff that she guessed must be snow had fallen over the forest, bedecking every branch with a thin coating of brilliant white. The novelty of the experience had worn off quickly for her, particularly after she realized that it had soaked her clothing and *piwafwi* with frigid water. The reality of snow on the surface was far less appealing than any account of the phenomenon she'd read in the comfort of her House library.

Overhead, the sky was sullen and gray again, but brighter than the previous day—bright enough to cause no little discomfort to the drow travelers. Since Quenthel didn't choose to drive them out into the sunlight after Pharaun had rested and studied his spells, they passed most of the day's bright hours sheltering deep in the cavern away from the light. The company didn't prepare to break camp until late in the day, when the sun was already beginning to sink into the west.

"Remind me to conduct some research into methods by which that infernal orb might be extinguished," remarked Pharaun, squinting up into the snow-laden sky. "It's still up there behind all those blessed clouds, burning my eyes."

"You're not the first of our kind to find its light painful," Quenthel replied. "In fact, the more you complain about it, the more it troubles me, so keep your whimpering to yourself and get about the business of casting your spell."

"Of course, most impressive Mistress," Pharaun said in an acerbic voice.

He turned away and hurried off across the snow-covered rocks and boulders before Quenthel could make a proper retort. The Baenre muttered a black curse under her breath and turned away as well, busying herself with watching Danifae as the battle captive stuffed Quenthel's bedroll and blankets into her pack. The rest of the company kept to a studious silence and pretended not to notice the interplay, either between Quenthel and Pharaun, or Quenthel and Danifae. They gathered up their own belongings and broke camp.

Halisstra picked up her own pack and followed Pharaun across the floor of the sinkhole, scrambling up after him along the hidden path that ascended to the forest floor. Standing in the clearing surrounding the sunken spot where the cavern mouth had undermined the hillside, she found that the forest was very dense and pressed in close on all sides. Everywhere she looked, the wall of trees and brush was the same, a verdant barrier with no landmarks at all, no distant mountains by which she could orient herself, not even an orderly plan of sand-covered streets to follow. Even in the most twisted caverns of the Underdark, one usually was offered only a handful of choices at a time—forward or back, left or right, up or down. In the forest, she might simply walk off in any direction she liked and eventually arrive somewhere. It was an unsettling and unfamiliar feeling.

She finished her careful examination of the forested hillside, and faced Pharaun again. The rest of the company watched him as well, variously standing or squatting on their heels and shading their faces with their hands as they awaited the wizard's guidance.

"If I say anything," said Pharaun, staring into the trees and speaking over his shoulder, "anything at all, mark it carefully. I may or may not understand exactly what it is I see."

He extended his arms wide and closed his eyes, whispering harsh syllables of arcane power over and over again as he turned in a slow circle.

The eldritch sensation of magic at work tugged at Halisstra, a feeling that was almost palpable, yet maddeningly distant. A strange, cold breeze arose, sighing in the treetops as it bent them first one way, then another, growing stronger moment by moment. Boughfuls of snow shifted and fell as the weird wind increased to a wild, shrieking gale. Halisstra raised a hand to shield her eyes from flying dust and grit. Through it all, she heard Pharaun's voice growing deeper, more powerful, as the spell took on a life of its own and seemed to drag itself from his throat. She lost her footing and slid awkwardly to one knee, her hair whipping around her head like something alive.

The magic of Pharaun's divination bore him aloft. Arms still outstretched, he revolved in the air as the winds circled with him. His eyes were blank and silver, cast upward to the heavens. A nimbus of green energy began to coalesce around the wizard's body, and he gave out a great howl of anguish. Bolts of emerald fire exploded from his halo to scour and blast at the boulders nearby. Each green ray sliced into rock like a rapier into soft flesh, causing the stones to split and flake with deafening cracks. Where each green bolt played, a black rune or pattern formed in the damaged stone, appearing as if etched by acid in the exposed rock. The designs made Halisstra's eyes ache to look at them, and from the air in the center of the clearing, Pharaun began to mutter in a horrible voice that somehow carried through the wind and thunder.

"Five days west lies a small river," the wizard intoned. "Turn south and follow its dark swift waters upstream another day, to the gates of Minauthkeep. The Masked Lord's servant dwells there. He will aid you and betray you, though neither in the manner you expect. Each of you save one will commit betrayal before your quest is done."

The spell concluded. The wind died away, the green energy dissipated, and Pharaun came slumping down from his lofty perch as if he'd been dropped from a rooftop. The wizard struck the hard earth awkwardly and crumpled, huddling with his face in the cold slush covering the ground. As the reverberations of the spell's violence fell away in the snowy wood, the black-etched runes carved into rocks and boulders faded as well, flaking away in tiny bits of ebon dust that evaporated within the space of moments.

The rest of the company straightened and exchanged dark looks.

"I can see why he's slow to cast that spell," Ryld remarked.

He moved forward and caught Pharaun by one feebly waving arm, turning him over and checking for any obvious signs of injury. Pharaun looked up and managed a weak grin.

"Good news and bad, I suppose," he said. "Tzirik seems to be alive and well, at least."

"The directions are clear," Valas said with care. "I think I can keep us heading west easily enough."

"What did you mean by that last bit?" Jeggred said to Pharaun, ignoring Valas. "About the betrayal?"

The draegloth tightened his fists.

"About each of us betraying someone? Why, I couldn't begin to guess," the wizard said. He coughed and sat upright, waving away Ryld's help. "It's the nature of the magic to offer cryptic predictions like that, threatening little riddles that you have little hope of solving until it suddenly becomes obvious that the event you feared has come to pass." He offered a wry chuckle. "If only one of us doesn't have some shocking act of treachery to pull off in the near future, I must say I'd like to know who's sleeping on the job. He'll tarnish our reputation if he's not careful."

Halisstra studied the rest of the company, noting the impassive faces, the thoughtful eyes. Danifae met her gaze with a slight smile and the merest flicker of her gray eyes toward Quenthel, a gesture so small and secret that no one save Halisstra could note it.

Despite the wizard's easy dismissal of the exact words of the divination, she wasn't pleased to learn that every one of her companions would at some point in the future commit some kind of treacherous act or another. Or, more likely, all but one of her companions. Just because Halisstra planned no immediate act of betrayal didn't mean she might not choose to take advantage of an opportunity arising later. She had not held her rank as First Daughter of House Melarn without developing a certain ruthless instinct for such things. If ruin had not come to Ched Nasad, Halisstra didn't doubt that at some point in the fullness of time she would have seriously plotted against her own mother to claim leadership of the house. Matron Melarn had unseated Halisstra's grandmother in the same manner and for the same reasons many hundreds of years past. It was no more or less than the Spider Queen's way.

"Well," Pharaun said as he pushed himself to his feet, still shivering. The wizard accepted his pack from Ryld, moving gingerly. "It seems I have provided a destination. So which way is west, Master Hune?"

Valas nodded toward the near side of the clearing and said, "There are a couple of game trails leading more or less toward the setting sun."

"Come," said Quenthel. "The sooner we set out, the sooner we arrive. I have no wish to spend one hour more than we must in this light-seared land. Master Hune, you will take your customary place as our guide. Master Argith, you will accompany him. Halisstra, you will bring up the rear and keep an eye behind us."

Halisstra frowned and shifted uncomfortably. That struck her as a job suitable for a male. In their travels over the past few days Jeggred had customarily brought up the rear. It didn't escape Halisstra that changing the order of the march kept Jeggred close by Quenthel, where the draegloth could protect the Baenre priestess from any attack. She likewise noted that Quenthel had referred to both Valas and Ryld as "master," while calling her only Halisstra.

There was no point in protesting, of course, so she only waited as the rest of the company filed off into the woods, following Valas's path. She unslung her crossbow and made sure the weapon was ready for quick use. After allowing the rest of the company a lead of about fifty yards, Halisstra set off after them.

ELEVEN

The surface woodland proved to be a strange and disquieting place. As the party moved away from the clearing's edge, the tangled underbrush vanished, leaving only an endless green hall of round trunks rising to the forest roof above, like the pillars of some dark elven hall somewhere in the Lands Below. Old, fallen logs lay scattered here and there, covered in bright green moss. Some were so large that the company had to detour hundreds of feet around them, or scramble awkwardly over or under. A dusting of snow had filtered to the ground, and cold water dripped steadily from the branches above. Unlike the lifeless desolation of Anauroch, the forest was filled not only with mighty trees and twining brambles, but all manner of small birds and animals. After a dozen heart-stopping starts, Halisstra soon learned to identify a number of discrete birdcalls and animal sounds and relegate them to the realm of the insignificant.

She had at first feared that she would easily lose sight of the company ahead, but away from the crowded foliage by the infrequent clearings, the underbrush consisted of ferns and other green plants rarely more than waist high. As darkness fell over the forest floor, her vision improved, and Halisstra felt more and more comfortable.

The drow marched on through the night, halting a little before daybreak to set up camp in an old ruined tower whose broken white stones were covered by moss. Smooth and delicately veined, the place showed remarkable elegance of form, and the lintel of its long-vanished door was carved in a flowering vine design—clearly the work of surface elves. After Pharaun checked the place for lingering spells that could be dangerous to drow, the company made camp to pass the painful bright hours of the day. Quenthel ordered Jeggred and Pharaun to keep watch, and the others enjoyed the shade and safety provided by the partial floors and graceful walls of the ruined tower.

At sundown they ate, broke camp, and set off again, in the same order as before, marching again through the night. They passed the next two days and nights in much the same way, resting while the sun was out and traveling by night. Valas even managed to shoot a small, hoofed animal a little before dawn at the end of their third night of travel, and Halisstra was surprised to find that its meat was light and succulent, better than that of a young rothé.

Toward the end of the day the clouds returned, darker and thicker than before, and as the daylight failed and the dark elves made ready for their fourth march on the surface, a soft snow began to fall, wet and heavy. It was eerily silent, as if the entire forest held its breath to keep from intruding on the moment. Halisstra watched vigilantly behind the company, taking a dozen steps forward and turning to scan the trail behind them, sometimes walking backward for several minutes at a time, glancing to the front only to be sure of her footing. If Pharaun's divinations were accurate, they should reach the stream at the end of that night or perhaps the next, which meant that House Jaelre and the Vhaeraunite priest were only a day beyond.

With the objective of their long journey so close at hand, it occurred to Halisstra that she had no reason why the heretic would consider helping them. Valas might have been an old acquaintance, but no cleric of the Masked Lord would aid priestesses of Lolth simply out of the goodness of his heart. Some price would have to be met, of that Halisstra was certain. Wealth, perhaps? Quenthel and her comrades carried many valuable gemstones. It was the easiest and most compact way to transport wealth through the wilds of the Underdark. Halisstra had stuffed her own pockets too before fleeing Ched Nasad. She doubted that a powerful Vhaerraunite would be so easily purchased, though.

Coercion might be possible, or they might have to barter some kind of service to win his aid. Danifae was occasionally useful in such arrangements. Any drow had at least one enemy in need of a setback.

She realized she'd fallen a bit behind, so she picked up her pace to take up position closer behind the main body of the company. She trotted easily through the darkness, her boots gliding through the snow, until she caught sight of Jeggred's hulking form and the smaller shapes of her companions moving ahead of her. Halisstra settled back into her pace, and turned to glance back down the trail.

Someone was there.

From all sides she heard the whisper-quiet sounds of soft feet stealing through the woods, then the sounds were abruptly cut off by a perfect, impenetrable silence that could only be magical.

Halisstra hissed in alarm, but heard nothing. She brought up her crossbow. Directly up the path a lanky male elf with skin as white as the snow darted toward her, armed with a gracefully curved war axe in one hand and a shorter hand axe in the other. His eyes glittered like green death in the night.

"Watch out!" she cried, trying to warn her companions, but again nothing broke the perfect silence.

Without a moment's hesitation she whirled and fired her crossbow at Jeggred, perhaps fifty yards ahead. She skewed her aim a bit, so instead of taking him between the shoulder blades the quarrel struck quivering into a tree beside the half-demon's head. The draegloth leaped and shouted—or so she guessed, anyway, since she couldn't hear it—but, more importantly, he turned to see what was happening behind him, and spied the surface elves stealing up from behind them.

An instant later, the elf axeman was upon Halisstra, whirling his two matched crescent blades in a deadly pattern of gleaming steel. He was shouting something too, a war cry perhaps. Halisstra gave up her fine crossbow to deflect the first stroke of the long axe, leaped back out of the reach of the shorter one, and hastily drew her mace, slinging her shield from her shoulder. The pale elf leaped forward to engage again, and they circled, trading skillful blows that failed to find their mark.

Halisstra could see more green-armored shapes flitting through the woods toward her, swords and spears glittering in the darkness. She redoubled her efforts and put the two-axe fighter on the defensive, hoping to batter down his defenses before she was surrounded by foes.

A brilliant, searing light detonated along the trail behind her, filling the darkened forest with the painful glare of daylight. The last thing she saw before the spell blinded her completely was a company of surface elves and human warriors, dashing up to join the fray.

There was only one thing Halisstra could do. Raising her shield to buy a moment's time, she ducked down, grasped a handful of dirt and dried leaves from the ground at her feet, and imbued them with magical darkness, making good use of the power shared by all drow. A heavy blow fell on her shield, without a sound, and she quickly scuttled away from the axeman, staying low to the ground and feeling her way along. Some of her enemies would be waiting for her to emerge from the impenetrable blackness—at least, that was what Halisstra would have done in their place. The wisest thing to do was to remain within as long as possible in the hopes that the surface dwellers had no more magic suitable for canceling or dispelling her field of darkness.

As with any drow noble familiar with battle, Halisstra knew to an instant how long her own dome of darkness would persist. In her case, she could sustain the magical gloom for almost three hours. If she lay still and quiet for a long time, the surface dwellers might very well think she'd slipped away. At the very least, she was reasonably sure she could outwait the spell of silence that covered the area. Once her hearing returned, she might be able to form a better guess as to what to do next.

Mace in hand, she groped her way to a large tree, leaned against its trunk, and settled down to wait.

Nimor stood patiently in the hall outside the council chamber, studiously allowing his shoulders to slump and his face to sag. He was supposed to be tired, after all. Dressed in the arms of an officer of House Agrach Dyrr, he'd purportedly fought his way free of the battle at Rhazzt's Dilemma in order to carry word of the attack to the matron mothers. Of course, the Agrach Dyrr garrison had already delivered the outpost to the army of Gracklstugh, but the matron mothers didn't know that yet.

Feigning exhaustion, despair, and resolve in the proper quantities was difficult for him, especially when his heart raced with excitement and his body quivered in anticipation. Long-laid plans had found their moment and unfolded slowly toward a terrible fruition. Through his own labors and toils he had altered the course of two great cities. Both moved ponderously and yet inevitably toward a terrible collision he had imagined months before, and with each hour events gathered speed and required less and less of his guidance. Soon he could allow himself to vanish from the stage once more, his great toils done, and make ready to reap the rewards of his labors.

To divert himself while he awaited the summons to the council in the chamber beyond, Nimor studied the hall with care. One never knew, after all, when a half-remembered doorway or a choice of exits might spell the difference between life and death. The Hall of Petition, as the place was called, formed the entrance to the matron mothers' secretive council chamber. The high ladies themselves rarely passed through this room. They had various secret and magical ways to travel from their palaces and castles to their seats within. Instead, the Hall of Petition was the place where all who had business with the council awaited the matrons' pleasure. Naturally, it was nearly empty.

Any drow who needed something simply begged it of one of the matron mothers, and most carefully and respectfully at that. Only those drow commanded to appear before the council waited in the Hall of Petition, and again, anyone whose presence was commanded had probably already made his report to one of the matron mothers beforehand. The hall was most commonly employed as a convenient place for persons of interest to the council to wait until called within to deliver her report, present her request, or more often plead her case and hear judgment.

Sixteen proud male warriors and wizards stood in or around the hall, two from each of the Houses whose matron mothers sat on the council. They were ostensibly designated as a guard for the entire council, but in truth each male spent most of his time carefully watching the males of rival Houses to make sure that no secret attack was afoot that day.

The floor, all of polished black marble with veins of gold, gleamed in the dim light of faerie fire globes set high in the ceiling, and great friezes along the walls showed the story of Menzoberranzan's founding.

Several minor functionaries scurried about the hall, bowing and scraping to all who deserved such obsequiousness, and imperiously disregarding any who did not. Nimor, wearing the arms of a minor officer of House Agrach Dyrr, fell somewhere in between.

To Nimor's great surprise, he was kept waiting only forty minutes before one of the chamberlains approached and gestured toward the door.

"The Council expects your report, Captain," he said.

Nimor followed the official into the council chamber itself, bowing to the high seats of the eight matron mothers. Each was attended by one or two of her daughters, nieces, or favorites. A grand archway to one side of the chamber led off to a set of smaller shrines and halls adjacent to the council, to which the matrons' attendants and secretaries could be dismissed should the matron mothers decide to discuss their business in private.

"Matron Mothers, Captain Zhayemd of House Agrach Dyrr," the chamberlain announced.

Nimor bowed again, and held the pose as he surreptitiously studied the matron mothers.

Triel Baenre sat at the head of the Council, of course. Petite and pretty, she seemed too young for the place of honor, though she was of course hundreds of years in age. Mez'Barris Armgo of House Del'Armgo sat next to her, then came the place where the Matron Mother of House Faen Tlabbar formerly sat. Nimor studiously did not smile, but he allowed his gaze to linger a moment on a young female who occupied Ghenni's place—Vadalma, the fifth daughter of the House. Either the first four destroyed each other squabbling for their mother's place, he reflected, or young Vadalma was much more accomplished than she looked.

Opposite the new Faen Tlabbar matron sat Yasraena Dyrr, graceful and lissome, well at ease in the chair she had occupied since Auro'pol's demise.

"Ah, I see my captain has arrived," Yasraena said to her peers. "Welcome, Zhayemd. You have endured much today, but I am afraid I must subject you to one more ordeal before you can be allowed your well-deserved rest. Tell the Council the tidings you brought me earlier."

"As you wish, Honored Matron," Nimor said. He glanced around at the highborn females and affected a trace of nervousness. "Matron Mothers, I have come from the garrison at Rhazzt's Dilemma. We have come under attack from a great force of duergar and their allies, including derro, durzagons, giants, and many slave troops. We do not expect to delay them for more time than it takes the duergar to bring their siege engines into play."

"I know that place," Mez'Barris Armgo said. "It lies three or four days' travel south of the city. Is your news that old? Why did your spellcasters not warn us through magic instead of sending you to report in person?"

"Our wizard was slain in the first assault, Matron Del'Armgo. He had the misfortune to be leading a patrol outside our defenses and apparently fell victim to the approaching duergar. When Mistress Nafyrra Dyrr—the commander of our detachment—realized we had no means to signal a warning, she dispatched me at once to carry a message back to Menzoberranzan. This all occurred earlier this morning."

"You have only answered one of the questions I posed, Captain," the Matron Mother of House Barrison Del'Armgo observed. "Rhazzt's Dilemma came under attack this morning, but the outpost lies more than thirty miles south of here, a journey of several days."

Nimor affected a trace of hesitation, and glanced deliberately at Yasraena Dyrr as if seeking guidance. The Matron Mother of House Agrach Dyrr simply inclined her head in assent.

"I made use of a somewhat unreliable portal to shorten my journey from several days to a few hours, Matron Del'Armgo," he said. "It lies a mile or two from the outpost and is somewhat difficult to use, as it functions only intermittently. The other side lies in a disused cavern in the Dark Dominion. My House has known of it for some time, though we did not trust the portal's magic enough to employ it except in a dire emergency."

"I have no doubt that Barrison Del'Armgo knows of similar portals in and around the city," Yasraena Dyrr observed. "Forgive us if we neglected to mention the existence of this one until today."

"The portal is irrelevant," Triel Baenre said, making a dismissive gesture of her hand. "The captain is here to make his report, and that is sufficient. Tell me what you observed of this duergar army."

"I would guess it to number somewhere around three to four thousand gray dwarves, plus a number of slave soldiers—mostly orcs and ogres. We noted the banners of eight companies in the attack, and many more held back in reserve. There could be more, of course, or the duergar may have deliberately attempted to deceive us by carrying false banners into battle."

"A raid," muttered Prid'eesoth Tuin of House Tuin'Tarl. "Your outpost is simply being tested, Captain."

Nimor shifted his feet and did his best to look determined, serious, and dutifully subservient.

"Mistress Nafyrra does not believe so, Matron Tuin," Nimor said. "We have fought off duergar raids on numerous occasions, but nothing like the onslaught we encountered this morning. If we are not besieged by the whole army of Gracklstugh, it's certainly close enough."

"How strong is your garrison?" Yasraena Dyrr asked.

"Our garrison numbers almost eighty warriors, and we have an excellent defensive position, Honored Matron. We can hold out for several days, but the outpost will fall when the duergar bring up their siege engines, or employ the right sort of magic."

"It should not surprise me to learn that this duergar onslaught is little more than a particularly large and aggressive raid," Vadalma of Faen Tlabbar said. "I am sure Matron Dyrr has reported what her males believe to be the case, but perhaps the matter should be investigated before we react in blind panic. A simple confirmation of the report, at the least. After we have properly assessed the scope of the threat, the Council can deliberate over the best means to address it."

"Under most circumstances, our young sister would be wise to suggest a more thorough assessment of the situation," said Yasraena. She had been well coached. Nimor lowered his gaze to keep his smile from showing. "However, my officers tell me that, if we wish to meet the duergar army outside the city, the place to do it is at the Pillars of Woe, between here and Rhazzt's Dilemma. A strong army dispatched quickly can hold the pillars against any conceivable assault, but if we delay too long, the duergar will reach it before we do. We would throw away a very significant advantage of position. We should, of course, seek confirmation of the report with all due haste, but while we're investigating, our soldiers should be marching."

"Shouldn't we simply stand on the defensive here, in the city cavern?" asked Mez'Barris Armgo. "We can fortify the approaches easily enough, and the duergar army would have a difficult time surrounding the city in its entirety while the threat of our own intact army remains within."

"If we allow the gray dwarves to infest the city," one of the other matron mothers said, "we shall surely see illithid, aboleth, and humanoid armies at our doorstep in no time at all. We have many enemies. Look at what happened to Ched Nasad."

The eight high priestesses exchanged somber looks.

"Clearly, the Council must reach some decisions quickly," Triel Baenre said, breaking her thoughtful silence. "We don't have much time if we wish to meet the duergar outside the city, so I will order half of Baenre's troops to make ready to march. I advise the rest of you to do the same. If we decide to stand on the defensive in the city cavern, we can have our soldiers stand down, but if we decide to march, we will want to be able to march soon."

"I favor a vigorous and aggressive defense of the city," said Yasraena Dyrr. "Hard exertion now may serve to deter further attacks later. I will order half the strength of House Dyrr to make ready at once." She studied the other matrons carefully and added, "Provided, of course, that some other Houses agree to shoulder a share of the risk and assist us. Either we all make the same commitment, or none."

"House Baenre guarantees Agrach Dyrr until the return of the expedition," Triel said briskly.

Nimor nodded to himself. He'd expected that the leader of Menzoberranzan's strongest House would choose to lead by example in this instance. Among other things, it deflected any predatory designs of the other Houses into an external activity, where the Baenre could be seen to be taking strong and decisive action to secure the city. Triel was badly in need of such measures.

She looked up at the various guards, advisors, and guests in the council chamber and said, "The matron mothers must discuss how best to meet this treacherous attack in private. Leave us."

"Captain Zhayemd," Yasraena Dyrr said, "I would like it if you took command of the Agrach Dyrr contingent and began your preparations at once. I know you have fought your way through great peril already today, but you have intimate knowledge of the field of battle, and I have the utmost confidence in you."

"I will serve to the best of my abilities," Nimor said. "With the goddess's aid, I will scour our city's foes from our territory."

He offered another deep bow to the matron mothers, and quietly withdrew.

🕷　　🕷　　🕷

The forest sounds abruptly returned, signaling the end of the spell of silence. Wind sighed in the treetops, a small brook ran somewhere nearby, and tiny rustles and scuttling sounds whispered in the darkness as the small creatures of the woods—or larger ones who knew how to be stealthy—moved about nearby. Halisstra listened for a long time, hoping to hear some sort of positive evidence that the surface dwellers had gone or that her comrades battled on somewhere nearby, but no ringing swords or thunderous spells split the night. She heard nothing as convenient as an enemy conversation to help her decide if her foes had left, or were instead crouched silently outside the darkness, waiting for her to emerge. Halisstra could be quite patient when it suited her, and she was not unused to hardship and danger, but the sheer nervous tension of stretching out to identify and categorize every tiny sound that came to her ears soon left beads of sweat trickling down her face.

If Quenthel and the others were nearby, I would hear it, she decided. The fight must have carried them far ahead by now.

Her heart pounded at the thought of being lost in the endless woods alone, a reviled enemy to any creature who walked the surface world.

Better to die trying to rejoin the others, Halisstra decided. At least I know where they're going, if I can manage to keep my course.

First, she needed to escape from the darkness that sheltered her. She did not choose to dismiss the magical gloom, deciding to leave it to continue until it failed in an hour or two. There was a small chance that her enemies might be waiting quietly outside for the darkness to fail before moving in. Halisstra groped in her belt pouch and withdrew a slender ivory wand. She felt very carefully to determine if it was the wand she needed, and when she was convinced that she had the right one, she tapped it against her chest and whispered a word.

Though there was no way for her to verify it, sitting on the forest floor in the magical darkness, the wand's magic had made her invisible. She stood as quietly as she could, cringing at every soft rustle or clink of her mail, and began steadily moving away.

Halisstra broke out into the open night much sooner than she expected—it seemed she had been sitting no more than six or seven feet from the edge of the darkness. Confident in her invisibility, she stood up straight and looked around. The forest looked much as it had before, except there was no sign of her companions or the woodsmen and surface elves who had attacked them. The moon was rising, and its brilliant silver light flooded the forest floor. She set off in what she hoped was a westerly direction, moving as quickly and quietly as she could.

She soon came upon the scene of a furious battle, if she read the signs right. Several large, blackened circles in the forest still smoldered. In other places the bodies of perhaps half a dozen surface elves and green-garbed human warriors lay where they'd fallen, most bearing the marks of sword, mace, and talon. Of the drow, there was no sign.

Halisstra tried to remember what she'd seen of the pale elves and their human allies, deciding that there might have been as many as fifteen to twenty of the surface folk.

"Where are your comrades, I wonder?" she asked the fallen warriors before moving on.

Halisstra only managed another half mile through the moonlit forest before she stumbled into the ambush. One moment she was stealing along, quick and confident, eager to catch up to the rest of the company and the familiar perils of their association, the next she was surprised by the appearance of a surface elf wizard who simply stepped out of a tree and hurled a spell at her, barking words of arcane might as he gestured with his hands.

"Quick!" he shouted. "We have her!"

Halisstra's invisibility failed at once, undone by the surface wizard, and from the foliage and tree trunks all around her a dozen of the pale elves and the green-clad humans abruptly appeared, weapons at the ready. They leaped at her, murder in their eyes, filling the forest with their war cries and shouts of exultation.

Recognizing the hopelessness of her plight, Halisstra snarled in pure drow rage and charged to meet the surface warriors, determined not to sell her life cheaply.

The first foe in her path was a hulking human with a bristling black beard, fighting with a pair of short swords. He launched into a spinning attack, stabbing one blade at her eyes to raise her shield and slipping the other low to gut her while her guard was high. Halisstra simply dodged aside and hammered down at his extended left arm with her mace, striking a heavy blow that cracked bone and jarred the blade from his injured hand. The man grunted in pain but kept at her, giving ground grudgingly as he continued to hew and slash with his one remaining sword.

Three more of his comrades moved up to engage Halisstra from all sides, and she was forced on the defensive, batting spear and blade aside with her shield and delivering crushing parries with her magical mace. The forest echoed with the sounds of steel on steel.

"Take her alive if you can," called the wizard. "Lord Dessaer wants to find out who these newcomers are and where they came from."

"Easier said than done," grunted the first swordsman, still holding his ground despite the loss of his off-hand blade. "She does not seem interested in surrendering."

Halisstra growled in frustration and abruptly turned on the elf to her left, slipping inside the point of his spear and rushing him. The fellow backstepped and brought in his weapon as quickly as he could, but she had him.

With a snarl of cold glee she smashed her mace hard at the bridge of his nose. The weapon struck with a deadly crack of thunder and blew apart the skull of her victim, who fell in a nerveless heap.

She paid the price for her aggressive move a moment later when the elf swordsman behind her jammed the point of his weapon into her left shoulder blade despite her cat-quick effort to twist away from the attack. Steel grated on bone, and Halisstra cried out in pain as the strength fled from her shield arm. A moment later an arrow fired from an archer standing off a bit struck quivering in the back of her right calf, buckling her leg.

"Now we've got her, lads!" called the elf swordsman.

He raised his blade for another stroke, but Halisstra allowed herself to crumple completely to the ground and rolled up under his guard, destroying his left hip with another thundering blow of her mace. The elf screamed and reeled away to collapse thrashing in the snow.

Halisstra tried to regain her feet, but the wizard hammered her with a blinding bolt of lightning. The force of the spell literally picked her up and flung her through the air, depositing her in a small, icy creek nearby. Halisstra's whole body jerked and ached from the wizard's energy, and she became aware of the distinct, charred scent of her own burned flesh.

She pushed herself up on one arm and responded by hurling a *bae'qeshel* song at him, a deadly, sharp chord that flayed the bark from the trees and kicked up the dusting of snow into a stinging storm of white. The elf wizard swore and covered himself with his cloak, shielding his eyes and enduring the deadly song.

Halisstra began another song, but the warriors splashed up to her, and the burly human with the beard silenced her with a hard kick to the jaw that knocked her sprawling again. All went dark for an instant, and when she could see again, no less than four deadly blades were poised over her. The heavy swordsman glared down at her over the point of his sword.

"By all means, continue," he spat. "Our clerics can question your corpse as easily as they can question you."

Halisstra tried to clear her head of the roaring pain and the ringing in her ears. She looked around and saw nothing but death in the eyes of the surface dwellers.

I can feign surrender, she told herself. Quenthel and the others must know I'm missing, and they will make efforts to find me.

"I yield," she said in the human's brutish tongue.

Halisstra allowed her head to fall back against the stream bank and her eyes to close. She felt herself jerked upright, her mail stripped from her, and her hands bound roughly behind her back. The whole time she studiously ignored her captors, keeping her mind sequestered from her situation by focusing on the exhaustive catechisms to Lolth she had been obliged to learn as a novice.

"She must be someone important. Look at this armor. I don't think I've ever seen its equal."

"We've a lyre here, and a couple of wands," muttered the ranger with the broken hand as he pawed through her belongings. "Be careful, lads, she may be a bard. We ought to gag her to be safe."

"Bring me that healing potion, quickly. Fandar is dying."

Halisstra glanced over at the elf swordsman whose hip she had shattered. Several of his companions knelt by him in the snow and mud, trying to comfort him as he writhed weakly in agony. Bright blood flecked the snow nearby. She watched the scene absently, her mind a thousand miles distant.

"Cursed drow witch. Thank the gods they don't all fight like that."

The elf wizard appeared in front of her, his handsome face taut and angry.

"Hood her, fellows," he ordered the others. "No sense letting her know where she is."

"Where are you taking me?" Halisstra demanded.

"Our lord has some things he would like to know," the wizard replied. His smile had a distinctly cold and wintry cast to it, and his eyes were as sharp as knives. "In my experience, most drow are so venomous they'd rather choke on their own blood than do anything sensible and useful, and I expect you'll prove no different. Lord Dessaer will ask you a few questions, you'll call him something impolite, and we'll take you out back and gut you like a fish. That's a damned sight better than our captives fare in your hands, after all."

The hood came down over Halisstra's face and was jerked tight around her neck.

Ryld crouched in the shadows of a great tree with a trunk so thick and tall it might have been the forest's Narbondel. Splitter rode between his shoulders, virtually unused in the company's most recent battle. He leaned out a little and carefully peered into the dappled moonlight and shadow of the forest floor, searching for a target. With Pharaun he'd waited quietly to guard the party's backtrail, hoping to turn the tables on the elves and humans who'd harried them so long. After several valiant attempts to bring the drow to close combat, the surface elves and their human allies had learned to respect the dark elf party's skill and ferocity. They soon fought a slow and stealthy battle of arrows in the dark, punctuated with quick ambuscades and quicker retreats.

An arrow hissed in the dark. Ryld jerked back just in time to glimpse a white-feathered shaft fly past, so close to the tree trunk that its fletching kissed the bark. Had he relied on the tree for cover, the expertly aimed arrow would have skewered him through the eye.

"No point waiting any longer, now," Pharaun whispered.

The wizard had greeted Quenthel's order to lay an ambush with a distinct lack of enthusiasm, and he wasn't at all unhappy to call the effort a failure and rejoin the rest of the band. He muttered the harsh syllables of a spell and gestured in a peculiar fashion, concentrating.

In a moment the wizard straightened and motioned to Ryld, *Come. I've created an image that will make it seem that we still stand guard here, but you and I are invisible to our antagonists. Follow me quietly, and stay close.*

Ryld nodded and moved off stealthily just behind the wizard. He took one last glance at the desolate forest behind them, wondering if the wizard's trick would work.

Halisstra is back there somewhere, he thought. *Most likely dead.*

The surface dwellers had shown no interest in taking prisoners, and in the logical part of his mind Ryld simply wrote off her loss as another casualty of battle, just as he might account for the untimely fall of any useful comrade. He'd fought enough battles over the years to understand that warriors die, but despite that, he found Halisstra's loss strangely unsettling.

Pharaun paused, turning in a slow circle as he searched for some sign of the rest of the company or any foes still on their trail. Ryld held still and listened. A gentle wind moved the treetops and sighed in the branches overhead. Leaves rustled, and branches creaked. A small brook trickled nearby, but he could detect nothing that might signal danger—or Halisstra's return.

Stupid to hope for such a thing, he told himself.

Something troubles you? motioned Pharaun.

No, the weapons master replied.

The wizard studied him, the brilliant silver moonlight gleaming on his handsome face.

Tell me you're not worried about the female!

Of course not, Ryld replied. *I'm concerned only because she's been a valuable comrade, and I don't like the idea of proceeding without her skill at healing. But I am not concerned on any other account. I am no fool.*

I think perhaps you protest too much, Pharaun signed. *It does not matter, I suppose.*

He started to say more, but at that moment a soft rustle behind them cut off his words. Wizard and swordsman turned together, Ryld's hand stealing to Splitter's hilt as he aimed his crossbow with the other hand, but from the bright shadows Valas Hune suddenly appeared. Of all the company, the Bregan D'aerthe seemed almost as skilled as the surface dwellers in the patient cat-and-mouse game of forest hunting.

Did you catch sight of any of our foes? the scout asked.

No, but someone saw enough of Ryld to shoot an arrow, Pharaun replied. *Since they seemed to guess where we were, we left an illusion and came to rejoin you.*

Any sign of Halisstra? Ryld asked.

No. Nor you, then? Valas replied.

Perhaps half an hour ago we heard sounds of fighting from back down the trail. It went on for a couple of minutes. That might have been her, Pharaun signed.

"There it is, then," Valas muttered under his breath. "Well, come on then. The others are waiting, and if we can't ambush our pursuers, we might as well keep moving. The longer they keep us here, the more likely it is that more of them will show up and join the fight."

The scout led the way as he hurried through the trees and brush, moving swiftly and silently. Pharaun and Ryld could not match the softness of his steps, but the wizard's magic seemed an adequate ruse, since they encountered no more hidden archers or spearmen. In a few hundred yards they came to a small, steep ravine, well screened by thick brush and large boulders. There they found Quenthel, Danifae, and Jeggred lying low, watching vigilantly for any sign of a renewed attack.

"Did you surprise the archers?" Quenthel asked.

"No. They located us quickly, and avoided a fight," Ryld replied. He ran a hand over his stubbled scalp and sighed. "This is not a good battlefield for us. We can't bring the surface elves to grips, not with the advantage they have in this terrain, but if we don't do anything, they'll eventually surround us and cut us to pieces with arrows."

Valas nodded in agreement and added, "They're working to find and flank us now. We've got a few minutes here, but we're going to have to move or fight soon. Ten minutes or less, I think."

"Let them come," rumbled Jeggred. "We killed a dozen of them not an hour ago when they stole up on us from behind. Now that we know the day-walkers are out there, we'll slaughter them in heaps."

"The next assault will most likely consist of a rain of arrows from archers we won't even be able to see," Valas said. "I doubt that the surface dwellers will oblige us by lining up for us to kill. Worse yet, what if the rangers sent for help? The next attack might come at daybreak with two or three times the numbers we've seen so far. I don't relish the thought of being showered with arrows and spells after the sun comes up and our opponents suddenly begin to see much better than we do."

"Fine," Jeggred snarled. "So what would you do, then?"

"Withdraw," Ryld answered for the scout. "Make the best speed we can and keep moving. With luck we'll outdistance our pursuers before the sun comes up, and maybe we'll find a good place to hide."

"Or maybe we'll reach territory controlled by the Jaelre," Valas added.

"Which may, of course, prove to be even more dangerous than playing cat-and-mouse with our friends the surface dwellers," Pharaun said. "If the Jaelre aren't fond of visitors. . . ."

"It doesn't matter if they are or not," Quenthel said. "We came to speak to their priest, and we will do so, even if we have to cut our way through half their House to do it."

"Your suggestion is not very encouraging, Master Hune," Danifae said. She bled freely from a wound in her right arm, where a hard-driven arrow had actually punched through her mail and transfixed her upper arm. As she spoke she worked awkwardly with one hand to bind the wound. "What happens if we fail to outpace our enemies? They seem well able to keep up with us in these damnable woods."

"One moment," Ryld said. "What about Mistress Melarn? She's back there somewhere."

"Most likely dead already," Valas said with a shrug. "Or a prisoner."

"Shouldn't we make sure of that before we leave her?" the weapons master replied. "Her healing songs are the only magic of that sort we have left to us. Common sense dictates—"

"Common sense dictates that we don't waste time and blood on a corpse," Quenthel interrupted. "No one came after me when—"

She stopped herself, then stood and walked over to help Danifae cinch her bandage.

"Our mission lies ahead of us, not behind," the Mistress of Arach-Tinilith said. "The quest is more important than any one drow."

Ryld rubbed his hand over his face and glanced around the company. Valas looked away, busying himself with some unimportant fastening of his armor. Pharaun stared at Quenthel with an expression that made it clear the wizard noted the priestess's hypocrisy, if nothing else. She had, after all, spent more time in Ched Nasad hoping to empty Baenre storehouses of their goods than seeking the renewed attention of Lolth.

Danifae stared off into the woods behind them, her brow furrowed with concern, but obviously unwilling to argue the point on behalf of her mistress.

Finally Quenthel turned to Pharaun and said, "Perhaps our skilled wizard has some magic that might help us discourage these cursed day-walkers from following too closely?"

Pharaun stroked his chin, and thought.

"Our chief difficulty in these circumstances," the Master of Sorcere said at length, "lies in the fact that our antagonists are able to use this terrain to their advantage, and our *dis*advantage. Should a forest fire suddenly arise, the smoke and flames would—"

Valas laughed and interrupted, "I'm afraid you know little of surface forests, Master Mizzrym. These trees are far too wet to oblige you with a forest fire now. Try again in a few months, after summer has dried them out."

"Oh," the wizard replied, "I can see that's true for *mundane* fire."

"You won't be able to prevent fire from sweeping back on us," Ryld said, the idea giving him some anxiety.

"Well, I can't be certain they won't, but my fires will burn in the manner I choose," Pharaun said. "As Master Hune observed, the forest is damp enough that the trees won't catch unless directly affected by my spell. We will, of course, have the advantage of knowing how and when the fires begin."

Quenthel thought for a moment, then said, "Very well, you may proceed."

Ryld felt his throat tighten and he stepped away from the group, quickly regaining control of himself.

The Master of Sorcere stood and reached into a pouch at his belt to withdraw a tiny silk purse. He emptied it into his hand. Red dust glittered in the moonlight. Pharaun studied the forest, turned to sense the wind, and spoke his spell quickly, casting the powder into the air. Bright crimson sparks appeared amid the falling dust, growing brighter and more numerous moment by moment. With another gesture, Pharaun scattered the burning motes across a great, wide arc of the forest before him.

As each tiny mote settled to the ground, it flared into life, growing into a spiderlike shape fully as large as a man's head. Wreathed in crimson flame, the fire spiders scuttled across the ground, moving deeper into the trees. Whatever they touched smoldered at first, then burst into flame. The wood was indeed wet, and the flames were smoky and slow to spread—but Pharaun had conjured hundreds of the spider creatures. The living motes of fire seemed to set upon the moss-grown trunks with a peculiarly savage ferocity, almost as if the presence of so much timber had provoked them into a frenzy of fiery destruction.

"Good, good," Pharaun murmured. "They like trees . . . they truly do."

"The fire's too slow to burn our pursuers," Quenthel observed.

"I've never heard of a surface elf who'd allow a fire such as this to burn unchecked in his precious forest," Pharaun said with a smile. "They'll be busy chasing down my spiders and extinguishing the flames for some time.

Quenthel watched the blaze a moment longer, and smiled.

"It may serve, then," she said. "Master Hune, take the lead. I mean to reach House Jaelre before we're troubled by the surface dwellers again."

※ ※ ※

Kaanyr Vhok folded his well-muscled arms and frowned.

"How many this time?" he asked.

Kaanyr surveyed the aftermath of a battle between the tanarukks of his vanguard and a titanic purple worm, a carnivorous giant over a hundred feet in length. The worm was dead, hacked to death by dozens of the half-demon's soldiers, but a handful of the Sceptered One's troops lay torn and crushed by the monster they had killed.

"Seven, my lord, but we slew the beast, as you can see."

The tanarukk captain called Ruinfist leaned on his huge greataxe, spattered with the foul juices of the creature. The orc-demon's left hand had been mangled in some battle long before, and was encased in a locked battle-gauntlet that served as a better weapon than the damaged hand it covered.

"The warriors heard it moving in the rock," Ruinfist continued, "but it came through the ceiling and dropped on them."

"I didn't bring you here to slay mindless worms," Kaanyr said. "Nor did I bring warriors to this spot to feed whatever monster happens by. This was a battle best avoided, Ruinfist. These seven warriors won't be with us when we meet the dark elves, will they?"

"No, my lord," the tanarukk growled. He lowered his head. "I will tell the patrol leaders to do what they can to avoid needless battles."

"Good," said Kaanyr. He offered the tanarukk a hard grin and clapped the creature on the shoulder. "Save your axes for the drow, Ruinfist. We'll be on them soon enough."

A hungry light flared in the tanarukk's eyes, and the demon-orc raised his tusked jaw again. He growled in assent and trotted off to go find his fellow captains.

"You did not discipline him?" Aliisza asked, slinking out of the shadows. "Mercy is not a quality I am accustomed to in you, love."

The cambion lord turned at her approach.

"Sometimes," he replied, "one soft word serves the purpose of two hard ones. Knowing which to choose and when is the art of leadership." Kaanyr nudged one of his dead warriors with his toe, and smiled. "Besides, how can I take offense at a show of the very fighting spirit I've worked so hard to instill in my Scoured Legion? It's the nature of a tanarukk to throw himself into battle and bring down his foe or die trying."

Aliisza looked at the purple worm and shuddered.

"I think that's the biggest worm I've ever seen," she murmured.

The half-demon's seat of power in the ruins of ancient Ammarindar was the better part of two hundred and fifty miles southeast of Menzoberranzan, and the Darklake was an obstacle in their path. Fortunately, tanarukks were fast, hearty, and could endure swift marches with few supplies. The dwarves of ancient Ammarindar had carved great subterranean highways through their realm, broad, smooth-floored tunnels that ran for mile after mile through the endless gloom. Kaanyr was somewhat disconcerted to think that the tremendous cavern of the Darklake lay somewhere a mile or two beneath his feet, but the old dwarven road offered far and away their best route to the environs of Menzoberranzan. If the road happened to be plagued by hungry monsters, well, any other route would have problems of its own.

He shook himself from his reflections and started to walk back toward the long file of his warriors, streaming past the scene of the battle in a ragged double-column.

"So, tell me again about this Nimor," Kaanyr said. "I can easily understand Horgar Steelshadow's motive in mustering this attack. The gray dwarves and the dark elves have fought many wars over the centuries. What I don't understand is what's in it for a drow assassin?"

"As best I can tell," Aliisza replied, "he hates the great Houses of Menzoberranzan enough that he'll destroy the city in order to bring about their fall."

"Such a purity of intent is rare in a dark elf. You know he's lied to you, of course."

Kaanyr suspected, as always, that Aliisza was holding something of her encounter with Nimor to herself. After all, she was an alu-fiend, the daughter of a succubus, and her weapons and methods were obvious.

"Lied?" she quipped. "To me?"

"I merely point out that that one should beware of dark elves bearing gifts," Kaanyr replied. "He might have convinced you it was in my best interest to bring my army here, but I don't believe for a heartbeat that your mysterious assassin doesn't have more to gain from this alliance than I do."

"That goes without saying, doesn't it?" she said. "If you see that, why did you agree to bring your army to the Pillars of Woe?"

"Because something is going to happen there," Kaanyr said. "My ambitions have reached the borders of old Ammarindar, and I don't care to arrest them there."

The cambion watched his fierce warriors marching by, staring past them to the dark visions that enthralled him.

"We'll be approaching from above and to the east," Kaanyr said, "perfectly positioned to flank a force trying to hold the Pillars against the approach of Gracklstugh's army. On the surface, that is why Horgar Steelshadow and his drow assassin want us there. It might suit their purposes to sit in the gorge a few days and let the drow decimate my soldiers before they attempt to force the pass. Being on the same side of an obstacle as our enemies carries a liability, as well as an opportunity. I wouldn't put it past Horgar to manufacture some excuse for a delay in order to let my tanarukks handle the brunt of the fighting."

Aliisza cozied up beside him and purred, "Until the battle is joined, love, you haven't chosen sides. The dark elves might pay, and pay well, for your assistance at a critical juncture of the campaign. Even if that assistance takes the form of simply not doing anything to aid the gray dwarves in their attack."

Kaanyr Vhok bared his pointed teeth in a wry smile.

"There is that," he admitted. "All right, then. We'll see what happens when the Pillars of Woe stand before us."

🕷   🕷   🕷

Halisstra was marched for several miles through the forest, gagged, hooded, her hands manacled behind her. The surface elves had healed the wound in her calf in order to keep her from slowing them down, but the rest of her injuries they didn't bother to tend. While they'd removed her mail and shield, they did permit her to keep her arming jacket against the cold night air—after searching carefully to make sure they didn't miss any hidden weapons or magical devices.

Eventually they reached a place where the forest floor underfoot gave way to stone, and she could hear the whispers and rustles of a number of people around her. The air grew warmer, and sullen firelight penetrated the hood over her eyes.

"Lord Dessaer," a voice close by said, "the captive Hurmaendyr spoke of."

"So I see. Remove her hood. I would look on her face," said a deep, thoughtful voice from somewhere ahead of her.

Her captors removed the hood, leaving Halisstra squinting in the bright light of an elegant hall made of gleaming silver-hued wood. Flowering vines wound along posts and beams, and a fire glowed to one side in a large hearth. Several pale elves watched her carefully—apparently guards of some kind, dressed in silver-hued scale mail with polearms and swords at their hips.

Lord Dessaer was a tall half-elf with golden hair and pale skin with a faint bronze hue to it. He was well-muscled for a male, nearly as big as Ryld, and he wore a breastplate of gleaming gold with noble accoutrements.

"Remove her gag, too," the elf lord said. "She'll have little to say otherwise."

"Careful, my lord," spoke the captor beside her, whom Halisstra saw was the black-bearded human she'd fought in the forest. "She knows something of the bard's arts, and may be able to speak a spell with her hands bound."

"I will exercise all due caution, Curnil." The lord of the hall moved closer, gazing thoughtfully into Halisstra's blood-red eyes, and said, "So, what shall we call you?"

Halisstra stood mute.

"Are you Auzkovyn or Jaelre?" Dessaer asked.

"I am not of House Jaelre," she said. "I do not know of the other House you name."

Lord Dessaer exchanged a worried glance with his advisors.

"You belong to a third faction, then?"

"I was traveling with a small company, on a trade mission," she replied. "We sought no trouble with surface dwellers."

"A drow's word is regarded with some skepticism in these lands," Dessaer replied. "If you're not Auzkovyn or Jaelre, then what was your business in Cormanthor?"

"As I said, it was a trade mission," Halisstra lied.

"Indeed," drawled Dessaer. "Cormanthor was not entirely abandoned during the Retreat, and my people object strongly to the drow effort to seize our old homeland. Now, I would like to know who exactly you and your companions are, and what you were doing in our forest."

"Our business is our own," Halisstra answered. "We intend no harm for any surface folk, and mean to be gone from this place as soon as our business is done."

"So I should simply allow you to go free, is that it?"

"You would do yourself no harm if you did so."

"My warriors engage in deadly battles every day against your kind," Dessaer said. "Even if you say you have nothing to do with the Jaelre or the Auzkovyn, that doesn't mean you're not our enemy. We do not ask quarter of the drow, nor do we extend it to them. Unless you succeed in explaining to my satisfaction why you should be spared, you will be executed."

The lord of the surface folk folded his arms before his breastplate, and fixed her with a fierce stare.

"Our business is with House Jaelre," Halisstra said. She drew herself up as best she could with her arms bound behind her. "It does not concern surface elves. As I said before, my company is not here to cause any trouble to you or your people."

Lord Dessaer sighed, then nodded to Halisstra's guards.

"Escort the lady to her cell," he said, "and let us see if she becomes more helpful with some time to fully consider her situation."

Halisstra's guards replaced her hood, covering her eyes again. She stood passively and allowed them to do so without protest. If her captors came to expect compliance from her, there was always the chance they might make a mistake and give her a chance to get out of her bonds.

Her guards led her out of the hall and back outdoors again. She could feel the deep chill of the air, and sensed the growing brightness in the sky even through her hood. Dawn was near, and the night was vanishing at the sun's approach. She wondered if her captors meant to lock her in some open cage, a place where the curious and malcontent could come by to jeer and torment her, but instead they led her into another building and down a short flight of stone steps.

Keys jangled, a heavy door creaked open, and she was led through. Her hands were unbound, only to be secured again in heavy iron manacles as rough hands maneuvered her into place.

"Listen well, drow," a voice said. "You will be unhooded and ungagged, at Lord Dessaer's command. However, the first time you attempt to work a spell, you will be fitted with a steel muzzle and hooded so closely you will labor for every breath. We don't go out of our way to mistreat prisoners, but we'll repay every trouble you cause us threefold. If we have to break your limbs and shatter your jaw to keep you docile, we will."

Her hood was removed. Halisstra blinked in the bright cell, illuminated by a hot beam of sunlight pouring in from a grate up in one corner. Several armed guards watched her carefully for any sign of trouble. She simply ignored them and allowed herself to slump against the wall. Her hands were chained together tightly, and the manacles were bound to a secure anchor in the ceiling, cleverly de-signed to take in any slack.

The guards left her half a loaf of some kind of crusty, gold-brown bread and a soft leather jack of cool water, and they exited the cell. The door was riveted iron plate, evidently locked and barred from outside.

So what now? she wondered, staring at the opposite wall.

From what little she'd seen of the surface town, Halisstra sus-pected that her comrades could break her out easily enough with a determined effort.

"Hardly likely," Halisstra muttered to herself.

She was a Houseless outcast whose usefulness did not overcome the simple fact that, as the eldest daughter of a high House, she stood as Quenthel's most dangerous rival in the band. The Mistress of the Academy would be only too happy to abandon Halisstra to whatever fate awaited her.

Who would argue against Quenthel on her behalf?

Danifae? Halisstra thought.

She allowed her head to drop to her chest and she laughed softly and bitterly.

I must be desperate indeed, to hope for Danifae's compassion, she thought.

Once dragged off as a battle captive herself, Danifae would find the situation deliciously, perfectly ironic. The binding spell wouldn't let Danifae raise a hand against her, but without specific instruc-tions, the battle captive would not be compelled to seek her out.

With nothing else to do but stare at the wall, Halisstra decided to close her eyes and rest. She still ached in calf, torso, and jaw from the injuries she'd sustained in her desperate last stand. As much as she longed to use the *bae'qeshel* songs to heal herself, she dared not. The pain would have to be endured.

With a simple mental exercise she distanced her mind from her body's pain and fatigue, and slipped deep into Reverie.

In Dessaer's audience hall, the half-elf lord watched his soldiers lead the dark elf away while he stroked his beard thoughtfully.

"So, Seyll," he said, "What do you make of this?"

From behind a hidden screen a slender form in a skirt and jacket of embroidered green glided forward. She was a full-blooded elf, thin and graceful—and she was also a drow, her skin black as ink, the irises of her eyes a startling red. She moved close to Dessaer and gazed after the departing soldiers with their hooded captive.

"I think she's telling the truth," she said. "At least, she's not a Jaelre or an Auzkovyn."

"What shall I do with her?" the lord asked. "She killed Harvaldor, and she damned near killed Fandar as well."

"With Eilistraee's grace, I will restore Harvaldor to life and heal Fandar," the drow woman said. "Besides, is it not the case that Curnil's patrol attacked her and her companions on sight? She was simply defending herself."

Dessaer raised an eyebrow in surprise and glanced at Seyll.

"You intend to give her your goddess's message?"

"It is my sacred duty," Seyll replied. "After all, until it was given to me, I was very much like her."

She inclined her head to indicate the absent prisoner.

"She's a proud one from a high House," Dessaer said. "I doubt she'll care to hear Eilistraee's words." He rested a hand on the drow priestess's shoulder. "Be careful, Seyll. She'll say or do anything to get you to lower your guard, and if you do, she'll kill you if you stand between her and freedom."

"Be that as it may, my duty is clear," Seyll replied.

"I will delay my judgment for a tenday," the Lord of Elventree said, "but if she refuses to hear your message I must act to protect my people."

"I know," said Seyll. "I do not intend to fail."

Chapter

THIRTEEN

The Houses of Menzoberranzan mustered for battle. From a dozen castles and palaces, caverns and strongholds, slender males in elegant black chain mail marched in proud columns or pranced along in the high saddles of riding lizards, pennons flying from their lances. Under normal circumstances each House might have sent hundreds more slave warriors, a rabble of kobolds, orcs, goblins, and ogres to drive into their foes before valuable drow troops were committed to battle, but armed slaves were something of a scarcity after the alhoon's uprising. Thousands of lesser humanoids had survived the revolt and its failure, as well as the dreadful reprisals that ensued, but the warriors among the slave races had naturally suffered the greatest losses. Even those who'd been allowed to surrender were certainly not to be trusted with weapons again.

Nimor sat in the saddle of an Agrach Dyrr war-lizard, and smiled in satisfaction as the forces of House Dyrr marched past before him. The companies gathered in a small, somewhat cramped plaza near the border between West Wall and Narbondellyn, ironically enough not very far at all from the compound of House Faen Tlabbar. Each drow swordsman carried a light kit in addition to his arms and armor, and a supply train of sorts was taking shape as each company brought its own pack lizards and attendants. Many of the common folk of the city had turned out to watch the mustering of the army, as it was easily the largest assemblage of soldiers the matron mothers had commanded since the ill-fated assault on Mithral Hall years before.

"I surmise that the Council meeting went well," said Dyrr, standing at Nimor's stirrup.

The undead sorcerer did not appear in his own shape, of course, nor even that of the aged male he affected within his own house. His current guise was that of a nondescript Agrach Dyrr wizard, young and hale, draped with the fine vestments of his House.

"Your matron mother was well coached," Nimor replied. He kept his voice low, even though no one stood close enough to eavesdrop. "We've got half the soldiers in the city mustering for battle."

"Yasraena has proven a useful front," the lich observed. "I have known a dozen or more Matron Mother Dyrrs, and from time to time I find that my female relations object to my . . . unique position within the House. Yasraena would kill me if she could, of course, but she knows that Agrach Dyrr would of necessity be destroyed should something unfortunate befall me. I have made her aware of certain long-standing arrangements in order to discourage her from surprising me."

Nimor chuckled dryly and said, "I suspect that you are rarely surprised, Lord Dyrr."

"Success follows preparation in equal measure, young Nimor. Consider that your lesson for the day." The lich affected a smile across his illusory features, and stepped away from Nimor's mount. "Good luck in your venture, Captain."

Nimor wheeled the war-lizard around as the last of the column passed by.

He turned back to the lich and said, "One more word. Narbondel was illuminated hours late a tenday ago, but every day since it has been illuminated on time, and it is whispered throughout the city that the Masters of Sorcere have misplaced their archmage."

Dyrr smiled and spread his hands.

"As Archmage Baenre may be unavailable for quite some time," the lich said, "it would please me to find the Masters of Sorcere determine on their own who among them should take Gromph's seat."

"Won't Matron Mother Baenre and the Council have something to say about that?"

"Not if the assembled masters realize the power they truly hold now," Dyrr said. "I am not a member of the Academy, of course, but a couple of young pups of my House are, and they keep me well-informed. The masters debate whether this is the time to break with tradition and name their own archmage, but half of them scheme to eliminate any fellow clever and bold enough to take the job, while the other half contemplate whether they might return to their own Houses and rule there. Breaking from the Council in such a way would mean civil war, and those few masters who don't realize the civil war is raging already are arguing to adhere to the status quo in fear of Lolth's return. Regardless, Sorcere is well and truly paralyzed by Gromph's absence."

The lich turned, leaning heavily on his tall staff, and ambled off with a dry, crackling laugh.

Nimor raised an eyebrow and watched the lich depart, considering his ally's words, then he trotted off after the column.

"Lieutenant Jazzt!" he called.

From alongside the marching column of House Agrach Dyrr's warriors, a small, scarred male detached himself and came trotting to Nimor's side. The soldiers marching in the expedition knew very well that "Captain Zhayemd" was no scion of their House, but it had been explained to them that the detachment's commander enjoyed Matron Mother Yasraena's complete confidence and had, in fact, been adopted into the leadership of their ancient clan—a common enough practice among the high Houses of the city. Nimor didn't doubt that Jazzt Dyrr, second cousin to the matron mother herself, had received some additional and specific orders concerning the circumstances under which he was to ignore Nimor's commands, but as Nimor intended to scrupulously honor his bargain with Agrach Dyrr, he was reasonably certain that the Dyrr officer would offer no trouble.

"Yes, Captain?" Jazzt said.

He was careful not to show any expression at all, simply regarding Nimor with the bland curiosity of a seasoned veteran.

"Form up the company there, beside the Baenre contingent. Tell the men to make ready for a long march. I hope to set out within the hour."

"Yes, Captain," Jazzt replied.

The lieutenant stepped back and saluted sharply, then turned and began to bark orders to the Agrach Dyrr soldiers. Nimor turned his mount aside and trotted across the plaza to a small tent bustling with activity. There, the highborn officers and commanders of each of the various House contingents had gathered, most with some number of sergeants and messengers in train. Several arguments on all manner of different topics—the order of march, the best place to halt at the end of the day, the fastest route to the Pillars of Woe—proceeded at the same time.

He dismounted, handed the reins of his war-lizard to a nearby slave, and strode into the midst of the confusion, pushing through to the partitioned area. He had to flash his insignia of House and rank to gain admittance. Inside, a knot of captains and officers from various Houses stood engaged in several different conversations at the same time. The occasion of raising an army and marching to war seemed to displace the normal rivalries and vendettas, at least for a time. Instead of dueling each other in the streets, the rakish fellows sought to outshine each other with deeds of valor and ruthlessness on the battlefield.

Nimor surveyed the commanders, noting the insignias of six out of eight great Houses, and another half dozen of the largest and strongest minor Houses. His eye fell on a male wearing the insignia of House Baenre, as the fellow held up his hands and raised his voice to capture the attention of the other officers.

"Go back to your companies and look to your supply trains," Andzrel Baenre, Weapons Master of House Baenre, said. "I want a list from each of you of the number of pack beasts and wagons in your train, and a general inventory of your stores. Return within the hour. Our female relations will doubtless debate many issues of high strategy, but it will fall to us to work out the details of supply trains and battle signals, and we still have much to discuss."

Andzrel was a tall, slender fellow who wore armor of blacked mithral plate and a dark cloak. His tabard proudly displayed the emblem of House Baenre, and his eyes held iron discipline, an expression of directness and purpose that was unusual in a drow of high birth, whether male or female.

The commanders broke up and strode from the tent, heading back to their detachments. Nimor allowed them to pass by. As he moved up to speak with the Baenre weapons master, the assassin muttered a spell.

"Master Baenre," Nimor asked, covering the last syllables of the enchantment.

"Yes," the weapons master said, blinking at Nimor. "I . . . uh . . ."

Nimor smiled, seeing the effect the enchantment had on the drow, and knowing that for quite some time, Andzrel Baenre and he would be very close friends.

"You are familiar to me, but I do not believe I know you," said Andzrel. "You wear the arms of Agrach Dyrr."

"I am Zhayemd Dyrr, and I command my House's company," Nimor replied. "Do you have any idea when the priestesses will deign to join us, or at least allow us to start on our way?"

"I believe the matron mothers are still deciding which of them will lead the expedition," Andzrel replied, seemingly recovered. "None of them trusts any of the others enough to voluntarily leave the city now, but they all think it's clear that someone had better be put in charge of the males."

Nimor laughed at that.

"You have a talent for plain speaking, sir." Nimor glanced around at the other captains and officers in the pavilion and added,

"I assume you've tallied which Houses are here, and how many troops—and of what type—each has brought? The priestesses will want to know that, and it will be helpful for us all to have an idea of who's marching next to whom."

He could think of other uses for the information, of course, but there was no need to mention that, was there?

"Of course," Andzrel replied. He pointed at a table in the outer portion of the tent, where several Baenre officers studied maps and reports. "I'll need you to give those fellows the strength of your complement, the number of infantry and cavalry, and some information on your supply train, as well. After which I would like to ask you some questions about the route of our march and the place we expect to meet the duergar army. I understand you're familiar with the region, as well as the composition and tactics of the duergar force."

Nimor straightened his cuirass and nodded earnestly.

"Certainly," he said. "I know them well."

❦ ❦ ❦

Halisstra was roused from her dreams by the sound of her cell door opening. She glanced up, wondering if perhaps the time had come when the surface folk would simply put her to the blade.

"I have no more to say to your lord," she said, though the thought crossed her mind that selling out her comrades was preferable to death by torture, especially if she could gain her freedom in the exchange.

"Fine," a woman's voice replied. "I hope then that you will consent to speak with me."

A slender figure slipped through the open door, which was closed and locked behind her. Veiled in a long, dark cloak, the visitor paused to study Halisstra then she reached up with hands as black as coal and slipped back her hood to reveal a face of gleaming ebony, and eyes as red as blood.

"I am Seyll Auzkovyn," the drow said, "and I have come to give you my lady's message: 'A rightful place awaits you in the Realms

Above, in the Land of the Great Light. Come in peace and live beneath the sun again, where trees and flowers grow.' "

"A priestess of Eilistraee," Halisstra murmured. She had heard of the cult before, of course. The Spider Queen held nothing but scorn for the weak, idealistic faith of the Dark Maiden, whose worshipers dreamed of redemption and acceptance in the World Above. "Well, I did come in peace, and I do seem to have found my rightful place in this tidy little cell. I expect wonderful flowers bloom just beyond the bars of my window, and I am more than a little thankful that the thrice-cursed sun shines no deeper into my prison." She laughed bitterly. "Somehow the holy message of your silly little dancing goddess rings a little false today. Now go away, and let me get back to the important business of preparing myself for the inevitable tortures that await me when the so-called lord of this fetid dungheap of a village loses his patience with my intransigent ways."

"You sound like me, when I first heard Eilistraee's message," Seyll replied. She moved closer and sat on the floor beside Halisstra. "Like yourself, I was a priestess of the Spider Queen who found herself a captive of the surface folk. Though I've lived here for several years now, I still find the light of the sun overly harsh."

"Don't flatter yourself, apostate," snarled Halisstra. "I'm nothing like you."

"You might be surprised," Seyll continued calmly, her placid demeanor unchanged. "Have the Spider Queen's punishments ever struck you as needless or wasteful? Have you ever failed to nurture a friendship because you feared betrayal? Have you ever, perhaps, watched a child of your own body, your own heart, destroyed because she failed at a senseless test, only to tell yourself that she was too weak to live? Did you ever wonder if there was a point to the deliberate and calculated cruelty that poisons our entire race?"

"Of course there's a point," Halisstra replied. "We're surrounded on all sides by vicious enemies. If we didn't take steps to hone our people to their finest edge, we would become slaves—no, worse yet, we would become *rothé*."

"And have Lolth's judgments in fact made you stronger?"

"Of course."

"Prove it, then. Offer an example." Seyll watched her, then leaned forward and said, "You remember countless tests and battles, naturally, but you can't prove that you were made stronger by them. You don't know what might have happened if you hadn't been subjected to those tortures."

"Simple semantics. Naturally I can't prove that things are other than they are."

Halisstra glared at the heretic, profoundly annoyed. She would have found the conversation irritating and irrelevant under the best of circumstances, but with her hands and feet chained together, slumped against the cold, hard wall of a stone cell with a painful shaft of sunlight slanting in, it was positively infuriating. Still, she had very little to occupy her mind otherwise, and there was a small chance that a display of enthusiasm for Seyll's faith might win her a parole of sorts. Lolth was completely intolerant of apostates, but to feign acceptance of another faith in order to win the freedom to betray the trust of one's captors . . . that was the sort of cleverness the Spider Queen admired. The trick, of course, was not to appear too eager, yet just uncertain enough that Seyll and her friends might come to hope for a true change in Halisstra's heart.

"You are annoying me," she said to Seyll. "Leave me alone."

"As you wish," Seyll said. She stood gracefully, and offered Halisstra a smile. "Consider what I've said, and ask yourself if there might be some truth to it. If your faith in Lolth is as strong as you think, surely it can withstand a little examination. May Eilistraee bless you and warm your heart."

She pulled her hood back over her head, and silently withdrew. Halisstra turned her own face away so Seyll couldn't see the cruel smile that twisted her features.

🕷 🕷 🕷

Rear guard, mused Ryld, seems to be the spot Quenthel saves for the person she deems least useful at the moment.

He paused to listen to the forest around him, seeking for any sound that might indicate an approaching enemy. He heard nothing but the steady patter of cold rain. Pharaun's fire-spiders had managed to set a smoky blaze in the woods behind them, but the rain had likely prevented the fires from burning too much of the forest. The weapons master glanced up into the sky, allowing the cold drops to splash on his face and noting the sullen silver glow behind the clouds.

At least the rain is washing out our trail, he thought.

After a hard march the previous night and lying low in a thick tangle of brush through a long, sunny day, they had resumed their hike in the evening only to meet a deluge soon after setting out. The forest floor was nothing but mud and slush.

Taking a moment to adjust his hood, Ryld set out again, trying hard not to hurry his steps too much. He would not be much of a rear guard if he closed up right behind the others, but on the other hand, the last thing he wanted to do was fall so far behind that he missed an innocent turn of the trail and wandered off alone into the endless woods. If Halisstra wasn't worth going back for, he was under no delusions as to what would happen if he managed to become separated from the rest of the company. He tramped on for quite some time, pausing every few dozen yards to listen and scan the forest.

Soon he became aware of the louder, more insistent sound of water in motion—a swift forest stream, dark and wide, that sluiced through muddy banks covered in thorns and bracken. A large log had been felled to cross the stream, its upper surface sawn flat to form a reasonably secure bridge. Quenthel and the others waited there, silently watching their surroundings. Ryld noted the crossbows pointed in his direction, and the acute attentiveness of his companions. Clearly the running battle with the surface folk had taught his comrades to be wary of the woods.

"Hold your fire," he called softly. "It's Ryld."

"Master Argith," Quenthel said. "I was beginning to wonder if you'd lost the trail."

Ryld bowed to Quenthel and joined the others. He took a moment to sit on the stump of the log, fishing in the pockets of his cloak for a small flask of duergar brandy. Normally he wouldn't risk diluting his senses with alcohol, but hours of marching in cold rain had soaked his clothing and left him chilled to the bone. The liquor brought a hot glow to the middle of his body with one good mouthful.

"Is this your stream?" he asked Pharaun.

"Yes," the wizard said without hesitation. "Here, we cross and turn to the south, following the river upstream. House Jaelre is not more than a couple of miles away."

He pointed at Ryld with one finger and muttered a magical syllable. The flask rose up from the weapons master's hand and bobbed through the air to the wizard, who promptly helped himself to a healthy swallow.

"My thanks," said Pharaun. "The gray dwarves may be odious churls, but they distill a good brandy."

"Don't drink too much," Quenthel said. "The Jaelre are as likely to shoot us as look at us. I need you alert and sharp-witted, wizard. Master Argith, keep up close with the rest of us from this point on. I'm more worried about what lies before us now than behind."

"As you wish, Mistress," Ryld said.

He held out his hand to Pharaun, who took one more small swallow and tossed the flask back to Ryld. The weapons master stood, shouldered his pack, and led the way across the bridge. The surface of the log was slick and uneven, and doubtless would have been trouble for a clumsy dwarf or awkward human, but the dark elves negotiated the crossing with ease.

On the other side, they found the overgrown remnants of an old stone road, cracked and broken by the twisting roots of countless trees and hundreds of years of frosts and thaws. Smooth white stone, expertly joined, marked it as the work of the ancient surface elves who once inhabited the forest. Ryld was not so poorly educated that he had not heard of Cormanthor, the great forest empire of the surface elves, or the fallen glory of its legendary capital city of Myth Drannor. Other than the names, though, he knew very little of who the builders of the forest empire had been and what had befallen them.

Moving slowly and carefully, the company advanced in an open skirmish line, prepared to defend themselves against any attack. They followed the old road for more than a mile, just as Pharaun had said they would, and they came upon the wreckage of old walls and battlements ringing some ancient stronghold. Green vines wreathed the walls, thriving despite the winter season, but the wall was cracked and holed in a dozen places. A rusted iron gate lay across the road where it pierced the walls, a barrier that had long since fallen into uselessness. Beyond the walls, a small stony tor rose from the forest floor, crowned by a large pentagonal keep of white stone. At first Ryld thought the place was whole and intact, but as he studied it, he realized that the tower-tops were holed and that more than one of the flying buttresses linking the outlying towers to the main body of the keep had collapsed with the years. Green vines knotted their roots in the riven stone, covering the ruins in a living blanket.

"Ruins," Jeggred growled in disgust. "Your insipid spells have failed you, wizard—or you have deliberately led us astray. Are you in league with our treacherous scout, perhaps?"

"My spells do not fail," Pharaun replied. "This is the place. The Jaelre are here."

"Then where are they?" the draegloth snarled. "If you—"

"Silence, both of you!" Valas snapped. He moved a few steps away from the gate, his footfalls as soft as those of a stalking leopard, an arrow lying across his bow. "This place is not as abandoned as it looks."

Ryld moved over to take shelter by a tottering old column of masonry, setting one hand on Splitter's hilt. Danifae and Pharaun did the same on the other side of the road, staring hard at the ruined keep. Quenthel, however, chose not to move at all.

Instead she stood confidently in the center of the path and called out, "You of House Jaelre! We wish to speak with your leaders at once!"

From a dozen places of concealment, stealthy shapes in dark cloaks that deceived the eye by mimicking the wearer's surroundings slowly stood, bows and wands pointed at the Menzoberranyr. One of the figures, a female carrying a double-ended sword, pushed back her hood and eyed the company with cold contempt.

"You are miserable spider-kissers," she hissed. "What do you have that the lords of House Jaelre could possibly want, other than your corpses feathered with our arrows?"

Quenthel bridled and allowed one hand to fall to her whip. The weapon writhed slowly, the serpent heads snapping their fangs in agitation.

"I am Quenthel Baenre, Mistress of Arach-Tinilith, and I do not bicker on doorsteps with common gate guards. Announce our arrival to your masters, so that we can get in out of this damnable rain."

The Jaelre captain narrowed her eyes and motioned to her soldiers, who shifted position and made ready to fire. Valas shook his head and lowered his bow, stepping forward quickly with one hand in the air.

"Wait," he said. "If Tzirik the priest is still among you, tell him that Valas Hune is here. We have a proposition for him."

"I doubt our high priest will have much use for any proposal of yours," the guard captain said.

"If nothing else, he'll find out why we came a thousand miles from Menzoberranzan to speak to him," Valas replied.

The captain glared at Quenthel, then said, "Lower your weapons and wait there. Do not move, or my soldiers will fire, and there are more of us than you think."

Valas nodded once, and set his bow down on the ground. He glanced at the others, and took a seat on the edge of a crumbling old fountain. The rest followed suit, though Quenthel didn't demean herself by taking a seat. Instead she folded her arms and waited with imperious displeasure. Ryld glanced around the courtyard full of hostile warriors, and rubbed his head with a sigh.

Quenthel knows how to make an impression, eh? Pharaun gestured discretely.

Females, Ryld replied, just as discretely.

He carefully reached into his cloak and withdrew the brandy flask again.

C h a p t e r

F O U R T E E N

The most doleful torment of incarceration, reflected Halisstra, was boredom, pure and simple. Like most of her extraordinarily long-lived kind, the priestess hardly noticed the passing of hours, days, even tendays when her mind was engaged. Yet, despite the wisdom and patience of her more than two hundred years, a few hours' confinement in a featureless stone cell seemed more onerous than months of the harsh discipline she endured in her youth.

The endless hours of the day crept by, a day in which her body longed to rest despite the painful glare of sunlight streaming in through that one cursed window. Meanwhile her thoughts veered wildly from praying for her comrades to return and rescue her to fomenting the most hideous and agonizing tortures she could imagine for each one for abandoning her to capture.

Eventually, she fell into Reverie, her mind empty of new schemes or old memories, and her awareness so dim and distant that she might have been sleeping in truth. Exhaustion had finally caught up with her, not just the sheer physical exhaustion of the long tendays of travel and peril through desert, shadow, Underdark, and forest, but a kind of mental fatigue rooted deeply in the grief she still carried for the loss of the House she was to one day rule. Halisstra might not have permitted herself to shed a tear for Ched Nasad, but the malignant truth of her plight had an odd way of surfacing in her thoughts, poisoning them with a cold, hopeless disbelief that was difficult to set aside. Long hours of imprisonment offered her the opportunity to exhume the hateful situation in its entirety and contemplate her loss of station, wealth, and security until her horrible fascination was in some way sated.

At dusk the guards brought her fresh food, a bowl of some bland but nourishing stew and another half loaf of bread. Halisstra found herself ravenously hungry, and she devoured the meal with little thought to the possibility of poison or drugs. Soon after she'd finished, the door to her cell was unlocked with a rusty scraping of iron, and Seyll Auzkovyn slipped inside again.

The priestess had shed her long, heavy cloak, and wore an elegant lady's riding outfit, an embroidered green jacket and knee-length skirt over a blouse of cream and high boots that matched the jacket. The sight of a drow priestess dressed as a noble surface elf struck Halisstra as jarringly incongruous.

"Did the surface lord dress you like that?" she sneered at the Eilistraee worshiper. "You seem almost a perfectly helpless gentlelady of the accursed sun elves in that outfit."

"How else should I dress?" Seyll replied. "I'm among friends here, and need not wear armor. Besides, I found that the skull and spider motifs of my previous wardrobe seemed to alarm the surface folk." She made a small gesture to the jailers outside, and the door was closed behind her. "Anyway," she added, "there are no sun elves here."

"They're all the same to me," Halisstra said.

"When you know them better, you'll be able to tell their kindred easily enough."

"I have no wish to know them better."

"Are you so certain of that? There is always advantage in knowing one's enemies . . . especially if they need not be your enemies."

Seyll knelt easily on the floor beside Halisstra and composed herself. She was young, not much more than a hundred, and pretty enough in her own way, but her carriage was . . . wrong. Her eyes lacked the hungering ambition or the cold appraisal Halisstra was accustomed to seeing mirrored in the faces around her. One could easily mistake Seyll's patient expression for a sort of submissiveness, the lack of the will necessary to achieve, and yet there was a calm assurance about her that hinted at strength held in check.

Halisstra's eyes fell to Seyll's hands, as the priestess smoothed her garments. They were strong, and callused like a weapons master's.

"I had the opportunity to examine the heraldry of your arms today, and study the devices. Melarn is a leading House of the city of Ched Nasad, is it not?"

"It was," Halisstra said.

She instantly regretted the slip. If the surface folk didn't know of Ched Nasad's fate, then she hardly needed to provide them with a gift of information. She had to set a price on anything she revealed.

"You were defeated in a House war?"

It was a reasonable guess on Seyll's part, as most drow Houses that vanished, lost status, or otherwise fell low usually did so because of the actions of other Houses.

"Not quite."

Seyll waited a long moment for Halisstra to elaborate, and when she did not, the Eilistraee priestess shifted tactics.

"Ched Nasad is a long way from Cormanthor. At least six or seven hundred miles, with the great desert of Anauroch and the phaerimm-haunted Buried Realms between here and there. Lord Dessaer is curious about the circumstances that would bring a high-ranking daughter of a powerful House of Ched Nasad into the lands of his people. To be honest, I am curious too."

"So this is to be the method of interrogation, then?" Halisstra said. "A sympathetic ear to garner the answers to questions asked in seeming friendship?"

"Some account of your purpose in Cormanthor must be made before Lord Dessaer will release you into my parole. If your business is as innocent as you say, you need not be imprisoned here."

"Release me?" Halisstra laughed long and quietly. "Ah, I see you have not lost your penchant for cruelty despite your apostasy, Auzkovyn. Did your surface friends ask you to play on a prisoner's hopes by offering freedom in exchange for cooperation, or did you suggest the tactic? Did you really think a single day in this accursed cell would reduce me to desperately grasping at phantom hopes?"

"The hopes I offer are not phantoms," Seyll said. "Tell us what you're doing here, show us that you're no enemy of the peaceful folk of Cormanthor, and you will have your liberty."

"You can't expect me to believe that."

"I am here, am I not?" Seyll answered. "Clearly some of our kind learn to live in peace with the surface folk."

"Of course you have nothing to fear among the surface folk," Halisstra retorted. "Your vapid, dancing goddess is too weak to threaten them."

"As I told you before, I was a priestess of Lolth when I was captured," Seyll said. She formed her hands into a gesture of supplication, a ceremonial pose Halisstra knew well. In the tongue of the abyssal planes where Lolth dwelt, Seyll mouthed the words of a high and secret prayer: " 'Great Goddess, Mother of the Dark, grant me the blood of my enemies for drink and their living hearts for meat. Grant me the screams of their young for song, grant me the helplessness of their males for my satiation, grant me the wealth of their houses for my bed. By this unworthy sacrifice I honor you, Queen of Spiders, and beseech of you the strength to destroy my foes.' "

The infernal words seemed to crackle with dark power, each harsh syllable charged with an evil potency that spread through the cell like a slick of poison. Seyll made a drawing motion of her hand, showing the manner in which the knife was to be wielded, and settled back on her heels.

Shifting back to Elvish, she closed her eyes and said, "Many hapless souls died beneath my knife, yet I found redemption and peace here. Whether the same awaits you is a question I cannot answer, but I offer myself as proof that you can walk these lands in peace if you wish."

Halisstra stared at Seyll, almost as if seeing her for the first time. She had been about to condemn the priestess once more as a weak failure, a traitor to the one true drow goddess, but the words died on her lips. No one but a priestess of high station would have been taught that rite, yet Seyll had decided to turn her back on Lolth. Not only that, but she still lived, and seemed to have found some amount of contentment in her decision. Halisstra had of course been indoctrinated over years of training to regard heresy, apostasy, as the vilest sort of crime imaginable. Yet in her years of sacrifice and abasement before the Spider Queen's altar she had never before encountered a true apostate. Oh, she'd slandered some of her rivals with false accusations of turning away from the Spider Queen, but actually sitting in the presence of someone who had committed the ultimate betrayal of the goddess, and—so far, at least—lived to tell the tale. . . .

"I want to challenge you to do something," Seyll said. "I believe you have the intelligence and the imagination for it, but we shall see. Imagine, for a moment, that you could live in a place where you can walk the streets without fearing an assassin's dagger in your back. Imagine that your friends—*real* friends—want nothing more from you than the pleasure of your company, that your sisters cherish your accomplishments instead of resenting your successes, and your children are not murdered for an accidental failing. Imagine that your lovers seek you out for who you are, and not your station or influence. Imagine that your goddess asks you to celebrate her with your joy, not your terror."

"There is no such—"

"You answer too quickly. I asked you to imagine it, if you can," Seyll said. She stood and moved away, turning her back on Halisstra. "I will wait."

"I can't imagine such nonsense. It's an empty fantasy, signifying nothing. We're not meant for such things; no one is, not dark elf, not light-elf, not even the insipid humans. Only a fool dwells on dreams."

"Yet, for the sake of argument at least, would it not seem a pleasant thing?" Seyll said over her shoulder. "You must entertain impossible dreams all the time. All thinking creatures do. Perhaps you've dreamed of having your enemies in your power, or of a lover you couldn't take, or of rising to the station you truly merit."

Halisstra snorted, truly irritated, and shook her hands in her manacles.

"If you can imagine the destruction of all your enemies at once," Seyll pressed, "you can certainly imagine the faithfulness of a friend or a goddess pleased by your loyalty, not your sacrifice."

"All gods demand sacrifice. You delude yourself if you think Eilistraee is any different. Perhaps you're simply too weak-minded to understand your bonds." Halisstra looked away and added, "You have succeeded in boring me again. You may leave now."

The priestess walked to the door. She rapped once on the rusty iron and waited, turning back to face Halisstra.

"What if I show you that you're wrong?" she said softly. "Tomorrow night we dance in the forest for Eilistraee's delight. I will bring you there, and you will see for yourself what our goddess demands of us."

"I will have no part of it," Halisstra snapped, finally irritated enough to forget her resolve to feign a grudging conversion to the surface dwellers' vapid beliefs.

"Your faith in your Spider Queen is so weak you can't bear to watch us dance?" Seyll asked. "Listen, watch, and judge for yourself. That's all I ask."

⚘ ⚘ ⚘

The endless black gale that shrieked up through the vertical streets of ruined Chaulssin welcomed Nimor's return with a barrage of gusts so powerful that even he was momentarily rocked on his feet. His white hair whipping around his head like a wild halo, the Anointed Blade paused a moment in his steps to allow the blast to die away.

He could not remain long in the City of Wyrmshadows, not while Menzoberranzan's army marched and the Agrach Dyrr contingent tramped along without him, but he wasn't in such a hurry that he couldn't tarry a moment in the hidden citadel of his secret House. Nimor Imphraezl was a prince of Chaulssin, after all, and the magnificent ruin, the hell-carved citadel, was his domain. He had not been born there, of course, nor had he spent his childhood years in the shadow-haunted city. The place was too perilous for the young, so the Jaezred Chaulssin fostered their princes in a dozen minor Houses in as many cities throughout the Underdark. From the time he reached adulthood and came into his ancient birthright, though, Nimor had regarded the windswept ruin as his own palace.

The gust passed, at least as much as any blast of wind ever did in the black chasm yawning around the city, and the assassin continued on his way. Menzoberranzan was little more than an hour distant through the Plane of Shadow, and so it was fairly easy for Nimor to manufacture an excuse to absent himself from the marching column to tend to some "personal matters." Even if Andzrel Baenre summoned the House captains to a sudden council of war during Nimor's absence, he took little risk in leaving for a short time. The army moved quickly, as armies go, but no one would find it overly suspicious for a noble to tarry in the city for a short time before riding out to catch up to the column.

He reached the great, spiraling stair cut through the heart of Chaulssin's stone mountain and ascended quickly, taking the steps two at a time. In the great hall at the top, he found the patron fathers assembled again, clustered together in twos and threes as they traded news and fomented plots to advance the House during their time of remarkable opportunity. Grandfather Mauzzkyl turned to level his fearsome glare upon Nimor as the assassin entered.

"Once again you keep us waiting," he said.

"I beg your forgiveness, Revered Grandfather," Nimor replied. He drew up into the circle with the others and made a small bow. The winds outside the chamber moaned eerily in the distance. "I was summoned to a council of war that I did not think it wise to miss."

"One might say the same of this gathering," observed Patron Father Tomphael.

Nimor forced a smile and replied, "I have been working for some time to cultivate a particular identity and level of responsibility among Menzoberranzan's defenders, Tomphael. That sort of effort is not to be lightly thrown aside. Until the revered grandfather instructs me otherwise, I will keep you waiting when it is necessary to protect our plots against the Spider Queen's favored—"

"Enough, Nimor," Mauzzkyl rumbled. "How do things proceed in Menzoberranzan?"

"Very well, Revered Grandfather. Crown Prince Horgar Steelshadow of Gracklstugh marches an army of nearly five thousand duergar on Menzoberranzan. The matron mothers have decided to meet the duergar in the field instead of awaiting a siege, since they fear the belligerence of other Underdark realms. I have, however, arranged for the crown prince's army to steal a march on the Menzoberranyr, and I also have command of a contingent of troops who can be turned at the right moment to help assure the outcome we desire. Finally, I have convinced the cambion warlord Kaanyr Vhok to bring his army of tanarukks against Menzoberranzan as well, though I am less certain of the Scoured Legion. Vhok may or may not show, and if he does, he has little allegiance to our cause."

"You intend to destroy the forces of Menzoberranzan in detail, then," Patron Xorthaul observed. The black-armored priest stroked his chin. "What if the Menzoberranyr prove more resilient than you expect, and defeat the duergar instead? Or Kaanyr Vhok proves unfaithful? It might have been better to lure a smaller force into your trap, Anointed Blade. Your first play is too risky."

"If I had presented the duergar as less of a threat, the matron mothers would have been sorely tempted to ignore them altogether. As matters stand, one of three results may come of the battle between Gracklstugh and Menzoberranzan. The duergar might win, it could be in effect a draw, or the drow could prevail. We're doing what we can to deliver Menzoberranzan's army into the crown prince's hands, but even if he fails to destroy the Lolthites outright, there is an excellent chance the duergar will badly maul the Menzoberranyr—in which case, the duergar may weaken our enemies so badly we can overthrow them ourselves. At the worst, if Gracklstugh is routed, well . . . other than the failure of our plan, we lose little."

"Remember, Patron Xorthaul, our strategy against Menzoberranzan is a strategy of attrition," Mauzzkyl said. "The city is too strong to take in one stroke, so we must bleed it to death with a dozen cuts."

"Menzoberranzan's wizards will certainly divine the existence of such a great army so close to their city," Patron Tomphael, himself a wizard, observed. "The matron mothers will recall their force, or reverse your ambush on the duergar instead."

"Our allies in Agrach Dyrr have helped us with this," said Nimor. "Gromph Baenre has vanished. The Masters of Sorcere are quite naturally testing each other's resolve and resources to determine who shall be the next archmage."

"There are many powerful wizards serving the city's Houses, Nimor," Tomphael replied. "They will not be distracted by an opportunity at Sorcere."

Nimor permitted himself a rueful nod and said, "True, but as we well know, House wizards tend to spend a lot of their time spying out the weaknesses of other Houses. So far, no one seems to have come forward to dispute the version of events I advanced to the Council."

"It would be no more than the better part of wisdom to set your plans with the assumption that your plots will be unmasked at the most inconvenient time possible," Patron Xorthaul said. "What will you do if some raw apprentice in some second-rate House happens to scry the approach of the crown prince's army, and the matron mothers recall theirs? They might stand a siege forever."

"Now you understand," Nimor said patiently, "why I went so far as to approach Agrach Dyrr with an open offer of alliance, and decided to risk bringing Kaanyr Vhok into the equation. We need the Fifth House against that very possibility, to admit Horgar's army—or the Scoured Legion—into the city, if it comes to that."

Mauzzkyl folded his arms and lowered his fiery gaze.

"In either case, we shall have them," the revered grandfather said, a smile of dark satisfaction twisting his features. "If Kaanyr Vhok betrays you, you still have Agrach Dyrr. If Agrach Dyrr betrays you, you have the cambion. I presume that Dyrr and Vhok know nothing of each other?"

Nimor said, "I thought it best to reserve at least one surprise against each of my ostensible allies, Revered Grandfather. It seemed wise to me to make certain that I would have as many options as possible, for as long as possible, in developing the attack on the city."

"Excellent. What assistance might we provide you?"

The Anointed Blade considered the question. He was sorely tempted to say none at all, and claim all the glory of the victory to come, but the time was coming when his ability to move from place to place would be limited by the role he played at the head of Menzoberranzan's army, and he needed help in handling Kaanyr Vhok. Besides, if the Sceptered One proved unfaithful, he could blame whomever had been sent to the warlord.

"We should gather our strength and be ready to strike when our allies play their part in reducing Menzoberranzan's defenses," he said.

"We do not have any great force at arms, Anointed Blade," Mauzzkyl said. "I will not commit the Jaezred Chaulssin to a pitched battle."

"I understand, Revered Grandfather." If they gathered all their strength in one place, the secret House would hardly amount to the numbers of a single minor House of Menzoberranzan—though the Jaezred Chaulssin could have an impact out of all proportion to their numbers. "I need one of my brothers to go to Kaanyr Vhok's Scoured Legion and steer the warlord in the right direction. My responsibilities in Menzoberranzan's army and my efforts to guide Horgar Steelshadow and the renegade Agrach Dyrr do not permit me sufficient time to look after Kaanyr Vhok as well as I would like."

Mauzzkyl nodded and said, "Very well. Zammzt, there is nothing left for you to do at Ched Nasad. I want you to go to Kaanyr Vhok and serve as our voice in his camp. Do whatever you must in order to keep his army aligned against Menzoberranzan, but you will answer to Nimor."

The plain-faced assassin replied, "Of course, Revered Grandfather."

He glanced over at Nimor, but did not allow his thoughts to show on his face.

"I approached the warlord through his consort, Aliisza," Nimor told Zammzt. "She is an alu-fiend and a sorceress of no small skill. She knows that I represent a society or order of some kind, so she should not be surprised to receive another of us."

Though I doubt she'll extend you the same welcome she gave to me, he told himself.

"When do you expect the Menzoberranyr to first encounter Horgar's army?" Mauzzkyl asked.

"Four days, I think."

"Do what you can to sow dissent and uncertainty, Anointed Blade," Mauzzkyl said. "The time for subterfuge and stealth is ending. The Jaezred Chaulssin leave the shadows and take the field. Destroy the matron mothers' army and bring your duergar allies to Menzoberranzan as quickly as possible. We will meet you there, and we will see if the Masked Lord favors us our not."

Nimor bowed again, then turned and strode away from the assembled patron fathers. Something would go amiss in his plan—something had to. One could not create such an elaborate collision of so many disparate forces without some of the components falling by the wayside. As best he could tell, though, the Jaezred Chaulssin were prepared. The longer he could keep secret the deadly maneuverings of his allies and his House, the better his chances for success.

Perhaps I will encourage Andzrel to appoint me chief of the expedition's scouts, Nimor thought. No need to trouble the Baenre with irrelevant reports of armies on the move, after all.

The dark elves of House Jaelre proved to be suspicious and ungracious hosts. Ryld had expected to be shown into an audience room of some kind, where they would meet a clan matriarch and bribe, threaten, or persuade her into allowing them to consult with the priest Tzirik. However, nothing like that occurred. Since they refused to surrender their weapons, the Jaelre drow ushered the company into a small, disused guardroom that had once warded the ruined castle's main gate.

"You will wait here until Tzirik chooses to receive you," the female commanding the watch told them. "If you attempt to leave this room, we will take that as a sign of hostile intent and fall on you at once."

"We are a high embassy from a powerful city," Quenthel said in response. "You mistreat us at your peril."

"You are slaves of the Spider Queen, and most likely spies and saboteurs," the captain replied. "Lolth holds no sway here, spider-kissing bitch."

She closed and locked the iron door before Quenthel could summon a suitable retort, though the fierce agitation of her snake-headed whip certainly hinted at the depths of her anger.

"Do we intend to remain confined here, like rabble locked up in a debtors' gaol?" Jeggred snarled. "I have half a mind to—"

"Not yet, Jeggred," Quenthel countered.

She paced back and forth angrily, her mouth working in silent fury. Pure ire fueled Quenthel with relentless energy. Confinement in a small room with her pent-up anger would be difficult for all of them.

Danifae watched her, then restrained Quenthel's agitated pacing with a gentle hand on the Baenre's arm.

"What is it, slave?" the priestess snapped.

"Your zeal is admirable, Mistress," Danifae said, "but, please, we must be patient now." She shielded her hands as best she could and added, *Remember, we may be watched.*

"She has a point, dear Quenthel," Pharaun said. "You don't want to start a fight against the very people we came to see. Your

245

hard words and proud manner play better at Arach-Tinilith than on another god's doorstep."

Quenthel turned a look of such icy hatred on the wizard that Danifae put up a hand to steady her. Danifae herself shot Pharaun a venomous look, contempt twisting her beautiful features.

"Silence, Pharaun," the battle captive snapped. "Your smug arrogance and endless baiting play better at Sorcere. At least the Mistress has the strength of her convictions—all you have is cynicism."

Danifae studied Quenthel's face and offered her a shy smile.

"Save your anger for later, Mistress," the battle captive said softly. "Surely the goddess will be more pleased if you exact an accounting of the faithless after you've wrung the usefulness from them than if you destroy the tools required to serve her."

Quenthel allowed herself to relax. She drew a deep breath, and took a seat at a barren wood table on which a flagon of water stood.

"Fine, then," Quenthel breathed. "We will see what happens."

That, Ryld guessed, was about as close as Quenthel would ever come to admitting that she had been wrong about something. With little else to do, the company settled down to endure whatever wait the Jaelre chose to test them with.

Long hours passed. The night faded into an overcast morning, which then gave way to a gray, rain-soaked afternoon.

Studying what portions of the old castle he could see from the slitlike windows, Ryld came to the conclusion that Minauthkeep was not half so ruined as it first appeared. The Jaelre had cleverly repaired much of the ancient structure while leaving the outward appearance mostly unchanged.

Eventually, as the wait grew interminable, the weapons master settled back against the wall of the chamber and allowed himself to drift off into a light trance, Splitter bared across his lap in case he needed it quickly.

He was roused from Reverie near nightfall, when the iron door of the chamber abruptly boomed with three forceful knocks. The lock turned, and the watch captain of the previous night entered, with several more Jaelre guards behind her.

"You are summoned before High Priest Tzirik," she said. "You are to disarm yourselves here. The wizard must consent to have his thumbs bound together, and the draegloth will be manacled."

"I will not," Jeggred snapped. "We're not your prisoners, to be dragged before your master in chains. Why should we do for you what you lack the strength to make us do?"

"You came to us, half-breed," the captain said.

"Mistress?" Danifae whispered.

Without taking her eyes from the captain's face, Quenthel drew out her whip. Weighing it in one hand, she seemed to struggle with herself, then she tossed it to the corner of the chamber.

"Yngoth, watch over our arms," she said to one of the hissing vipers. "Strike dead any who would tamper with our belongings in our absence. Jeggred, you will permit yourself to be bound. Pharaun, you as well."

Ryld sighed and set Splitter on the floor, kicking the blade to within striking distance of Quenthel's vipers. Valas discarded his kukris as well. With a grimace of distaste, Pharaun stepped up and held out his hands. A Jaelre drow tied his thumbs together with stout cord, a measure that would make it very difficult for the mage to make the complex gestures and passes needed for many of his spells. Jeggred's large upper arms, the long ones with the wicked claws, were chained together, but his smaller humanoid arms were left free.

The draegloth rumbled.

"Be still, nephew," Quenthel said, then she turned to the Jaelre captain. "Take us to the priest."

The watch captain nodded to her soldiers, who formed up in a tight phalanx around the Menzoberranyr, swords drawn. They marched the company out of the guardroom and into the depths of the keep. The company was shown into a large hall or gallery appointed as a shrine to Vhaeraun, the Masked Lord. Ryld studied the temple with some interest. He'd never set foot in a place dedicated to any deity but Lolth. At the upper end of the hall, across from the entrance, a great half-mask the size of a tower shield hung from the wall, overlooking the shrine. The symbol was made of beaten copper, with two black disks to mark the eyes.

Two males waited for them. The first was young, dressed in black leather armor that showed off a well-muscled chest. A curved kukri was thrust through his belt, and a small green asp was coiled around his arm. His left leg was encased in an awkward harness of iron and leather, and he moved stiffly. The second was unusually short and stocky, with brawny shoulders and a bald pate, dressed in a breastplate of black mithral and masked with a ceremonial veil of black silk.

"The visitors, my lords," the watch captain said.

The veiled priest studied them. His expression was virtually unreadable behind the veil.

"Valas Hune, as I live and breathe," he said at last. "Well, this is a surprise. I haven't seen you in more than fifty years." He hesitated a moment longer, then strode forward boldly and clapped the Bregan D'aerthe scout on the shoulders. "It has been too long, old friend. How are things with you?"

"Tzirik," Valas said. He smiled back, his dour face stretching with unaccustomed enjoyment, and he took the priest's hand in a firm grip. He glanced around the chamber. "I see you have finally achieved the Return you were always talking about. As far as how things go with me, well, that will take some explaining."

Tzirik studied the company carefully.

"A Master of Sorcere," the priest said, "and another of Melee-Magthere."

"Master Pharaun Mizzrym, an accomplished wizard," Valas replied, "and Master Ryld Argith, a weapons master of no small skill."

"Gentlemen, if Valas vouches for you, you are welcome guests in Minauthkeep," the priest said. When he looked at the others, his face hardened, geniality fading into sharp appraisal.

"The draegloth is Jeggred," Valas said, "a scion of House Baenre. The lesser priestess is Danifae Yauntyrr, a highborn lady of Eryndlyn, late a battle captive. The leader of our company is—"

"High Priestess Quenthel Baenre," Quenthel interrupted, "Mistress of Arach-Tinilith, Mistress of the Academy, Mistress of Tier-Breche, First Sister of House Baenre of Menzoberranzan."

"Ah," Tzirik said. "We rarely have dealings with those of your persuasion, let alone a priestess possessed of so many impressive titles."

"You will find me possessed of more than titles, priest," Quenthel replied.

Tzirik's face went cold.

"Lolth may rule in your buried cities," he said, "but here in the night of the surface world, Vhaeraun is the master." He turned and gestured to the crippled male behind him. "In the interest of common courtesy, may I present my cousin, Jezz of House Jaelre."

The younger male limped forward.

"You are a long way from home, Menzoberranyr," he said in a rasping voice. "That, more than anything, spared you. The spider-kissers we feud with come up from Maerimydra, a few miles south of here, but we have not met folk from Menzoberranzan in quite some time."

He laughed softly, finding humor in some private joke. Tzirik smiled as well, but the smile did not reach his eyes.

"Jezz refers to the ironic fact that we are Menzoberranyr ourselves, or at least were, once upon a time. Almost five hundred years ago the wise and beneficent Matron Baenre ordered our House destroyed for the twin perversions of being governed by males and following the Masked Lord. Many of my kin died screaming in the dungeons of Castle Baenre. Of those who escaped, many more died in the long, hard years of exile in the lonely places of the Underdark. You must understand how ironic it is for a Baenre daughter to place herself in our power. If nothing else comes of whatever business you bring before me, Valas, you will have my gratitude for this." He moved closer and folded his powerful arms. "So, why do you seek me, Baenre?"

Quenthel kept her face impassive.

"We need you to commune with Vhaeraun," she said, "and ask your god a few questions on our behalf. We are willing to pay and pay well for your trouble."

Tzirik's eyebrows rose.

"Really? And why would Vhaeraun want me to do this for you?"

"You will, of course, discover what it is that brings us here, and what your god knows of it."

"I could torture you for a few years and discover as much," the priest said. "Or, for that matter, having agreed to ask the Masked Lord your questions, I might not see fit to share the answers."

"True, perhaps," Quenthel said, "though I think you might find that we are far from helpless, even with our weapons back in our chambers. Before we make a trial of that, let us see if we can reach an agreement of sorts."

"She's bluffing," Jezz remarked. "Why deal with these venomous creatures? Spare your friend if you like, but slay the priestesses at once."

"Patience, young Jezz. There is always time for that later," Tzirik said. He paced away, then looked back to Quenthel. "What is it you wish to learn?"

Quenthel squared her shoulders and met the priest's gaze evenly.

"We wish to know what has become of Lolth," she said. "The goddess refuses us our spells, and has done so for many months now. Since we do not have access to the magic she normally grants us, we have no way to ask her ourselves."

"Your fickle goddess is testing you," Tzirik said with a laugh. "She's withholding your spells simply to see how long you remain loyal."

"So we thought at first," Quenthel said, "but it has been nearly four months now, and we can only conclude that it is her will that we should seek the answer for ourselves."

"Why ask a priest of Vhaeraun?" Jezz asked. "Surely the priestesses of a neighboring city could be persuaded to intervene on your behalf."

"They have lost contact with the goddess, too," Danifae answered. "I came from Ched Nasad, where we had experienced the same silence as the priestesses of Menzoberranzan. We have reason to believe that all the drow cities throughout the Underdark are in the same situation. Lolth is speaking to no one, drow and lesser races alike."

"That would explain the retreat of Maerimydra," Jezz said quietly to Tzirik. "If their priestesses are powerless, they might be too busy with their own difficulties to cause any trouble for us."

"The facts would seem to fit," Tzirik replied. He turned his attention to Pharaun. "What of your vaunted wizards? Could they not summon up demons and devils aplenty and question them as to your goddess's mysterious silence, or use divination spells of their own?"

"We found that the infernal powers knew little more than we did," Pharaun said. "It seems as if Lolth has barred contact with the neighboring layers of the Abyss, sealing the borders of her realm against other powers." He raised his thumb-bound hands and made a small self-deprecatory gesture. "That is what I surmised from the reports of my colleagues investigating the matter, at any length. I did not do so personally, as the archmage has instructed me not to conjure such beings on pain of a particularly grotesque death."

Tzirik studied the Menzoberranyr, then paced over to consult with Jezz. The two Jaelre spoke together quietly, while the Menzoberranyr waited. Ryld surreptitiously studied the guards nearby, calculating which of them he could disarm in order to provide himself with a weapon if it came to that. He still wore his dwarven breastplate, and felt reasonably confident that he could wrest a halberd away from one of the guards before he was run through—though it might be a better move to use his belt knife to sever Pharaun's bonds as the first step in any kind of fight.

He was interrupted in his planning when Tzirik and Jezz returned to the company.

"I will intercede with Vhaeraun on your behalf," the high priest of the Jaelre said, "not least because I, too, would like to know what Lolth is up to. However, I think it is fair to expect a service for a service, and as you have approached me and not the other way around, I will seek Vhaeraun's guidance only after you have completed your task."

"Fine," grated Quenthel. "What do you wish us to do?"

"Three days west of here lie the ruins of Myth Drannor, once the capital of the old surface elf realm of Cormanthyr," Tzirik said. "During the course of our exploration of the ruins, we have come to suspect that a book containing secret and powerful lore—the Geildirion of Cimbar—is buried in the secret library of a ruined wizard's tower. We have need of the knowledge that is in the Geildirion, for it will help us to master the ancient magical wards our long-lost surface cousins raised about their realm. Unfortunately, demons, devils, and fiends of all kinds plague the city's ruins, and the tower itself is home to an unusually powerful beholder mage. We have sent two expeditions to the tower, but the beholder destroyed or drove off our scouts with ease. I have no wish to throw away the lives of more of my charges, but I would dearly like to possess that book. Since you seem to be the best Menzoberranzan has to offer, perhaps you can succeed where our warriors have so far failed. Bring me the Geildirion, and I will seek Vhaeraun's insight regarding Lolth's silence."

"Done," Quenthel replied. "Provide us a guide to this place, and we will get your book for you."

Jezz laughed softly and said, "You might not be so quick to agree, if you knew how dangerous the beholder really is. You will earn our aid, that is for certain."

FIFTEEN

At nightfall, Seyll, accompanied by a young drow woman and a pale elf maiden, came for Halisstra. The priestess of Eilistraee was armed and armored beneath her green cloak, a long sword at her hip. She wore high leather boots, and carried a bundle under one arm.

"It's raining," she said as she entered the cell, "but our senior priestesses say it will be clear later on, when the moon rises. Tonight we will go to honor our goddess."

Halisstra shifted in her chains and rose.

"I will not honor Eilistraee," she said.

"You need not participate. I am simply offering you the opportunity to observe and draw your own conclusions. You challenged me to demonstrate that my goddess is not a cruel or jealous one. I stand ready to offer proof."

"Doubtless you think to ensnare me with some beguiling enchantments," Halisstra said. "Do not think I will be duped so easily."

"No one will attempt to work any magic on you," Seyll replied.

She set down her bundle and unwrapped it. Inside was a large leather case, boots, and a cloak not unlike her own. "I have brought your lyre, in the hopes that you might honor us with a song if you feel so inclined."

"I doubt you will take much pleasure in the *bae'qeshel* songs," Halisstra said.

"We will see," the priestess said. "You've been manacled here for three days, and I'm offering you a chance to get out of your cell."

"Only to be returned here when you're done hectoring me about your goddess."

"As we discussed before, you need only offer Lord Dessaer an accounting of yourself to be free," Seyll said. She produced a set of keys and dangled them in front of Halisstra. "Xarra and Feliane are here to help me escort you safely to and from the spot of our ceremony tonight, and I'm afraid I must insist on keeping your hands bound."

Halisstra glanced at the other two women. They wore chain mail beneath their cloaks, too, and also carried swords at their hips. She had little wish to watch some meaningless drivel in Eilistraee's name, but Seyll offered her a chance to get out of her cell. At the very worst, Seyll's vigilance would not lapse, and no opportunities for escape would arise, leaving Halisstra no worse for wear. At best, Seyll and her fellow clerics might make a mistake that Halisstra could capitalize on.

In either case, she would at least have an opportunity to spy out some of the town and the surrounding forest, which might come in useful if a chance to escape came up later—and there was always the chance of that.

"Very well," she said.

Seyll unlocked Halisstra's manacles, and helped the Melarn priestess to don the winter clothing and cloak she'd brought. She knotted a strong silver cord around Halisstra's hands, and the small party left the palace dungeons and ascended into a cold, rain-spattered night.

Elventree was not really a town, nor an outpost, nor an encampment, but something in between. Ruined walls of white stone crisscrossed the place, hinting at the old ramparts and broad squares of a good-sized surface town, but most were crumbling with age. Many of the original buildings were nothing more than empty shells, but a number of them seemed to have been appropriated by the town's current residents, who had covered the old buildings with wooden latticework or permanent tents in order to turn the proud old structures into humble, semi-permanent woodsmen's homes. Great gnarled trees rose from the cracked pavement of ancient courtyards, and many structures actually stood well off the ground in their mighty branches, linked by swaying catwalks of silver rope and white planks. A handful of the town's original buildings still stood more or less intact.

Halisstra saw that she had been imprisoned beneath an old watch-tower. Across the square an elegant palace rose through the trees, illuminated by hundreds of soft lanterns. Lord Dessaer's palace, she surmised. The sound of distant song and laughter drifted through the air.

The priestesses of Eilistraee led Halisstra along an old boulevard that quickly carried them out of the town and into the dark, rainy forest. They marched for quite some time, the silence of the night broken only by soft footfalls on the forest floor and the constant pattering of the rain—which did indeed slacken noticeably as they went on, giving way to a partial overcast through which stars on occasion appeared.

Halisstra had had about all of the World Above that she cared to endure, but she occupied herself by quietly working at the knots of the rope binding her hands while keeping an eye on her captors, hoping they would relax their vigilance. Xarra, the drow, walked in front, while Feliane marched at the rear. Seyll stayed close by Halisstra at all times, either a little before her or a little behind.

"Where are you taking me?" Halisstra asked as the walk dragged on.

"A place we call the Dancing Stone," Seyll answered. "It is sacred to Eilistraee."

"The forest looks all alike to me," said Halisstra. "How can you tell one part of it from another?"

"We know this trail well," Seyll replied. "In fact, we're not all that far from where we first encountered you and your companions. They abandoned you, and haven't been seen since that night."

Halisstra took a sip from her own flask to hide the smile that flitted across her features. The apostate priestess had made a mistake, and she didn't even realize it. If they weren't far from where she'd been captured, it stood to reason that she could follow the directions of Pharaun's vision from there and have a reasonable chance of locating the Jaelre drow. Regardless of what else she accomplished that night, it had already been worth her while.

They came to a loud, rushing creek, its bed strewn with large boulders. Xarra crossed first, leaping lightly from rock to rock and continuing into the woods on the far side, keeping watch for any danger. Seyll followed, a few steps ahead of Halisstra, her eyes on the uncertain footing beneath her. Halisstra started to follow. The rushing water was loud, even though the creek was shallow and not at all wide. The moon slipped behind the clouds, momentarily darkening the forest floor.

Halisstra scented opportunity.

She quickly hopped two rocks into the stream and halted, as if studying her next step. Instead she pitched her voice low and began a *bae'qeshel* song, the sound covered by the noisy creek. Seyll continued to pick her way ahead, and behind Halisstra the surface elf Feliane stopped, waiting for her to cross.

It was difficult with her hands bound, even as loosely as they were, but the power of the enchantment was in Halisstra's voice, not her hands. Even as Feliane lost patience and hopped forward to aid her, Halisstra turned around and fixed her red eyes on the pale girl's face.

"Angardh xorr feleal," she hissed. "Dear Feliane, would you draw your sword and free me of these troublesome bonds? I am afraid I will fall."

The charm ensnared the young priestess easily. With a blank expression, she drew her blade.

"Of course," the elf murmured vacantly.

She drew the razor edge carefully through the cords on Halisstra's wrists. Halisstra glanced over her shoulder at Seyll and carefully moved to shield Feliane's work with her body.

"What's wrong?" Seyll called.

"Don't answer," Halisstra whispered to the girl. She kept her hands together and turned carefully to face the priestess. "A moment!" she called. "I'm not certain of this step with my hands bound. The next rock seems slippery."

Seyll glanced at the creek, then retraced her steps, leaping one rock to the next as she came back toward Halisstra and Feliane. Halisstra twisted to look back at Feliane, standing behind her with her sword drawn.

"Dear Feliane," she said sweetly, "may I borrow your sword for a moment?"

The girl frowned slightly, perhaps aware somewhere in the depths of her enchantment-fogged mind that something was not right, but she extended the sword's hilt to Halisstra. Again concealing the movement with her body, Halisstra took the blade in her hand.

"Here," said Seyll. The Eilistraee priestess reached the next boulder and set her feet carefully, extending a hand. "Take my arm, and I will steady you."

Halisstra spun with the quickness of a cat and buried Feliane's sword beneath Seyll's outstretched arm. The priestess gasped in cold shock and crumpled at once, slipping from her perch to fall awkwardly in the icy stream. She slumped down the moss-covered boulder and came to rest leaning against the stone, sitting waist deep in the rushing water.

Halisstra withdrew the sword and turned back to Feliane, who stared at her with dumb amazement.

"Seyll's been hurt, girl," Halisstra snapped. "Quick, run back to Elventree and fetch help! Go!"

The pale elf maiden managed only one jerky nod before she whirled and raced off. Halisstra leaped over Seyll's rock and dashed quickly over the path. Xarra, the younger drow priestess, emerged suddenly from the wooded banks ahead of her, returning to find out what had delayed the others. To her credit, Xarra took in the situation with a single glance. She raised her crossbow and took quick aim.

Halisstra threw herself aside, twisting in midair as she sprang. Xarra's quarrel hissed by her torso so closely she felt it tug at her coat as it flew past.

"You missed your shot, girl," Halisstra snarled.

Xarra dropped her crossbow and reached for her sword. She died before the blade had cleared her scabbard, spitted through the throat. Halisstra straightened and looked down at the body, her heart pounding. The stream sang loudly beside her, and the air smelled of rain and wet leaves.

What next? she wondered.

Her prized mail, mace, and crossbow were in Lord Dessaer's keeping in Elventree, and as much as she wanted to recover her possessions, it didn't seem likely that she would be able to without the assistance of the Menzoberranyr. Her best move would be to arm herself as well as she could, take what provisions she could from Seyll and Xarra, and strike out in search of the Jaelre. With luck she would find them before Dessaer's rangers found her.

Halisstra thrust the sword through her belt and ventured back out into the stream to see if Seyll was carrying anything of use. She splashed down into the cold stream beside the Eilistraee priestess, gathered her up beneath the arms, and hoisted her back onto the stone slab in order to get a better look at her gear. The armor was clearly magical, as was the shield slung over Seyll's shoulder and the sword at her belt. Halisstra began unfastening the mail, intending to strip it from Seyll's body.

Seyll's eyes fluttered, and she groaned, "Halisstra. . . ."

Halisstra recoiled, startled above all else, and somewhat repulsed to find that she was stripping the corpse of someone who was not quite dead yet. She glanced down at the stone and studied a coursing rivulet of blood streaming from Seyll's side to the foaming water of the creek. The priestess's breath sounded wet and shallow, and bright flecks of blood stained her lips.

"I hope you will forgive me, Seyll, but I have need of your arms and armor, and you will be dead in a very short time," Halisstra remarked. "I have decided to decline your gracious invitation to join your observances tonight, as I have pressing business elsewhere in the forest."

"The . . . others?" Seyll gasped.

"Xarra had the decency to die swiftly and without awkward conversation. The surface girl I charmed and sent running off into the forest."

Halisstra unbuckled Seyll's sword belt and dragged it loose, setting it well out of the dying drow's reach. She set to work on the armor fastenings.

"While I admire your determination to save me from myself, Seyll, I can't believe you didn't see this as a likely outcome of your attempt to convert me."

"A risk . . . we are all . . . prepared to take," Seyll managed. "No one is beyond redemption."

She mumbled something more and reached up to interfere with Halisstra's work, but the Melarn priestess simply batted her hands away.

"A foolish risk, then. Lolth has punished your faithlessness through my hand, apostate," Halisstra said. She pulled off Seyll's boots and undid the leggings of her mail. "Tell me, was it worth it, to follow the path that led you to a cold and pointless death here in this miserable forest?"

To Halisstra's surprise, Seyll smiled, finding some last reservoir of strength.

"Worth it? Upon . . . my soul, yes." She laid her head back and gazed up into Halisstra's face. "I . . . have hope for you still," she whispered. "Do not . . . concern yourself . . . with me. I . . . have been . . . redeemed."

Her eyes closed for the final time, and the wet sound of her breathing halted.

Halisstra paused in her work. She had expected anger, resentment, perhaps even fear or scorn, but forgiveness? What power did the Dark Maiden hold over her worshipers that they could die with a blessing for their enemies on their lips?

Seyll turned away from the Spider Queen, she told herself, and through me the Spider Queen exacted her vengeance. Yet Seyll died with calm assurance, as if she had escaped Lolth finally and completely with the ending of her life.

"The Spider Queen take your soul," she said to the dead priestess, but somehow she doubted that Lolth would.

🕷   🕷   🕷

"A swift march is our surest path to victory," Andzrel Baenre said, addressing the assembled priestesses.

Nimor stood to one side and watched the Baenre weapons master, one of only a handful of males invited to take counsel with the assembled females. All of the great Houses, and no less than sixteen of the minor ones, were represented in the hastily mustered Army of the Black Spider, named for the banners under which they marched. Nearly thirty high priestesses—at least one from almost every House, and in some cases, several high priestesses from the same House—filled the great command pavilion provided by the Baenre contingent, watching Andzrel like predatory cats while reclining, sitting, or standing as rank and opportunity dictated. Nimor and the other few males stood, of course. No mere male would be seated while a high priestess remained standing.

"We lead some four thousand drow soldiers and twenty-five hundred slave soldiers into battle. By all reports it would seem that we are evenly matched with the duergar army that marches up from the south, but we do not intend to meet the duergar in a fair fight, of course." The word "fair" sent a wave of chuckles echoing through the tent. Andzrel used a slender baton to direct their attention to a large map inked on rothé-vellum. "We can stop a force significantly stronger than our own by picking the right ground to fight for. The place we will halt the duergar advance is here, at the Pillars of Woe."

"If I decide that your plan has merit, you mean," drawled

Mez'Barris Armgo of House Barrison Del'Armgo. "Triel Baenre may trust in your judgment, but I intend to think for myself, boy."

A tall, powerful female, the matron mother of the Second House was the ranking priestess present and nominally in command of the entire expedition. Each of the Houses had contributed some number of its priestesses to command their contingents in battle, ranging from unblooded acolytes to first daughters and matron mothers. Weapons masters such as Andzrel and males—including Nimor in his role as Zhayemd Dyrr—commanded warbands, companies, and cavalry squadrons, attending to the endless details of organizing the army of Menzoberranzan.

"My cousin presents House Baenre's views, Matron Mez'Barris," Zal'therra Baenre rasped. "Matron Triel endorses the weapons master's battle plan."

Foremost of Triel Baenre's cousins, Zal'therra looked nothing like the petite Matron Mother of House Baenre. She was tall and broadly built in the shoulders, a strapping female with a remarkable amount of physical fortitude and a coarse, intimidating manner. She and Mez'Barris were two of a kind in physique, yet the Matron Mother of House Del'Armgo possessed a brilliant, vicious cunning that was nothing more than a sullen streak in the Baenre priestess. Mez'Barris fixed her red eyes on the younger woman, but did not respond.

Andzrel knew better than to speak while the two females sparred. He waited through a moment of silence before he continued the briefing.

"Here is Rhazzt's Dilemma," he said, "where Captain Zhayemd of Agrach Dyrr reported the duergar vanguard yesterday morning. It lies about twenty-five miles south of the Pillars of Woe, at the lower end of the canyon. Assuming the worst, we can expect the duergar to storm the outpost and force the entrance by sometime late today, perhaps tomorrow if we're lucky. Duergar are hearty soldiers and can march all day long, but they're slow, and their army will be burdened with a long supply train and heavy siege engines. Ascending the gorge will be difficult going. It seems that, in the worst case again, they should reach the Pillars in five days—more likely seven or eight."

"How do you know the gray dwarves haven't overrun the outpost already?" a priestess of Tuin'Tarl asked.

"We do not, Mistress Tuin'Tarl. The duergar wizards and clerics are preventing our efforts to scry the surroundings, a common tactic in warfare of this sort." Andzrel nodded to Nimor and added, "That is why it is essential to deploy a screen of capable scouts, to find out through mundane means what our wizards cannot see. Zhayemd of Agrach Dyrr is charged with the command of our reconnaissance."

Andzrel waited a moment to see if the priestess had any more questions, then went on, "In any event, our armies travel faster than the gray dwarves, and we have a much easier route. I would expect our vanguard to reach the Pillars of Woe three to four days from now. If we hold the upper exit from the gorge, the duergar will never break our defenses. As you can see, it is something of a race, and therefore we should make all possible speed."

"What plan do you have for battle, Zal'therra?" asked another priestess, the mistress of the House Xorlarrin contingent.

Nimor smiled at the remark. Zal'therra had certainly been instructed by Triel to rely on her House weapons master's advice in planning the battle, but the high priestesses naturally talked past Andzrel as if he wasn't even there.

"Andzrel will present it," the Baenre priestess replied, as if she'd just finished explaining it all to him and choose to allow him to show off her genius.

If the weapons master took note of the slight, he did not show it.

"We will build a strong, well-anchored line across the mouth of the gorge. A few hundred troops should suffice for this, but we will commit a thousand. The remainder of our soldiers will be held in reserve and secure various small passageways and flanking caverns in the vicinity." Andzrel set down his baton and faced the assembled priestesses, his face expressionless except for the keen glitter of determination in his eyes. "I mean to allow the duergar to come to us, and break them between the Pillars of Woe. When they have hurled their strength on us in vain, we will pursue them back down the gorge and slaughter them and their minions in heaps."

"And what if the duergar choose not to force the Pillars?" Mez'Barris asked, addressing Andzrel directly.

"The duergar are invading our lands, Matron Mother, so the burden of action is on them. If they decide not to try the Pillars, we will wait them out—our supply lines are much shorter than theirs. In a matter of days they will have to choose between going forward and going back."

Mez'Barris gazed at the map, considering Andzrel's answer.

"Very well," she said. "I want to see just how quickly we can reach the spot you have in mind. Extend the march by two hours a day. If we reach the Pillars of Woe in three days, we should have time to rest before battle is joined. I want our fastest forces to make a dash for the Pillars, just in case. There is no reason we couldn't have a couple of hundred scouts at the top of that gorge in a day and a half. Now, if you will excuse us, I wish to discuss with my sister priestesses the best use of our talents in the upcoming conflict."

Andzrel offered a shallow bow, and withdrew from the room. Nimor fell in beside the Baenre weapons master as they left the black pavilion, flanked by a handful of other officers. The tent stood in a large, round tunnel crowded with soldiers and pack lizards, banner after banner of various Houses stretching out of sight up and down the passage.

"Zhayemd," said Andzrel, "I want you to assume command of our vanguard, as Matron Mother Del'Armgo suggests. Take your Agrach Dyrr cavalry and make speed tomorrow and the next day. Our lack of information about the duergar army makes me nervous. I'll have some of the other riders join you, so that you'll have a strong company to hold the pass if worse comes to worst."

"I must consult with our high priestess," Nimor said, though he had no intention of doing any such thing. The weapons master, still under Nimor's powerful and lasting enchantment, would trust him anyway. "I believe she will support the suggestion, though."

"Good," Andzrel said as they reached the Baenre camp. He clapped Nimor on the shoulder. "If you find the duergar somewhere they're not supposed to be, report back at once. I want no foolishness out of you. You are the eyes of our army."

Nimor smiled and said, "Do not worry, Master Andzrel. I intend to leave nothing to chance."

※   ※   ※

Jezz the Lame crouched awkwardly in the shadow of a ruined wall, gazing across a small square at a large, round tower a stone's throw away.

"There," he said. "The beholder's tower. There's a flight of stairs leading up to the door, which we have previously found to be unlocked but guarded by deadly magical traps. You'll see several small windows in the upper levels, perhaps large enough for a small drow to slip through. We haven't tried those, though."

Ryld, who crouched just behind the Jaelre, leaned out to take a look for himself. The tower was much as Jezz had described it, surrounded by the sprawling ruins of Myth Drannor. After using Pharaun's magic to speed their travel to the old elven capital and resting a few hours to prepare, the company had spent most of the night fighting their way through the ruins.

Myth Drannor was little more than a great wreckage of white stone overgrown with trees and vines, but once it had been something more. The old surface elf city might not have been as large as Menzoberranzan or as infernally grand as Ched Nasad, but it possessed an elegance and beauty that equaled, if not exceeded, the best examples of drow architecture.

Ryld cast a careful glance to the rooftops.

"No sign of devils," he said. "Perhaps we've slain enough that they've decided not to trouble us anymore."

"Unlikely," Jezz said with a snort. "They've drawn back to organize another attack, and await the arrival of more powerful fiends before trying us again."

"In that event, we should take advantage of the respite to do what we came to do," Quenthel said. She too moved up to study the tower. "I see nothing that encourages me to change our plan. Pharaun, cast your spell."

"As you wish, dear Quenthel," the wizard began, "though I must say that I do not entirely agree with the stratagem of—"

Angry glares from every other member of the company silenced Pharaun before he finished his protest. He sighed and fluttered his hand.

"Oh, very well."

The wizard straightened and carefully spoke the words of his spell, the potent syllables ringing with magical power. An intangible wave seemed to roll over Ryld and the others. In its wake, Ryld felt strength and quickness drain from his limbs, and Splitter seemed to grow heavier in his hand, its gleaming blade suddenly dulled. Ryld was no wizard, but like any accomplished drow he had over the years armed himself with various magical devices and enchantments to increase his speed, his strength, the toughness of his armor, the deadliness of his weapons. Pharaun's spell temporarily abolished all magic in the vicinity, leaving Ryld without the benefit of a single enchantment, and the other drow were similarly affected. The strangest effect of all was the sudden inertness of Quenthel's fearsome whip. One moment the snakes hissed and writhed of their own accord, alert and vicious, and in the next they dangled like dead things from the weapon's haft.

"Stay close to me, if you wish to stay within the spell's effect," Pharaun said.

He licked his lips nervously. Within the zone of antimagic he'd just created, he could cast no spells, and his own formidable array of enchanted devices and protections were inert, too. The wizard readied his hand crossbow, and loosened his dagger in its sheath.

"I feel like I'm going up against a dragon with a dinner knife," he muttered.

Ryld clapped him on the shoulder and stood. He sheathed Splitter and drew his own crossbow.

"Yes, but your spell pulls the dragon's fangs," he said.

"Get moving," Quenthel said.

She looked more than a little uncomfortable herself. Evidently she didn't care for the unmoving silence of her weapon. Without waiting, she loped across the courtyard and bounded up the steps leading to the tower's door. The others followed, blinking in the light of the approaching dawn. Ryld made a point of keeping watch on the ruined streets and walls behind the party, watching for the return of any of Myth Drannor's monstrous denizens. The last thing they needed was a band of blood-maddened devils to descend on them while they'd suppressed their own magic.

At the door of the tower, Quenthel stepped aside for Jeggred. The hulking draegloth moved up and wrenched the door open, bounding inside. Masonry cracked and clattered to the stone steps. Quenthel followed hard on his heels, then Danifae and Valas. Ryld looked around one last time, and noticed Jezz hanging back.

"You're not coming?" he asked the Jaelre.

"I intend to observe only," Jezz replied. "Defeating the beholder is your task, not mine. If you survive, I'll join you in a few minutes."

Ryld scowled, but ducked inside. They were in a foyer of some kind, illuminated by slanting rays of dim light from holes in the ancient masonry. At the far end of the room, a second door stood. Once the foyer might have been a grand and impressive hall, but the tiles of the floor were cracked and split by deep green mold, and the proud banners and arrases that hung on the walls were little more than tattered rags. Pharaun stood close by, examining an intricate symbol clearly etched on one block of the floor. The whole emblem was a little larger than his hand, with a great complexity of curving lines and characters.

"A symbol of discord," the wizard observed. "If we were not protected by the antimagic field, it would have caused us to fall on each other with murderous fury . . . but we hardly need a symbol for that, do we?"

"The next room?" Ryld asked.

Jeggred was already by the door. The draegloth opened it and quickly bounded through, followed by the others, into a round chamber not unlike the bottom of a well. Several of the floors above had long since collapsed, burying the ground floor in rubble and wreckage, with great wooden beams protruding from the mess. Heaps of masonry taller than a drow impeded movement.

Ryld stared into the empty space above, searching for any sign of the monster that was supposed to lurk there. The others did as well, but all was still.

"I see no beholder," Jeggred said.

Ryld was about to reply when something above them responded in a horrible, croaking voice, "Of course not, fools. I do not wish to be seen!"

An instant later the creature lashed out at them. From somewhere high overhead, near the top of the ruined tower, several brilliant rays of magical energy—the deadly beams each of the monster's eyes could fire in order to wound, paralyze, charm, or even disintegrate its foes—lanced downward at the drow, followed by a great blue bolt of lightning conjured by the unseen monster. Ryld could not see the magic's source.

The rays and crackling bolt of electricity abruptly winked out just over the drow's heads, negated by Pharaun's zone of null magic. The creature tried again, bringing different rays to bear and incanting some horrible spell in its deep, droning voice, but those were no more successful.

Ryld aimed his crossbow up the shaft and guessed at the spot from which the rays had stabbed down at them, loosing his bolt with practiced skill. A squeal of pain overhead told him that he'd guessed his target well. Valas, Danifae, and Pharaun fired too, while Jeggred snatched up a good-sized brick in one fighting claw and hurled it up into the darkness with surprising swiftness. Not all of their barrage struck home, of course. Even if it had been visible, a beholder's thick chitinous hide could deflect many attacks, and scoring a square hit on the creature when it was garbed in invisibility was more than a little difficult. Still, a couple of quarrels struck home.

The beholder mage obviously comprehended the nature of the company's defense very quickly on its own. Instead of striking directly at the dark elves, it turned its deadly gaze on the wreckage of the upper floors. With one eye ray it burned through the base of a heavy wooden beam projecting from the tower's stone wall, and with another it seized the timber in a telekinetic grip and flung it down at

Valas, who was plying his shortbow to great effect. The scout threw himself aside just in time to avoid being crushed beneath the massive timber, but lost his balance and fell amid the rubble. Dust and the cracking of stone filled the air. The beholder instantly went to work on another wooden beam. In the meantime the creature changed its droning incantation and began another spell.

"We need to climb higher," Quenthel said. "The creature is above Pharaun's spell."

"Do you propose that I should jump?" Pharaun asked. He ducked a head-sized chunk of masonry clattering down from above, and took aim with his crossbow again. "The antimagic that protects us also prevents us from flying or levitating up to get at—"

"For Lolth's sake," Ryld exclaimed. *Sign!*

Valas slipped and scrambled over to one side, seeking a better vantage. The scout drew his shortbow carefully, and loosed another arrow. The beholder above let out a horrible screech. The eye rays winked out, and debris stopped falling from overhead.

The beholder retreated back above the next intact floor, Valas signed. *We'll have to go up and get it.*

Ryld studied the interior walls of the ruined towers carefully. Perhaps four of the lower floors were missing, leaving at least two or three intact above the ceiling of the highest floor they could see. At a guess, it was at least a sixty-foot climb, and the masonry was old and damaged. A skilled climber could make good use of the wreckage of the beams that formerly supported the lower floors, but it was nothing he cared to try.

I don't like the climb, he replied.

Nor do I, Danifae added. The creature knows we're protected by anti-magic. Will it expect us to abandon the spell in order to get to it?

"Possibly," said Pharaun. At a sharp look from Ryld he signed, *One wonders if perhaps we should have studied this situation at greater length before agreeing to the task the Jaelre set us.*

Pharaun, like the others, moved carefully across the floor of the chamber, peering upward.

The wizard craned back his head and called, "Ho! Beholder! As we are at something of an impasse, will you consent to parlay?"

Quenthel fumed.

"You speak for us, wizard?" she growled.

From the heights of the tower overhead the deep, rasping voice came again.

"Parlay? On what account? You have invaded my home, impudent fools."

"Pharaun—" Quenthel started.

"You have a book we want," the wizard replied, ignoring the high priestess. "I guess it's called the Geildirion of Cimbar. Give it to us, and we'll trouble you no more."

The beholder fell silent, evidently considering the offer. Quenthel stared daggers at the wizard, but like the others, she listened for the beholder's reply.

"The book is extremely valuable," the creature replied finally. "I will not yield it up because some whelp of a dark elf demands it of me. Retreat, and I will consent to spare your lives."

Quenthel snorted and said, "As if we expected anything different." She made a small wave of her hand to call the others' attention to her, and signed, *On the count of three, Pharaun will dismiss his spell. Danifae and Ryld—you will follow me up the shaft. Pharaun, when we reach the halfway point, you will then teleport yourself and Jeggred to the floor above and take the monster unawares while it focuses its attention on defending the shaft. Valas, you remain here and cover our ascent with your bow. Come up as quickly as you can once we reach the top.* The Baenre did not wait to entertain any refinements to her plan, beginning her countdown at once.

One, two . . . three!

Pharaun made a curt gesture and dismissed his spell of antimagic. Ryld felt the arcane power of his belt, his gauntlets, and his sword flood back into his limbs. He drew Splitter and ascended into the shaft, using the levitation charm with which his Melee-Magthere insignia was imbued. With luck, the sword's ability to disrupt enchantments would shield him from the worst of what the beholder mage could send their way.

Quenthel and Danifae rose alongside him, three black, graceful forms sliding smoothly up into the darkness. Pharaun moved up beside Jeggred and watched their progress, one hand on the draegloth's white-furred shoulder.

The ceiling of the shaft featured a circular opening at one side, cluttered somewhat by the remnants of the old stairwell that once climbed the tower. Ryld peered at the opening, expecting incandescent death at any moment.

The beholder mage did not disappoint him.

A brilliant green ray flashed into existence, lancing toward Ryld. He parried it with Splitter, and felt a tingle in the hilt as the greatsword destroyed the insidious ray. Beside him, Danifae yelped and swerved aside from another tremendous bolt of lightning that arced out to sear all three dark elves, leaving the odor of charred wood and ozone in the air.

Arrows hissed up from underneath, whistling past the weapons master as Valas fired at the unseen foe. Ryld snarled in defiance and willed himself upward with more haste. Another spell struck Quenthel—some kind of dispelling magic that snuffed out her levitation. She flailed her arms and plummeted to the floor below. Ryld reached out to catch her, but the Baenre was simply not close enough. She struck the floor at the bottom of the shaft after a fall of close to forty feet. Quenthel crashed into the rubble like a falling meteor, and vanished in dust and wreckage.

"Keep going!" shouted Danifae. "We're almost at the top!"

The beholder mage must have reached the same conclusion. A moment later, a barrier of solid ice appeared, walling off the top of the shaft and trapping the drow beneath it.

"Damn!" swore Ryld.

Danifae glowered at the barrier and said, "Maybe we can—"

At that moment, Jezz the Lame appeared on the floor of the chamber. He wheeled and hurled a spell back through the doorway, then slammed the door shut.

"Whatever it is you're doing, finish it," the Jaelre called. "The devils have returned in force!"

Ryld looked up at the sheet of ice covering the top of the shaft, then down again at the rubble-strewn floor. Quenthel lay half-buried in the shattered masonry, unmoving. Spells rumbled above the ice, sure signs that Pharaun and Jeggred had found their foe, but the creature's barrier had effectively cut the company in half. Abandoning the effort to get at the beholder mage might give the monster the chance to destroy the company in detail, but Quenthel was dead or injured below.

"Up," Ryld decided. "Going back is no good. Valas, Jezz, aid Quenthel!"

He came up beneath the gleaming white ceiling and struck at the icy wall with Splitter, using the sword's ability to rend enchantments. Razor-sharp shards of ice flew from the spot he struck, but the sword failed to undo the beholder's magic. Ryld cursed and tried again, with no more success.

Below them, the door to the tower boomed with a heavy blow. Valas quickly shouldered his bow and scuttled over the heaps of masonry and rubble filling the bottom of the shaft, heading toward the spot where Quenthel had fallen.

Jezz the Lame growled something and worked a spell, clogging the tower's foyer with a mass of sticky webbing. He mouthed the words of another spell and arrowed up into the air, leaving Valas and Quenthel on the floor of the shaft.

"Forget the priestess," he called to Valas. "Come, if you want to live!"

The scout grimaced in frustration.

"I can't climb and carry her!" he snapped as a second blow at the door splintered wood and bent iron.

The ancient door would not withstand another blow. Valas glanced up the shaft and down at Quenthel, and reached down and unfastened her House Baenre brooch from her shoulder. Her snake-headed whip stirred in agitation, and Yngoth actually struck at the scout, but Valas scrambled back and fixed the brooch to his tunic.

"I'm trying to save your mistress," he barked at the whip.

The scout moved close and grasped Quenthel under the arms, using the power of her own brooch to levitate away from the floor.

Meanwhile, Ryld measured the icy barrier in front of him.

"All right, then," he muttered.

He backed up, set his feet as best he could against the shaft's wall, and drew Splitter back for the mightiest blow he could muster. With a cry of rage, he struck the wall a tremendous blow, Splitter's blade shearing through the magical ice even as waves of excruciating cold washed over him. He ignored the pain and swung again, and again—and the sheet of ice cracked into a dozen pieces and fell away to the floor below. Without waiting for the others, Ryld hurled himself up into the beholder's lair.

Chapter

S I X T E E N

Within a day of Seyll's murder, Halisstra began to wonder if she might have been better off going with the Eilistraee priestess and feigning conversion. It might have been a strategy unlikely to reunite her with her comrades, but it would have meant that she would have enjoyed shelter, food, and the opportunity to perhaps regain her equipment, instead of an interminable march through the freezing woods. As dawn approached, she could find no better shelter than a small, damp hollow surrounded by drow-high boulders and bare trees. Shivering, she shrugged off her stolen backpack and searched it thoroughly, hoping against hope that she had somehow overlooked some key implement or a scrap of food.

Seyll and her followers had not anticipated a wilderness sojourn of more than a few hours. They carried no more gear than Halisstra would have, had she decided to venture out to a well-known cavern a mile or two from Ched Nasad. They certainly hadn't equipped themselves for the convenience of their captive's escape.

With the crossbow she'd taken from Xarra and the *bae'qeshel* songs at her command, she had a fair chance of dropping any game she came across, but in her hours and hours of wandering she'd not seen anything larger than a bird. Even if she did succeed in killing something for her dinner, she had no means to cook it, and Halissra was beginning to suspect that the forest itself conspired against her.

She was reasonably sure that she'd managed to keep heading west after her escape from the heretic. If Seyll hadn't been lying when she said they were near the spot where Halissra had been captured, the Melarn priestess was no more than one or two nights' march from the small river Pharaun had described in his vision. Since the river ran south to north somewhere in front of her, it seemed a difficult target to miss as long as she kept moving west.

Halisstra tried to keep the sunset and moonset ahead of her, and a little to her left, since they'd be somewhat south of her at this time of year—or so she'd gathered from watching Valas navigate the woods over the past few days. Of course, she had no way of knowing whether to turn upstream or downstream when she did reach Pharaun's river, since she couldn't be sure that she'd struck the stream at the spot the wizard anticipated. For that matter, she was unlikely to know for certain whether she'd found the right stream at all. She'd already crossed a dozen small brooks in a day and a half, and while she didn't think any of them could properly be called a river, she simply didn't have enough experience of the surface world to be sure.

"Of course, that all presumes that I haven't been wandering in circles for hours," Halisstra muttered.

It could be that the most sensible thing to do would be to abandon the notion of searching for the Jaelre, and pick the straightest course out of the forest she could find. Sooner or later, she might find civilization again, and beg, borrow, or steal food and other supplies—or charm a guide who could lead her to the Jaelre.

She closed her eyes, trying to build a mental picture of Cormanthor and the lands around it. She was in the eastern part of the forest, she knew—so was her best course east, toward the rising sun? There was little on that side of the forest except for the human settlement of Harrowdale, if she recalled her geography. Or was she better off turning south? Several more dales lay in that direction, so her odds of reaching civilization seemed better that way, even if that meant she would have a longer trek to reach the eaves of the forest. North she ruled out at once, since she was fairly certain that Elventree lay in that direction. Any way she went, she would be turning her back on the Jaelre and her sacred mission, at least for a time.

"This would be easier if the goddess would consent to answer my prayers," she grumbled.

When she realized what she'd said, she couldn't help but glance around and put a hand to her mouth. Lolth did not look kindly on complainers.

She passed a cold, wet, and miserable day hunched down among the rocks of her small hiding place, drifting in and out of Reverie. More than once she wished she'd had the presence of mind to order Feliane to guide her to the Jaelre, or at least give up her cloak and pack before dashing off in a panic. Lord Dessaer's rangers were most likely on her trail, of course, and they would not show her much mercy if she fell into their hands again. Even so, Halisstra was beginning to feel that a quick execution by the surface elves might be preferable to a long and lonely death by starvation in the endless forest.

At nightfall she rose, gathered her belongings, and scrambled out of her hiding place. She stood on the forest floor, looking toward the direction she reckoned west, then south, and west again. South might offer a better chance of finding a human or surface elf settlement, but she couldn't bring herself to abandon the hope of rejoining her comrades. Better to try one more march west, and if she still hadn't found Pharaun's river by dawn, she'd think about giving up the effort.

"West, then," she said to herself.

She walked for a couple of hours, trying to keep the moon left of her, even though she felt it rather than saw it. The night was cold, and high thin clouds scudded by overhead, driven by a fierce blast of wind that didn't reach down to the shelter of the trees. The woods were cold and still, probably pitch black by a surface dweller's standards, but Halisstra found that the diffuse moonlight flooded the forest like a sea of gleaming silver shadow. She paused to study the sky, trying to gauge whether she was allowing the moon's passage to affect her course too much, when she heard the faint sound of rushing water.

Carefully she stole forward, trotting softly through the night, and she emerged at the bank of a wide, shallow brook that splashed over a pebbly bed. It was wider than any she'd seen yet, easily thirty to forty feet, and it ran from her left to her right.

"Is this it?" she breathed.

It seemed large enough, and it was about where she'd expected to find it—a march and a half from the place where she'd been captured. Halisstra crouched and studied the swift water, thinking. If she made the wrong decision, she might follow the stream into some desolate and unpopulated portion of the woods and die a lonely death of hunger and cold. Then again, her prospects weren't very bright no matter what she did. Halisstra snorted to herself, and followed the stream to her left. What did she have to lose?

She managed another mile or so before the night's walk and the cold air made her hunger too great to be borne any longer, and she resolved to stop and make a midnight meal of whatever supplies she had left. Halisstra shook her pack off her shoulder and started to look around when an odd whirring sound fluttered through the air. Without even thinking about it, Halisstra threw herself flat on the ground—she knew the sound too well.

Two small quarrels flew past her, one sinking into a nearby tree trunk, the other glancing from her armored sleeve. Halisstra rolled behind the tree and quickly sang a spell of invisibility, hoping to throw off her assailants' aim, when she happened to glance again at the bolt. It was small and black, with red fletching; the bolt of a drow hand crossbow.

Several stealthy attackers moved closer through the wood, their presence indicated only by the occasional rustle of leaves on the ground or a low signaling whistle. Halisstra carefully stood, still hiding behind the tree.

In a low voice she called, "Hold your fire. I killed the Eilistraeen priestess who carried these arms. I serve the Spider Queen."

Her voice carried the hint of a *bae'qeshel* song that gave her words an undeniable sincerity.

Several drow stalked closer, their feet rustling softly in the underbrush. Halisstra caught sight of them, furtive males in green and black who prowled through the moonlit forest like panthers. They peered into the darkness, searching for her, but her spell concealed her well enough.

She set her hand to the hilt of Seyll's sword and shifted slightly to ready her shield in case they found a way to defeat her invisibility.

One of the drow in front of her paused a moment and replied, "We've been looking for you."

"Looking for me?" Halisstra said. "I seek an audience with Tzirik. Can you take me to him?"

The Jaelre warriors halted. Their fingers flashed quickly, signing to each other. After a moment, the warrior who had spoken straightened and lowered his crossbow.

"Your company of spider-kissers came to Minauthkeep three days ago," he said. "You were separated from them?"

Hoping that Quenthel and the others had done nothing to make enemies of the Jaelre, Halisstra decided to answer honestly.

"Yes," she said.

"Very well, then," the stranger replied. "High Priest Tzirik ordered us to find you, so we'll take you back. Why, and what becomes of you there, is up to him."

Halisstra allowed her invisibility to fade, and nodded. The Jaelre drow fell in around her and set off at a quick pace toward the south, following the stream. She might have had no idea where she was, but the Jaelre seemed to know the woods well enough. In less than an hour, they came to a ruined keep, its white walls gleaming in the moonlight. The stream passed a stone's throw from the fortress.

I had the right stream, Halisstra noted with some surprise.

She'd kept her course for two nights and veered only a couple of miles too far to her right, it seemed. She thought about what would have happened if she'd crossed the stream and continued. The thought made her shiver.

The Jaelre scouts led Halisstra into the ruined keep, past watchful guards who crouched in hidden places and kept an eye on the forest all around. She discovered that the place was in much better repair than it seemed from outside. Her guards escorted her to a modest hall whose only furnishings were a large fire and an array of hunting trophies, mostly surface creatures Halisstra did not recognize. She waited for a long time, growing hungrier and thirstier, but eventually a short, solidly built male of middle years appeared, his face covered in a ceremonial black veil.

"Lucky me," he said in a rich voice. "Twice in three days servants of the Spider Queen have called upon my home and asked for me by name. I begin to wonder if Lolth wishes me to reconsider my devotion to the Masked Lord."

"You are Tzirik?" Halisstra asked.

"I am he," the priest said, folding his arms and studying her. "And you must be Halisstra."

"I am Halisstra Melarn, First Daughter of House Melarn, Second House of Ched Nasad. I understand that my companions are here."

"Indeed they are," Tzirik said. He offered a cold smile. "One thing at a time, though. I see you wear the arms of a priestess of Eilistraee. How did you come by them?"

"As I told your warriors, my company was attacked by surface elves some distance away from here five days ago. My companions escaped the attack, but I was captured and taken to a place called Elventree. There, a female who called herself Seyll Auzkovyn called on me in my cell, and sought to indoctrinate me in the ways of Eilistraee."

"A rather simpleminded notion," Tzirik observed. "Continue, please."

"I allowed her to believe I might be swayed," Halisstra said. "She offered to take me to a rite they were to hold two nights ago out in the forest. I found an opportunity to escape as we traveled to their ceremony."

She glanced down at the mail and weapons she wore. The naivete of the female still surprised Halisstra. Seyll had not seemed like a stupid drow, not by any stretch of the imagination, and yet she had fatally misjudged Halisstra.

"In any event," she finished, "I took the liberty of borrowing some things Seyll had no more use for, since the good people of Elventree confiscated my own weapons and armor."

"And now you would like to be reunited with your comrades?"

"Provided they're not dead or imprisoned, yes," she replied.

"Nothing like that," said the priest. "They asked me to provide an unusual service for them, so I thought of something they could do for me by way of compensation for my time and trouble. If they succeed, they should return in a day or two. The question is, will you be here to greet them?"

Halisstra narrowed her eyes and remained silent. The high priest paced over by the fire and took a poker from a stand by the hearth. He prodded at the crackling logs.

"The comrades who abandoned you to captivity among the surface folk told me a very unusual story," said the priest. "Doubtless you're thinking to yourself, 'How can I know how much they told Tzirik?' You can't, of course, so the wisest thing to do would be to tell me everything."

"My companions may not appreciate that when they return," Halisstra said.

"Your companions will never know you were here if you fail to satisfy my curiosity, Mistress Melarn," Tzirik said. He set down the poker, and lowered himself into a seat by the fire. "Now, why don't you start at the beginning?"

※　　※　　※

Ryld crouched in the thick embrace of a deadly, acidic fog, trying hard not to draw breath despite the fact that he panted for air. His skin burned as if liquid fire had been poured over his body, and ugly welts were already rising wherever his ebon skin was exposed to the air. To stay where he was invited nothing less than a slow, agonizing death, but the vapors clung to his limbs like soft white hands, impeding his every movement. The cursed beholder lurked somewhere in the chamber, but where?

A brilliant bolt of lightning illuminated the white murk, lashing out with a dozen crackling arcs as it plowed through the mist. The weapons master threw himself aside and fell slowly to the floor, cushioned by the clinging mists, as a mighty thunderclap shook the stones of the chamber and rattled his teeth in his head.

"Pharaun!" he shouted. "Where is the damned—?"

He instantly regretted speaking, as needles of hot pain filled his nose and throat.

"Against the east wall!" the wizard replied from some distance away.

The Master of Sorcere fell at once into another spell, rushing his words as he tried to cast as quickly as possible. Meanwhile the beholder mage droned its horrid spell-song, muttering the black words of half a dozen incantations at once. Lightning flashed again, followed by the whining shrieks of conjured missiles arrowing for their targets, and the cries, shouts, and curses of his companions.

Ryld finally reached the floor, where he found himself fetched up against one curving stone wall—the only landmark he could make out in the horrible mist. Without pausing for thought, he scrabbled forward at the best speed he could, hoping to emerge from the acidic fog before it burned the flesh from his face.

Goddess, what a mess! he thought, slashing and cleaving at the thick tendrils of fog with Splitter.

The beholder had been waiting for them to resort to magic to ascend the shaft, and it had scoured the company with every spell at its command.

"The devils are coming up after us!" Jezz shouted from somewhere beyond the burning fog. "Finish this thing quickly so that we can get what we came for and leave!"

Finish it quickly, Ryld thought with a grimace. That's a novel idea.

He surged forward and suddenly found himself free of the deadly, clinging fog. No one else stood nearby, though he could hear his companions battling in the mists behind him.

"Damnation!" he muttered.

Clear of the unnatural fog, it was apparent that the whole floor of the tower had once been a royally appointed suite of rooms. A thick red haze of dust on the floor might have once been a plush carpet, and the walls were finished in patterns of orange and gold tile to form the image of a surface forest with its normally green leaves for some reason rendered in reds, oranges, and yellows. Ryld coughed, his eyes streaming from contact with the noxious fumes. Evidently he'd blundered through an archway into a different chamber, but another doorway led out of the room on the far side.

"Where in all the screaming hells am I?"

Something screeched in rage ahead, and the room beyond the arch flared brightly with magical fire. Ryld hefted Splitter and dashed into the next room, right into the middle of a fierce skirmish.

Danifae and Jezz battled against a pair of lean, scaly devils almost ten feet tall, horrible fiends with huge wings who fought with razor-sharp scourges and barbed tails that dripped with green venom. Several lesser devils hissed and surged behind the two already in the room, pressing forward and looking for a chance to join the fight.

"The devils are upon us!" Jezz cried.

The Jaelre fought with a curved knife in one hand, and a deadly white spell-flame wreathing the other. One of the big devils sprang at Jezz and hammered its iron chains past the Jaelre's defenses, spinning the surface drow to the floor. The creature stooped over the dazed Jaelre and reached for his throat.

Ryld glided forward, feinted high to bring the devil's weapon up to guard its face, and crouched low to take off its leg at the knee. The huge fiend roared in pain and toppled, its wings fluttering awkwardly as black blood spurted from the horrible wound. Ryld moved in close and reversed his grip on Splitter to finish the monster on the ground, but it replied with a flurry of slashing claws and snapping teeth, while lashing its barbed tail at him so quickly that only the stoutness of his dwarven breastplate saved him from being spitted on the wounded devil's sting.

Ryld parried furiously, battling for his life, as yet more devils—a group composed of man-sized creatures who were armed with knife-like barbs jutting from their scaly bodies—swarmed closer, their fanged faces twisted in hellish glee.

"Dark elves to feast on!" they gloated. "Drow hearts to eat!"

"We've got to get out of here!" Danifae cried. "We can't hold them!"

She whirled her morningstar with skill and strength, dueling the other big devil and a pair of the smaller ones who snatched at her from her flanks.

"There's no place to go," Ryld snapped. "The beholder's behind us!"

He could feel deadly spells flying in the chamber behind him, the reverberations of thunderbolts and the soul-searing chill of slaying spells that made his flesh crawl.

This isn't working, he thought. We're split in two, fighting two dangerous enemies.

They needed to regroup and focus on one foe or the other, or abandon the field all together and try again later. Presuming, of course, that the denizens of Myth Drannor allowed them to retreat at all. More than likely, they'd all die here, surrounded and over-whelmed by endless hordes of bloodthirsty demons. Quenthel and Valas were likely dead already.

Enough, Ryld snarled to himself. We didn't come all this way to be defeated here!

He redoubled his attack, stepped inside the big devil's reach, and drove Splitter's point through the creature's scaly neck. It flailed violently at him, but it was dying, and its convulsions gouged stone and clawed at the air instead of mauling Ryld. The weapons master leaped over the creature's body to engage the smaller barbed devils already moving toward him.

Jezz rejoined the fray, pulling out a scroll from his belt and hur-riedly reading off an abjuration that blasted several of the lesser devils back to whatever infernal realm they had crawled out of.

Two more instantly replaced their banished comrades.

"We have to move!" the Jaelre cried. "The beholder is our enemy. The devils are just a distraction!"

Ryld grimaced again. If they tried to flee, they'd be pulled down from behind. Still, he started backing his way toward the door leading to the beholder, praying that the creature was not in a position to see them. He gave ground grudgingly, unwilling to blunder into another fight while one still raged.

To his surprise, one of the devils on the other side of the chamber dropped out of view, and another one shrieked as a serpent-headed scourge sank its fangs into the back of its neck. Struggling through the ranks of the devils, Valas and Quenthel limped into sight. The scout supported the badly injured priestess, warding her side with one of his kukris while she lashed and flailed with her deadly scourge.

Danifae and Ryld took advantage of the devils' momentary disadvantage to press home attacks against their immediate foes. Quenthel slumped to one wall, fumbling with Halisstra's healing wand at her side, while Valas drew his second knife and darted into the fray, slashing and stabbing the devils from behind.

"Hurry!" Quenthel gasped. "A pit fiend and a dozen more devils are just behind us."

Ryld cut down another of the barbed devils, while Danifae splattered the brains of a second across the chamber wall with a two-handed blow of her morningstar. In the space of a few moments, the dark elves cleared the room of devils. Jezz produced another scroll and quickly read off a spell, sealing the doorway behind Quenthel and Valas with a crackling sheet of sparking yellow energy.

"That will only hold the creature for a moment," he cautioned.

The Baenre looked around the chamber. The fall in the shaft must have hurt her badly. Blood caked the side of her head, and her eyes didn't seem to want to focus. One arm hung limp at her side, but she held herself upright.

"Where's the beholder," she asked, "Pharaun, and Jeggred?"

Ryld jerked his head at the archway behind him. Another spell rumbled through the air.

"Back there somewhere," he said. "The beholder—"

He was interrupted by the sudden, sickening awareness of an overwhelming presence approaching Jezz's barrier, something unseen that seemed to shake the very stones of the tower with its footfalls.

"The pit fiend comes," Danifae reported, panting for breath, her eyes wide with alarm.

"Go," Quenthel said, waving them forward with her good arm.

Without another word, the dark elves scrambled for the other exit, plunging into the next room heedless of the spells that thundered and crawled in the space beyond.

🕷   🕷   🕷

Triel Baenre stood on a high bridge of House Baenre, gazing toward Narbondel. The creeping ring of radiance that slowly climbed the mighty stone column marked the passage of time in Menzoberranzan. The glow stood near the pillar's upper end, which meant that the day would soon be done. Not for the first time it struck her as ironic that a race that had been driven from the world of light almost ten thousand years in the past would have the slightest use for marking the passage of days and nights in the manner of the surface folk, when the night was eternal and changeless in the Underdark, but it had proven somewhat useful over the years to remember the endless march of unseen days in the world above. It helped in dealing with those who had more use for the custom, such as merchants who brought a few of the surface's more exotic and desirable goods down to the City of the Spider Queen.

Not that many of those had visited Menzoberranzan of late. War was hard on commerce.

The other question that came to Triel's mind as she looked out over Narbondel and the city below was somewhat less abstract: Who would be coming in an hour or two to cast the spells that renewed

Narbondel's fiery ring? The office of archmage still belonged to her brother Gromph, missing for more than a tenday, but the Masters of Sorcere would not permit the high seat to remain empty for much longer. She'd learned that several of the more ambitious masters already maneuvered for the post. Doubtless Pharaun Mizzrym would have been among them if he had remained in the city, but the errand to Ched Nasad had fortunately removed the hero of the hour from Menzoberranzan at the very moment that he might have put his fame to its best use. She turned her head slightly and spoke over her shoulder to the loyal Baenre guards who stood a respectful distance behind her.

"Send for Nauzhror," she said. "Tell him I desire his counsel on a matter of some importance. He may attend me in the chapel."

Triel made her way to the great temple of Lolth that lay in the center of House Baenre's Great Mound, her attention far from her surroundings as she contemplated the multiplicity of troubles that had descended over the city in the past few months. She was almost grateful to the duergar for providing her with a cause to which she could rally the Council, and through them the dozens of lesser Houses that comprised Menzoberranzan's strength. A victory in the tunnels south of the city would do much to restore House Baenre's preeminence.

On the other hand, another setback could be disastrous. Even if Baenre remained the wealthiest and most powerful House, the Council might see fit to remove House Baenre as the First House. None of them alone, perhaps not even any two of them together, could hope to defeat House Baenre, but what if all seven of the other Houses on the Council agreed that it was time to pull down the strongest among them?

"Lolth preserve us," Triel muttered, and shivered with true fear.

In terms of numbers of troops, magical might, and sheer wealth, the other Houses had always possessed the wherewithal to destroy House Baenre if they chose to unite against the First House. What they had never possessed was the blessing of the goddess for an act of such impropriety. If the Spider Queen returned her attention to

Menzoberranzan and destroyed the Second through the Eighth Houses for their presumption the day after they obliterated House Baenre, well, Baenre would hardly be helped by it. Without Lolth's wrath to deter the ambitions of the other great Houses, a unified attack against Baenre seemed more like an inevitability than a possibility.

The trick, mused Triel, is to keep the other Houses from settling thorny issues such as who would be First House after Baenre's fall, and tempt some of the smaller Houses with the places of the larger ones.

If Houses such as Xorlarrin or Agrach Dyrr could be convinced that they would advance with more certainty by supporting Baenre against a conspiracy of Barrison Del'Armgo and Faen Tlabbar than they would by turning against the First House, then House Baenre could withstand almost any threat from its lesser neighbors.

She paused at the door to the chapel, examining the notion with acute distaste. Could she really feel that House Baenre needed *allies?* The old Matron Baenre had not governed with anyone's consent. She had ruled the city because she was so strong no one could contemplate resisting her will.

Triel scowled and gestured at the chapel guards, who pulled open the doors and bowed before her.

Her sister Sos'Umptu awaited her in the chapel. Sos'Umptu had Quenthel's height, but took after Triel's thoughtful reserve as opposed to the willfulness of Quenthel or her unlamented sister Bladen'Kerst. Sos'Umptu possessed a calculated, deliberate maliciousness that she kept in careful check, never picking a feud she could not win. She briefly lowered her eyes, the minimal gesture of respect Triel's position demanded, then straightened.

"Any news from the army, eldest sister?" she asked in a soft voice.

"Not as yet. Zal'therra tells me that Mez'Barris has dispatched a small force to go ahead and seize a strategic pass in the path of the duergar army, which seems sensible enough. The rest of the Army of the Black Spider follows as fast as it may."

"It is a difficult situation. I wonder if perhaps you should have led the army in person."

Triel frowned. She was not accustomed to having her actions openly scrutinized by anyone, but if she couldn't survive the criticism of her family, how could she hope to cow the other matrons?

"Given the unusual situation," Triel replied, "I felt it wisest to remain close to the city."

"Perhaps. The problem is simple, of course—if the army is defeated, the blame will naturally attach to you. If the army triumphs, you have made a hero of Mez'Barris Del'Armgo."

"As well as Zal'therra and Andzrel," Triel pointed out. "I admit I have more to lose than to gain, but I will not second-guess myself now."

She studied the chapel, gazing up at the great magical image depicting the Queen of Spiders. While Sos'Umptu watched, Triel performed a perfunctory obeisance.

"You have not observed the goddess's rites as closely as you might over the last few tendays," Sos'Umptu said.

The goddess has not observed us for far longer, Triel found herself thinking.

She hurriedly thrust the blasphemous thought from her mind, horrified that something so irreverent could ferment in her head. She maintained her outward calm with the ease of long practice, returning her attention to her sister.

"We are confronted by yet another challenge," Triel said. "The Masters of Sorcere clamor for Gromph's replacement. House Baenre has placed archmages on Sorcere's throne as we liked for many hundreds of years, but this time, I am weighing the value of supporting the candidate of another House for the position. It might be . . . expedient."

Sos'Umptu's eyes widened by the thickness of a blade, and she said, "You seek my counsel?"

"As Gromph has absented himself, and Quenthel is far away, I find that the children of my formidable mother are in short supply. Very few females—and even fewer males—understand the lessons Mother taught us." Triel snorted in irritation. "Not even all our siblings, for that matter. Bladen'Kerst understood nothing but strength and cruelty, and Vendes was simply murderous. I have need of a sharp mind, a subtle mind, trained by my mother, and it occurs to me that I have allowed you to lurk in this chapel far too long." Triel moved a half-step closer and hardened her expression. "Understand that you advise me at my pleasure, and do not mistake consideration for indecision. I will brook no questioning of my right to rule."

Sos'Umptu nodded and said, "Very well. I think we should presume that Gromph has been killed. He would not have lightly abandoned his duties, and there are at least two reasons someone might have killed him. Either someone wanted to strike against the archmage himself, or someone wanted to strike against the leading wizard of House Baenre. If the former, well, whomever becomes archmage next will either be the culprit, or the next target. Why should we hurry to place a Baenre wizard weaker than Gromph into that position, when there is at least some chance we might lose whomever we promote?"

"I don't like the idea of surrendering such an important post to another family, but I like the idea of losing another skilled wizard even less," Triel mused. "Especially when we might forge a stronger tie with another House by allowing them to advance their candidate, who would then become the target of whatever power was strong enough to destroy Gromph."

"I don't understand," Sos'Umptu replied. "You seek *allies?*"

"It occurs to me that we might do well to ally ourselves with a great House of middle rank, perhaps two," said Triel. "It seems a sound precaution against any effort by the Second or Third Houses to rally the rest in common cause against us."

Sos'Umptu stroked her chin and said, "You believe matters have become as dangerous as that? Mother would never have agreed to such a thing."

"Mother lived in a different time," Triel said. "Do not compare me to her again."

Triel fixed her eyes on her sister until the priestess dropped her gaze. Sos'Umptu was clever, but not strong. If she joined forces with Quenthel, or maybe a cabal of the more capable cousins such as

Zal'therra, she would be a threat to Triel, but until then she could be trusted—within reason.

"What if Gromph's assassination was an attack on House Baenre," Triel asked, "and not simply a means to open the post of archmage?"

"In that case, we would be well advised to raise another Baenre wizard over Sorcere. Failing to do so would make us seem weak, and if the other Houses perceive us as vulnerable, they might be tempted to try the very thing you fear."

"Your advice does not provide me much comfort, Sos'Umptu," Triel grated. "And I am concerned, not afraid."

"There is another possibility," Sos'Umptu said. "Delay. Maintain that Gromph is still Archmage of Menzoberranzan for as long as possible. For that matter, spread the story that you have sent him off on a special mission and he will not be back for a while. The longer we delay, the more likely it is that events will make the circumstances of his disappearance clearer. If the Army of the Black Spider finds victory in the tunnels to the south, then your position might be strengthened enough that you can do as you will with the archmage's post."

Triel nodded. It was a sound piece of advice. Though she hated to admit that if Lolth continued to refuse her spells she might face a challenge for the leadership of the House, it didn't hurt her to begin strengthening her own ties to Sos'Umptu. She might need all the sisters she could get.

The door to the chapel creaked open, and a plump male dressed in elegant black robes entered. He resembled nothing so much as a housecat that had been fed too much, satisfied with his own superiority. Nauzhror Baenre was Triel's first cousin once removed, the son of one of her mother's nieces. His familiar, a hairy spider as well fed as the wizard himself, perched on Nauzhror's shoulder. He was accounted a Master of Sorcere, the only Baenre so recognized other than old Gromph himself, and was reputed to be an abjurer of some skill. Younger than Gromph, he had a habit of maintaining an insouciant smirk that made it hard to gauge what he was thinking.

Try as she might, Triel could not imagine him wearing the robes of the Archmage of Menzoberranzan.

"You sent for me, Matron Mother?"

"I am going to make it known," Triel said, "that my brother Gromph is engaged in a mission of great importance and secrecy, and will return to resume his duties as Archmage of Menzoberranzan in due time. In the meantime, I am going to allow the Masters of Sorcere to designate a substitute to attend to the responsibilities of the position. You will support the best candidate from either House Xorlarrin or Agrach Dyrr."

Nauzhror's smirk failed him.

"M-matron Mother," he stammered. "I . . . I had thought that perhaps I should assume the—"

"Are you Gromph's equal, Nauzhror?" Triel asked.

The abjurer might have been soft in appearance, but his eyes betrayed a hard and calculating mind—and a pragmatic one, as well.

"Were I the archmage's equal, Matron Mother, I would have challenged him for his title already." He thought for a moment, reaching up to stroke the spider that sat on his shoulder. "In time I expect to equal and perhaps surpass his skill, but I must study the Art for many years before I can call myself his peer."

"As I thought. Consider this, then," Triel said. "Whomever engineered Gromph's disappearance will most likely make short work of you if you presumed to call yourself Archmage of Menzoberranzan. The day may come when you realize your ambition, cousin, but that day is not today."

Nauzhror did not hesitate to incline his head and reply, "Yes, Matron Mother. I will do as you command."

"You are now acting House Wizard of House Baenre, Nauzhror. If it turns out that my brother is no more, you will hold the position in earnest, but for now I have need of your spells and counsel. Settle your affairs in Sorcere for the time being. I will have your personal effects brought here."

Nauzhror genuflected and said, "I thank you for your confidence in my abilities, Matron Mother."

"My confidence in your abilities extends exactly this far, cousin: Do not get killed," said Triel. "As of this moment, any male with the least aptitude for wizardry in House Baenre is yours to train. We need a cadre of skilled arcanists to equal those fielded by Del'Armgo or Xorlarrin."

"Such a collection of talent cannot be produced overnight, Matron Mother. It will be the work of years to match Xorlarrin's strength in wizardry."

"Then it is a work best begun immediately."

Triel studied the corpulent wizard and found herself hoping against hope that her House's future did not rest in his oily hands.

"There is one thing more, Nauzhror," she said as the wizard stepped away. "Consider it your first duty as House Wizard." Triel moved close and fixed her eyes on his, daring him to smile into her face. "You will find out what has happened to my brother."

🕷   🕷   🕷

Ryld barreled through a short, curving corridor, Jezz and Valas at his heels. Danifae helped Quenthel to stagger along behind them. The weapons master followed the corridor back to his right, and emerged into a large hall or ballroom of some kind. The beholder mage drifted there, a hulking monstrosity in the form of a chitin-covered orb six feet across, its ten eyestalks writhing as it hurled spell after spell at Pharaun and Jeggred. The wizard stood encased in a globe of magical energy, some kind of defensive spell that protected him while he dueled spell-for-spell with the monster. Jeggred stood immobile, his face locked into a needle-fanged grimace as he struggled to throw off the influence of some baneful spell or another.

"Persistent insects," the beholder snarled as it caught sight of Ryld and the others. "Leave me be!"

The creature floated back through an open archway, retreating to another portion of its lair.

Pharaun turned wearily to face the others. One side of his clothing was spattered with smoking holes, where some kind of acid had burned him, and he trembled with fatigue.

"Ah, I see my worthy companions have at last elected to join me," he observed. "Excellent! I was afraid you might miss the pleasure of hazarding life and limb against a murderous foe."

"What's wrong with Jeggred?" Quenthel managed.

"He's ensnared by a holding spell of some kind, and I expended all of my dispelling magic in my duel. If you can free him, please do so. I wouldn't want to be selfish, and keep the beholder all to myself."

"Shut up, Pharaun," Danifae rasped. "We have to finish the beholder, quick. There's a pit fiend and a dozen more devils just behind us, and we're about to be caught between the two."

The wizard grimaced. A dangerous light flickered in his eyes as he looked at Danifae, then at Jezz the Lame.

"If your magical tome is this much trouble, perhaps we should keep it for ourselves," the Master of Sorcere observed.

"Tzirik will not share the results of his divinations with you if you betray us," the Jaelre said simply. "Decide what is more important to you, spider-kisser, and do it quickly."

"Stop it, Pharaun," Ryld said.

He moved over to where Jeggred stood frozen, and laid Splitter alongside the draegloth to break the enchantment that held him. The half-demon blinked his eyes and scowled, slowly straightening.

"One problem at a time," Ryld continued. "Do you have any magic that can keep the devils off our backs long enough for us to defeat the beholder?"

The wizard answered, "No, they'd be among us in just a moment, and that would be a scene, wouldn't it? The—wait a moment, I have an idea. We won't keep out the devils. In fact, we'll let them in."

Infernal power crackled and snapped in the room behind them.

"That's the pit fiend destroying my wall," Jezz said. "Explain quickly, Menzoberranyr."

Pharaun began chanting a spell, and weaving his hands in the arcane gestures necessary to shape and control his magic.

"Do not resist," he told the others. "Ah, there we go. I've covered us all with a veil of illusion. We're all devils now."

Ryld glanced down at himself and noted nothing different, but when he looked back up, he saw that he was standing in the middle of a company of barbed devils. He recoiled momentarily, and noticed the other devils flinching too. Faintly, as though draped in a diaphanous gauze, he could see the natural forms of the other dark elves beneath their scaly exteriors.

"I can see through this," he warned.

"Yes, but you're expecting it," said the devil who stood where Pharaun had. "This should create no small amount of confusion for our foes, but we must move quickly. We want the devils to come upon us while we're dealing with the beholder."

The wizard glided across the chamber, following the beholder, and the rest of the company fell in behind him, hurrying after Pharaun as the howls of the pursuing devils rose in the corridor behind them. They climbed a spiraling stair and found the beholder waiting for them in what seemed to be a large throne room. The monster hesitated as the company burst in, cloaked in their devilish guises.

"The dark elves are not here," the beholder rasped. "Search the rest of the tower. They must be found!"

"I'm afraid you are mistaken," Pharaun laughed, and he hurled a blast of lightning at the creature that charred a dinner plate sized patch of its chitinous hide.

At the same time, Valas fired a pair of arrows that sank into its armored body, while Ryld, Jeggred, and Danifae broke into a charge.

The creature recovered from its surprise with incredible alacrity, whirling to flay the attacking drow with its deadly rays and spells. Jeggred was flung across the room with a telekinetic ray, while Danifae had to throw herself flat to avoid the incandescent green sweep of a disintegrating ray. Ryld got three steps farther before no less than three of the monster's thin eyestalks whipped around, spotting him at once and lashing out with more spells. A hail of incandescent bolts of energy streaked out to meet his charge, punching into his torso like the blows of a dwarven warhammer. Ryld grunted in pain, and stumbled to the hard floor.

At that moment, a flood of devils climbed up out of the staircase behind them, pouring into the room. In the space of half a dozen heartbeats, the scene descended into complete chaos, as the devils thronged the room, some turning angry glares on the beholder, others simply halting in confusion, surprised to find so many of their fellows already in the room.

From the floor Danifae pointed up at the beholder and screeched, "The beholder is in league with the dark elves! Slay it! Eat its eyes!"

The devils paused just long enough for the beholder to scour their front ranks with deadly spells, and they set upon it, flinging themselves at the monster. Rock-hard talons clawed and gouged at the beholder, while devils exploded under bolts of white fire or crumbled into lifeless stone beneath the beholder's eye rays.

Ryld had been about to leap up and engage the monster again, but he caught Pharaun's cautioning gesture, and feigned injury. The wizard's strategy was brilliant—let the beholder and the devils battle, and their foes might destroy each other.

"Weak-minded fools!" the beholder hissed. "The dark elves have deceived you!"

Still it wreaked terrible devastation with its spells and eye rays, trying to repel the devils' attack. The stink of charred flesh and the eldritch sensation of deadly magic filled the air.

A palpable sense of *wrong* flitted across Ryld's heart, and a hulking pit fiend climbed into the room. The mighty devil stood twice as tall as a drow, its torso rippling with muscle, its vast black wings mantling it like a cloak of ebon glory. It took in the scene with a malignant, measuring gaze, and Ryld's heart sank as he realized that the powerful fiend was not in the least deceived by Pharaun's illusion.

With one absent gesture the huge devil conjured up a great, seething orb of black fire in its claw, and hurled the sinister blast at Pharaun. The dark blot exploded in a tremendous explosion of evil flame that rocked the tower to its foundations, throwing Pharaun a dozen feet through the air and scorching him terribly as lesser devils and drow alike were sent flying like ninepins.

"They are right here!" the creature bellowed in a voice like a roaring forge. "Destroy the dark elves!"

The pit fiend started to call up another infernal blast, but Jeggred—still veiled in his devilish guise—hurled into the mighty fiend's flank, clawing and tearing with abandon. The great devil roared in rage, staggering under the draegloth's assault.

"Lolth's sweet chaos," Ryld muttered.

Which was more dangerous, the beholder mage or the pit fiend? The beholder still blasted any devil it saw, veiled drow or not, and most of the pit fiend's minions had fallen already. The pit fiend hammered and slashed at Jeggred, who stood toe-to-toe with the infernal lord, giving as good as he got.

The weapons master glanced between the two enemies, hesitated only a moment, and decided. Silently as an arrow whispering through the dark, Ryld scrambled up and leaped forward, aiming a tremendous cut at the beholder's round body. The beholder mage spotted him at once and blasted a bolt of lightning in his direction, but he tumbled aside and kept coming. Another eye fixed on him, and the beholder's drone took on a peculiarly horrid and deadly sound. Rather than wait to find out what spell the monster could cast with that eye, Ryld altered his path and bounded into the air, reaching out to sever the tentacle cleanly with Splitter's gleaming blade.

The beholder's drone broke in a piercing shriek of pain. The monster whirled to face Ryld with its jaws gaping, but the weapons master took careful aim and severed another waving eye before ducking down and scrambling beneath the bloated sphere of the hovering creature's body. None of the beholder's eyes could see directly beneath its own bulk.

Dropping to one knee, Ryld shortened his grip on Splitter, and thrust the greatsword up into the chitinous underside of the monster. Black, thick gore streamed down the blade, and the huge monster shuddered and shrieked again.

"Well done!" Jezz cried.

The Jaelre renegade commenced to bark out arcane words, his hands weaving in mystical patterns. He conjured up a seething missile of mystic acid that burned another eyestalk from the beholder's body as the monster rolled and twisted in agony.

Ryld yanked out his sword and rolled aside even as the beholder tried to crush him beneath its bulk, its jaws snapping at him. He found himself looking directly at the front of its body, where its great central eye had once gazed out from an armored carapace. The central eye was nothing but an empty socket. An old lesson came to the weapons master's mind: a beholder that wished to learn magic had to blind itself in order to do so.

The lesser eyes flailed and twisted on their tentacles, trying to focus on Ryld. The weapons master saw his opportunity and his target at the same moment. With one swift bound he drove Splitter like a lance straight through the empty central socket and deep into the creature's alien brain. With grim determination he sawed the greatsword in and out, side to side, while dark gore spurted and streamed from the awful wound.

The beholder gave one great shudder, its jaws snapped shut, and its waving eyestalks—those that remained—went limp. It sank slowly toward the floor.

Ryld glanced up and saw another devil closing on him, apparently having discerned his true form through the illusion, and he snatched out his short sword to gut the fiend as it threw itself on him. The devil knocked him to the floor, its foul blood pouring out all over him. Ryld gagged in revulsion and shouldered the jerking corpse aside, wrenching his sword out of the creature's midsection with his right hand while he dragged Splitter clear of the beholder mage's eye with the left. He shook his head to clear his eyes of the blood of his foes.

By the chamber's entrance, Jeggred sprawled to the ground beneath another terrible spell from the pit fiend, a roaring column of fire that blackened the draegloth's fur and might have incinerated him outright if not for the half-demon's native resistance to fire.

Jeggred screeched and rolled across the floor, trying to smother the burning embers, but as the pit fiend followed to strike at him again, Danifae appeared in front of it and dealt the monster a mighty blow that cracked its kneecap. The devil staggered and flared its wings for balance—and Valas buried three arrows in its back, sinking each shaft feather-deep between the fiend's shoulder blades.

Ryld started forward cautiously, preparing to engage the devil lord in his own turn, but Pharaun, blistered and smoking, rose from the spot where the devil's fireball had blasted him, and lashed out with a brilliant spray of iridescent colors that caught the pit fiend as it turned to confront the archer. A green ray carved a deep, black, boiling wound in the center of the pit fiend's torso, while a virulent yellow ray exploded with crackling arcs of electricity as it grazed the devil's hip. The monster staggered back two steps, and toppled, a smoking corpse. The chamber fell silent as the echoes of its thunderous fall died away.

Pharaun picked himself up gingerly, cradling one arm close to his body. One hand and part of his face were mottled and pink, abraded horribly by the fleeting touch of the beholder's disintegration ray, while his robes smoked with the fading effects of the dark fireball the pit fiend had conjured. The other dark elves slowly relaxed their guard, glancing around in some surprise to find no more foes on the field, and no life-threatening injuries among their number. Quenthel fumbled at her belt and produced Halisstra's healing wand, which she began to use to repair her own injuries, murmuring quiet prayers as she wielded the device.

"That," said Pharaun, "was not easy. We should have demanded something more from the Jaelre for our services."

"You came to us, spider-kisser," Jezz said.

He limped up to study the beholder's corpse where it sprawled on the steps of the ancient dais. Valas and Danifae followed, both keeping an eye on the stairwell behind them.

"Spread out and search for the book," said the Jaelre. "We must locate the Geildirion and withdraw before all the devils in Myth Drannor descend upon us."

Jezz followed his own advice at once, ransacking a set of dusty workbenches and cluttered scroll racks along the far side of the beholder's room.

Ryld sat down on a step and started to scrape the blood from Splitter's blade. He was exhausted. Jeggred, on the other hand, threw himself into the search, hurling heavy pieces of disused furniture aside and pulling down bookshelves. It occurred to Ryld that the draegloth was unlikely to find that the beholder had stashed a valuable book underneath the wreckage of a dusty old couch, but it seemed to keep the half-demon occupied. Ryld settled for staying out of the draegloth's way.

"Hold still, all of you!" Pharaun said sharply.

The wizard spoke a spell and commenced to turn slowly in a circle, studying the whole room intently. The rest of the company, including Jezz, halted their hurried ransacking and watched him impatiently. Pharaun continued past Jeggred, past Valas, and halted as he faced a blank wall. He smiled in a predatory fashion, evidently pleased with himself.

"I have defeated the defenses of our deceased adversary," he said. "That wall is an illusion covering an antechamber."

He gestured again, and part of the wall not far from Ryld abruptly vanished, revealing a large alcove or niche filled with ramshackle bookshelves cluttered with various old tomes and scrolls. Jezz hopped awkwardly to the bookshelf and started rifling through the titles, shoving each into a satchel at his hip.

"Ryld, Jeggred, keep watch," said Quenthel. She stood straighter, and the dazed look in her eyes was gone, but she frowned as she replaced the healing wand in her pack. "Valas, tidy up the beholder's gold and jewels. There's no point in leaving the loot here, and one never knows when it might be helpful." She looked over at the Jaelre sorcerer, who stood holding a great tome covered in green scales. "Well, Master Jezz, is that the book you wished to recover?"

Jezz blew dust from the cover and ran his slim fingers over the rough leather. He smiled, his handsome face twisting with glee.

"The Geildirion," he breathed. "Yes, this is the tome. I have what we came for."

"Good," said Quenthel. "Let's get out of here while we can. I think I've had all I can stand of this place."

SEVENTEEN

Halisstra sat in a window bench, alone in the apartment set aside for her, and plucked idly at the strings of her dragonbone lyre. She'd been confined to the room for two days, and she found herself growing more than a little weary of incarceration.

Whatever I manage to find in this whole venture, she promised herself, *I will not be locked up again.*

She had expected torture, magical compulsion, or worse during her interrogation, but Tzirik seemed to have taken her at her word. More than a few drow would have indulged themselves in the opportunity to torture a prisoner regardless of whether she was being truthful or not, leading Halisstra to wonder if Tzirik was waiting for word of Quenthel and the others before doing something that might anger them. Halisstra didn't think the Mistress of Arach-Tinilith and her comrades had managed to cow the entire House, but it was entirely possible that their competence had persuaded Tzirik not to look for trouble without good cause.

She looked out the narrow, barred window. Dawn was fast approaching. The sky was already growing painfully bright in the east, though the sun had not yet risen. Halisstra could make out the endless green forest of Cormanthor, rolling away from her for mile after mile.

A knock at the door startled her, followed by the jingling of keys in the lock. She looked around and stood as Tzirik entered the room, dressed in a resplendent high-collared coat of red and black.

"Mistress Melarn," he said, offering an indulgent bow, "your comrades have returned. If you'll come with me, we shall see whether they had some good reason for abandoning you in the wilds of the World Above."

Halisstra set down her lyre and asked, "Were they successful?"

"In fact, they were, which is why I intend to set you at your liberty now. Had they failed, I'd planned to use you as a hostage to compel them to try again."

She snorted in amusement, and the priest escorted her from the room. He led her through the elegant pale halls and corridors of Minauthkeep. A pair of Jaelre warriors trailed them, dressed in cuirasses dyed a mottled green and brown, short swords at their hips. They came to a small chapel, decorated in the colors of Vhaeraun, and there they found Quenthel, Danifae, and the rest of the company waiting.

"I see you have survived the rigors of Myth Drannor and returned to tell the tale," Tzirik said by way of a greeting. "As you see, it seems I have found something of yours, just as you have found something of mine."

Halisstra studied the faces of her former companions as she appeared. Most showed some degree or another of surprise—a raised eyebrow, an exchange of glances. Ryld offered her a warm smile before dropping his gaze and shifting his feet nervously, while Danifae actually came forward to clasp her hand.

"Mistress Melarn," she said. "We thought you lost."

"I was," Halisstra replied.

She was surprised to find how relieved she was to be back among her former companions—though they were interlopers from a rival city—and her scheming battle captive. Danifae might not have been Halisstra's ornament anymore, but the binding spell was still there, making her the only ally Halisstra had left in the world.

"Where have you been?" Quenthel asked.

"I was subjected to several days worth of effort to convert me to the worship of Eilistraee, if you can believe such a thing," Halisstra answered. "Lolth granted me an opportunity to slay two of the Eilistraen clerics and escape."

Though her heart glowed with dark pride at her accomplishment, Halisstra found herself feeling a bit disappointed by the results of her treachery. She was no stranger to the traitor's dark art, but it seemed as if she had only managed to do what was expected of her.

"Undoubtedly the surface folk set you free to see what you were up to," Quenthel said. "It's an old trick."

"So we thought, too," Tzirik said. "However, we investigated Mistress Melarn's story and found it to be true. It's almost comical, the naivete of our sisters in Eilistraee's worship." He paused and rubbed his hands together. "Be that as it may, Jezz informs me that you helped him recover the tome we needed."

"We *helped* him?" Jeggred growled.

"His task was to bring back the book," Tzirik replied, "not to battle the denizens of Myth Drannor."

"You have your book," Quenthel said. Ignoring Jeggred's snarl, she folded her arms and fixed her eyes on Tzirik. "Are you ready to fulfill your end of the bargain?"

"I have already done so," the priest replied. He glanced up at the bronze image high on the wall, and made a small genuflection. "Whether or not you returned alive, I intended to consult with the Masked Lord and find out for myself what takes Lolth from you. Your story made me quite curious."

Quenthel virtually ground her teeth in frustration.

"What did you learn, then?" she managed.

Tzirik savored his knowledge, responding with a deliberate smirk as he paced away from the company and took a seat on a small dais that stood to one side of the chapel.

He steepled his fingers together and said, "In all essentials your story is true. Lolth does not grant her priestesses spells, nor does she reply to any entreaties."

"We already knew as much," Pharaun observed.

"But I did not," the priest answered. "In any event, it seems that Lolth has, in some manner, barricaded herself within her infernal domain. She denies contact not only to her priestesses, but all other beings both mortal and divine, which would explain why the demons you conjured up to question about the Spider Queen's doings were unable to assist you."

The Menzoberranyr stood silent, considering Tzirik's answer. Halisstra was puzzled, as well.

"Why would the goddess do this?" she wondered aloud.

"In the spirit of candor, I will admit that Vhaeraun either does not know or does not wish for me to know," Tzirik said. He fixed his cold gaze on Halisstra. "For the moment, divine capriciousness seems as good an explanation as any."

"Is she . . . alive?" Ryld asked quietly. Quenthel and the other priestesses turned angry glares on the weapons master, but he ignored them and went on. "What I mean to say is, would we know if she had been slain by another god, or sickened, or imprisoned against her will?"

"If only we were so lucky," Tzirik said, laughing. "No, Lolth still lives, however you might define that for a goddess. As to whether she has sealed herself into the Demonweb Pits, or been sealed in by another power, Vhaeraun did not say."

"When will this condition end?" Halisstra asked.

"Again, Vhaeraun either does not know or does not wish for me to know," Tzirik said. "The better question might be, will it end? The answer to that is yes, it will end in time, but before you take too much comfort in that I must remind you that a goddess may have a very different sense of what we would consider to be a reasonable wait. The Masked Lord might have been referring to something that would happen tomorrow, next month, next year, or perhaps a hundred years from now."

"We can't wait that long," Quenthel murmured. Her expression was distant, fixed on events in faraway Menzoberranzan. "A resolution must be reached soon."

"Take up the worship of a more caring deity, then," Tzirik replied. "If you're interested, I would be happy to discourse at length on the virtues of the Masked Lord."

Quenthel bristled, but held her tongue—a feat of remarkable self-control for the Baenre priestess.

"I decline," she said. "Does the Masked Lord have any other advice for us, priest?"

"In fact, he does," Tzirik replied. He shifted in his seat, leaning forward to convey his point to Quenthel. "These were the exact words he spoke to me, so take note of them. 'The children of the Spider Queen should seek her for answers.' "

"But we have," Halisstra cried. "All of us, but she does not hear us."

"I don't think that's what he meant," Danifae said. "I think Vhae-raun is suggesting that we won't learn anything more unless we go to the Demonweb Pits ourselves, and beseech the goddess in person."

Tzirik remained silent and watched the Menzoberranyr. Quenthel paced in a small circle, considering the idea.

"The Spider Queen requires a certain amount of initiative and self-reliance in her priestesses," the Mistress of Arach-Tinilith said, "but she also demands obedience. To go before her in her divine abode in the expectation of answers . . . Lolth does not smile on such effrontery."

Halisstra fell silent, thinking furiously over what Tzirik suggested. Ventures into other planes of existence were not unknown, of course. Pharaun's spell had carried the company across the Plane of Shadow, after all, and there were many more universes that mortals armed with the right magic could reach, a multitude of heavens and hells, wonders and terrors beyond the confines of the physical world, but the notion of attempting such a journey without Lolth's explicit invitation terrified Halisstra.

"The penalties for failing to understand the goddess's will in this matter would be severe indeed," Halisstra said.

"Have we not just heard the goddess's will?" Danifae asked. "She led us to this place and this question through her silence, just as surely as if she had placed the commands directly in our hearts. She might be angered if we fail to do this."

Halisstra was accustomed to a feeling of certainty when it came to interpreting the Spider Queen's wishes. Before the divine silence had fallen over the priestesses of Lolth, she'd known the rare touch of the goddess's whispers in her mind. It didn't happen often, of course—she was only one priestess, and Lolth was served by un-counted thousands—but she knew what it felt like to understand to the depths of her soul what the Spider Queen wished, and how she could accomplish it. Halisstra felt nothing. Lolth's will, evidently, was that she should figure it out for herself.

Halisstra glanced up, where the bronze mask of Vhaeraun hung over a black altar. The foreignness of the place seemed palpable, a tangible expression of everything she had lost. Instead of standing before the ancient altar in the proud temple of House Melarn, Lolth's divine certitude thrumming in her very soul as she performed the rites of sacrifice and abasement the Spider Queen demanded, she stood alone, lost, an interloper in the temple of a pretender god, groping blindly for a hint of Lolth's intentions for her.

She imagined standing before Lolth, her soul naked to her god-dess, her eyes blasted by the sight of Lolth's dark glory, her ears scoured by the sound of the Spider Queen's sibilant voice. Perhaps it was effrontery to think that Lolth would erase her doubts, supply answers for her questions and a balm for her wounded heart, but Halisstra discovered that she did not care. If Lolth chose to discard her, to punish her, then she would, but then why had she destroyed Ched Nasad and House Melarn if not to bring Halisstra before her and receive her plea?

"I agree with Danifae," she said at last. "I cannot see what the point of this has been, other than to summon us before the goddess's throne. We will find our answers in her presence."

Quenthel nodded slowly and said, "I read her will in the same way, sisters. We must go to the Demonweb Pits."

Ryld and Valas exchanged worried looks.

"A sojourn to the sixty-sixth layer of the Abyss," Pharaun observed. "Well, I have dreamed of the place. It would be interesting to see if the reality matches my dream from years ago, though I have to say, I do not relish the thought of meeting Lolth in person. She minced my soul to pieces when I had that vision. It took me months to recover."

"Perhaps we should return to Menzoberranzan and report what we have learned before we consider anything rash?" Ryld asked, clearly alarmed by the prospect of descending into the infernal realms.

"Now that I understand the goddess's will, I do not wish to delay in obeying it," Quenthel said. "Pharaun can use his sending spell to apprise Gromph of our intentions."

"More to the point," Valas said, "how exactly does one get to the Demonweb Pits?"

"Worship Lolth all your life," Quenthel replied, a dark look clouding her eyes, "then die."

Halisstra glanced at the high priestess, then looked at the scout and said, "Were the goddess granting us our spells, we could do it easily enough. Without them, it is not so easy. Pharaun?"

The wizard wrung his hands.

"I will learn the proper spells at the first opportunity," he said. "I suppose I will have to locate a wizard of some accomplishment who happens to know the right spells, and persuade him to share one with me."

"That will not be necessary, Master Pharaun," Tzirik said. He stood up from his seat and descended the dais, powerful and confident. "As it so happens, my god has not seen fit to deprive me of my spells. I have an interest in seeing for myself what transpires in Lolth's domain. We can leave as soon as tonight, if you like."

✷ ✷ ✷

Company by company, the Army of the Black Spider marched proudly into the open cavern behind the Pillars of Woe. It was nothing compared to the vast cavern of Menzoberranzan, or the incomprehensible gulf of the Darklake, but the plain at the head of the gorge was still impressive, an asymmetrical space perhaps half a mile across, its ceiling rising a couple of hundred feet overhead. Innumerable columns supported its roof, and shelflike side caverns twisted away on all sides like highways beckoning in the dark.

Nimor surveyed the place from astride his war-lizard, watching as the great Houses of Menzoberranzan filed into the cavern, forming up in glittering squares beneath a dozen different banners. He'd had more than two days to reconnoiter the various crevices, caves, and passages leading to the open spot. The strategic value of the Pillars of Woe was obvious. Only one road lead south through a torturous canyon, yet several tunnels met where he'd led the drow, each leading into Menzoberranzan's Dark Dominion.

"A good place for a battle," he said, nodding to himself with satisfaction.

His mount, vicious and stupid beast that it was, still seemed to dully sense the impending conflict. It hissed and pawed at the pebble-strewn floor, its tail twitching in agitation.

Nimor waited near the center of the scout line holding the gap between the Pillars, at the head of a force of almost a hundred Agrach Dyrr riders. Those among his scout force who had any other House allegiance lay sprawled among the rocks and crevices of the gorge below, where Nimor and his men had slaughtered them soon after reaching the Pillars of Woe.

Nimor ached to go riding up to greet Mez'Barris Armgo, Andzrel Baenre, and the rest of the army's priestesses and commanders. He could see their pavilion, already rising in the center of the cavern.

The difficulty with a betrayal spanning a whole battlefield, he thought, is that one simply can't be everywhere at once to savor the moment in its entirety.

He noted a lean runner-lizard pelting from the command pavilion toward where his company waited.

"It seems I am wanted, lads," he called to the Agrach Dyrr soldiers waiting behind him. "You know what to do. Wait for the signal. When it comes, hold nothing back."

Nimor kicked his war-lizard into motion and rode back a short distance to meet the messenger. The rider was a young fellow in the livery of House Baenre—no doubt a favored nephew or cousin, given a relatively safe task in order to gain a blooding without too much risk. He wore no helmet, allowing his hair to stream out behind him like a mane. A bright red banner fluttered from a harness secured to his saddle.

"You are Captain Zhayemd?" he called, slowing his lizard to greet Nimor.

"I am."

"Your presence is requested at the command pavilion immediately, sir. Matron Del'Armgo wants to know where the gray dwarves are, and how best to dispose the troops."

"I see," Nimor replied. "Well, ride on back and tell her I'll be along presently."

"With respect, sir, I am to—"

Three great horn blasts, two short followed by one long, bellowed up from the space between the Pillars of Woe, echoing so loudly it seemed the rock itself had given voice to the cry. The messenger broke off and twisted his mount around, padding past Nimor to peer back toward the Pillars.

"Lolth's wrath, what was that?" he said.

"That," said Nimor, "would be the signal for the duergar attack."

From the depths of the gorge beneath the Pillars of Woe came the ground-shaking rumble of an army on the move. Below Nimor's line of scouts, hundreds of duergar lizard riders suddenly rose from beneath carefully arranged blankets of camouflage and pelted up and into the gap Nimor's scouts were supposed to hold. Behind the duergar cavalry, rank upon rank of duergar infantry ran forward, shouting their uncouth war cries, hammers and axes raised high. The Agrach Dyrr riders scrambled to their saddles, taking position to bottle up the charge between the mammoth columns of rock—and, as arranged, they wheeled in unison and dashed to one side, leaving the line unguarded.

"The Agrach Dyrr! They betray us!" the messenger shouted, horror and shock on his face.

He wrenched his mount around, but Nimor leaned out from his saddle and ran the boy through. The young Baenre clutched at his wound, swaying, and toppled from the saddle. Nimor slapped his sword against the lizard's rump and sent the beast bolting off back into the main cavern, the dead messenger dragging behind it with his feet tangled in the stirrups.

Nimor spurred his mount up onto an uneven shelf of rock about fifteen feet above the cavern floor, overlooking the Pillars. From that vantage he could see most of the cavern.

"A good view of the fray, my prince!" he called. "What a magnificent day for your triumph, eh?"

"I'll tell you in a quarter-hour if we have a victory or not."

From the shadows at the back of the ledge, Horgar Steelshadow emerged. He and his personal guards were warded by a well-crafted illusion, invisible to anyone below, unless one knew precisely where to find them.

"Do not come closer, Nimor," the crown prince said. "I do not wish someone below to notice you disappearing into a wall, and become overly curious about what might be up here."

"Surely you mean to join the battle, Prince Horgar? I know you are a dwarf of no small valor."

"I will venture into the fray when I'm certain I will not need to issue any more orders, Nimor. In another few moments you won't be able to hear a fellow shouting in your ear."

Nimor turned his attention back to the battle. The Agrach Dyrr riders, well clear of the Pillars, charged madly in a circle, skirting the perimeter of the cave and avoiding the main mass of the Menzoberranyr army. Their task was to get to the rear and aid the Agrach Dyrr infantry in sealing the tunnel through which the Army of the Black Spider had just come.

Duergar cavalry streamed up and through the gap, overrunning the positions that had been supposedly held against them and spilling out onto the cavern floor. Several of the House contingents in the van of the march milled about in evident disorder, surprised to find themselves suddenly faced with a thundering charge in an open field instead of siege-work and camp-building behind a stout line.

Other Houses responded to the sudden assault with adroitness and valor. The huge Baenre contingent raised a fierce war cry of their own, and dashed forward to seize the pass before any more duergar could flood through it.

"A bold move, Andzrel," Nimor said, not without admiration. "Unfortunately, I think it's too late to put the cork back in that bottle."

Nimor flicked his war-lizard's reins and positioned himself for a better view of the cavern center. He'd expected the mad rush of motion, the sight of armored ranks surging forward to crash and retreat like the bloody surf of an iron sea, but the sound of the battle was intolerable. Caught by rock above, below, and to all sides, the roars, screams, and clang of weapons on shields became completely indistinguishable, growing into a single great thundering sound that continued to build and build as more and more warriors became embroiled in the fighting.

"The noise will stand to our advantage," he cried over his shoulder to Horgar, though he could not hear his own words. "The commanders of the Army of the Black Spider must decide how to respond, and give the appropriate orders."

"Aye," the gray dwarf monarch answered. Nimor had to strain to understand him. "The middle of a fight is hardly the best time to draw up your plan of battle!"

A brilliant lightning bolt tore into the duergar ranks, followed by a thunderclap audible even over the din of the battle. Exploding balls of fire and scathing sheets of flame streaked across the battlefield, as wizards on each side began to make their presence felt.

Nimor frowned. A handful of powerful wizards could decide the issue, even in the teeth of the ferocious duergar assault and the duplicity of his allies in Agrach Dyrr, but there were wizards among the duergar troops, too, many of them disguised as common riders and infantrymen. As the drow mages struck at the attacking gray dwarves, they gave away their own positions. Duergar wizards answered each bolt of lightning, each blast of fire, in kind, and in moments the cavern was filled with flashes of painful light and ruddy fire, the air hot and acrid with the mighty magic thrown heedlessly from one side to the other.

Try as he might, Nimor couldn't tell whose magic would prevail, as the whole terrible scene descended into complete anarchy. In the space of a few dozen heartbeats, the sheer mass of Menzoberranyr troops in the middle of the cavern checked the initial rush of the duergar charge, the two armies tangling in a long line of contact that snaked across the cavern floor for hundreds of yards. Standards waved and fell, war-lizards reared and plunged, as the great charge bogged down into a thousand individual duels.

Rushing columns of heavily armored duergar pressed through the seams where dark elf Houses met, streaming in and around their desperately battling foes. Nimor smiled grimly. The dark elves had very little notion of how to weld their companies together to make an army into a single weapon, but each House contingent was a small army of deadly, seasoned veterans by itself. The duergar assault had smashed the Army of the Black Spider into twenty smaller forces that swarmed and stung back like a basket of scorpions that had been kicked over.

"Our victory is still in question, Nimor," Horgar called from above. "The cursed wizards have checked our first assault!"

"Yes, but you have forced the Pillars, have you not?" Nimor shouted back. "I'd thought the initial charge would break the Menzoberranyr outright, but it seems the House armies are not so easily swept away."

As he surveyed the battle, Nimor thought the gray dwarves, with advantage of surprise, would most likely be able to defeat the Houses of Menzoberranzan in detail, but it would be a long hard day of fighting to reduce the dark elf force. House Baenre, in particular, had managed to close the Pillars of Woe for the moment, and the longer Andzrel held the pass, the better the dark elves' chances were.

Fortunately, Nimor had taken steps against this very possibility. The Menzoberranyr seemed heavily engaged to the front with the gray dwarf assault. It was time to slip his knife between Menzoberranzan's ribs while their swords were locked.

"Now, Aliisza," he said into the raging air.

Nimor wheeled his mount around, drew his sword, and spurred his war-lizard down into the confused fray. Mez'Barris Armgo and Andzrel Baenre were somewhere near the center of the fight, and he intended to make sure they did not escape the destruction of their army.

❀   ❀   ❀

A little less than half a mile away, crowded into a small tunnel that descended from the east toward the upper field at the head of the Pillars of Woe, Aliisza stood with her eyes closed, her mind focused on the spell that allowed her to observe Nimor. By virtue of the magic she used, she heard his every word as if he'd spoken clearly in a quiet room. She shook herself and allowed the spell to dissipate.

"It's time," she said to Kaanyr Vhok.

"Good," the warlord said. His pointed teeth were bared in a fierce smile, anticipating battle. He glanced at the assassin Zammzt, who stood nearby. "Well, renegade, I suppose this is your lucky day. I will throw my warriors against the dark elves, not your duergar allies."

Zammzt inclined his head and replied, "I assure you, you will not regret it, Warlord. Destroy this army, and Menzoberranzan will lie naked before you."

Kaanyr strode past the alu-fiend and the dark elf to the place where his standard-bearers stood.

"Sound the charge!" he cried.

Instantly, a dozen bugbear drummers struck their instruments, sounding a simple three-beat ruffle, repeating three times. Thronging the tunnel below, the tanarukks of Kaanyr Vhok's Scoured Legion howled in bloodlust and pressed forward, stamping their feet and clashing their axes as they poured down the tunnel. Kaanyr drew his own molten sword and joined his charging troops, as his guards and standard-bearers hurried to keep up. Aliisza caught her breath at the sight, and took to the air to wing after Kaanyr's standard. A battle like this didn't come along every day, after all.

Ahead of the charging tanarukks, one of the cavern walls on the flank of the Army of the Black Spider seemed to shimmer, and abruptly vanished, revealing a gaping tunnel mouth that had been concealed by a clever illusion. The screaming horde of slavering tanarukks poured from the hidden roadway, streaming out to take the drow army from behind while the great Houses were engaged by the duergar riders who had come up through the Pillars of Woe. Aliisza glimpsed Kaanyr's red banner flying proudly at the head of the force, and the Scoured Legion slammed into the battle.

Only a handful of minor Houses stood in the path of the onrushing horde. The wave of bloodthirsty orc-demons overran them, a spear of red-hot iron punching deep into the army's flank. Aliisza found herself whooping in exultation and terror, gripped by the terrible spectacle and helpless to express her excitement in any other way. The Army of the Black Spider was hopelessly entangled in the very battle it did not want to fight, a wild melee in open terrain against the combined armies of Gracklstugh and Kaanyr Vhok. Like islands in a swirling sea of foes, each House of Menzoberranzan stood alone against a tide of steel and spell, battling for its life.

The alu-fiend alighted atop a blunt stalagmite and stared down at the battle below her.

Ah, Nimor, she thought. What a great and terrible thing you have done!

🕷   🕷   🕷

Nimor Imphraezl, Anointed Blade of the Jaezred Chaulssin, waded through a scene such as all the devils in all the hells could hardly have imagined. The blood of dozens of highborn drow mingled on his rapier and splattered his black mail. His war-lizard was long gone, burned out from under him by a lightning bolt hurled by a Tuin'Tarl wizard, and his limbs ached with fatigue and a dozen minor wounds, but Nimor grinned savagely, giddy with the results of his deadly work.

"Who has accomplished something now, Revered Grandfather?"

he laughed aloud. "Zammzt may have delivered Ched Nasad into your hands, but I have brought low the favored city of the Spider Queen!"

The battle had raged for several hours. Instead of holding an impregnable line between the Pillars of Woe, the Army of the Black Spider had found itself beset on all sides by a foe who'd picked the terrain and the moment to strike. Of course, like a great dumb beast with a mortal wound in its belly, a broken army could take a long time to die, thrashing and convulsing for hours as its blood slowly ran out. In the battles of the World Above, perhaps the defeated drow would have thrown down their arms and hoped for good terms from the victors. In the ruthless calculus of warfare in the Underdark, quarter was neither given nor asked. The gray dwarves had no intention of allowing a single dark elf to survive the day. The warriors of Menzoberranzan knew that, and they fought to the death.

Some of the smaller Houses were smashed apart and scattered throughout the cavern, leaving drow in pairs or threes to sell their lives as dearly as they could. Bands of duergar, bugbears, ogres, and other soldiers loyal to the Crown Prince of Gracklstugh roamed the cavern, drunk on slaughter as they hunted the wretched drow whose companies had been scattered by the assault. Some Houses stood where they were in the great cavern, fighting furiously as the duergar tide rose higher and higher, assailing them from all sides, and some of the Houses held together and tried to cut their way out of the fray, hoping to snatch survival from the specter of a catastrophic defeat.

The soldiers of Barrison Del'Armgo had been driven into a narrow, twisting side-tunnel, and forced from the field. Retreating through a passage only twenty feet wide, the proud warriors of the Second House held off repeated duergar assaults. Mez'Barris was penned in and unable to join with any other Houses, while her supplies burned along with the rest of the train, fired by the Agrach Dyrr infantry who had brought up the rear of the day's march. Del'Armgo would have a long and hungry march home.

House Xorlarrin's company, well stocked with the potent wizards the House was famed for, was caught near the center of the cavern, far from any place of relative security. The Xorlarrin mages kept five times their number of duergar at arm's length for most of the day by raising walls of fire and ice, and lashing out with sweeping blasts of destructive energy—but their wizards were tiring, exhausting their spells. Hundreds of duergar lancers mounted on war-lizards waited for the chance to ride down the Xorlarrins when their arcane defenses failed.

The proud company of House Baenre, more than five hundred strong, stood like a rock as lesser Houses were shattered and pulled down around them. As Nimor had predicted, Andzrel Baenre had been forced to relinquish the Pillars of Woe soon after seizing them, and his forces had slowly battled their way across the cavern to the tunnel mouth through which the Army of the Black Spider had marched only hours before. The Baenre turned their full attention on the Agrach Dyrr who barred escape back down the path of the march. Quarrels, javelins, and deadly spells flew thick and fast as the two Houses battled furiously. While the Baenre outnumbered the treacherous Agrach Dyrr more than two to one, the warriors of the First House were obliged to defend themselves against attacks on all sides while they tried to cut their way through to escape.

Nimor stalked toward the thick of the fighting, picking his way past the dead and the dying. Fortunately, he'd readied several spells of invisibility for the day, otherwise he would have been waylaid time and time again by raging tanarukks or grim duergar anxious to slay any drow they encountered. Hundreds of Horgar's Stone Guards clashed with the Baenre footsoldiers ahead of him, while the Agrach Dyrr barricaded the mouth of the main tunnel on the opposite side. Nimor carefully skirted the fight, catching sight of Andzrel and Zal'therra beneath the Baenre banner.

The Baenre leaders led their soldiers into the thick of the battle against the Agrach Dyrr, slowly but surely cutting their way through the warriors of the treacherous House. A tight knot of bodyguards surrounded them.

The assassin grinned, seeing his opportunity. The Baenre leaders had committed themselves to the fray. If he could destroy them, he would decapitate the Baenre contingent, and if their force disintegrated, there was an excellent chance that nothing of the Army of the Black Spider would survive the day.

Nimor spotted Jazzt Dyrr, who stood back from the melee, directing the Agrach Dyrr soldiers. The nobleman held his hand to a bloody slash across his ribs. The assassin hurried over and released his invisibility.

"A job well done, my kinsman," he shouted to Jazzt. "Continue to hold the Baenre on this side, and the crown prince's guard will grind them to nothing."

Jazzt looked up. Fatigue and pain faded from his face as he surveyed the fight.

"Easier said than done," he said. "The Baenre fight like demons, and more than a few of our own lads won't be going home." He straightened, and offered Nimor his hand. "I had my misgivings about you, Zhayemd, but your plan seems to be unfolding well enough. I'd say we could use you here, but I take it from the blood all over you that you're keeping yourself busy."

"The great Houses still hold in the center of the cavern floor, but this is the spot of decision," Nimor replied. His eyes were fixed on the Baenre banner. "Lend me whatever lads you can. I mean to kill the Baenre commanders."

"Good, we need the help," Jazzt replied. He gestured sharply, and brought up a reserve of a dozen seasoned warriors. "You lads, you go with Zhayemd. Take the Baenre banner!"

Nimor readied his rapier and dagger while the fresh fighters gathered behind him. The melee edged closer, as the Baenre continued to claw their way toward escape. He could see the Baenre standard, waving above the center of the fight. Andzrel himself stood near the forefront, surrounded by the best House Baenre had to offer, while Zal'therra hobbled along a few steps back. The priestess was struggling with a bad wound in her hip, and she had her arm around another Baenre as the line advanced.

Nimor waited until the leading Baenre guardsmen were within a spearcast of his soldiers, and shouted, "Up and at them, lads!"

With a ragged cheer the warriors of Agrach Dyrr dashed forward from their hiding places, some firing crossbows into the Baenre before discarding the weapons and drawing blades. Quarrels hissed in the tunnel mouth. Some bounced from the armor of the Baenre guards and priestesses, but other quarrels struck home. The Baenre guards readied themselves for Agrach Dyrr's charge as best they could. Zal'therra hopped to one side of the tunnel and defended herself with a huge, black, two-headed flail, unwilling to trust her injured leg enough to press into the skirmish but still far from helpless—as an Agrach Dyrr soldier learned when she expertly tripped him and followed up with a blow that pulped the wretch's skull. In a moment the din of steel on steel and the awful sound of steel in flesh filled the corridor, accompanied by the screams, grunts, and curses of the fighters.

Andzrel, unlike his kinswoman, threw himself into the fight, wielding a double-ended sword with expert skill and lashing out with brutal spinning kicks to hammer his foes to the ground while they parried his flashing blades. Nimor watched in admiration as the furious assault swayed back and forth, then, the Agrach Dyrr making way, he approached the Baenre weapons master.

"Greetings, Andzrel," he called. "Your master of scouts must report that the duergar seem to have slipped past our line at the Pillars of Woe, and now pose a considerable danger to the Army of the Black Spider."

Andzrel Baenre fell still as the skirmish swept away from him. Hard anger seethed beneath his disciplined manner.

"Zhayemd," he spat. "You have made a grave mistake in confronting me. You would have been wiser to savor the fruits of your treachery from afar."

"We shall see," Nimor replied.

He leaped forward and aimed a murderous thrust straight for the center of the Baenre's torso, but Andzrel was not unprepared. The weapons master twisted aside and brought up his double-sword in a spinning parry that deflected Nimor's blade, and whirled in close to slam his armored elbow against the side of the assassin's head. Had

Nimor been the slight drow he appeared to be, the blow might have fractured his skull. Instead it merely jolted him, hard. He responded by spinning the other way and bringing up his off-hand dagger in a hidden slash that scored Andzrel beneath the breastplate. The weapons master took half a step back and leaped into the air, planting his boot in the assassin's ribs, but Nimor merely grunted and threw Andzrel back with contemptuous strength.

Andzrel rolled and came up with his sword high, his eyes wide.

"What in all the goddess's hells *are* you?" he muttered.

Before Nimor could compose a suitable answer, the weapons master's hand flashed down to his boot and he hurled a knife straight for Nimor's throat. The assassin threw his arm in front of his face and caught the blade in the meat of his left forearm. He snarled and pulled it out, blood spattering the dusty cavern floor.

Andzrel didn't wait for him, of course. The Baenre followed his thrown dagger by hurling himself forward and rolling under Nimor's guard, trying to run him through with a quick jab.

Nimor jumped clear over the weapons master, pulling his feet up close to his body, and landed on the other side. As Andzrel reversed his thrust and came back up, Nimor punched his rapier through the Baenre's breastplate and scored a deep wound in the weapons master's side. Andzrel grunted and stumbled, losing his balance. He sprawled to the ground at Nimor's feet, his two-ended sword flat on the ground below him.

"A good effort," Nimor said, drawing back his sword to finish off the Baenre.

Before he could strike, a globe of amber energy encased him. Magical force halted the thrust of his blade as surely as if he'd tried to skewer Narbondel, and resisted his knife as well.

"What in the Nine Hells?" Nimor demanded.

The assassin snarled in rage, even as he realized that the sounds of battle in the tunnel had increased threefold at the same instant. He glared out of the sphere, trying to determine where it had come from and what was happening.

Outside, dozens of fresh Baenre troops poured into the fight from the tunnel behind the Agrach Dyrr, catching Jazzt and his footsoldiers between hammer and anvil. The Agrach Dyrr blocking the tunnel were quickly driven away or killed, clearing the retreat for the House Baenre contingent. Nimor watched in cold wrath as the Baenre began to stream past his magical prison, reinforcing their embattled kin. In the space of a few moments, the battle rolled away from him and back into the main cavern.

Nimor glanced back down the tunnel, and found himself looking at a tall, round-bodied wizard in the colors of House Baenre, who studied the amber globe with a smirk of self-satisfaction. Zal'therra and Andzrel both stared at the newcomer as well.

"Nauzhror," said the priestess. Blood streamed from her injured hip. "Your timing is impeccable."

"A fortunate accident, really," the wizard purred. "The matron mother instructed me to obtain news from the field, and so I scried the army, found the battle underway, and noted your difficulties. I made use of a very valuable scroll to raise a gate and bring you some help." He turned and studied Nimor in the globe of energy. "Isn't this fierce fellow Captain Zhayemd of Agrach Dyrr?"

"So he says, anyway," Andzrel gritted. "Can you destroy him in that sphere?"

"Not right away. It simply captures someone for a time, encapsulating the victim in an impervious shield of magical force. It will fade in a short while, after which you may kill him at your leisure."

"Later, then," Andzrel said, dismissing the question of the trapped Nimor.

With one hand he groped for a small vial at his belt—a healing potion, Nimor guessed—and drank it down. He glanced back at the fighting, his face expressionless as he studied the savage melee.

Zal'therra limped up beside him and said, "Make ready to charge. With Nauzhror's reinforcements, we can turn the tables on these cursed dwarves and tanarukks." She looked over to the wizard. "How many soldiers did you bring?"

"Only a single company, I fear. The matron mother did not want to risk any more of our strength in a lost battle, if things go poorly."

Zal'therra began to protest, but Andzrel set a hand on her arm.

"No," he said, "the matron mother was right. Now that we've secured our line of retreat, we must withdraw any Houses we can from the fight. The duergar and their tanarukk allies have won the day."

Nauzhror's eyes widened and he asked, "Is it as bad as that?"

"If we move swiftly," Andzrel answered, "we will bring a good portion of our soldiers off the field yet. Once we've got the important Houses out of the fray, we can make a fighting retreat all the way to Menzoberranzan if we have to. There is no time to lose, if we want to save Xorlarrin and Tuin'Tarl. Fey-Branche is all but gone, I haven't the faintest idea what happened to Barrison Del'Armgo, and Duskryn and Kenafin were swept away by the tanarukks. Menzoberranzan can't lose any more drow here."

"Your retreat will only delay the inevitable," Nimor said. "You can't stop it now."

Andzrel leaned on his two-bladed sword and threw a dark look at Nimor.

"On second thought," the weapons master said, "I'll detail a few lads to wait for this sphere to fade. I see no reason to let him live a moment longer than I have to." He met Nimor's eyes with a cold expression. "Your House will rue the day you betrayed our city, traitor."

Nimor tried the force globe again, to no avail. Andzrel, Zal'therra, and the Baenre wizard turned away and followed their soldiers into the renewed battle, while several Baenre guards trotted back and took up stations surrounding the sphere of force.

"I'll see you in Menzoberranzan," Nimor promised the Baenre.

The Anointed Blade invoked the power of his ring, and disappeared from the force globe into the welcoming shadows.

Four hours later, the company stood again beneath the bronze mask of Vhaeraun in the chapel of Minauthkeep. Battered, filthy mail had been laboriously cleaned, broken links mended, arming coats laundered. Those who had lost their packs, bedrolls, or other gear carried replacements purchased from Jaelre merchants. For the first time since leaving Gracklstugh Halisstra felt clean, rested, and reasonably well prepared for the next step in her journey. She sorely missed the mail she'd worn as First Daughter of House Melarn, and the thundering mace her mother had given her a century past, but she still had her lyre, and Seyll Auzkovyn's mail and sword were not entirely useless substitutes.

The sword in particular seemed a fine piece of work. It carried a potent virtue of holiness that made it tingle unpleasantly in the dark elf's grip, but Halisstra suspected its blade would be unbearable to any fell creature who felt its bite. Considering the fact that she intended to descend into the Abyss itself, where such creatures would likely set upon the company in numbers, she was willing to endure the sword's distasteful enchantment for a time.

Tzirik had donned a suit of black mithral plate armor decorated with grotesque demonic figures and chased with gold filigree. A wickedly spiked mace hung at his belt, and he wore a great masked helm in the shape of a demon's skull. He radiated confidence and energy, as if he'd waited a long time for the opportunity to serve his god with worthwhile stakes at hand.

"As you know," said the priest, "there is more than one way to leave this plane of existence and venture into the dimensions beyond. I have examined the issue at length, and I have decided that we shall travel in astral form. Now, if—"

"That would require us to leave our bodies comatose while our spirits journeyed to the Abyss," Quenthel interrupted. "Why would you even hope I might consent to that?"

"Betrayal," Jeggred rumbled. "He intends to have his comrades slit our throats while our bodies lie uninhabited."

The draegloth took a step forward, baring his fangs at the Vhae-raunite priest.

"I choose to travel in astral form for two reasons, Mistress Bae-nre," Tzirik replied, ignoring Jeggred. "First, it is marginally safer, in that if someone's roving spirit happened to be killed while visiting the Demonweb Pits, that person would not truly be dead—he would awaken here, unharmed. A spirit is a difficult thing to destroy, after all. Second, as far as I can tell, we have no real alternative. I have already attempted to plane shift bodily to the Demonweb Pits, and the spell failed outright. I believe the barrier or seal of which the Masked Lord spoke prevented the direct transference of a physical body into Lolth's demesnes."

"Yet you believe you'll be able to carry our astral forms there, when the realm is still sealed?" Halisstra asked.

"I know of only two ways to take you to the Demonweb Pits, and if one doesn't work, the other must," Tzirik said with a shrug. "The Masked Lord himself has instructed me to take you there, so there must be a way. Still, if you happen to know of any permanent gates or portals connecting our world with the Abyss, or the Demonweb Pits itself, I suppose you could make use of such a device."

"Show me that physical travel will not work," Quenthel said.

"Step close," Tzirik said from behind his mask, his voice carrying a certain dry amusement, "and join hands with me."

The drow shuffled close and joined hands in a circle with Tzirik, who took a place between Quenthel and Danifae, laying his left hand over their joined hands and leaving his right free to make the gestures necessary for the spell. He collected himself, then chanted out a rolling, powerful prayer whose unholy words filled the air with a nearly tangible darkness.

Halisstra watched carefully to make certain that the priest cast the spell correctly, and as far as she could tell, he did. For a moment she thought it would work, as the Jaelre chapel grew misty and faint around them, and her body seemed to somehow drop away from the world without moving an inch—but then she sensed through some preternatural perception an impediment, a barrier that prevented the company from materializing again in a new place and seemed to almost jolt them back to Minauthkeep. She reeled drunkenly as her senses whirled.

"That happened the last time I tried it," Tzirik said.

Thunder gathered in Quenthel's brow, but she managed to keep her calm as she detached her hand from Danifae's and steadied herself against Jeggred.

"Pharaun," the high priestess said, "what did you observe?"

The wizard raised an eyebrow, perhaps surprised to be consulted by the Baenre, and said, "It seems plausible enough. If we travel by projecting our spirits into the Astral Plane, we won't be going directly from this plane of existence to the Abyss. We'd actually traverse the astral sea and approach Lolth's domain as spirits. It may be that the mysterious barrier we encountered does not bar such an approach." The wizard smoothed his robes, considering. "And that might explain why our conjured demons couldn't manage the trick either. They do not travel between planes by astral projection, as they have no souls."

Quenthel muttered something to herself, folded her arms, and turned back to Tzirik.

"Fine," she said. "You have convinced me. Where do you intend to leave our bodies?"

Tzirik walked over to one wall of the chapel and depressed a hidden stud, revealing a secret chamber behind the bronze mask of Vhaeraun. It was not large, but eight elegant old divans—furnishings that might have dated back to the castle's days as a home to the surface elves of Cormanthyr—were arranged in a tight circle in the room, heads together, feet outward.

"Only a handful of my people know of this room's existence," said the priest, "and I have instructed them to make no intrusion for as long as may prove necessary. You need not fear any harm here."

Ryld, who stood a little behind Jeggred, turned away from Tzirik and gestured subtly to Pharaun and Halisstra, *So if our spirits are defeated while we are astral, we return to our bodies. What happens to our spirits if someone sticks a knife in our bodies?*

Death, the wizard replied. *A cautious fellow would make sure his body was someplace safe and guarded by trustworthy sorts before sending his spirit off to some other plane.*

Ryld grimaced, but made no other reply.

The company followed Tzirik into the small room. Halisstra stared with some trepidation at the old couch in front of her, knowing that she was doing so but unable to look away. She wasn't the only member of the company regarding the divans like a collection of coffins; Quenthel must have been having the same thoughts.

She looked up from the couch to Tzirik and said, "We will leave behind a guard. Someone I trust will be here to watch over our bodies until I return, just as someone you trust will be watching over you."

"Ah," Tzirik said. "You are a dark elf indeed. Do as you will."

"He might mean to have this whole castle descend upon whomever we leave behind," Jeggred snarled. "Best leave two, maybe three."

"Our sentry's only duty will be to cut Tzirik's throat before he's overwhelmed," Pharaun said. "The question is, who stays?"

Quenthel glanced at Ryld, then her eyes slid toward Halisstra. For a moment Halisstra feared that Quenthel meant to leave her behind in order to deny her the audience she sought with Lolth, but even as her heart thudded in apprehension she realized that the last thing the Baenre would want—if she truly viewed Halisstra as a threat, anyway—would be a Melarn conscious and alone with her own helpless body. Quenthel's eyes narrowed as she weighed the same considerations, and she turned to Jeggred.

"You must stay here," she said to the draegloth.

Jeggred contorted himself in a spasm of anger.

"I am not going to sit here staring at your living corpses while you face the perils of the goddess's realm! Mother told me to guard you. How can I do that when you leave me behind?"

"You will be guarding me," Quenthel said. "No harm can come to me in astral form. It is here that I will be vulnerable, and I trust no one else with the task. It must be you, Jeggred."

The draegloth waved all four arms in protest and said, "You of all people know what awaits you in the Demonweb Pits, Mistress. You will need my strength there."

"Cease this at once," the Mistress of Arach-Tinilith commanded. Her eyes flashed, and her whip rippled and spat. "It is not for you to question me, nephew. You will discharge your obligation in the manner I direct."

Jeggred subsided into a sulking silence. In disgust he turned away and threw himself down on the stone floor, shucking his pack and bandoleer. Quenthel glanced at the others, and nodded at the couches.

"Come," she said. "The goddess awaits."

Tzirik waited while the Menzoberranyr chose divans and stretched out. He moved to the last one and sat down, then glanced over at Jeggred.

"If you will be staying here, half-demon, you should know that some of my kinfolk will be accompanying you on your vigil. Do not cause them any trouble, and I think you will find that they will be happy to leave you alone."

Jeggred sneered in answer, and Tzirik laid himself down awkwardly in his plate armor, arranging his mace so that it lay at his side.

Halisstra found that she was lying between Ryld and Danifae. She glanced over at the weapons master. Ryld's expression was taut and nervous. Clearly, astral travel was something beyond his experience too.

If our spirits are doing the traveling, why do we need all our weapons? he motioned to her.

They're part of you, she replied. *Your consciousness includes your belongings in your definition of yourself. Therefore, when your soul roams free from your body, your mind will imagine for you an astral copy of anything you have close at hand.*

"Reach out and take each other's hands," Tzirik said. "Make sure you have a good grasp. I do not want to leave anyone behind."

The priest started to chant again in his melodious voice. Halisstra stared at the ceiling and reached out to grasp Danifae with her right hand, and Ryld with her left.

Perhaps I should imagine for myself some good strong drink, Ryld observed.

He reached out and caught Halisstra's hand in his strong grip before she could reply.

Behind her, unseen on the other side of the circle, Tzirik continued his spell, speaking the harsh words of the magic with confidence and ease. Halisstra felt an electric jolt race through her body from hand to hand as the magic began to take life, joining her to Ryld and Danifae with a strange, tingling sensation. A sense of detachment swept through her, as if she'd all at once become weightless. She seemed to be floating up and out of herself, drawn by some irresistible force tugging on her in a direction she could not relate to up or down, left or right. The stone ceiling wavered and grew dim, pulling away from her faster and faster.

And she was gone.

Triel Baenre stalked gracefully past the ranks of her battered soldiers, her face held rigidly expressionless by nothing more than sheer iron determination. The exhausted troops stood at attention for her as best they could in the narrow tunnel. She'd had Nauzhror transport her immediately to the scene of the retreat to view with her own eyes the scope of Menzoberranzan's defeat, and she found that she did not like what she had seen. She did not like it all.

The passage was the better part of ten miles long, one of the main thoroughfares leading from the way-meeting at the Pillars of Woe to the shell of twisting passages and wild caverns known as Menzoberranzan's Dominion. It seemed that every second or third soldier she passed carried some obvious injury—a bandaged torso here, an arm in a sling there, a fellow using a broken spear shaft as a crutch against the other wall. The wounded did not bother her, though. What Triel found truly disconcerting was the fatigue and moroseness of the soldiers. She'd expected to find them tired, of course—Andzrel had marched the army for a day without halting to salvage something from the disaster of the Pillars of Woe—but she hadn't expected to find her soldiers so . . . *defeated*. They'd been beaten, and they knew it.

Andzrel trailed a respectful step behind the matron mother, not presuming to speak until addressed.

"How bad were the losses?" she finally asked, not looking at her weapons master.

"For the whole army, somewhere around a quarter to a third of our strength, Matron Mother. Some Houses fared much better or much worse than that, depending on the fortunes of battle."

"And House Baenre's contingent?"

"Ninety dead, forty-four seriously wounded," Andzrel replied. "About a quarter of our strength."

"We were fortunate to save that much, Matron Mother," Zal'therra added. "Some of the minor Houses were slaughtered to a male in—"

"I did not address you," Triel said.

She folded her arms and tried not to let the sick horror in her stomach show.

It will be a miracle if the Council doesn't rise in open revolt against me, the matron mother thought. Thank the goddess that Mez'Barris is lost somewhere, and Fey-Branche so badly weakened. Byrtyn Fey must guard her response with half her House army destroyed, and I will have some time to consider what must be done before I have to confront Mez'Barris, Lolth willing.

Then again, she thought, what was left of the Council, anyway? Faen Tlabbar, the Third House, was in the hands of an untried girl, and Yasraena Dyrr was not likely to present herself at the next meeting, was she? She and all her filthy House were barricaded in their castle, awaiting the arrival of their duergar allies, and apparently quite prepared to stand a siege.

That left Zeerith Q'Xorlarrin, Miz'ri Mizzrym, and Prid'eesoth Tuin as the only matron mothers she need concern herself with.

To distract herself from the unpleasant prospect ahead, Triel turned to face Andzrel and Zal'therra. More than anything, she longed to punish the weapons master and her cousin Zal'therra for leading her army into a disastrous ambush, but as far as she could tell, Andzrel's skill and Zal'therra's decisiveness had most likely extricated the Army of the Black Spider from a dreadful mauling. Menzoberranzan's army was battered, but intact.

"Where are the duergar now?" she asked.

"About three miles south of us," replied Andzrel. "House Mizzrym currently serves as rear guard, though I've sent almost a hundred of our own soldiers to stiffen the defense." Triel understood what Andzrel really meant—he'd put Baenre soldiers beside the Mizzrym to make sure that another betrayal of the sort Agrach Dyrr had engineered didn't take place. "The Scoured Legion advances through another passage to our east, circling around us. We don't dare try to make a stand in this tunnel, or the tanarukks will get by us."

"It would only take a hundred soldiers to hold this tunnel against almost any force, wouldn't it?" Triel asked.

"Yes, but the duergar have enough war wizards in their ranks, and siege engines in their train, that they wouldn't be halted for long by a rearguard action."

"Try it anyway," Triel grated. "Use slave troops, and leave enough officers behind to make sure they don't break and run. We need time, Weapons Master, and that's what rear guards are for."

Andzrel didn't argue the point, and Triel paced away to gather her thoughts. Drow rebels, slave revolts, duergar armies, dark treachery, a missing archmage, and tanarukk hordes—it was hard to see how matters could get much worse. Where could she even start to address any of these problems? Assault Agrach Dyrr, without the magical might of the city's assembled priestesses? Pick another spot to meet the duergar, and allow the tanarukks to sweep past?

"How did this happen?" she muttered aloud.

"Agrach Dyrr was in league with our city's enemies," Zal'therra replied. "They contrived to make up the vanguard of our army, and instead of holding the Pillars of Woe against the gray dwarves, they led us into a trap. They must be obliterated for their treachery."

"I was not speaking to you," Triel growled, and this time she could not restrain herself.

Though she knew Zal'therra was not to blame for the disastrous battle, she had to strike out at something. She slapped the girl, hard, rocking her to her heels despite the fact that Zal'therra towered almost a foot taller than her, and outweighed her by thirty pounds.

"You must come to expect treachery, you simpleminded fool!" Triel snarled. "Why were there no Baenre officers among our scouts? Why did you take no steps to verify the reports the Agrach Dyrr fed to you? If you had exercised even the most minimal amount of caution, our army would not be in tatters."

Zal'therra shrank back, saying, "Matron Mother, we all approved of Andzrel's plans—"

"Andzrel is a *weapon,* Zal'therra. Our House army is a *weapon.* Yours is the hand that must wield those weapons against our enemies. I sent you out to exercise your judgment and make decisions, to use your head and *think!*"

Triel whirled away to keep herself from striking Zal'therra again. If she did, she didn't think she'd be able to stop, and like it or not Zal'therra was probably the most promising of her cousins. Triel wouldn't be around forever, and she needed to give thought to leaving House Baenre with at least a few competent priestesses in the event that the day came when she would have to have her sisters murdered.

"Matron Mother," the girl managed, her eyes wide with fear, "I apologize for my failure."

"I never asked for an apology, girl, and a Baenre should never offer one," the matron mother rumbled, "but I will give you the opportunity to demonstrate that you have some redeeming portion of merit and resourcefulness. You will take command of the rearguard."

Triel gestured toward the south. There was an excellent chance that she was sending her cousin to her death, but she needed to know if Zal'therra had the wits and the resolve to become a leader of House Baenre, and if she found a way to survive the assignment and obtain any degree of success at all, Triel might consider permitting her to live.

"Make the duergar fight for every step they take toward Menzoberranzan," Triel added. "Your survival depends on your success. If you abandon this tunnel before three days pass, I will have you crucified."

Zal'therra bowed, and hurried off. Triel turned back to the weapons master.

"Understand that I do not hold you blameless, either," she said in a low voice. "You were the author of our grand strategy, and I committed the full weight of House Baenre's power and prestige to your battle plan, which has led us to a disaster the likes of which we have not seen since Mithral Hall. In any other circumstances, I would have you dumped into a pit of hungry centipedes with your tendons slashed for your failure, but . . . these are unusual times, and there exists the small possibility that your skill and grasp of strategy may prove useful in the days to come. Do not fail me again."

"Yes, Matron Mother," Andzrel said, bowing low.

"So," she continued, "where do we stop the duergar and their allies?"

Without hesitation, the weapons master replied, "We do not, Matron Mother. Given the losses we have already suffered, I advise withdrawing back to Menzoberranzan and preparing for a siege."

"I do not like that option," Triel snapped. "It reeks of defeat, and the longer an army sits on our doorstep, the more likely it is that they'll be reinforced by the arrival of some other enemy, such as the beholders or the mind flayers."

"That is possible, of course," Andzrel said, his voice carefully neutral, "but the gray dwarves will not find it easy to maintain a siege around Menzoberranzan, a hundred miles from their own city. I don't think the duergar can wait us out for more than a few months, and I doubt they have the numbers to take the city by storm. Our best course of action is to make the duergar set their siege, and see what kind of a threat we're really facing. It would provide us the opportunity to crush House Agrach Dyrr in the meantime."

"You're afraid to face the duergar in battle again?" Triel rasped.

"No, Matron Mother, but I will not advise a course of action that hazards the city on a battle for which we are not prepared, not unless we have no other choice. We are not yet at that point." He paused, then added, "We can always gather our strength within the city and sally in force in only a few days, if we see the need or the opportunity."

Triel weighed the weapons master's advice.

"I will return to Menzoberranzan and set the matter before the Council," she said at last, "but, until you're ordered otherwise, continue your withdrawal. I will have our captains in the city make ready to withstand a siege."

Halisstra opened her eyes and found herself drifting in an endless silver sea. Soft gray clouds moved slowly in the distance, while strange dark streaks twisted violently through the sky, anchored in ends so distant she couldn't perceive them, their middle parts revolving angrily like pieces of string rolled between a child's fingertips. She glanced down, wondering what supported her, and saw nothing but more of the strange pearly sky beneath her feet and all around her.

She drew in a sudden breath, surprised by the sight, and felt her lungs fill with something sweeter and perhaps a little more solid than air, but instead of gagging or drowning on the stuff she seemed perfectly acclimated to it. An electric thrill raced through her limbs as she found herself mesmerized by the simple act of respiration.

Halisstra raised her hand to her face in an unconscious desire to shield her eyes, and she noticed that her eyesight was preternaturally keen. Each link of her mailed gauntlet leaped out in perfect symmetry, its edges boldly defined, the leather of her gloves gleaming with discrete layers of oils and stains.

Words failed her.

"You have not ventured here before, Mistress Melarn?" said Tzirik from somewhere behind her.

Halisstra craned her neck back to look for him, but in response the entire vista seemed to revolve and spin in one quick, smooth motion, bringing into her view the floating forms of her companions. The Vhaeraunite priest stood—no, that was not right, *floated* was better—a dozen yards from her, his armor as sharp as the edge of a knife, his cloak rippling softly in a breeze Halisstra could not feel. He spoke softly, yet his voice carried with a marvelous clarity and precision that made it seem that he stood within arm's reach.

"I would have expected a priestess of your stature to be familiar with the astral realm," the priest added.

"I know something of what to expect, but I have never had the occasion to journey to other planes," she replied. "My knowledge of this place is only . . . theoretical."

She noted that each of her comrades seemed every bit as sharply defined, as tangible and real, as Tzirik himself. From some spot she could not easily perceive—somewhere in the middle of their backs, or perhaps the napes of their necks—sprang a slender, gleaming tendon of silver light.

Halisstra reached around behind her head and felt her own cord. The warm, pulsing artery vibrated with energy, and when her fingers brushed it, a powerful jolt quivered through her torso as if she'd just plucked the heartstring of her own soul. She jerked her hand back, and resolved not to try to touch her cord again.

"Your silver cord," Tzirik explained. "A nigh indestructible bond that ties your soul to its rightful home: your body, back in Minauth-keep." The priest offered a cruel smile. "You will want to be careful of it. There are few things that can part an astral traveler's cord, but if something did, that traveler would be destroyed in an instant."

Halisstra watched as Ryld felt for his own cord and touched it. His eyes widened and he snatched his hand back just as swiftly as she had withdrawn her own.

"How long do these things get?" the weapons master asked.

"They are infinite, Master Argith," Tzirik said. "Don't worry, they fade to intangibility within a foot or two of your skin, so you won't be tripping over your own cord. In fact, it has the habit of keeping itself out of your way, quite without a thought on your part."

Halisstra glanced around the company, watching as the Menzo-berranyr struggled to adjust themselves to their new environment. Ryld and Valas flailed their limbs slowly as if trying to tread water. Quenthel held herself as stiff as a blade, her limbs locked tight to her sides, while Danifae drifted languidly, her long white hair stream-ing behind her. Pharaun merely waited, his eyes sparkling with dark amusement as he watched the efforts of his companions. Tzirik glanced around, studying their surroundings, and nodded.

"This is something of a timeless place," he said, "but time does pass here, so I suppose we should begin our journey. Follow me, and stay close. You may think you can see forever from here, but things have a way of vanishing in the mists."

He glided off without moving, arms folded, his cloak whipping silently behind him.

Follow him how? Halisstra wondered, watching the priest go, but somehow in conceiving the desire to keep the priest close by, she found herself leaping forward with such alacrity that her next impulse was to yelp out loud, if only to herself, "Stop!"

And she did, so quickly and with so perfect an end to motion that her mind told her she *must* lurch forward, as if she had tried to stop too suddenly from a run. She managed to throw herself into a violent circle before she stopped completely. Fortunately, she was not the only one having trouble.

Danifae scowled prettily as she tried to make herself go anywhere at all, and Ryld and Valas had somehow collided with each other and clung together, unwilling to trust themselves to the void again.

"Oh, in the name of the goddess!" Quenthel growled, watching them. "Simply clear your minds and think of where you want to go."

"With all due respect, Mistress, where is it that we should desire to go?" Valas asked as he disentangled himself from Ryld.

"Concentrate on following the priest," the Baenre replied. "He cast the spell, so he will be able to find the portal leading into the Demonweb Pits. It may take many hours, but you will find that time passes strangely here."

With that, Quenthel moved off in pursuit of Tzirik.

Halisstra closed her eyes, took a deep breath, and concentrated on trailing the priest at a comfortable distance. She closed up quickly and smoothly, and this time she didn't allow herself to react in panic. Soon enough the rest of the company sailed along beside her, keeping together easily as they became more and more accustomed to the strangeness of the Astral Plane. Halisstra indulged herself by experimenting with her mode of locomotion, at first orienting herself horizontally so that she felt like she flew like a bird through the pearly void, then trying to face her direction of travel so that she felt as if she was walking swiftly without moving her legs.

As it turned out, it didn't really matter what she did with her body as long as her mind remained focused on staying near her companions, and the true immateriality of the astral sea began to seep into her understanding. She was only a spirit, weightless, perfect, yet she was in a place where spirits became tangible. Somewhere beyond the endless pearly expanse that met her eye lay the realms of the gods, a thousand infinite concepts of existence where the divine beings who ruled over the fate of all Faerûn—of all the worlds, for that matter—had their abodes. She could spend a hundred drow lifetimes exploring the domains that touched on the astral sea, and not even come close to seeing them all.

The thought made her feel small, almost insignificant, and she pushed it from her mind. Lolth had not called her to the Demonweb Pits for her to be overawed by the silver void of the Astral Plane. She had called Halisstra and the others to stand before her, capable and confident, to profess their faith and adoration. For what other purpose could the goddess have done all that she had done by withdrawing her power from her faithful, by permitting the fall of Ched Nasad, by causing the endless toils and tribulations that had assailed the First Daughter of House Melarn?

There is a purpose, Halisstra told herself, a purpose that will be made clear to me soon, if I keep my faith strong and do not falter.

The Queen of the Demonweb Pits has brought us this far. She will bring us a little farther.

NINETEEN

How long it took them to cross the Astral Plane, Halisstra could not begin to say. She'd never realized before the extent to which the routine processes of one's body measured the days. Her astral form didn't grow tired or hungry, and didn't know thirst or discomfort of any sort. Without the minor actions of looking after the body's needs—taking a sip from a waterskin when thirsty, halting to take a meal during their day's march, or even stopping to sink deep into Reverie and while away the bright hours of daylight—time simply lost its doleful count.

From time to time they caught glimpses of phenomena other than the endless pearly clouds and twisting gray vortices that streaked the surrounding sky. Strange bits of matter drifted through the astral sea. On several occasions they passed boulders or hillocks of rock and dirt that hovered in space like miniature worlds, some nearly the size of mountains, others only a few yards across. Weird, empty ruins graced the larger of them, the abodes of astral sojourners or long gone residents. The strangest things they came across were whirling pools of color slowly revolving in the astral medium. The hues ranged from bright, shining silver to blackest midnight shot with angry purple streaks.

"Don't stray too close to any of the color pools," Tzirik had said. "If you enter one you will be ejected into a different plane of existence, and I have no desire to wander into strange worlds looking for a careless traveling companion."

"How will we know which one will lead us to the Abyss?" Valas Hune asked.

"Do not worry, my friend, the spell Vhaeraun has granted me also confers a certain affinity for the destination I conceived when I shifted my spirit to this plane, and I am leading us more or less directly to the nearest color pool that will serve our purposes."

"How much longer must we travel?" Quenthel asked.

"We are drawing near," the priest answered. "It's hard to tell here, of course, but I would guess we are within four or five hours of our destination. We've already traveled for almost two days."

Two days? Halisstra thought. It seemed much less.

She found herself wondering what might have transpired back in Faerûn in two days. Did Jeggred still maintain his vigil over their inert bodies? He couldn't have been entirely remiss in his duties, as they were all still alive, but how many more days would pass before they reached their destination, beseeched the goddess for an audience, and managed to return to their native plane?

Absorbed in her own thoughts, Halisstra kept to herself for the balance of the journey, scarcely noticing that her companions did the same. It came as a surprise to her when Tzirik slowed his effortless flight and finally arrested his motion all together, facing a whirlpool of black with silver streaks that slowly churned in the astral medium a short distance from the travelers.

"The entrance to the Sixty-sixth Layer of the Abyss," the priest of Vhaeraun said. "So far our journey has been uneventful, but once we set foot within Lolth's domain that is bound to change. If you have any second thoughts about this quest, Mistress Baenre, this would be the time to express them."

"I have no reason to fear the Demonweb Pits," Quenthel sneered. "I intend to do what I came here to do."

Without waiting for the priest she arrowed forward and plunged herself into the whirling, inky blot. In the blink of an eye her gleaming astral form was lost to view, swallowed by the maelstrom.

"Impatient, isn't she?" Tzirik remarked.

He shrugged and moved into the color pool himself. Like Quenthel, Halisstra sensed a certainty in the moment, and she did not mean to let any quailing sway her from her intended course. She entered the pool of swirling night a heartbeat behind Tzirik, her teeth bared in a defiant snarl.

There was no sensation at first, though the pool swallowed her sight completely the moment she plunged within it. The medium seemed much the same as the rest of the Astral Plane—a weightless, cool, perfect nothingness—but the swirling current of the revolving pool caught her at once, tugging on her with some strange non-dimensional feeling of attraction or acceleration that dragged her psychic form in a direction she couldn't even begin to comprehend. It didn't hurt, but it felt so alien, so dislocating, that Halisstra gasped in shock and distress, shuddering violently in the grip of the astral maelstrom.

Goddess, help me! she pleaded in the silence of her own mind, as she flailed her arms and tried to extricate herself from the spinning mass. There was another long moment of indescribable motion, and—

She was through.

Halisstra swayed drunkenly with the return of gravity and struggled to catch her balance. She opened her eyes and found herself standing on something silver-gray, a steeply sloping ramp or wall top that dropped away an incredible distance before her. The rest of the party stood close by, looking around in silence as they rubbed their limbs nervously or fingered their weapons.

All around there was nothing but a black, smothering emptiness darker and more forbidding than the blackest chasm of the Underdark. Her nostrils filled with a foul, acrid scent, and a soft muttering updraft streamed constantly from below. Halisstra glanced into the abyss at her left hand and saw something gleaming there, a dull silver strand several miles away that sloped down through the darkness. Lesser strands intersected it at odd intervals, and as she followed some of them with her eyes she saw that they climbed back up slowly and met the very ramp or buttress on which she stood. The hot, stinking breeze grew momentarily stronger and actually managed to induce a great, gentle swaying in the monstrous strand.

"It's a spiderweb," Ryld muttered. "A gigantic spiderweb."

"This surprises you?" Pharaun said with a sardonic smirk.

Danifae took a couple of cautious steps down the surface of the strand. The whole thing was easily thirty or forty yards in diameter, yet because its surface was round, it was difficult to feel comfortable walking more than a dozen feet or so from the centerline of the strand. She knelt and brushed her fingers over the strand's surface, and grimaced.

"Sticky, but not dangerously so—and we appear to be completely physical again." She straightened, and stretched languidly. "Do I have two bodies now? One here, and one back in the Jaelre castle?"

"In fact, you do," Tzirik said. "When one leaves the astral sea and enters another plane, the traveling spirit constructs for itself the physical body it expects. You might say that your spirit must undergo a sort of condensation to resume a physical existence on another plane. When you leave this place, your spirit will return to the Astral Plane, while this shell you have created for yourself will simply fade away into nothingness."

"You seem well acquainted with the rigors of planar travel," Halisstra observed.

"Vhaeraun has called me to his service in the planes beyond Faerûn on several occasions," Tzirik admitted. "In fact, I have been in the Demonweb Pits before now. All the gods of our race reside here, each in their own domain within this great chasm of webbing. My previous business did not take me to Lolth's domain, though, and that was a good many years ago."

Quenthel scowled and said, "All of the Demonweb Pits are Lolth's domain, heretic. She is the queen of this entire layer of the Abyss, and the other so-called gods of our people exist here only at her sufferance."

"I am certain you have correctly parroted your faith's beliefs on the matter, and so I will not argue the point with you, priestess of Lolth. For our purposes, the exact relationship of our pantheon's deities is not very important."

Tzirik turned his back on Quenthel and surveyed the black gulf surrounding the party. He waved his hand in a sweeping gesture.

"Somewhere below us we will find some kind of gate or border marking the place where this entryway opens to Lolth's own domain—which, as I understand it, is much like the rest of the Demonweb Pits, except subject to her every whim and caprice."

"If the plane is infinite, then the spot we seek might be infinitely far away," Pharaun observed. "How are we to get from here to there?"

"If we had simply materialized at some random point in this reality, you would be correct, wizard," Tzirik replied. "However, the astral spell is not a random means of travel. We are not too far from what we seek—an hour's march, perhaps a day's, but not much farther. Since we know that Lolth's domain lies at the very nadir of this place, I would propose that we need only descend this strand and continue to descend each time we come to an intersection. In the meantime, be alert."

"There will be others," Quenthel added. "The souls of the recent dead. If you see anyone you recognize as a worshiper of the Spider Queen, we will follow them."

If Lolth is still calling them home, Halisstra thought.

The others seemed to be thinking the same thing.

The armored priest hefted his mace in his hand, adjusted the grip of his shield, and set off directly down the titanic gray strand, shoulders squared. The Menzoberranyr exchanged looks, but turned to follow, picking their way down the steeply pitched column of webbing behind the Jaelre priest.

The surface of the strand proved surprisingly easy to negotiate. Its surface was tacky, rather than truly adhesive, and it was composed of rough fibers that provided a sure footing. It was springy enough that it cushioned the jarring footfalls of the sharply descending walk.

At first Halisstra thought the place was as empty as the silvery seas of the Astral Plane, since the vast distances from strand to strand of the webbing gave the whole place a sense of immense vacancy. Yet the farther she went, the more she became conscious of an active malevolence in the very air of the place, as if the entire plane watched their intrusion and seethed with anger. Strange, rasping rustling and oddly insectile tittering sounds rode on the fetid updraft from below, a crawling sound of distant movement and activity that carried no small menace with it.

Sometimes Halisstra spied motion on neighboring strands, even though the sagging gray cables were miles away across the bottomless space. She could make out frenetic activity here and there, the creatures or objects responsible so far distant that it was impossible to guess what they might be. More than once she sensed presences in the airy voids around their strand, slow, foul things that glided on the noisome exhalations from below, wheeling and drifting closer to the drow travelers as if sizing up an easy meal.

They began to pass corpses at odd intervals, hulking forms of nightmare that combined the worst features of spiders and demons. Great rents had been torn in the chitinous shells of the monsters, limbs twisted off, hairy thoraxes crushed and oozing sour green paste. Winged vulture-demons lay in shabby piles of filthy feathers, their foul beaks agape in death. Bloated, froglike things hung suspended in the ropy fibers of the great strand, swaying slowly in the hot stench of the place. Some of the demons still clung to life, too horribly damaged to do more than quiver and rasp, or croak dire threats at the drow as the company carefully climbed down past them.

"This place is a charnel house of devils," Ryld muttered, holding one hand over his nose and mouth. "Is it always like this?"

"I saw nothing like this on my previous visit," Tzirik said. "What it means, I cannot say, but I would not care to meet that which tears apart demons."

"It is not like I recall, either," Quenthel said. Her face was set in a thoughtful frown, her voice quiet and strained. "Change is the essence of chaos, and chaos is an aspect of Lolth."

"Indeed," Pharaun said. The fastidious wizard held a handkerchief to his nose and picked his way around a huge spider corpse whose bulbous abdomen had burst entirely, strewing the strand with its horrid contents. "It seems not unlikely that they did this to themselves. Demons are violent creatures, after all. In the absence of a powerful, commanding presence, they often turn on each other."

"An absence . . ." Halisstra repeated. She frowned, studying the carnage. "There are no drow bodies here."

Having descended a goodly ways, the neighboring strands were closer, and the intersections more frequent. Halisstra could see more broken forms clinging to the tattered strands nearby. Whatever battle had raged there must have spanned dozens of strands and miles of gaping darkness.

"The Spider Queen . . ." said Halisstra. "She has abandoned the denizens of her own plane, just as she has abandoned us. Much as we have done in Ched Nasad, the demons of her realm have destroyed each other." She closed her eyes, trying to shut out the awful sight. The smell soured her stomach and left her light-headed with nausea. "Goddess, what is the *purpose?*" she murmured aloud.

"The Spider Queen will explain her purposes if she sees fit to do so," Quenthel answered. "We can only beseech the restoration of her favor, and trust that we will find approval in her eyes."

"We can also move along a little quicker, and stop gawking," Valas Hune called. He was at the rear of the band, an arrow laid across the string of his double-curved bow. The scout stood peering up the strand behind them, his face pinched in a worried frown. "Excuse the interruption, but we have company. Something is following us down the strand."

Halisstra followed the scout's gaze upward, swaying awkwardly as she lost her balance. She hadn't realized just how far they'd descended until she looked back up the massive strand, sloping upward steeper and steeper into the darkness overhead. Something was following them, a crawling horde of tiny, spiderlike figures that swarmed over the strand's entire circumference, heedless of whether they clung to the web's top, sides, or bottoms. They were still many hundreds of yards behind the company, but even at that distance Halisstra could tell that they were ogre-sized monstrosities, and the alacrity of their pursuit certainly didn't seem to be a good sign.

"I don't like the looks of that," Ryld said.

"Nor do I," Quenthel agreed. "Pharaun, do you have a spell prepared that can bar their passage?"

The Master of Sorcere shook his head and answered, "Not without risk of severing the strand, I fear, and I find myself strangely unwilling to chance that. I could instead confer a spell of flying on enough of us to perhaps abandon this strand and reach another, or we could simply descend to that strand below us by levitation."

He pointed at a slender, almost wispy web a long distance below them and a little to one side.

"Save your magic," Quenthel decided. "That strand will do. Master Argith, carry Valas and Danifae."

She slid down the side of the great strand they stood on, and pushed herself off into the darkness. One by one, the others followed. Halisstra risked one more glance at the scuttling terrors behind them, and hastened to follow the Baenre priestess. She scrambled down the curving side of the monstrous cable, and leaped out into the dark.

$$\text{\ss} \qquad \text{\ss} \qquad \text{\ss}$$

Three days after his victory at the Pillars of Woe and twenty miles closer to Menzoberranzan, Nimor stood in the shadows at the mouth of the Lustrum, a wondrously rich mithral mine. Near the entrance, a wedge-shaped vault soared upward for hundreds of feet, widening as it climbed, but down on the cavern floor it was cramped and broken with the shattered remnants of huge boulders. The miners—slaves and soldiers of House Xorlarrin, or so he believed—had abandoned their tools and their homes in the face of the advancing duergar army, carrying off as much mithral ore as they could manage. Nimor gazed up at the narrow black rift above him.

The mithral mine was an interesting bit of decoration, but it was only one of the reasons he was there. The Lustrum stood between the army of Gracklstugh and the army of Kaanyr Vhok. The duergar stayed to the left and came up on Menzoberranzan's southwest side, while the tanarukks pushed right and approached the city from the southeast. The drow army retreated ahead of them, in full flight for the dubious safety of their home city. Menzoberranzan's Mantle—the great halo of twisting caverns and passageways ringing the city—offered the invading armies a thousand paths by which they might approach.

Of course, the matron mothers hadn't left their outer demesnes completely undefended. Nimor glanced down at the green shards of one of the city's infamous jade spiders, huge magical automatons of stone that guarded the city's approaches. The wreckage of the one at his feet still smoked with acrid black fumes from the stonefire bombs that had destroyed it a few hours before. They were clever and deadly devices, but without cadres of magic-wielding priestesses to hurl all sorts of awful dooms and blights on invaders, the jade spiders were not sufficient to the task of halting the two approaching armies.

How much longer until Menzoberranzan's great castles lie shattered like this device? Nimor mused.

The Anointed Blade was interrupted in his reflections by the tramp of dwarven boots and the angry scrape of iron on stone. The armored diligence of Crown Prince Horgar Steelshadow approached, escorted by a double file of the duergar lord's Stone Guards. Nimor winced at the resounding clangor of the duergar soldiers.

One would think they'd get their fill of hammer blows and noise back in their city, he thought.

He brushed off his tunic and went down to meet his ally.

"Well met, Crown Prince Horgar. I am pleased that you honored my request for a parley."

The duergar lord threw open the armored door in the side of his iron wagon, and stepped down to the cavern floor. Marshal

Borwald followed a step behind, his scarred face hidden by a great iron helm.

"I have been looking for you, Nimor Imphraezl," Horgar replied. "You vanished after guiding our vanguard to this maze of tunnels. What business did you have elsewhere that was more pressing than our assault on Menzoberranzan, I wonder?"

Victory had transformed the crown prince's dour pessimism into a kind of ferocious hunger for more victories, and Horgar's lairds echoed their ruler's attitude. Where before the sight of the assassin brought black scowls and dark mutterings, the lairds of Gracklstugh had come to acknowledge his presence with gruff nods and open envy of his successes.

"Why, Crown Prince, my business concerned the upcoming assault," Nimor said with a laugh. He kicked aside one of the jade shards from the ruined construct. "Once I'd shown your men how to disable these things it seemed to me that your army had matters well in hand, so I took the liberty of reporting to my superiors, and spying out how matters stand in the city."

The duergar prince frowned, his brows knitting in thought.

"You felt free to gamble with the tanarukk army," said Horgar. "They might have turned on us as easily as upon the Menzoberranyr, you know."

"Under normal circumstances, perhaps, but there is opportunity in the air. I can smell it, Kaanyr Vhok can smell it, and I think you can, too. We stand at a fulcrum on which many great events might be made to turn."

"Empty platitudes, Nimor," the gray dwarf growled.

He folded his thick arms and stared into the darkness, waiting. After a short time, a scuffling and snorting drifted through the darkness, followed by quick and heavy steps.

Bearing an iron palanquin the size of a small coach on their hairy shoulders, a score of tanarukks loped into the cavern, bestial eyes aglow with red hate, axes and maces gripped in their powerful fists. The gray dwarves and the orc-demons glared at each other, nervously muttering and fingering their weapons.

The door to the palanquin creaked open, and Kaanyr Vhok slowly straightened out of the chair. The half-demon warlord was resplendent in his armor of crimson and gold, and his fine-scaled skin and strong features bespoke presence and charisma in a way that Horgar's duergar churlishness and suspicious manner could never match. The alu-fiend Aliisza followed sinuously, stretching her wings as she emerged. Finally, Zammzt climbed out of the warlord's coach.

"Well, I have come," Kaanyr said in his powerful voice. He studied the assembled gray dwarves, and regarded Nimor as well. "We have driven the dark elves back to their city in disarray. Now how do we finish the job? And, more importantly, how shall we divide the spoils?"

"Divide the spoils?" Horgar rasped. "I think not. You will not help yourself to part of my prize after my army shouldered the brunt of the hard work in defeating the drow at the Pillars of Woe. You will be paid fairly for your assistance, but do not presume to claim a share of my victory."

Kaanyr's handsome brow creased in an angry frown.

"I am not a beggar crying out for your largesse, dwarf," the cambion said. "Without my army's approach, you would still be fighting your way toward Menzoberranzan, one step at a time."

Horgar started to compose an angry retort, but Nimor quickly stepped between the gray dwarf and the half-demon and raised his arms.

"My lords!" he cried. "The only way the Menzoberranyr can defeat you is if the two of you turn on each other. If you cooperate, if you combine your efforts intelligently, the city will fall."

"Indeed," said Zammzt. The plain-faced assassin stood by Vhok's palanquin, shrouded in his dark cloak. "There is little point in dividing the spoils of a city that you have yet to capture. There is even less point in allowing the effort of dividing the spoils to prevent the city's fall in the first place."

"That may be true," Kaanyr said, folding his powerful arms across his broad chest, "but I will not be forgotten when the city is plundered. You brought me here, assassins."

"You brought me here, as well," Horgar rumbled, "and you brought the Agrach Dyrr. I suspect that your secret House will be hard-pressed to honor your promises to all three of your allies. Which of us do you mean to betray, I wonder?"

For the first time, Nimor found himself wondering if perhaps he had arrayed too many enemies against Menzoberranzan all at once. That was the nature of diplomacy in the Underdark, after all. No alliance outlived its usefulness, not even by a heartbeat.

To his surprise, he was rescued by Aliisza.

The alu-fiend draped herself at Kaanyr's side and said, "He will not honor his promises to either of you, as long as the city stands. How can he? We will all go home empty-handed if you cannot come to an agreement."

Nimor inclined his head in gratitude, making a very conscious effort not to allow his eyes to linger on Aliisza for too long when she stood next to Kaanyr Vhok. Somehow he doubted that she'd shared with her master the exact details of her visit to Gracklstugh, and he didn't want to give the half-demon any reason to become curious.

"Lady Aliisza's wisdom is as great as her beauty," he said. "For the sake of avoiding argument, I propose this: To Horgar, five-tenths of Menzoberranzan's wealth, populace, and territory; to Kaanyr Vhok, three-tenths; and for my own House, two-tenths, out of which I will come to terms with the Agrach Dyrr. All subject to final negotiation and adjustment when Menzoberranzan is ours, of course."

"My army outnumbers the cambion's by better than two to one, so why does he gain a share better than half of my own?" Horgar said.

"Because he is here," Nimor said. "Take your army and go home if you like, Horgar, but look around you before you depart. We stand at the Lustrum, the mithral mines of House Xorlarrin. Menzoberranzan controls dozens of treasures such as this, and its castles and vaults are filled with the wealth of five thousand years. If you do not fight, your share will be nothing."

That was the other reason Nimor had chosen the Lustrum as the place to hold his parley. It served as a tantalizing reminder of the true prize that waited.

Horgar's eyes darkened, but the duergar prince turned aside to study the chasm and the gaping adits nearby. Marshal Borwald leaned close and whispered something to the crown prince, and the other lairds muttered among themselves. After a moment, Horgar shifted his thick hands to his belt and cleared his throat.

"All right, then. Subject to final negotiation, we agree. So how do you intend to reduce the city?"

"You will crush Menzoberranzan between your two armies," Nimor said. "Given your victory at the Pillars of Woe, the Lolthites are committed to awaiting your assault in the city proper, but thanks to this maze of passages surrounding the city, they can't know where you'll make your attack. That means the Menzoberranyr will have to maintain a strong force in waiting somewhere near the city's center to respond to whatever point is threatened. The Scoured Legion will provide that threat, and when we force the Lolthites to commit to battle, the army of Gracklstugh will commence its attack and break into the city."

"It's not a bad plan," Kaanyr Vhok observed. "However, it is exactly what the Menzoberranyr must expect us to try, given the situation. They'll be very careful in committing their strength to any one threat."

"Aye," Horgar said. "How will you draw them out, now that you've taught them caution at the Pillars of Woe?"

Nimor smiled. It didn't escape him that Horgar and Kaanyr were examining the tactical problem of defeating Menzoberranzan, instead of quarreling over what they expected to gain from their efforts.

"My brothers and I expect to help in that regard," he said. "We're not numerous but we're well-placed, and, my lords, you have forgotten House Agrach Dyrr."

Horgar and Kaanyr exchanged a nod, even a smile.

Prepare well, Menzoberranzan, Nimor thought. I'm coming.

"I never imagined so many demons in my life," Ryld grunted. He leaned on Splitter, watching as a huge, bat-winged, bloated form spiraled feebly down into the darkness, vainly trying to fly with its wings savaged by blows of the weapons master's greatsword. He straightened and wiped the back of one hand across his brow. "It's getting hotter, too. I hope we're close to whatever we're looking for."

Halisstra and the rest of the company stood nearby, swaying with nausea or trembling with fatigue as the environment and their exertions warranted. For what seemed like hours, they'd continued to fight their way down strand after strand. Sometimes they descended for miles past strands that were empty or held nothing but corpses, but more and more frequently they encountered demons that were alive and hungry. Most of the infernal creatures threw themselves headlong into battle as if all reason had deserted them, but a few retained enough of their intelligence to employ their formidable magical abilities against the interlopers.

With fang, claw, sting, and unholy sorcery the denizens of the Demonweb Pits scoured and scored the drow company. It didn't help that Quenthel had commanded Pharaun to hoard his spells carefully so that the company met each new demonic threat with steel, not the wizard's magic.

"Save your breath, Master Argith," Quenthel said. She slowly straightened from her own fighting crouch, her whip splattered with the gore of a dozen demons. "We must press on."

The company hadn't gone more than another forty yards before their strand shuddered, and an enormous taloned hand appeared from beneath. Clawing its way around from the unseen bottom side of the web, a massive, bison-headed demon with foul, coarse fur sprouting from its shoulders and back hauled itself to the top of the strand and bellowed a vast challenge.

"A goristro!" Pharaun cried. "What in all the hells is that doing here?"

"Some pet of Lolth's that's gotten loose, I don't doubt," Tzirik replied.

The Vhaeraunite priest began to chant a spell, while the others leaped into action. Before the monster could clamber to its feet, Valas feathered it with at least three arrows, the black shafts sprouting from its shoulders and thick neck like pins in a cushion. The goristro snorted in pain and anger, and reached out one hulking hand to pick up the corpse of a small spider-demon nearby. It flung the corpse at Valas, catching the scout as he fished in his quiver for more arrows. The impact staggered Valas, who stumbled and slipped down the side of the strand, cursing in several languages.

Ryld ran forward with Splitter held high, Quenthel at his side, while Halisstra and Danifae carefully tried to circle the beast to one side as best they could on the narrow strand, hoping to surround it on all sides.

Tzirik finished his spell and shouted out a deep, rolling word of power, creating a great whirling disk of spinning razors across the goristro's torso. Blades bit and blood flew, but still the monster came on undeterred.

"What will it take to stop this thing?" Halisstra called. "Does it have any weaknesses?"

"It's stupid," Pharaun replied. "Barely sentient, really. Don't meet it blow for blow."

The wizard gestured and struck the monster with a gleaming green ray of energy that chewed into the goristro's chest, while Tzirik moved in behind Ryld and Quenthel to help them against the monster. The weapons master and the high priestess leaped and slashed at the creature's belly and torso, while dodging the ponderous blows of its enormous fists. One glancing blow spun Quenthel to her hands and knees, but she managed to scramble out of the way before the creature could finish her off.

"Noooot stuuuupiiiid!" roared the goristro.

It lifted one hoofed foot and stamped it down on the strand with such astonishing power that the whole miles-long cable thrummed like something alive. The shock wave threw all of the drow into the air, yet the goristro had failed to anticipate the consequences of its mighty stomp, for the shock threw it into the air as well. The monstrous demon landed awkwardly on its side and slid off the strand, catching itself by one arm dug into the upper surface. It scrambled and kicked, its struggles shaking the strand even more.

Quenthel picked herself up from the trembling surface, and weaved her way past the brute's arm to look down at its face. With a deliberate motion, she flicked her snake-headed whip at one of its beady eyes and destroyed the organ in a sickening burst of gore. The goristro howled in agony and recoiled, losing its grip on the strand and tumbling down into the abyss. Its bellows of rage continued for a long time, diminishing as it fell away from them. She didn't bother to watch it fall. Instead she turned to the rest of the company.

"Get up," she snarled. "We're wasting time."

Halisstra picked herself up from the web and glanced around. Valas scrambled back into view from his precarious position on the side of the strand. Danifae climbed to her feet as well. They followed after Quenthel as the Mistress of Arach-Tinilith set off again at once, moving at an impatient lope as she bounded down the strand. Halisstra was too tired to keep up the pace for long, but she had even less energy for an argument with the single-minded priestess, and so she merely set her jaw and endured.

They reached the bottom—almost.

For some time they'd noticed converging strands drawing closer to their own, and Halisstra could see the reason why. A great ring of webbing a dozen times thicker than any of the gray strands was suspended below them, binding the ends of the strands together. Its circumference was so great that Halisstra could hardly describe a curve at all in the ring's vast arc. In the center there was some-thing—a titanic black structure or island of sorts hanging in the mighty web. The drow paused, surveying the scene, until Valas broke the silence.

"Is that it?" he said in a low voice.

"The entrance to Lolth's domain," Tzirik answered, "lies some-where within that ring."

"Are you sure?" asked Ryld.

"I am," Quenthel replied for the priest.

She didn't look aside or hesitate, but simply set off again at the same hard pace.

As the strand approached the central ring its steep pitch gradually flattened and thickened somewhat, and for the first time in seemingly endless hours and miles the company found itself traversing something like level ground instead of picking their way down the sloping cable. More demonic and spidery corpses appeared, some half-buried in the strand as if they'd fallen from the limitless heights above—which they most likely had.

The travelers reached the thick ring and crossed one more stretch of twisted webbing only to find that the structure in the center was some kind of immense stone temple, a baroque building of gleaming black obsidian miles in diameter. Spiked stone buttresses soared across the bottomless space, linking the structure to the ring around it. Vast dark plazas of smooth stone large enough to swallow cities surrounded the temple's flanks. Without speaking, the company picked their way over to one of the colossal flying buttresses and advanced toward their goal.

Halisstra found herself trembling, not with exhaustion, but with a combination of terror and ecstasy as she realized that she must soon withstand Lolth's scrutiny in the flesh.

I am worthy, she told herself. I must be.

The demons that had plagued their progress through the webs didn't seem to care for the black temple. In any event, no more of the monsters pursued the company once they left the web behind them. For a long time the dark elves simply walked onward, crossing the huge outer plaza, as the walls of the temple came closer and closer, revealing their dark details.

Quenthel oriented their march on a sharp-edged break in the cyclopean wall, a huge cleft that must have been the temple's portico. From time to time they passed the strange, inanimate forms of large, spiderlike beings that seemed to be sculpted from fluid black stone. Oddly enough, the petrified forms grew smaller and smaller the closer they came to the cleft. Halisstra dismissed the mystery from her mind, concentrating only on the goal before her.

At last they reached the mouth of the temple, and looked upon its entrance. A vast face confronted them, the face of a cruelly beautiful dark elf, her features calm and still as if in contemplation. Perfect black stone barred the entrance from one side to the other, sculpted into the image of the Spider Queen's visage. Only her half-lidded eyes showed any animation at all. Gazing down blankly at the tiny supplicants below her, Lolth's eyes gleamed with a roiling, hellish glee focused entirely on whatever thoughts or processes lay behind them.

The company stood gazing up in wonder and terror, and Quenthel prostrated herself before the image of her goddess. Halisstra and Danifae joined her at once, groveling on the cold black stone. Even the males dropped to the ground, lying on their faces and averting their eyes. Tzirik, as a priest of Vhaeraun, settled for taking one knee and lowering his gaze respectfully. He didn't serve the Queen of the Demonweb Pits, but he and others of his faith certainly recognized her divinity.

"Great Queen!" called Quenthel. "We have come from Menzoberranzan to beseech you to restore your favor to your priestesses! Our enemies encroach on your holy city and threaten your faithful with destruction. We humbly beg you to instruct us in what we must do to find approval in your eyes. Arm us with your holy might once more, and we will hunt your enemies until their blood fills the Underdark and their souls fill your belly!"

The face did not respond.

Quenthel waited for a long time, still prostrate, then she licked her lips and uttered another prayer. Halisstra and Danifae joined their pleading to hers, and they begged and pleaded with every prayer, every invocation, every catechism they had ever been taught, scraping and groveling at the temple door. The males simply waited, still stretched out on the black stone. After a time, Tzirik moved off a short distance and sat down with his back to the face, communing with his own god. Halisstra ignored him and continued her supplications.

Still the face did not respond.

The three priestesses kept up their pleas for what must have been hours, but finally Quenthel pushed herself upright and gazed full on the visage of Lolth.

"Enough, sisters," said the Mistress of Arach-Tinilith. "The goddess plainly does not deign to answer us at this time."

"Perhaps we are in the wrong place," Pharaun suggested. "Perhaps we must go farther in order for you to offer your prayers."

"There is no place farther to go," Tzirik said, rejoining the party. "Vhaeraun informs me that this is the only point of approach to Lolth's domain through the Abyss. If she refuses to hear you at this spot, she will not hear you anywhere else in this plane."

"But why does she continue to ignore us?" Halisstra asked in a plaintive voice. She climbed to her feet, her heart sick with longing. After all that had happened—the fall of her House, the destruction of her city, the travails of the quest—to stand before Lolth's temple and be ignored was simply incomprehensible. "What more do we have to do?"

Tzirik shrugged and said, "I cannot answer that question."

"Apparently Lolth can't, either," Halisstra said.

She ignored the disapproval and fear that flickered across Quenthel's features, and strode up angrily to stand within arm's reach of the towering face.

"Hear me, Lolth!" she cried. "Answer me! What have we done to earn your displeasure? Where are you?"

"Speak with respect!" hissed Quenthel, her eyes wide with terror.

Ryld quailed, but managed to find the strength to take a couple of steps forward.

"Mistress Melarn . . ." he said, "Halisstra, come away from there. No good—"

"*Lolth!*" Halisstra screamed. "Answer me, damn you!"

She struck the cold stone of the face with her fists, flailing away in futility, in anger. Her mind went empty as animal fury rose up to overthrow her reason. She screamed curses upon her goddess, she battered at the uncaring face until her hands were bruised and bloody, and still no answer came. After a time she found herself huddled against the cold stone, weeping, her hands broken and useless. Like a lost child, she cried with all the ache in her heart.

"Why? Why?" was all she could manage to say through her sobs. "Why have you abandoned us? Why do you hate us?"

"You speak heresy," Quenthel said, her voice hard with disapproval. "Have you no faith left, Halisstra Melarn? The goddess will speak in her own time."

"Do you really believe that still?" Halisstra muttered.

She turned her face away and gave herself up to her tears, no longer caring what Quenthel, or Danifae, or any of the others thought. She'd had her answer from Lolth.

"Weak . . ." she heard Quenthel whisper.

Standing a short distance from the rest of the company, Tzirik sighed and said, "Well, that's that, I suppose. Lolth hasn't chosen to break her silence for you, so now I have something I must do."

He raised his arms and made a complex series of passes, while muttering dire words of power. The air crackled with energy. Quenthel's eyes widened as she recognized the spell the Vhaeraunite spoke.

"Stop him!" she screeched, whirling to face the priest.

She started forward, raising her deadly whips, but Danifae caught her arm as she rushed past.

"Carefully!" hissed Danifae. "Our bodies are still in Minauthkeep."

"He's creating a gate!" Quenthel snapped. "Here!"

"What are you doing, Tzirik?" Pharaun said with some alarm.

The wizard recoiled a step and prepared a defensive spell, but Danifae's warning was just enough to cause him to hesitate before interfering.

Ryld and Valas held their hands as well, uncertain of what would happen if they harmed the cleric whose spell had brought them to Lolth's door. The weapons master and the mercenary drew their weapons but halted there.

"Pharaun, what should we do?" Ryld said.

Before the wizard could answer, Tzirik finished his spell. With an enormous tearing sound, a great black rift appeared in the air beside the Jaelre priest.

"I am here, my lord!" he cried into the rift. "I stand before the Face of Lolth!"

And from the depths of blackness within the rift, a voice of ineffable power, of terrible potency, answered, *"Good. I come."*

The blackness seemed to stir, and from the rift stepped something that had the size and shape of a lean, graceful drow male, but was obviously something more. Dressed in black leather, a purple mask draped over his face, the being radiated puissance and presence, his form almost quivering with the potentialities he contained. Even Halisstra, absorbed in her own misery with her back turned to the scene, whipped her head around as she sensed the being's arrival. With imperious ease, the being surveyed the plain of dark stone and the black temple.

"It is as I thought," he said to Tzirik, who had fallen prostrate at his feet. *"Rise, my son. You have done well, and brought me to a place from which I was barred."*

"I have only done as you commanded, Masked Lord," Tzirik said, standing slowly.

"Tzirik," Quenthel managed in a strangled voice, "what have you done?"

"He has opened a gate for me," the being who could only be a god said, with a cruel smile on his face. *"Do you not recognize the son of your own goddess, priestess of Lolth?"*

"Vhaeraun," Quenthel breathed.

The god folded his arms and drifted past the company of Menzoberranyr to confront the perfect stone visage, giving the mortals no further thought. He made a small shooing gesture with his left hand, and Halisstra, still huddled before the face, was violently hurled aside. She flew spinning through the air and landed badly at least thirty yards away, tumbling to a halt on the fluted ebon stone of the plaza.

"Dear Mother," Vhaeraun said, addressing the face, *"you were foolish to leave yourself in such a state."*

The god spontaneously began to grow, his radiance increasing as he soared to a height taller than a storm giant, scaling himself to the task at hand. He held out his hand, and from out of nowhere a black, gleaming sword made of shadows appeared in his grip, sized to his towering form.

A spearcast distant, Halisstra groaned and raised her eyes from the cold stone under her aching body. The Menzoberranyr stood paralyzed by indecision. Tzirik, on the other hand, watched smugly as Vhaeraun levitated upward to confront Lolth's gaze directly, blade in hand. With careful deliberation, the Masked Lord drew back his sword of shadows, his mask twisting into a rictus of hatred.

And Vhaeraun hewed at the Face of Lolth with all his godly might.

TWENTY

The sound of Vhaeraun's sword hammering at the great stone barrier shook the entire plane. Each blow set the great black fane at the web's center shuddering with the force of an earthquake, and from the center the reverberations pulsed through the immense gray cables that soared up into the endless night. Even though each stroke knocked her back down to the cold flagstones, Halisstra managed to stumble over to the company of Menzoberranyr, who, like her, staggered from side to side, trying to keep their balance in the face of Vhaeraun's assault.

Tzirik stood aside, still rapt with the glory of his god's presence, somehow able to ignore the damage the Masked Lord was wreaking as the shock waves passed through him with no effect. At each blow, a tiny network of glowing green cracks in the Face of Lolth seemed to spread just a little wider. Despite the incalculable force of each stroke of the god's blade, the visage of the Spider Queen seemed almost, but not quite, invulnerable to his assault.

The goddess does not respond, Halisstra thought in bleak amazement. She doesn't care.

She fell to her hands and knees amid the rest of the company, who ignored her, stupefied as they were by Vhaeraun's wrathful assault. Ryld knelt behind Splitter, averting his eyes and stoically enduring the punishing blows. Valas danced about in agitation, waving his arms, jerking his legs up and down like a spider on a pin. The scout didn't know whether to watch, run, or hide, and seemed to be trying to do all three at once. Pharaun levitated a foot or two above the ground to avoid the trembling impacts, shielding himself with some kind of spell as his eyes flicked from his companions to the god to Tzirik and back to Vhaeraun. Danifae, crouched nearby him, rolled with easy grace, keeping her feet beneath her as she watched each blow with a fierce, measuring gaze. Quenthel stood as stiffly as a statue, hammered by each tremor, her arms wrapped around her torso as if to hold in her distress. She watched the scene with a sick fascination, incapable of anything more.

Pharaun managed to break himself free of his indecision. He drifted close to Quenthel and seized her by the arm.

"What's happening here?" the wizard shouted in her ear. "What is he doing?"

The Baenre ground her teeth in frustration.

"I don't know," she admitted. "This is all wrong. It's not the same. There are no souls here."

"What souls?" the wizard asked. "Should we interfere?"

Both Ryld and Valas glanced up at that, their faces stricken.

"He's a *god*," Ryld managed to call out above the deafening clamor. "What do you propose we do?"

"Fine, then. Do we stay and watch, or do we leave? This doesn't seem to be a safe place to be," Pharaun replied.

Another shock wave lashed through the company, causing the wizard's spell shield to flare brightly.

"I'm not sure we can leave, even if we want to," Ryld said. He jerked his head at Tzirik, who watched the scene with an expression of dark joy behind his mask. "Don't we need him?"

"Should we leave, even to save ourselves?" Valas added. "We would seem to be culpable for—this." The scout shielded his eyes from the sight of Vhaeraun's efforts. "What happens when he breaches the temple? Mistress, what will happen? Is Lolth in there?"

Quenthel let out a shriek of despair.

Danifae fell at Quenthel's feet and asked, "Mistress, have you been here? Have you been here before?"

"*I don't know!*" the Mistress of Arach-Tinilith shouted.

She jerked her arm away from Pharaun and stormed over to Tzirik, weaving as the ground trembled underfoot. She spun him away from the facade of the temple, tearing him away from the dark adoration of his god, and gripped the breastplate of his armor with her hands.

"Why is he doing his?" she demanded. "What have you done, heretic?"

Tzirik blinked and shook his head, his eyes behind his mask still full of the glory of his epiphany.

"You do not know what you are witnessing, priestess of Lolth?" Tzirik said. He laughed deeply. "You have the rare good fortune to be present at the destruction of your goddess." He disentangled Quenthel's hands from his armor and took a step back, his voice rising in exultant glee. "You wish to know what is going on here, Lolthite? I will tell you. The Masked Lord is going to unseat your Spider Queen and overthrow her black tyranny forever! Our people will finally be freed of her venomous influence, and you and the rest of your parasitic kind will be swept away as well!"

Quenthel snarled in feral rage, "You will not live to see it!"

Her whip sprang into her hand, and she drew her arm back to flay the triumph from Tzirik's face. Before she'd even started her lash, Vhaeraun—a bowshot distant, his back to the company as he chiseled and bludgeoned at the growing crack in the stone visage—waved his left hand without turning around. From beneath Quenthel's feet a column of seething black magma exploded, hurling her dozens of feet into the air with bone-breaking force. Tzirik, standing almost within arm's length, was untouched, but the rest of the company scattered to avoid the hot, stone-shattering impacts of great round blobs of the molten rock.

The god didn't even break his hammerlike rhythm of blow after blow. He struck again and again, even as Quenthel plummeted back down to the flagstones of the plaza, screaming as gobs of the infernal rock clung to her flesh and burned. Valas and Ryld ran to her aid. Danifae cringed, but kept her eyes on the god engaged in his assault.

Pharaun studied the scene, and shook his head.

"This is insane," he muttered.

He made a curious gesture with his hand and disappeared, teleporting away to some presumably safer locale. Halisstra saw him leave, and stood staring for one long moment before another impact of Vhaeraun's sword threw her to the ground. She lay there, defeated, while Quenthel thrashed and shrieked in agony nearby.

"Ah," breathed Vhaeraun. The god backed away from the face, which was split by a glowing green scar from the center of the forehead straight down the bridge of the nose and across the lips to the cleft of the chin. *"Mother, have you nothing to say even now? Will you die in silence?"*

The face remained impassive, the roiling light in the introspective eyes unchanged, but once again something seemed to tear the very fabric of the cosmos with a horrible ripping sound. A black gash appeared in the air near the face, and from it stepped another divine form.

Where Vhaeraun was lean and impossibly graceful, the newcomer was a thing of nightmare. Half spider and half drow, it clutched an armory of swords and maces in its six thickly muscled arms, and each of its chitinous legs ended in a vicious pincerlike claw. Its face, perversely enough, was that of a handsome drow male.

"Depart, Masked One," the spider-god commanded in a tortured, burbling voice. *"It is forbidden for you to intrude here."*

"Do not presume to stand between me and my destiny, Selvetarm," Vhaeraun snarled.

The monstrous spider-god Selvetarm waited no longer, but

darted forward with blinding speed, weaving his sextuple blades in an irresistible assault that might have dismembered a dozen giants in the space of two heartbeats.

Vhaeraun whirled aside, dancing through the storm of steel as if he chased Selvetarm's weapons instead of the other way around, parrying blows he found too inconvenient to elude and riposting with supernal grace. When the gods' weapons met, thunderclaps shook the ground.

Halisstra pushed herself upright, gaping in amazement. She might have stood transfixed at the scene indefinitely, but Ryld appeared at her elbow.

"We need your healing songs," he hissed. "Quenthel is badly burned."

What does it matter? Halisstra wondered.

Still, she climbed to her feet and made her way over to the fallen priestess. Quenthel writhed on the ground, hissing between her teeth as she strove unsuccessfully to master her pain. Ignoring the impossible duel that raged back and forth between the two deities, Halisstra focused on the Baenre's injuries and managed to begin the discordant threnody of a *bae'qeshel* song. She laid her hands on Quenthel's burns and wove as best she could, finding a momentary calm in the exercise of her talents for a tangible and immediate end. Quenthel's thrashings eased, and in a moment she opened her eyes. Her spells cast, Halisstra merely slumped down again and stared at the battling gods.

"What do we do?" she whispered. "What can we possibly do?"

"Endure," Ryld replied. He gripped her arm with one iron hand and met her eyes. "Wait and watch. Something will happen."

He looked back toward Vhaeraun and Selvetarm, too.

Valas rose from Quenthel's side and made his way over to Tzirik, crouching to keep his balance.

"Tzirik! What happens to this place, to us, if Vhaeraun defeats Selvetarm and destroys the face? Can you get us out of here?"

"What happens to us does not matter," answered the priest.

"Maybe not to you, but it matters greatly to me," Valas muttered. "Did you bring us here only to die, Tzirik?"

"I did not bring you here, mercenary, you brought me," the priest replied, giving Valas only a fraction of his attention. "None but the Spider Queen's priestesses could get this close to her temple, not even the Masked Lord. As to what happens when Vhaeraun defeats Selvetarm, well, we shall see."

He turned his full attention back to the dueling gods.

The Masked Lord and the Champion of Lolth fought on furiously. Ichor oozed from several black wounds in the half-spider's chitinous body, and dripping black shadow flowed from a handful of sword cuts that had kissed the graceful Vhaeraun. While the gods strove together in the realm of the physical, exchanging blows at a dizzying rate, they also confronted each other magically and psychically at the same time. Spells of terrible power blasted back and forth between them, deadlier even than Selvetarm's six weaving weapons. Their eyes locked on each other with a tangible contest whose potency tugged at what was left of Halisstra's reason, even from a hundred yards away. Missed blows and deflected spells caused terrible damage all around the two deities, gouging great craters in the walls of the temple and the flagstones of the plaza, and more than once coming perilously close to annihilating the mortal onlookers through sheer mischance.

"Treacherous jackal!" snarled Selvetarm. *"Your perfidy will not be rewarded!"*

"Simpleminded fool. Of course it shall," Vhaeraun retorted.

He leaped in among Selvetarm's flurrying blades and punched his shadow sword deep into the spider-god's bulbous abdomen. The Champion of Lolth shrieked and recoiled, but a moment later he seized Vhaeraun's ankle with one pincer and jerked the god to the ground. As quick as a cat he rained a torrent of deadly blows down on the Masked Lord.

Vhaeraun responded by invoking a colossal blast of burning shadowstuff that plunged straight down from some impossible height overhead and bathed both gods in black fire. Selvetarm roared in divine anguish, even as he hammered again and again at Vhaeraun.

With a horrible grinding sound that Halisstra and the other

onlookers felt in their very bones, the stone plaza disintegrated beneath them.

Still locked in their furious struggle, the two deities fell through the great temple island into the black abyss that waited below. Their roars of rage and the ground-shaking clamor of their weapons grew fainter and fainter as they fell away into the pit.

"They're gone," Ryld said numbly, stating the obvious. "Now what?"

No one had an answer for him, as the company gaped at the castle-sized shaft into nothingness the gods had left behind them. Distant flickers of light still danced from their battle, far below. For the space of several minutes the drow did nothing, climbing back to their feet, no one speaking at all. Tzirik merely folded his arms and waited.

"Did they destroy each other?" Valas ventured at last.

"I doubt it," Danifae said.

She looked thoughtfully at the glowing green crack that split Lolth's face, but said nothing more.

"If Lolth didn't care to respond to Vhaeraun's assault, I doubt she'll have anything to say to us," Ryld said. "We should get out of here."

The weapons master turned to speak to Tzirik, only to find that the Jaelre priest was locked in rapt attention, staring off into nothing, his expression alight with adoration.

"Yes, Lord," he whispered to no one. "Yes, I obey!"

Even as Ryld stepped forward to question the priest, the Jaelre priest gestured and spoke an unholy prayer. A whirling field of thousands of razor-sharp blades like that he'd used against the goristro sprang into existence a short distance around him, barricading Tzirik behind a cylindrical wall of tumbling metal.

Ryld yelped a curse and leaped backward, throwing himself out of the path of the murderous blades.

Tzirik ignored the weapons master, continuing with whatever task Vhaeraun had assigned him. With fumbling fingers the cleric drew a case from his belt and extracted a scroll, unrolled it, and began to read aloud from the parchment, beginning the words of another powerful spell while protected from the Menzoberranyr by his deadly barrier.

Halisstra looked up at him in dull surprise, trying to discern what spell the Jaelre priest was casting. It was difficult to bring herself to care any longer.

Even as Halisstra sank back down in apathy and despair, the fight rekindled in Quenthel. She surged up, groping for her whip.

"It's another gate!" she screamed. "Do not let him finish that spell!"

§　　§　　§

A few hundred yards distant, cloaked in darkness and drifting vapors, Pharaun sat cross-legged on the hard stone, hurrying to finish his spell. He'd watched the two gods battle to a standstill and plummet out of sight, but he was committed to his course and did not intend to stop. The spell of sending could not be cast quickly, and if he attempted to rush it, he would lose it all together. In the part of his mind that was not absorbed in the shaping of the magic, he wondered with no little trepidation whether the gods' omniscience might be complete enough to note his presence, note that he was casting a spell, and deduce why he was casting it—and whether the gods would deign to stop him. As best he could tell from his safe distance, though, Vhaeraun and Selvetarm were occupied with their fierce battle and were unlikely to be paying him much attention.

He completed the spell and whispered the message it would carry for him through the incalculable distances of dimensions and space, "Jeggred. We are in mortal peril. Slay Tzirik's physical body at once. We will return quickly, but guard us until we do. Quenthel commands it."

Pharaun sighed and stood, his expression thoughtful. The sending was reliable, but he didn't know for certain the effects of attempting it from another plane of existence. Nor did he know how long it would take his words to reach Jeggred back in Minauthkeep, or if the draegloth would choose to do as he asked even in Quenthel's name . . . or even if the cursed half-demon was still alive and free to kill the high priest.

The Master of Sorcere had a good sense of what to expect if all went as he hoped. It was only a matter of time, and not much at that.

"This would not be a good time to become obstinate, Jeggred," Pharaun muttered, even though his sending was gone already. "For once, do as I ask without question."

Warily, he began to creep back toward the distant cleft in the temple's massive wall.

❊   ❊   ❊

Surrounded by his tumbling wall of blades, Tzirik stood aside from the rest of the company, quickly and expertly reading aloud from his scroll. He didn't bother explaining to the Menzoberranyr what Vhaeraun had told him to do, or why he was doing it. He simply proceeded as if they were not there at all, though he'd taken the precaution of raising a blade barrier to keep them from interfering.

Ryld and Valas stood close to the deadly, spinning razors, watching helplessly as the priest droned on. Danifae and Quenthel crouched a little father back, equally helpless, the determination to do something battling with their inability to discern what, exactly, they could do. Halisstra stood watching as well, but she merely waited to see what form her doom would take.

"Tzirik, stop!" cried Valas. "You have put us all in sufficient peril today. We will not allow you to continue."

"Kill him, Valas," Danifae said. "He will not listen, and he will not stop."

The scout stood paralyzed as the priest's chant approached the final, triumphant notes. His shoulders slumped, stricken with defeat. Without warning, Valas brought up his shortbow and fired.

The first arrow was deflected by a whirling blade in the magical barrier, but the second passed through cleanly and pierced Tzirik's gauntleted hand. The priest cried out in pain and dropped his scroll, which fluttered to the stone plaza, unexpended.

The Jaelre whirled on Valas, eyes afire with hate through his masked helm, and said, "Are you still the bitches' errand-boy, Valas? Don't you see that you're nothing but a well-heeled dog to them? Why do you persist in giving the Spider Queen your loyalty, when you could take the Masked Lord for your god and know true freedom?"

"Lolth will do as she will," Valas answered. "I, however, am loyal to Bregan D'aerthe, and to my city. We can't allow you, or even your god, to deflect us from our quest, Tzirik."

Tzirik's face clouded and he said, "You and your companions will not gainsay the will of Vhaeraun. I refuse to permit it."

He crouched and raised his shield, snarling out the words of another divine spell. Valas fired again, but his arrows only ricocheted from the priest's shield. Tzirik finished his spell and placed his wounded hand on the ground. A powerful tremor blasted through the stone and bludgeoned the Menzoberranyr, flinging them about like dolls and ripping open great cracks in the substance of the stone plain, crevices that led into absolute blackness below.

Valas staggered back and forth, trying to keep his balance as the stones cracked and buckled beneath him. Danifae steadied herself and snapped off a shot with her crossbow that passed through the blades and struck Tzirik a ringing hit on the breastplate, but the bolt shivered into pieces on the priest's armor.

Quenthel managed a desperate, off-balance leap to keep from toppling into a gaping crevice beneath her. She rolled awkwardly, and came up with a short iron rod in her hand. The high priestess barked a command word and discharged a white sphere of some magical, viscous substance at the priest, but Tzirik's seething blades ripped apart the viscid glob in a spray of gluey strands.

"Get up, Halisstra," Quenthel hissed. "Your sister priestesses need you!"

The powerful tremors took Halisstra's feet out from under her the first time she tried to stand. She shook her head and tried again.

My sisters need me? she thought. Strange, as our goddess apparently has no use for any of us who serve as her priestesses. If Lolth chooses to turn her back on me, to spurn my faithfulness and devotion, then the least I can do is return the favor.

Throughout Halisstra's life she had willingly joined ranks with her worst enemies, her most bitter rivals, when something rose to threaten the absolute dominion over dark elf society she and her sister priestesses shared. Staring off into the endless, empty expanse of the Demonweb Pits, she found that she would not take one single step in Lolth's name.

"Let him do as he will," she said to Quenthel. "Lolth has taught me not to care. If we managed to preserve Lolth's very existence today, do you think she would be grateful? If I tore my own heart out and laid it on the Spider Queen's altar, do you think she would be pleased by my sacrifice?"

Bitter laughter welled up in her throat and Halisstra gave herself over to it, even as Tzirik's tremors subsided. Her heart ached with a hurt that could rend the world in two, but she could not find a voice for it.

Quenthel stared at her in horror.

"Blasphemy," she managed to whisper.

The Mistress of Arach-Tinilith gathered up her whip and turned on Halisstra, but before she could strike, Tzirik struck with another spell, scouring the entire party with sheets of incandescent flames that raced back and forth across the stone plain like water sloshing on a plate. Halisstra threw herself flat and cried out in pain. The others cursed or cried out, scrabbling for cover that did not exist.

"Leave me!" Tzirik commanded from within his cage of whirling steel.

He stooped down and picked up his scroll, while the Menzoberranyr picked themselves up from the smoking stones.

Ryld rose slowly, his flesh seared at face and hands, and watched as the cleric started to cast his spell again. The weapons master eyed the spinning blades surrounding the priest, and with the quickness of a big cat, he gathered up his legs and sprang into the barrier, crouching low into the tightest ball possible. Droplets of blood splattered nearby as the whirling magical blades sparked and sliced against the weapons master's dwarven armor, drawing blood in a dozen places—but the Master of Melee-Magthere was through the barrier.

He staggered to his feet with an animal grunt of pain, Splitter gripped awkwardly in his slashed hands, but he managed to drive at Tzirik with the point of the greatsword. Once again the cleric was forced to drop his scroll. He parried the thrust with his shield and lashed back with his spiked mace.

Ryld avoided the blow only by leaping backward, so close to the whirling blades that sparks flew from his shoulders as the razors kissed his back. He recovered and glided forward again, spinning his deadly sword and slashing quickly at the Jaelre cleric.

Valas, standing outside the whirling blades, reached up to the nine-pointed star token on his breast and touched it. In the blink of an eye he vanished, reappearing inside the barrier behind Tzirik. He dropped his bow and drew his kukris, but Tzirik surprised him.

Turning his back on Ryld, the strong cleric took three power-ful strides and slammed his heavy shield into the Bregan D'aerthe even as Valas got his knives in hand. With a roar of anger the Jaelre shoved Valas back into the curtain of deadly razors and sent the scout stumbling through, spinning and screaming as the blades sliced his flesh.

Ryld made Tzirik pay by darting forward to strike out with a full double-handed slash across the torso that spun the priest half around, but the cleric's plate armor held against the blow. In re-sponse, Tzirik leaped in close to Ryld, inside the fighter's reach, and rained down a barrage of wicked blows with the spiked mace, driving the weapons master back.

Ryld gathered himself for another assault, but at that moment Quenthel hurled herself through the blades as well. One sliced her calf deeply and sent her stumbling when she passed through, and she went to one knee with a gasp of pain, blocking Ryld. Tzirik stepped back out of reach of the Baenre's whip, and quickly called out a spell.

Ryld froze in place as the cleric ensnared him, freezing his will and paralyzing his muscles.

Quick as a snake, Tzirik turned on Quenthel and hammered her to the ground even as she tried to stand on her injured leg. Avoiding the hissing serpent heads, Tzirik kicked her whip back outside the curtain of blades, and turned to crush Ryld's skull while the weapons master was helpless before him. The bronze mace drew back for the lethal blow—and Tzirik was sent reeling away from his intended victim, battered by a powerful blast of sound.

Halisstra, standing just on the other side of the blades, followed with a second *bae'qeshel* song and scoured the cleric again. She would not fight for Lolth again, but she would fight for her companions, Ryld in particular.

"Do not kill the priest," she called to her companions. "We need him to bring us home!"

"What do you suggest, then?" Danifae snapped from beside her. "He seems intent on destroying us!"

"Indeed," said Tzirik.

The Jaelre priest recovered from Halisstra's spells and lashed out with one of his own, calling down from the black skies above a column of crawling purple fire that blasted Halisstra and Danifae. The cleric wheeled to confront Quenthel, who was just gathering herself to leap at his back. He hefted his mace.

"I take great pleasure in slaying clerics of the Spider Queen," Tzirik said. "When you awake in Minauthkeep, I'll slay you again there."

He advanced on her, his cruel eyes alight as Quenthel hobbled awkwardly, seeking to dodge the inevitable blow.

Tzirik's breastplate simply vanished. The cleric halted in consternation, and glanced down. All other pieces of his full plate armor remained in place, but then—slowly—his arming coat vanished as well, revealing the smooth black flesh of his torso and chest.

"What in the Masked Lord's name?" he muttered, and glanced up just in time to turn away from Danifae, who shot a bolt at his heart that instead caught the cleric's shield. His mystification turned abruptly and instantly to pure terror. *"No!"* he screamed. *"N—"*

Some unseen force ripped open Tzirik's bare chest and began to pluck the gory ribs one by one out of his jerking torso. Blood and bits of bone splattered all around, yet the cleric impossibly kept to his feet as he was flensed alive before the astonished Menzoberranyr.

Halisstra, who had seen many terrible things at Lolth's altars, recoiled in horror. With a cold, distant part of her mind, she noted that the flesh and bone torn out of Tzirik simply faded away, just as his armor had.

It's not happening here, she realized. Tzirik is being murdered, but back in Minauthkeep.

One final obscene blow seized the contents of Tzirik's chest cavity and literally strewed them abroad. The Jaelre priest sank to his knees as his eyes rolled up in his head. From some immense distance a shining silver cord appeared, tethered to the priest's back. It recoiled sharply into his astral body with a psychic force that plucked at Halisstra's very soul, and Tzirik was gone, as if he had never existed.

"Gods . . ." Valas managed to say, then he grunted in shock.

All of them felt it at the same instant—a violent wrenching of their psyches that rent the stone plain and the black temple into a thousand silvery shards.

Halisstra opened her mouth, a scream of terror welling up inside her, but before she could draw another breath she was yanked away into oblivion.

❧   ❧   ❧

Halisstra awoke with a start, sitting bolt upright from the musty old divan in Tzirik's hidden chamber. It took her a moment to understand that she was alive. The experience of having her soul wrenched from the Demonweb Pits back to Faerûn in an instant by Tzirik's destruction was not something she cared to repeat. It took her a moment longer than that to understand that she was no longer in any physical pain.

Where she did ache, though, was in her heart. A great, hot hurt throbbed in the center of her being, a grief so keen and vast that Halisstra could not imagine anything that could swallow it.

She pressed her hand to her chest as if to smooth out the ache beneath her breastbone, and slowly looked around. The others in the company were rising, too, all variously dazed or groggy from their experience. To her right, Tzirik lay still on his couch, his body torn apart. Blood splattered the walls of the chamber, and awful pieces of the Jaelre cleric lay discarded on the floor. Beside the priest's ruined corpse squatted Jeggred, licking blood from his white fur. A pair of Jaelre warriors lay close at hand, their throats torn out.

"Mistress?" the draegloth asked Quenthel. "What happened? What did you learn?"

Quenthel's eyes fell on Tzirik's corpse and the dead Jaelre guards nearby, and she scowled.

"What in the goddess's name were you thinking?" she asked the draegloth. "Why did you slay him?"

"The guards? They seemed likely to object to my work on the heretic," answered Jeggred.

"No, not them," the priestess said, "Tzirik!"

Jeggred's eyes narrowed, and a low growl began in his throat. The half-demon straightened and paced around the couches toward Pharaun, clenching his claws.

"Wizard, if you caused me to fail in my duty to—"

"Pharaun . . ." Quenthel said, frowning as she struggled to collect her thoughts. It didn't take her long. Recollection dawned in her eyes, and she wheeled to glare at the Master of Sorcere. "You abandoned us in the middle of the Demonweb Pits, when we needed you the most. Explain yourself!"

"I deemed it necessary," Pharaun said. "We were in mortal danger, but we could not flee without Tzirik's complicity, and it seemed clear to me that Tzirik had no intention of going anywhere. The best method for escape I could contrive was to direct a sending to Jeggred, and instruct him to slay Tzirik's material body. As the priest is the one who cast the spell of astral travel, his death ended it for all of us—rather more abruptly than I would have liked, but

I could think of no other options. I told Jeggred you ordered it, since I was not certain he would kill the cleric simply because I asked him to."

"Your cowardice ripped us away from the one place we had a hope of winning our answers," Quenthel growled.

"No," said Halisstra. "Pharaun's prudence engineered our escape from an impossible situation, in the one manner that had any hope of working."

"What is the point of escaping, when we failed to complete our quest?" the Baenre demanded.

"Answers? There were no answers to be had, Quenthel," Halisstra said. "We could have abased ourselves before her until the end of time, and the Spider Queen could not have cared less. The quest was pointless—and it was a quest you were never certain of anyway. Or were there storehouses to raid in the Abyss?"

"I let your blasphemy and pridefulness pass in the Demonweb Pits, girl, but I will not do so again," Quenthel said. "If you speak to me again in such a manner, I will have your tongue torn out at the roots. You will be punished for your lack of faith, Halisstra Melarn. The Spider Queen will visit unimaginable torments upon you for your lack of respect."

"At least that would be a sign that she lives," Halisstra replied.

She stood and began to gather her belongings. In the stone halls beyond their chamber, she could hear distant shouts of alarm and the clatter of many feet coming nearer. It seemed almost beneath her notice.

"The Jaelre are coming," Danifae said. "They might have something to say about the evisceration of their high priest."

"I would prefer not to have to cut my way out of this castle," Ryld offered. "I've had my fill of fighting today."

With a low growl, Quenthel tore her attention away from Halisstra and studied the small chamber. She chewed her lip in agitation, as if wrestling with an idea she didn't like, then she muttered a curse and turned to Pharaun.

"Do you have a spell that can get us out of here?"

Pharaun smirked, obviously pleased that Quenthel had been forced to resort to his powers so quickly after condemning his actions.

"It's a bit of a stretch, but I think I can teleport us all at once," he said. "Where do we wish to go? I can't bring us safely into the Underdark, but other than that. . . ."

"Anywhere but here," Quenthel replied. "We need time to consider what we've seen and learned, and what we must do next."

"The cave mouth the portal from the Labyrinth led to," Valas said. "It's several days' march from here, and not heavily traveled."

"Fine," Quenthel snapped. "Take us."

"Join hands, then," Pharaun said.

He placed his own hand over Ryld's and Halisstra's, and spoke a short phrase just as the first blows sounded on the panel of the secret door. In the blink of an eye they stood on the cold, mossy ground of the cave mouth in the forest clearing. It was close to dawn. The skies to the east were pearly gray, and cold dew lay heavy around their feet. The glen was as empty and cheerless as it had been the first time the company camped there, a little more than a tenday past. Most of the snow had melted off, and icy water trickled into the sinkhole and ran out of sight beneath the hill.

"Here we are," the wizard announced. "Now, if nobody minds too much, I believe I am going to find the most comfortable spot I can in the cavern below and sleep like a damned human."

He clambered down the slippery rocks without waiting for a response.

"Take your rest later, wizard," Quenthel called after him. "We must determine what we need to do next, the meaning of the things we saw—"

"What we saw has no meaning," Halisstra said, "and what we do next does not matter. I'm with Pharaun."

She summoned up the strength to leap lightly from boulder to boulder, descending back into the comforting and familiar darkness of the cavern below.

Behind her Quenthel fumed and Jeggred rumbled in displeasure, but Ryld and Valas shouldered their packs and followed Pharaun down into the cave. Danifae turned to the Baenre priestess and rested one hand on her shoulder.

"We are all troubled by what we've seen," the battle captive said, "but we're exhausted. We'll all think more clearly when we have had some rest, and perhaps then the goddess's will might be more plain to us."

Grudgingly, Quenthel nodded in assent, and the rest followed into the cave. Halisstra and Pharaun had already thrown themselves down on the pebbled floor of the cavern a few dozen yards from the entrance, shucking their packs and leaning back against the walls. The rest of the Menzoberranyr filed in slowly and picked out their own spots, collapsing wherever they happened to stop moving.

Seyll's bloodstained armor seemed unbearably heavy on Halisstra's shoulders, and the hilt of the Eilistraeean's sword jammed painfully into her ribs. She was too tired to find a better position.

"Will no one tell me what happened in the Demonweb Pits?" Jeggred railed. "I have waited in that empty stone room for days, guarding your sleeping bodies faithfully. I deserve to hear what happened."

"You will," Valas answered. "Later. I don't believe any of us rightly know what to make of it. Give us time to rest, and to reflect."

Rest? Halisstra thought.

She felt as if she could sleep—sleep in the unconscious and helpless manner of a human—for a tenday and not feel healed of the fatigue she carried. Her mind refused to reflect any longer on why Lolth had abandoned her, yet she had something in her heart that demanded examination, a grief that would not permit her the refuge of the Reverie until she had found some way to let it out.

With a sigh, she pulled her satchel close and opened it, taking out the leather case of her lyre. She carefully unsheathed the heirloom, running her fingers over the rune-carved dragonbone arms, touching the perfect mithral wire.

At least I still have this, she thought.

In the silence of the forest cave, Halisstra played the dark songs of the *bae'qeshel*, and softly gave voice to her unbearable grief.

CHECK OUT THESE NEW TITLES FROM THE AUTHORS OF R.A. SALVATORE'S WAR OF THE SPIDER QUEEN SERIES!

VENOM'S TASTE
House of Serpents, Book I
Lisa Smedman

The New York Times Best-selling author of *Extinction*.
Serpents. Poison. Psionics. And the occasional evil death cult. Business as usual in the Vilhon Reach. Lisa Smedman breathes life into the treacherous yuan-ti race.

THE RAGE
The Year of Rogue Dragons, Book I
Richard Lee Byers

Every once in a while the dragons go mad. Without warning they darken the skies of Faerûn and kill and kill and kill. Richard Lee Byers, the new master of dragons, takes wing.

FORSAKEN HOUSE
The Last Mythal, Book I
Richard Baker

The New York Times Best-selling author of *Condemnation*.
The Retreat is at an end, and the elves of Faerûn find themselves at a turning point. In one direction lies peace and stagnation, in the other: war and destiny. *New York Times* best-selling author Richard Baker shows the elves their future.

August 2004

THE RUBY GUARDIAN
Scions of Arrabar, Book II
Thomas M. Reid

Life and death both come at a price in the mercenary city-states of the Vilhon Reach. Vambran thought he knew the cost of both, but he still has a lot to learn. Thomas M. Reid makes humans the most dangerous monsters in Faerûn.

November 2004

THE SAPPHIRE CRESCENT
Scions of Arrabar, Book I
Available Now